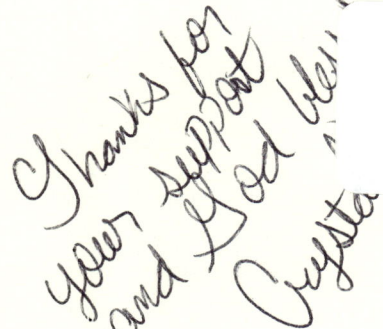

Thanks for
your support
and God bless
Crysta

MW01610051

Grace Beyond
the Border

Crystal Grant

PublishAmerica
Baltimore

ISBN: 1-4241-1569-8
PUBLISHED BY PUBLISHAMERICA, LLLP
www.publishamerica.com
Baltimore

Printed in the United States of America

Dedicated to:

Richard and Nancy Grant: Your constant support and leadership has made me the person I am today. A girl couldn't ask for better parents. I love you so much!

Richy: I appreciate so much the time you put in helping me with my ideas. You don't know how I need your input and creativity.

Holly: You've kept me on track through the years, not only as my practical younger sister, but my best friend. Thanks.

Emily: Little sister, you brighten days and certainly make life interesting! Keep smiling and dreaming!

The folks at Irondale Assembly: You'll never know how much you've blessed me through the years. You are like family to me.

And to my Heavenly Father. You've taken my dream and made it a reality. I give You all the glory.

Prologue

Two men walked from within the boundaries of their huge, multi-million dollar home, the younger one carrying a travel bag. He was broader of shoulder and stouter, but the resemblance between the two men was striking. Both had clear blue eyes and a wide, set jaw. Their hair was dark, though the older one wore his hair cropped shorter.

They walked silently down the broad, brick-lined walkway, lined on either side with tall, groomed cedar trees. The sun had lowered itself behind the white marble building, so the air was cooler than it had been. A few people—employees—moved about the yard, cutting grass and trimming the trees, but the men ignored them.

At last, they stopped at the end of the walk, an expensive black Firebird parked in front of them. They turned to each other.

"Well, younger brother," the older man smiled, "It's another trip to the US for you, I guess. How long are you planning on staying this time?"

With a smile, the other man shrugged. "Depends on how well my stay goes. Sure you won't come with me, Marlon?" he asked with a glint in his eye.

Marlon threw his head back and laughed out loud, his white teeth flashing. "Only if you don't want me to step foot back in Mexico!" he answered. "No, Reuban, you better go without me again."

Reuban shrugged again, a teasing smile lighting his handsome face. "Just checking."

The brothers grew serious. "You be careful, Reuban," Marlon said.

"Aren't I always?' Reuban returned. "Don't you worry, big brother, I won't lead the authorities to your doorstep."

"I'm glad to hear it," Marlon said. "Things have been going too good for the last two years. I don't want that to change."

Reuban nodded, and then changed the subject. "You need a girl, Marlon."

"Where did that thought come from?"

"I don't know," Reuban answered. "But you've been living alone for too long. It's time you had someone special again. I know you have Felina, but…"

Marlon cocked his head. "Can't say the thought hasn't crossed my mind lately. But I'd like someone from the States this time. I can't find anyone worth my time down here anymore."

With another charming grin, Reuban asked, "Want me to keep my eyes open?"

"It wouldn't hurt," Marlon said thoughtfully.

"I'll keep that in mind."

After a few more words, mostly about the business taking Reuban across the border into the States, Reuban climbed into his car and put on shiny sunglasses. "I'll see you in a couple of months!" he called, as he revved the engine up and roared down the driveway.

Marlon stood and waved until his brother was out of sight. He turned back to his house with a sigh. He could not help but feel slightly envious of Reuban's freedom. He could remember when he had moved about as he pleased without worrying about the law looking over his shoulder.

Never one to feel sorry for himself for long, Marlon spoke out loud. "Don't fret, Marlon Ferraro. You've got a beautiful life down here. What more could you get if you had the freedom Reuban has? I can get whatever I want right here in Mexico."

Indeed, it was true. There was seldom a time that either of the Ferraro brothers did not get what they wanted. Especially Marlon.

Chapter One

Edwardsville, Kansas
Friday evening, February 28th

"Alana, honey, do you know where the extra BBQ sauce is?"

Alana Crewe looked up when she heard the voice of her pastor's wife. "Um, yeah, I think it's in the fridge in the kitchen," she answered, her tone light. "I'll get it."

"Thank you, Alana!"

Alana moved with a quick step from the table she had been working over. Her long, silky brown hair fell over her shoulder as she walked, and she brushed it back. She ran up the steps to the kitchen and entered.

"Rachel, Maggie needs the extra BBQ sauce," she called.

Rachel Johnson appeared from another room, holding a big bowl of potato salad.

"You shouldn't be carrying that!" Alana scolded, quickly taking the heavy bowl from her friend's grasp.

Rachel laughed as she put her hand on her swollen stomach. "Well, I have to admit, Junior did not like the feel of that bowl at all! He was kicking something fierce!"

"I don't blame him!" Alana sided with the unborn baby. "Where's the sauce?"

"Here." Rachel handed Alana two extra bottles. "I'll be out in a minute with the vegetable salad."

"Okay, I think the meat is about done," Alana said, trying to balance the potato salad and the two bottles of BBQ sauce.

"Do you need help?"

"No, I got it!" she said, pushing the door open with her foot.

"Oh, good!" Maggie sighed when Alana returned. "I was worried we would run out!"

"We've got plenty," Alana assured, setting the big bowl on the table, which was already laden with food.

The yard of Tim and Rachel Johnson was full of members of the New Hope Fellowship Church. The air was full of laughter and banter. The kids were running in and out among the adults, trying unsuccessfully to stay out of the way. Teen girls from Alana's Sunday school class were sitting together, engulfed in talk of anything that seemed important to them. They paused at times to greet their teacher when she passed, intent on helping where she could. It was clear that everyone was having a good time.

Their pastor, Kenneth Nelson, was grilling the meat and playfully arguing with his wife as to how much sauce the hamburgers needed. The women of the church had brought plenty of food, and everyone's mouths were watering at the aroma of salad, baked beans, and desserts.

"All right everyone!" Maggie called out, just as Rachel set her salad on the table. "It's time to eat!"

Cheers cut her off and she laughed at their enthusiasm. "All right, all right!" she finally said. "Let's pray, and then you can eat! Kenneth?"

The gray-haired pastor took his cap off and bowed his head. Everyone else, including the kids, followed suit.

"Heavenly Father, we want to thank You for this beautiful day You've given us to enjoy. Thank you for the blessings You've given us in family, friends, and food. Bless this food to the use and nourishment of our bodies, and keep us safe and strong in You, no matter what the circumstance. Amen!"

Almost immediately, lines formed around the food. Alana held back, content to wait until the lines went down some before she filled her own plate. She took a soda from a cooler and sat down at a picnic table. Several called to her, advising her to get in line. She just smiled and shook her head.

"Aren't you going to eat?" Dinah Bower asked as she sat down next to her, carrying her own plate.

"Oh, yeah," Alana said. "I just don't like going up there when there's a big line."

Dinah's boyfriend, Curtis Roper, joined them just then. "Aren't you going to eat?" he asked Alana.

Alana laughed. "Yes!" she assured him. She eyed his plate, heaped high with salad, rolls, beans, and pork steaks. "You're not very hungry, are you?"

"This is just the beginning," he said, his blue eyes sparkling with merriment.

Dinah tucked her shoulder-length hair behind her ear. "You're such a pig, Curtis!"

Curtis pretended to be hurt. "Oh, that hurt! You've just killed my appetite."

"Well, then, just let me throw your plate away, if you're not hungry," Alana teased, reaching across the table.

Grabbing his plate, Curtis shot her a threatening look. "Back away from my food!" he ordered.

Alana laughed at his possessiveness. She noticed the line had grown shorter and stood up. "Save my seat, will you?" she asked. She hated to stand in the middle of a crowd looking for a place to sit.

"Sure," Dinah agreed, setting her purse on Alana's seat. "There, that'll keep it."

Alana then made her plate, her stomach grumbling loudly. When she returned to her spot, she saw Dinah's cousin, Belinda, and her new husband Tommy Wells sitting with Curtis and Dinah.

"Hi, Alana," Belinda greeted. "Is that all you're eating?"

Alana looked down at the salad and hotdog she had selected. "Yes, why?'

Belinda sighed. "No wonder you're so slim!"

Alana grunted. "You mean skinny!"

"What's the difference?" Curtis asked, stuffing a roll into his mouth.

Alana shrugged. "Nothing, I guess."

"Skinny doesn't sound as nice," Dinah answered for her.

"Yeah," Alana nodded.

The young adults talked easily while they ate, though Alana did not join the conversation much. The two couples were always fun to be around and she just enjoyed their company.

The meal was declared a hit by all, echoed by groans of agreement. Soon after, Curtis announced he was ready for volleyball.

"Come on, Alana," Dinah invited. "Let's play."

Alana loved volleyball, so she followed them to the court, which had been set up a safe distance from the table.

"I'm captain!" Curtis announced, grabbing the ball.

Dinah was the second captain and soon the two were picking their teammates. Alana stood quietly, secretly praying she would not be the last one picked. She was pleased when Curtis picked her fairly early. Her pleasure grew when Belinda, Tommy, and another guy from her church named Rob were on her team. She felt pretty comfortable with all of them and knew she would be able to enjoy the game.

Dinah had chosen her brother, Jesse, and three other guys from the church—Ted, Rick, and Bobby by name. "Okay, we're ready!" she shouted, her green eyes flashing with challenge. Ted got ready to serve the ball.

Curtis turned to his teammates. "Okay, here's our strategy—"

"Look out!" Alana called out.

The ball soared over the net and hit him in the back of the head.

"Ouch!"

"Well, we're off to a great start!" Belinda groaned, throwing her arms up.

Dinah gave two thumbs up. "Love the strategy, keep it up!"

Alana tried to ask Curtis if he was all right, but she was laughing too hard to get it out.

"Oh, don't worry about him," Dinah told her. "He's got a hard head!"

Curtis rubbed his head and frowned at his girlfriend. "Thanks, Dinah," he complained.

Ted served the ball again, and this time Curtis paid attention. Tommy hit the ball back with such force that Dinah failed block it.

"Our ball!" Curtis cheered.

Belinda served and got the team three points before Curtis blundered again and missed the ball.

Alana laughed at the bickering between her captain and Belinda. The game went on, both teams staying close in score. Curtis's team was down by one when Jesse fell hitting the ball and rolled completely under the net, knocking Alana off her feet. Curtis, not paying attention, fell over the both of them, his foot coming out and tripping Belinda.

The entire court burst into laughter, quickly joined by church members were watching the game from their lawn chairs. Laughing harder than anyone were the ones involved in the pileup. Curtis stood up and helped Alana to her feet.

"Well, that was an experience!" he laughed.

"Yeah, and we didn't get that point, so we lost," Belinda complained.

"That's not fair!" Curtis cried.

"Yes it is!" Dinah said.

"It was your teammate that ran into us!"

Alana stood back and let the others argue over the point, shaking her head at their antics. At last, it was agreed that Curtis would serve the ball again. His team played hard, but still ended up losing the point, which allowed Dinah's team to win, a fact that she rubbed in playfully.

They played two more games before dusk made it hard to see the ball. It was only then that they realized that most of the families had already gone home. The girls helped Rachel put the rest of the food and dishes away.

"Thanks for the help," Rachel said sincerely when it was just Alana and

Dinah left in her kitchen. "I think the BBQ went over pretty well, don't you?"

Alana nodded and Dinah said, "Definitely."

"The highlight of the evening had to be the pileup on the volleyball court though!" Rachel said, smiling.

"Oh, thanks!" Alana groaned. "I can't believe that happened!"

Dinah was laughing again. "And you were down at the bottom!"

"I know!" Alana gasped. "It's a wonder no one got hurt!"

"I'm glad everyone had a good time," Rachel spoke again.

Alana looked at her watch. "I hate to run, but Dad will be looking for me if I don't get home."

"Oh, go ahead," Rachel said. "I'll see you at church Sunday."

"And here again Thursday for Bible study!" Dinah piped up.

Alana gave them both a wave and quietly slipped out the door.

Rachel shook her head. "She is so sweet."

"I know. Curtis and I both love her to death."

"I guess you're pretty close to her, aren't you?"

Dinah cocked her head, her silky hair falling over her shoulder. "Not really." At Rachel's look of surprise she went on quickly. "It's not that I don't want to be. She seems to hold herself back, you know? Like she's afraid to open up too much."

Rachel nodded as she lowered herself to a seat across from Dinah. "I know what you mean. I've been able to get to know her better in the last year or two, but she's pretty backwards. I think she's very insecure, and that causes her to guard herself."

"What does she have to be insecure about?" Dinah questioned. "I mean, she's pretty, smart, and she's got a great family."

"I don't know," Rachel admitted. "Sometimes people struggle with their self-image for no apparent reason. She is a very special person, though, and I pray she will realize one day that she has a lot to offer the world." She looked at Dinah. "I encourage you to try to get closer to her, Dinah. I think you would find a very dear friend."

Dinah nodded. "I intend to. She is so nice, but at the same time, she seems kind of lost, you know? It's not that I feel sorry for her, because I don't. I would just like to show her that I want to be friends with her."

With a smile, Rachel agreed. "That's what she needs—good friends to keep encouraging her."

Curtis stepped in just then, after helping Rachel's husband put away tables and chairs. "Ready, Dinah?"

The two women promised to see each other on Sunday and Dinah and Curtis took their leave.

It was after ten o'clock when Alana arrived at home. Her mother, Sharon Crewe, was waiting up for her.

"Did you have a good time?" she asked her daughter.

Alana smiled. "Yes, I did. Did you see us all crash into each other playing volleyball?"

Sharon chuckled. "Yeah. Looked to me like everyone was having fun."

"Well, I sure did."

Sharon stood and hugged Alana. "I'm glad to hear it. You've worked too hard lately. Don't stay up too late, okay?"

"I won't," Alana promised. "I'm heading for bed now."

The house was quiet as she went up the steps. Her brother and sisters were apparently already sleeping. Her own bed looked inviting, so she quickly changed her clothes and climbed in. She picked up her Bible, but knew she would not be able to keep her eyes open long enough to read her nightly portion. She prayed instead.

"Father, thank you so much for this day. I love being with my church family. Each one makes me feel so special. Help me to do what I can to encourage and uplift those around me. I don't want to always take what I can. I want to give of myself as I'm able. Let your light shine through me. Help me tomorrow at work. As always, let me be a witness to the lost."

Her words faded as she felt sleep crowding in. She put her Bible safely back on her nightstand, rolled over, and went promptly to sleep.

Thomasville prison, Nebraska
Saturday morning, March 1st

Jack Norris strolled down the sidewalk, taking a deep breath of the fresh air. He tilted his rugged face towards the sun, soaking up its light. As he turned his attention to where he was walking, he caught sight of his probation officer and frowned.

Kelly White returned the frown. "This is your last chance, Norris," he said. "I've stuck my neck out for you too many times. You blow it again, you're back in for who knows how long."

Rolling his eyes, Jack pushed his way past the shorter man. "Just leave me alone, White," he growled.

"I mean it!" Kelly snapped. "Now, you have an appointment to meet with me Tuesday morning at nine o'clock. Do *not* be late, or I'll have the law on your tail so fast you won't know what happened!"

Jack Norris went on walking, pretending not to hear the officer calling after him. He did not have any plans for the immediate future, but he knew one thing for sure—by Tuesday morning, he would be far from Nebraska.

Chapter Two

Alana woke up every Saturday morning at five o'clock so she could be at work by six-thirty. This day, however, she groaned when her alarm rang. She got up and dressed in a knee length khaki skirt and white knit blouse. She pulled a blue blazer on over that and rolled the sleeves up slightly, grunting slightly at the stiffness in her arms.

"A little too much ball last night," she murmured, as she painstakingly brushed her hair. Deciding to make it easy, she left it hanging loose. After washing her face and applying light makeup, she looked at her reflection in the mirror.

"Well, not sensational, but it will do," she mumbled. She grabbed her purse and tiptoed quietly down the stairs.

Sharon was already there, putting a muffin on a plate for Alana. "Good morning," she greeted, handing the plate and a glass of juice to her.

"Thanks, Mom," Alana said, sitting down and taking a big bite. "I didn't know if I would have enough time to fix breakfast for myself."

"I figured you would have a hard time getting up this morning," Sharon observed.

Alana ate hurriedly and threw her mother a kiss when she was done. "I better go!"

"You look nice," Sharon complimented.

"Thanks!" Alana said with a pleased grin.

Sharon smiled as her daughter ran out the door and hopped into her black '96 Cougar.

Alana listened to the radio as she drove to work, humming along with the oldies, her favorite kind of music. Soon the huge department store loomed into view. She parked in the employees' lot and began the long walk to the front doors.

Darings', considered to be one of the most successful stores in the countries, boasted a store in every state. The business was now spreading to different parts of the world, including Taiwan, London, Paris, and just recently Mexico. Alana could not help but feel a little pride in her job.

She had worked for the business since she was sixteen—over five years ago. Working her way from cashier to customer assistance management, she now had a position in the accounting office. She liked her job, enjoyed most of the people she worked with, and thought highly of her store manager, Dick Browning. The employees were expected to dress and act as professionals. It was a nice place to work.

Now, as Alana made her way through the neat aisles, she was greeted by several other associates. She returned each one in her usual quiet, sincere way, unaware of the smiles she left behind her. After locking her purse up in her locker, she went to find her supervisor, Barb.

"I'll be doing some extra work in the next room, so if you need anything, just call," she said as she let Alana in the office.

"Sure," Alana assured. She closed the door behind Barb and turned to her work. She was halfway through the day's paperwork when her favorite co-worker, Stacey Martin, arrived.

"Hey, girlfriend," Stacey greeted. "How did your BBQ go?" She did not attend church anywhere, but she was aware of how active Alana was in her own church.

"It went great," Alana exulted. "You should've been there!" She went on to tell her of the disastrous volleyball game.

"Sounds like you had a bunch of nuts on your side!" Stacey joked.

"Curtis is a big nut all by himself," Alana said.

Falling easily into their routine of work and chatter, the girls were able to get a lot done by the time Alana was ready for her meal break. Just as she was filing her papers away, Brian Wheeler entered the office.

Alana could get along with most everyone at *Darings'*, but Brian was an exception. He was the youngest assistant manager and seemed to enjoy getting under her skin.

"Not quitting already?" he asked when he saw what she was doing.

"I'm going for my hour break," Alana said calmly, not pausing.

"You've only been here for three hours, haven't you?" he asked. "You know the rule. You have to be clocked in for four hours before you can take your hour."

"I have been here for almost four hours, Brian," Alana informed. "By the time I put all this away, it will be four."

Brian was looking through the key cabinet as he taunted her. "Well, I know how you are about trying to get out of work if possible."

Alana did not respond to that, knowing it was not true. She continued went on with what she was doing, trying to ignore him.

Brian found his keys and moved over to where she sitting. He picked up a stack that still needed to be separated and filed. "Is this all you have left?" he asked lightly.

"Yes."

"Well, I guess I *can* get some work out of you when you're in the mood." He moved to put the stack back on the counter when the papers slipped from his hand and flew out all over the floor.

"Brian!" Stacey exclaimed.

Alana sat up straight in her chair and clenched her jaw.

"Oh, I'm so sorry," Brian said, the glitter in his eye belying his words. "Hope it don't take you too long to clean up. I'd hate for you to be late for your break."

"You could at least offer to help clean it up!" Stacey growled.

Brian held up the keys and reached for the door. "Sorry, but the Houseware Department needs this right away. Don't want to keep the customer waiting." He sailed out without another word, but sent Alana a cocky grin.

"You really should tell Dick about his behavior towards you, Alana," Stacey advised as she knelt on the floor to help pick up the papers.

"Nah," Alana shook her head. "I don't want to bug him with petty stuff. He's got enough on his mind."

Stacey was not convinced, but she did not argue. "Why don't you go on? I don't mind cleaning this up."

"No, I won't leave you with a mess."

"But it'll cut your hour short!" Stacey objected.

Alana shrugged. "Oh, well."

With Stacey's help, Alana was able to gather the papers and file them in ten minutes. She sighed, knowing that she would have to come back from her meal that much earlier, but she didn't complain.

After a bite at the café housed within the mall, Alana took a stroll through the store. She still had a few minutes before she had to go back to work. As she walked, she prayed silently and was able to turn her frustration about Brian's treatment over to the Lord. She felt better when she returned to the office and Stacey went to her meal.

The rest of the day went by without any more disturbances from Brian. Apparently the business outside would not allow him any spare time to bother

her, for which Alana was thankful. At three o'clock, Alana said goodbye to Stacey and took her leave for the day. She had the next day off, and she would be back on Monday evening. Her whole family was home when she arrived, her seventeen-year-old sister doing homework at the kitchen table.

"Hey, Sis," Alana called.

"Hi. Can I borrow your peach sweater?" Andrea asked abruptly.

Alana scoffed. "Well, now that's a sincere welcome!'

Andrea smiled sheepishly. "Sorry. I've been meaning to ask, and I only just now remembered."

"What do you need it for?"

"Some of the girls are going to the skating rink, and it can get pretty cool in there."

With a cocked brow, Alana asked, "And will there be any guys there?"

Andrea dipped her head slightly and admitted, "Yeah, some guys from church are going, too."

"Sure, you can borrow it," Alana said generously.

Her blue eyes sparkling, Andrea thanked her and went back to her homework.

Alana moved to the living room, where her brother, Anthony, and Sharon were watching television. "Hello."

"Hi, dear," Sharon returned. "How was work?"

"Fine." Alana did not see any reason to tell her mother of Brian's rude behavior. "Where's Dad?"

"He and Audrey went to the store for some ice cream," Anthony answered, not taking his eye off the screen.

"Are you hungry?" Sharon asked.

"Not right now. I think I'll follow Andrea's example and get some homework done."

Alana went to her room and took off her blazer. She pulled her book bag to her desk and began pulling textbooks out. She was in her last year at Edwardsville Community College and would be graduating in May with her Associate's Degree in elementary education. From the time she was very young, Alana had dreamed of becoming a first grade teacher. In the fall, she planned to attend Kansas City University and work towards her Bachelor's degree.

"Some day," she muttered, opening an algebra book, "some day I will be done."

Curtis grabbed the ringing phone. "Y'ello!' he called.

"How's it going, Curt?"

"Hey, Jason!" Curtis greeted his closest friend. "Haven't heard from you in a while."

Jason admitted that he had been busy lately. "But, I have good news."

"You just saved a bunch of money on your car insurance by switching to Geico?" Curtis joked.

"Well, yeah," Jason teased, "but that's not what I called about." He paused expectantly.

"Well, out with it already!" Curtis cried.

Jason laughed. "You never were the patient one, even when we were kids."

"No, I wasn't," Curtis agreed. "Now, what's the news?"

"I'm coming for a visit."

Thrilled, Curtis said, "Great! What's the occasion? Or, did you just miss your old buddy so much that you just had to make the trip?"

"Hate to burst your bubble, but it's nothing like that," Jason replied. "Actually, I've been working on a transfer."

Curtis was surprised. "Really? You having problems over there?"

Jason immediately denied that possibility. "No, it's nothing like that. I've been praying about it. I've been feeling restless, and I really feel God moving me elsewhere. When I asked him where, Edwardsville came to mind."

"That'd be great!" Curtis exclaimed in his exuberant way. "We can always use another good cop."

"Your little town getting a bit rowdy?"

"Are you kidding?" Curtis scoffed. "Last week there was a speeding ticket given out for the first time in months. We're so quiet around here that you just might find yourself getting bored after the excitement of the big city."

Jason chuckled into the phone. "Well, Curtis, after the excitement of the big city, I just may be ready for a nice, quiet little town like Edwardsville."

"So, when you coming?"

"Well, I want to check the place out first," Jason informed. "I have a meeting with the police chief, and I want to make sure there's a good church."

"I can help you out there," Curtis cut in. "I'm going to the best church in the area."

"Is that so?" Jason asked, slightly amused.

"Sure. You wanna visit it when you come down?"

"Yeah, sounds good," Jason accepted.

The men talked for a few more minutes, during which Jason informed that he would be arriving the next Friday evening and would spend the weekend at Curtis's house. By the time they hung up, both were greatly looking forward to seeing each other again.

Chapter Three

On Sunday morning the New Hope Fellowship Church gathered for its morning service. The crowd was not especially large, but there was a strong feeling of family and friendship among its members. Alana arrived with her family and sat in their usual seat, halfway back on the right side of the sanctuary. Dinah and Curtis were sitting behind her.

"Did you have trouble getting up yesterday morning?" Dinah asked before the service began.

"A little," Alana confessed. "My arms were a little sore, too."

"I hurt all over," Curtis complained. "Course, I was doing most of the work, so it's no wonder."

Alana did not have time to respond, for Kenneth Nelson had just stepped to the pulpit. She shot Curtis a playful glare before turning around.

Kenneth opened the service with a prayer, and then the Sunday school classes left to go to their separate rooms. Alana followed her teen girls, all of them chattering nonstop.

She had been teaching for just over a year. She loved her girls, each of them bringing something different to the Bible discussions.

There were the cousins, Sarah and Jennifer Benson, blonde, freckled, and talkative. Their outgoing personalities made them popular both at church and school.

Curly-headed Maria Parks was shy and did not say much, though her brown eyes sparkled with a warmth and joy, brought about by the relationship she had with the Lord. She had only been a Christian for a few months, and her enthusiasm was refreshing to Alana.

Thirteen-year-old Breanna Smith still resisted turning her life over to God, though Alana and her other students prayed for her regularly. Breanna came from a difficult home life and at this point did not understand how God could have allowed her parents to abandon her. A godly couple within New Hope had adopted Breanna two years ago, and Alana hoped that their unwavering love, the support of the church, and most importantly, the gentle persuasion of the Holy Spirit would touch the bitter girl's heart.

Finally, there was Lizzie Matthews, the newest member of the class. She had turned thirteen just a few weeks ago and was thrilled to now be in the teen class. She thought highly of Alana and mimicked her style of dressing and acting. Alana was aware of her adoration and was very careful in everything she did. She wanted to keep a godly example before Lizzie and the rest of the girls, always pointing the way to the One who cared about them more than anyone else possibly could.

It was a small class, but for the most part, there were few problems. They all got along well with one another, and were very respectful of Alana.

"What's the lesson on today?" Maria asked.

"Job," Alana answered. "Does anyone remember what his story is?"

"Wasn't he the one that had a lot of bad stuff happen to him?" Jennifer asked.

"Yes, can you name some of them?"

Sarah raised her hand. "Didn't he lose his animals?"

"Aw, that's sad," said Breanna, a devout animal lover.

"Yes, he did," Alana answered. "But it was worse than just losing a few pets. Back in those days, those animals were a source of income for them. By losing his stock, Job lost his wealth, so it was a *very* devastating blow."

"He also lost a lot of his servants," Maria pointed out.

"And his kids," Jennifer added.

"What else?" Alana prompted, pleased with their remembrance.

"He got sick," Maria said.

"Yes," Alana nodded. "He got horrible boils that were very irritating and painful. Think about getting chicken pox, only they're much bigger and they hurt."

"Ouch," Breanna breathed.

Alana smiled. "Exactly. Now, we've talked about everything that Job has lost. What was the one thing he never lost?"

The girls were stumped. Maria, looking puzzled, asked, "His wife?"

Alana hid her smile. "No, although it's true nothing happened to her. Anyone else have any idea?" No one did. "In all the tragedies that Job went through, he never lost his faith in God."

"Duh!" Sarah exclaimed. "We should have known that!"

"How do you think you would react if your life was a mess and you began losing the people that were precious to you? What if you were sick all the time and suddenly penniless?"

"I'd be angry at God," Breanna answered honestly.

Alana knew Breanna was thinking of the events in her own life. "It would be very difficult to trust Him in hard times," Alana said gently. "I know we all have trouble understanding why God allows bad things happen. The Bible is full of examples of people experiencing times of hardship, and some of them lost faith. We have to remember though, that no matter what, God loves us and He wants our lives to be full of His glory. He is with us at all times, and He never leaves us. He just shares our pain."

The teens were looking up at Alana seriously. She had obviously given them something to think about. As they went a little deeper into the lesson, reading some passages from the Bible, they got involved with the discussion, some asking questions that made Alana really think through before she answered. By the time the hour was up, she felt that she had made some headway with presenting the message to them. Even Breanna seemed to understand what they had discussed. As she made her way back to her seat, Alana prayed that the seeds of the gospel would take root in her heart.

Kenneth approached her before he returned to the front. "Would you care to sing a special for us today, Alana?"

"Oh, uh, I suppose," Alana stammered.

"Good," Kenneth smiled before moving away.

Her stomach was immediately filled with butterflies. She took several deep breaths. This happened every time she was asked to sing. Although she loved singing, she did not like being in front of everyone.

After the opening prayer, Kenneth turned the podium over to Alana. She took one last deep breath and lifted the microphone to her mouth.

"Amazing Grace, how sweet the sound
That saved a wretch like me!
I once was lost, but now I'm found
Was blind, but now I see."

Her poignant voice filled the building. As the notes rose and fell, she felt her heart swelling as the words sank into her soul. She was able to forget where she was and sing her praise. Her voice grew even deeper and richer, stirring the congregation as they listened.

"Thru many dangers, toils, and snares
I have already come.

'Twas grace that led me safe thus far
And grace will lead me home.

When we've been there ten thousand years
Bright shining as the sun,
We've no less days to sing God's praise,
Then when we first began."

As if on cue, the congregation joined her in the last chorus, many of them with closed eyes. "Praise God, praise God, praise God, praise God." Their voices rose and fell in worship of the Lord they all loved and served so diligently.

As soon as the last note faded, Alana turned the microphone back to Kenneth, who was beaming, and made her way back to her seat. Her mother reached over and patted her arm, pride evident on her face. Her father looked over at her and winked.

Kenneth then moved on to the sermon and Alana listened intently to the message. The pastor spoke of the Old Testament sacrifices, comparing them to the sacrifice that Jesus made when He died on the cross. He then went on to explain Salvation's plan, describing how a sinner sacrifices his old life for God's will. Alana was moved by Kenneth's choice of words and his fervor.

After the service was dismissed, Alana was immediately besieged by a small crowd complimenting her song. She thanked each one humbly, not feeling like she deserved it.

Dinah's face finally appeared. "Good job, Alana," she winked.

"Thanks," Alana said. "I didn't expect this kind of reaction."

"What kind of reaction?" Belinda asked, joining their conversation.

"To her song," Dinah supplied.

"Oh, that was really good, Alana!" Belinda told her.

Alana chuckled.

"How's school going?" Dinah asked.

"Good," Alana said, gathering her purse. "I have only two months, and I'll graduate with my Associate's. Then I can start working towards my Bachelor's. I'm really looking forward to it."

"When is your graduation?" Belinda asked.

"May sixteenth," Alana supplied.

"Is it an open invitation?" Dinah asked. "Or do we have to have tickets?"

Alana shook her head. "It's open. Why?"

Dinah made a face. "Because I want to make sure I make it, that's why!"
"Oh."

"Don't sound so surprised, Alana," Belinda laughed.

"Well, I just didn't think anyone wanted to go," Alana said without thinking.

"What?" Dinah exclaimed. "Why wouldn't we want to go?"

Shrugging, Alana felt uncomfortable. She had not meant to sound pathetic.

"I will definitely be there," Dinah declared, as Belinda nodded in agreement. "I like to support my friends' accomplishments."

They were outside now, the sun shining brightly above them. "Thanks, girls," Alana said sincerely. "I'd love to have you there."

Before joining her family at their SUV, Alana found Rachel already seated in her car, waiting on her husband.

"How are you feeling?" Alana asked.

With a bright smile, Rachel answered, "I'm good, just tired. I'll be glad when it's all over, but I have to say, I really don't mind being pregnant."

"Why would you, with all the special treatment you're getting?" Alana teased. "But, I'm not as patient as you. I can't wait to see the little guy."

"Just a couple more months, and everyone will be able to meet him."

"Do you have a name, yet?" Alana knew the trouble Rachel and Tim were having in finding a name for the baby.

Rachel made a face. "No, not yet."

Alana heard her brother call for her. "I better go before they leave me. I'll see you later."

"Don't forget about the Bible study!" Rachel reminded her as she hurried off.

Des Moines, Iowa
Monday afternoon March 3rd

Bob Shaw smiled at the women as they exited his store. The sisters had just bought an expensive watch for their mother and the sale made Bob more than pleased. His jewelry shop was one of the more successful businesses on this side of the lane, brought about by his hard work and good business sense.

There was only one other customer in the store, so Bob went now to offer his assistance to the man. He was wearing a long trench coat and a wide brimmed hat.

"Can I help you, sir?" Bob asked politely, his smile in place.

The man did not look at him, but he shifted his position. "You can give me all the cash in your drawer."

"Huh?" Bob squeaked. The black gun that had suddenly appeared in the man's hands made him blink. "Now, wait a minute!"

The thief stepped closer, shoving the gun against Bob's ribs. "You do what I said," he growled, "and now!"

The feel of the cold metal made the owner's knees shake. "O-okay, just don't do anything!"

The man grabbed Bob's arm and shoved him towards the register. "Just get my cash!"

With shaking hands, Bob opened his drawer and fumbled with the money. He took the canvas bag the gunman tossed at him.

"Just give me all the bills."

With every bill that he pushed into the bag, Bob's heart sank lower. It had taken him years to build his business to this point. This robbery would seriously set him back. "Here you go," he said, fairly throwing the bag at the robber. "Now, leave, please!"

Jack Norris turned pale green eyes onto the jeweler, a sneer on his unshaven face. "Have a nice day!" he said, just before bringing the gun up and smashing it over Bob's head. With the crack against his skull, Bob slumped to the floor. The man in the trench coat stalked out of the shop and moved down the sidewalk without a backwards glance.

Chapter Four

The halls of Edwardsville College were not crowded now. With it being after three o'clock, most of the students had already left for home. Alana had taken a later class so she would not have to do any night classes this semester. She slung her backpack over her shoulder, on her way to see her advisor.

"So, are you excited about graduation, Alana?" Dianna Akin asked with a smile.

"Yes, definitely," Alana answered as she sat in the chair across from the counselor. Dianna had been her source of advice and assistance for over three years, so she was very comfortable talking to her about anything of concern.

Dianna herself had found Alana Crewe a joy to work with. The last three years had not been easy for Alana, but she always tried her best in her schoolwork. The fact that she was now so close to graduation was a bigger accomplishment than many gave her credit for. Because of finances, Alana had had to take a couple semesters off, setting her back. Last year, her grandmother had died, and the loss had hit Alana hard. Dianna alone knew how difficult it had been for Alana to keep her grades up, but she managed to get through that semester with all A's and only one B.

"Well," Dianna said, flipping through Alana's paperwork, "it looks like everything is here. The only thing you have to worry about is passing your classes, but I have no concern there."

Alana smiled. "Thanks for the confidence."

"You've earned it," Dianna replied. "I don't say this to a lot of my students, but I really am proud of how you far you've come. You've done a good job, and I will be glad to give you a good recommendation for your next school."

"I really appreciate that," Alana said. "I wouldn't have been able to do it without your help."

"I was glad to do it. I look forward to seeing you walk the aisle in your cap and gown."

Thursday evening, March 6th

"Alana, it's about time!"

Alana smiled at the group of girls gathered in Rachel's living room. She deposited her purse in the kitchen and joined them.

"Rachel made us hot dogs." Belinda held up her plate.

Sitting between Bailey Hawk and Christy Nelson, Kenneth and Maggie's granddaughters, Alana reached for the bowl of chips being passed around. "You shouldn't have gone through all this trouble, Rachel," she objected.

Rachel smiled and shrugged. "It was no trouble." She was sitting in her favorite stuffed chair, her hand resting lightly on her swollen belly.

Dinah arrived a few minutes later and Rachel started the weekly study. They were talking about Esther, what she did for her people and of her faith.

"What appeals to you the most about Esther?" Rachel inquired at one point.

"I like the fact that she put aside her own safety to think of her uncle and her people," Belinda answered.

"I think it's neat that she didn't forget where she came from," Christy said thoughtfully.

"What I mean is, she was a queen now. No one had to know anything more than that about her, but she lowered herself to be willing to share the same fate as the rest of the Jews."

Rachel nodded. "She was a very strong young woman, someone that ladies today can learn from."

"She didn't let herself be controlled by her fear," Alana spoke up. "She stayed in control at all times. She was in a very dangerous position, but she never lost control."

"I know what you mean," Dinah nodded. "We hear so much about bad things happening to girls every day. I just watched on the news the other day of a girl being abducted near Kansas City. Sometimes I wonder, what would I do if it was me?"

Belinda shook her head. "I'm a nervous person by nature," she confessed. "I'm afraid I would completely lose my head if I was put in a bad position."

Alana cocked her head. "I don't see myself giving up," she reflected. "I think anyone who tried to attack me would have a fight on their hands."

Dinah laughed. "You're such a nice person; I can't imagine you fighting anyone!"

Alana laughed with her. "I know. But I probably don't have anything to worry about anyway."

"Why?" Dinah asked.

With a shrug, Alana said simply, without thought, "Who's going to waste their time coming after me?"

The statement was immediately met with cries of outrage.

"Good grief!" she laughed. "I didn't mean to start an uproar! I was just making a comment."

"Girl, you need to stop talking like that," Belinda was saying.

"Really!" Bailey agreed.

"Do you really want to see me in a position like that to prove your point?" Alana asked.

"No!" Belinda said quickly.

"Good!" Alana chuckled. "Then we can change the subject."

Dinah looked over to see a troubled expression on Rachel's face. "Are you okay?"

"Hmm?" Rachel turned a preoccupied gaze to the girl.

"Is it the baby?" Alana asked, concerned.

"Oh, no, I'm fine," Rachel insisted. "I was just thinking."

Once she convinced the girls that she really felt fine, they returned to their previous conversation. Rachel forced her attention back to the meeting, trying to shake off the sudden cloud that had hung over her.

"Alana! Wait up!"

Alana turned and waited for Dinah to join her.

"Were you serious about what you said in there?" Dinah asked, looking bothered.

"About what?"

Dinah put her hands on her hips. "You know very well what I'm talking about."

Fidgeting with the strap on her purse, Alana smiled. "I really didn't mean for it to sound that way."

The blonde stepped into Alana's path and crossed her arms. "What did you mean, then?"

"Dinah, come on, it's not that big a deal!" Alana attempted.

"I'm not leaving until you talk to me."

Sighing, Alana looked away. Uncomfortable now, she wished she had never opened her mouth. "I've never had a very high opinion of myself," she finally admitted.

"Why not?" Dinah demanded. "You are so pretty and so smart!"

"Well, I don't know about that," Alana contradicted.

"Listen to you!" Dinah reprimanded. "You're doing it again!"

Alana could not help but laugh and Dinah joined her. "Okay, I know I shouldn't be that way," she amended. "I've always had the habit of comparing myself to others." When Dinah began shaking her head, she held her hand up. "I can't help it. Especially when I see all these cute couples around me. Look at Belinda and Tommy. They're *so* happy together, and then there's you and Curtis."

"Curtis is a *clod*," Dinah whined, as if she were trying to make Alana feel better.

"You know he's not," Alana said around her laughter. She grabbed her friend by the arm, noticing how distressed she was getting. "You don't have to put yourselves down to make me feel better. I'm not saying I resent you guys! I love watching the two of you together. You are so outgoing, and Curtis is such a gentle guy, even if he is a clod. You make an adorable couple, and I can't wait for the time that you announce your engagement."

The last comment caught Dinah unaware and she blushed. "Don't say that!"

"Why? Aren't you looking forward to it as well?" Alana teased.

"Well, yeah," Dinah giggled.

"Okay, then," Alana laughed.

Dinah threw her arms around Alana's shoulders, surprising her with the impulsive move. "You'll find someone who loves you as much as Curtis and I do! Just wait and see." she predicted.

Alana returned the hug gratefully. "We'll see, but thanks."

Friday, March 7th

The Crewe family had always been close. As the oldest child, Alana took her position in the family seriously, building strong relationships with each one of her siblings. Anthony and Andrea always knew they could go to their oldest sister about anything and seven-year-old Audrey practically idolized her.

Despite their bond, work and school had made it difficult for the family to spend time together, especially as the kids grew older. Alana and Anthony were both working part time jobs, and Alana and Andrea also had school. When Anthony started college that fall, it would get even more difficult to get together. Sharon saw this and made it routine for the family to share dinner together on Friday evenings. The kids grew accustomed to this rule and made sure they did not plan anything during that time.

Alan said grace, always adding a line of thankfulness for the family that God had blessed him with. The talk around the table was of anything of concern to them and often bounced from subject to subject. Alan and Sharon believed it was important to stay in touch with the events of their kids' lives, so as to better support and encourage them.

So on this Friday, Anthony filled his parents in on the ball team that he and his co-workers were attempting to put together. He worked at a sports shop, and although he had never been much of an athlete, he did enjoy baseball. It seemed he was having trouble getting enough teammates to make up a whole team.

Andrea was having trouble with algebra and revealed her frustration. She was a senior that devoted herself to excellence. She planned to get a job after school ended to help pay for her education, in the same way that her older brother and sister had. Anthony, the math whiz, offered to help her later that evening.

Audrey was full of talk of the "herd of horses" she had seen that day when she had gone with Alan to the grocery store. Her excitement grew as she described the way they "raced with the car." Alan winked at his family and disclosed that it had been three horses that had trotted alongside the SUV as it got ready to turn off the road.

The talk was light and uplifting. Alana always felt better when she left the table. She loved her family, as it should be. As a shy person, she had trouble opening herself up to others, but she felt comfortable talking to her parents about anything that came up in her life. She considered Andrea her best friend. And then there was Anthony.

At nineteen, he was two years younger than her, and sometimes acted out of selfishness or self-centeredness. They fought at times, like other brothers and sisters, and his harsh words sometimes hurt. Through it all, though, she knew that he loved her, and five minutes later they would forget what they had even argued about.

Audrey was Alana's shadow, her ray of sunshine. Ten years younger than Andrea, she had been a surprise to all of them when Sharon found out that she was expecting a fourth child. Instantly the whole family had been taken by the child and at times Alana wondered how dull their life would have been if Audrey had not been born.

Just before nine o'clock that evening, Audrey called Alana into her room after Sharon tucked her into bed.

"Will you read to me, Allie?" Audrey was the only one who shortened Alana's name. She did the same thing with Anthony and Andrea, calling them Tony and Andie.

"Sure, kiddo." This was a nightly routine for the two. After saying good night to the rest of the family, Audrey would pick out a book for her sister to read. The little girl would then crawl onto Alana's lap as they sat on the bed. Alana read out loud, letting Audrey point out objects of interest to her. This night, as Alana was turning the light out, Audrey asked, "Will you always read to me, Allie?"

Alana smiled at the little girl. "Sure, kiddo. As long as you want me to."

Audrey grinned as she snuggled down into her covers. "Then I want you to read to me every night for the rest of my life!"

Curtis shuffled across the living room, his eyes blurry. He opened the door and stared out into the darkness. "Did you have to interrupt my sleep?"

Jason Banks laughed as he stepped into the light of Curtis's house. "Sorry, dude, it took me longer to get out of the city than I expected."

"Save it for later," Curtis grumbled. He locked the door, turned the lights out, and said over his shoulder, "Good to see you. You know where the extra room is. Have a good night. See you in the morning."

Still laughing, Jason followed his friend from the room, knowing that he would get a warmer welcome in the morning, when Curtis was more awake.

Sure enough, before the sun was even completely out of the shadows, Curtis caught Jason up in a bear hug. "It's been too long, man!"

"That's not the impression I got last night," Jason joked, returning the brotherly embrace.

"Well, that's your fault!" Curtis insisted. "What did you expect, arriving after midnight? Did you think I was going to stay up all night for you?"

Jason put his hands up in surrender. "All right, all right. I'm sorry."

Curtis grinned. "Good."

Sunday, March 9th

The Sunday school lesson was another success for Alana. The girls seemed to be growing more interested in the things of the Lord, and she hoped and prayed it would be only a matter of time before Breanna would make her decision for Christ.

She found her seat and smiled back at Dinah and Curtis, immediately noticing the strange guy sitting with Curtis.

"Oh, hey, this is Jason Banks," Curtis spoke up, seeing her curious glance. "I was unlucky enough to have him as a best friend growing up."

Alana smiled as Jason said, "Gee, thanks, Curt."

Jason was tall, dark headed, with rugged good looks and clear blue eyes. His warm personality radiated from the sincere smile he gave her, making Alana feel strangely at ease with him at once.

"Well, my air-headed friend gave my name, but he seems to have forgotten yours," Jason said jokingly.

"Oops."

"I'm Alana. Alana Crewe."

"Oh, I've heard a lot about you."

Surprised, Alana cast a suspicious glance at Curtis. "Great."

"Jason's a cop, Alana," Curtis informed. "He's thinking about transferring over here, just to be closer to me."

Jason immediately denied the last comment.

"Where do you live now?" Alana questioned.

"In Topeka," Jason answered.

"Really?" Alana's brows rose. "And you're trading the exciting city for a small town like Edwardsville?"

Jason shrugged. "Well, I feel like God's moving me here, for whatever reason. At least for the time being."

"Oh, I see," Alana replied. "He's certainly not someone you want to argue with."

Jason smiled. "No, I've definitely found that out."

After the service, Curtis took Jason around to the rest of the members. Everyone seemed especially pleased to meet Curtis's friend, especially the single females. Jason caught more than one admiring glance turned his way, but he took it in stride. He found the people to be friendly and warm, and he was impressed with Kenneth's sermon. He told him so when he had the opportunity.

"Thank you, young man," Kenneth said. "I'm glad to hear that you're considering moving to the area. From what I hear from your buddy there, we could use some more young men like you."

Casting a sideways look at Curtis, who was grinning goofily back at him, Jason responded, "I'm looking forward to the move. I'm supposed to talk to the police captain tomorrow."

"Well, we'll be praying that everything goes all right," Kenneth assured.

Chapter Five

"I don't think our copier is working right," Stacey said, running her hand through her short red hair.

"What's wrong with it?" Alana asked.

Stacey held up a page. "It's printing the pages all blurry."

"Maybe it just needs to cool down."

Shutting the printer off, Stacey flopped down on her chair. "Is it time to go home yet?"

Alana laughed. "Not for another two hours."

They were interrupted by the ringing phone, which Stacey promptly answered. "They need a loan at the service desk," she announced after she hung the phone up.

The girls put the money in a cash bag and walked up together. They were surprised to see how busy it was.

"When did the rush start?" Stacey asked Pamela, the head Customer Courtesy Manager.

Pamela shook her head. "In this place, you can never tell when it's gonna get busy."

They caught sight of Dick Browning just then, talking on the phone. Alana could hear his side of the conversation.

"I'm sorry, ma'am, we don't carry that item…Well, we try our best to offer as much as we can to our customers…I can call some other stores and see if they carry it. They may be able to ship it here in a few days…Yes, I will notify our home office and tell them about this problem…Well, I am sorry for your inconvenience. Have a nice day."

He hung up the phone and looked at Alana, who was stifling her laughter. "Boy, the things these customers ask for!" he declared.

"Another unhappy customer, Dick?"

Dick wiped his brow. "She wanted to know why we didn't carry pigs' tongues."

"Pigs' tongues?" Alana repeated. "Good grief!"

"But you know our motto," Dick reminded.

"The customer is always right," Alana quoted, giving a salute. "And their needs come before our means."

"That's right," Dick sighed.

"I think that is way overrated," Stacey said.

"Nonetheless, it's the customers that provide us with a paycheck," Dick pointed out. "So, we must do everything in our power to provide anything they need, even if it's…pickled carrots!" he blurted out.

"Pickled carrots!" Alana laughed. "How weird is that?"

"There's no such thing," Stacey said. "Is there?"

Alana stifled her laugh, trying not to attract attention. "No, goofball."

"I was just making a point," Dick said with a grin.

"If anyone ever asks for pickled carrots, then you'll really have problems!" Alana declared, just before she and Stacey left the front for their own office.

Police captain Wade Harmon shifted the papers he was reading and looked over the top of them to the young man sitting across from him. "This is quite an arrest record you have," he observed.

Jason nodded and said simply, "Thanks."

Wade had been in the force for over thirty years, and he knew a good cop when he saw one. Just from reading his records he could tell that Jason Banks was an excellent law enforcer. "So, why do you want to transfer here?" he asked, setting the papers on his desk.

"I just feel that it would be a good move for me," Jason explained. "I think I've done a good job in Topeka, but I'm ready for a change."

"Why didn't you just try for a higher position?"

Jason shrugged. "I enjoy working the streets."

Wade steepled his fingers and rested them against his lips. "Well," he said finally. "From our discussion and your record, I see no reason why I wouldn't approve the transfer. I'd be happy to have you on my team, even though we really don't have much excitement around here. I'm sure your present boss will hate to lose you."

Jason stood and shook the older man's hand. "Thank you, sir. I look forward to working with you."

"What do you think?"

Alana turned to Stacey, who was holding a slinky nightgown up to her. "Stacey!" she exclaimed, looking around to make sure no one was watching.

The two young women were taking a break from the office and were walking around the store, "window shopping," as Stacey called it.

"I think it's cute," Stacey said, hanging the gown back on its rack.

Wandering out of that department, they studied shoes and house ware appliances.

"Hey, look at that!" Stacey suddenly gasped.

Alana looked to where Stacey was pointing. A tall, dark, very good looking man was ahead of them, looking over the men's boots. Alana smiled, catching Stacey's wide-eyed stare, and walked in his direction.

"Alana!" Stacey shrieked. "What are you doing?" She knew how out-of-character it was for Alana to approach strangers, especially men.

Alana marched right over to the man, feeling uncommonly bold, with Stacey gawking at her as if she had lost her mind. "Doing some shopping?" she asked, aware of Stacey following closely behind.

Jason was startled to be spoken to and twisted his head around. "Alana!" he greeted. "Yes, to answer your question, I was doing some shopping. Which boots would you suggest?" he asked, half joking.

Staring at the row of men's lace up boots, Alana said, "They all look the same to me."

Jason chuckled.

"Did you have your meeting with the captain today?"

Surprised that she would remember, Jason nodded. "Yes, I did."

Cocking her head, Alana asked, "How do you think it went?"

He took a deep breath. "He seems to be a hard, tough man, but I think he's fair. The meeting went fine. I expect the transfer to go through pretty quickly now."

"So you're moving to the area?"

"Looks that way."

Alana smiled. "Curtis will be glad."

"Yeah," Jason agreed. "It's been a long time since we've shared a neighborhood. I'm looking forward to having him nearby again."

Finally remembering the girl behind her, Alana said, "Oh, this is my co-worker, Stacey Martin. Stacey, Jason Banks."

Jason shook Stacey's hand with a warm smile.

"Where have you been hiding him, Alana?" Stacey asked bluntly, a gleam in her eye.

Jason chuckled as Alana's face went red. "We just met at church yesterday."

"I see."

Jason spoke to Alana again. "So you work here?"

"Yeah, I do," she replied, trying to forget her embarrassment.

"Obviously not in the shoe department," Jason teased.

"No," Alana laughed. "I work in the Accounting Office. We both do."

Jason seemed impressed. "Good position."

"But no fun," Stacey put in, making a face.

"So, when do you head back to Topeka?" Alana asked.

"Actually, that's where I'm headed now," Jason informed. "I just stopped by here to see if I could find a pair of boots. My old ones are about to fall apart."

"Well, have a safe trip," Alana offered.

"Thank you. I should be back in a week or two. I'm going to start moving my stuff down here."

"Oh, good, maybe I'll see you then." Alana knew it was time to go back to work, so she said her goodbyes and moved away. As soon as the office door was shut, Stacey attacked.

"Why did you never tell me about him? He's gorgeous!"

"Stacey!" Alana objected. "I just met him yesterday! He's a friend of Curtis's, and obviously a very nice guy, but that's it!"

Stacey crossed her arms. "You must be crazy!"

Alana shook her head. Stacey was always trying to pair her up with someone. "For all I know, he's probably got a girlfriend."

"If he does, he's leaving her in Topeka."

"Stacey, he's not going to show any interest in me, so just drop the subject, please!"

Stacey did, shaking her head in exasperation. Alana was relieved to put her mind back to her work and forget the whole conversation.

It was Tuesday night before Curtis heard from Jason again, and when he did, Jason told him that he was coming to Edwardsville on Wednesday to look for a place to live.

"You know of any apartments or houses for rent?"

"Mm, I might know of a couple," Curtis told him.

"Good, that'll make my search easier. I'll only be in town overnight."

"How 'bout we make a day of it?" Curtis suggested. "I'll get some friends together and we'll all go apartment hunting with you. It would be a good chance for you to get to know my group, and someone else may know of a place for you to try."

"Sure," Jason agreed. "Sounds fun."

Wednesday morning, March 12ᵗʰ

At seven in the morning, the young adults from New Hope Fellowship Church gathered in the parking lot outside of *Darings'*. Alana was there, as well as Curtis and Dinah. Belinda and Tommy also joined the group, and Bailey and Christy. Dinah's brother Jesse was the last one to show up, except for Jason.

"Ah, he's late," Curtis groaned. "I told him to be here at—oh, there he is!"

The group rowdily greeted Jason as he pulled up in his beat-up Chevy truck.

"All right, I've already introduced everyone, right? Good, let's go!" Curtis called.

Everyone separated into groups and formed a line as they drove out onto the road. Curtis was in the lead, as he had the directions to the first place Jason wanted to check out. Alana found herself in a car with Bailey, Jesse, and Belinda. Bailey and Jesse were both finishing their first year of college, so much of the conversation rotated around school.

Everyone was in high spirits as they arrived at the first location. It was a rather nice spot with a small house on a neatly trimmed lot. Curtis went to find the landlord, who unlocked the door and let them explore the place.

"Seems nice," Dinah said to Alana.

When Jason asked how much the monthly payments were, however, everyone had to refrain from gasping. Jason thanked the man kindly and told him honestly that the amount asked for was a little above his means.

"It was nice, but not that nice!" Belinda exclaimed as they all went back to their cars.

Alana had to admit that this had been a good idea of Curtis's. She could imagine that it would be easy for someone to get discouraged house-hunting with no luck. Having friends around kept the atmosphere light. Jason seemed too busy laughing and talking with Curtis's friends to be bothered.

Someone suggested stopping for lunch around noon. Everyone agreed wholeheartedly. They stopped by a fast food joint for burgers and shakes. Alana dug down in her purse for her wallet. When she could not place it immediately, she set it on a table and searched.

"Oh, no," she whispered, realizing that she did not have it. Thus, she had no money to pay for her lunch. *I must have left it on my desk,* she thought, frustrated with herself. *I wonder if I could borrow money from Dinah.* She hated to ask. What if no one had extra cash? She was not about to deprive anyone else.

"Um, I'll just take a water," she told the cashier.

Alana took the cup and moved away from the counter. She found a cluster of tables for her crowd and sat down, sipping her water. She frowned angrily at herself, especially when her stomach growled.

You knew we'd be stopping for lunch! she scolded herself. *Why didn't you make sure you had your money with you?*

No one had noticed Alana's scant order. No one but Jason. He took his tray and joined her, catching her frown just before she saw him.

"You're not going to eat?" he asked.

"Oh, no, I'm just having water," Alana said, smiling a little too widely.

Jason looked at her. "You're not hungry?"

"I'm fine."

"That's not what I asked you."

Now Alana's frustrated smile was directed at Jason. "Why are you so worried about my eating?" She was surprised and little ashamed at her abruptness.

"Because I'm afraid you're going to go hungry because you refuse to ask for money. Right?"

Alana blinked. "What makes you think that?" she continued.

Jason reached in his pocket and withdrew a ten dollar bill. "I've left my billfold at home too many times to count," he said quietly, aware that they were about to be joined. He slid the bill over to her. "Go get you something."

Alana objected. "I can't take—"

"Just go." Jason's voice was soft, but firm, and Alana suddenly found she could not argue with it. She took the money and rose from the table, relieved that he had not made a big deal over it. "Thank you," she said quietly.

"Are you just now ordering?" Curtis asked her, setting his tray by Jason's.

Alana smiled sweetly. "I was trying to figure out what I wanted."

By the time four o'clock rolled around, Jason had at last settled on a place. It was a two bedroom house, with a combined kitchen and living room area. "It'll be plenty of room if I ever have friends over," Jason surmised.

"Not that you have many," Curtis joked.

The house was set just a few miles out of Edwardsville, so he would have privacy, but not be cut off from the town.

Everyone was tired but pleased when they headed for home. Alana showered and headed straight for bed. She did not remember until just before she fell asleep that she still owed Jason for her meal. "Oh, man," she thought drowsily. "I'll have to make sure I pay him back."

Friday night was reading night; or at least it was in Alana's schedule. Her weeks were usually so full that she did not have much time to spend engrossed in a good book. So she set aside two hours every Friday night, just before going to bed, to read. She was more often than not joined by Andrea. The sisters talked sometimes but usually just enjoyed one another's company.

This night, however, Andrea broke the silence. "What do you think your first kiss will be like?"

Alana raised her eyes from the book. "Where did that question come from?"

"This book made me think of it."

"Another romance?"

Andrea smiled. "Yeah. Do you ever think about it, though?"

Alana shrugged. "Sometimes. But it doesn't do any good to think about it unless you have a pretty good idea who you're going to share it with."

"That's true," Andrea agreed. "Who do you want to share it with?"

Closing the book, Alana sat up and crossed her legs on the bed. "I don't know. How about you?"

The blush on her sister's face answered her question.

"Is there something you want to share with me, Sis?"

"Oh, I haven't kissed, if that's what you're getting at," Andrea said. "But, Brent asked me out today."

Alana's eyes widened. "He did? What did you say?"

Andrea rolled her eyes in self-disgust. "The dumbest thing a girl could ever say! I asked him why!"

"What? Why on earth would you ask him something like that?"

"Who knows?" Andrea shrugged. "I mean, how many reasons are there for a guy to ask a girl out?"

The girls stared at each other for the space of several heartbeats, and then doubled over with laughter. They could be heard from downstairs, where Alan and Sharon were sharing a last cup of coffee before heading to bed.

"I hope they don't wake Audrey up," Alan said with a smile.

Meanwhile, Alana was finally regaining her composure. "Okay, after you asked him why, what did you say?"

Andrea dissolved into giggles again.

"Come on, Andrea!" Alana tossed a pillow at her. "Get serious!"

"Well," Andrea cocked her head. "I told him I'd go with him to the school play next week."

"Oh, Andrea!" Alana exclaimed. "That's great! Brent is such a great guy!"

"I know!"

A little while later, after getting absolutely no reading done, Andrea went to her own room and Alana stretched out in her bed. She smiled at the thought of her little sister dating.

She took a deep breath and brought the covers up to her chin, suddenly growing sober.

When will it be my turn?

Chapter Six

Jefferson City, Missouri
Early Friday morning, March 14th

It was after midnight and the city was as quiet as it was ever going to get. Jack Norris knew he was going to have to get out. He had spent a week in Jefferson City, and noticed some people looking at him strangely. No doubt, his parole officer had got the word out that he had skipped town and had his picture in every newspaper.

"No matter," Jack muttered, creeping close to a red four-by-four. "I'm not going back to that place. And nobody, including my nosy parole officer, is going to get in my way."

The driver's door was unlocked. Staying low, Jack reached under the steering wheel and cut a few wires. In just a few minutes, he had the vehicle running. Norris grinned as he sat up straight. "This is a nice jeep," he said out loud. "I might just have to keep it for a while before I ditch it."

The jeep pulled out into the highway, heading southwest. He really had no idea what he was going to do in the future, but for now, things were going fine. Things would look even better in Kansas. The more miles he could get between him and Thomasville Prison, the more chance he had of keeping his freedom.

"Might even go down south for a while," he continued his monologue. "Maybe visit some old friends."

Monday, March 17th

"I know now for sure it was God who moved me to transfer," Jason told Curtis as they carried boxes into Jason's new house.

"Why's that?"

"Because there was no other way for that transfer to go through so quickly.

41

I'm already employed with the Edwardsville police, and Wade said I could start work Wednesday."

Curtis was amazed. "Maybe He just knew I needed my best friend around again."

They were in the living room now and deposited their boxes on the floor. The house was cluttered with boxes, trunks, and furniture, and a musty smell hung in the air.

"House will have to be aired out," Jason mused.

They made several trips until all of Jason's things were in the house. "This is going to take forever," Curtis complained.

"Hey, I didn't ask for your help," Jason pointed out. "You volunteered."

"Dinah's always telling me I open my mouth before I think."

With a chuckle, Jason said, "Sounds like a smart girl. When the two of you going to get married?"

"Oh, I don't know," Curtis said, rummaging through Jason's things. "To be honest, the subject has never come up. Besides, I want to make sure I can support her."

With Curtis's help, Jason managed to move the living room area into some semblance of order. Unpacking pictures, he and Curtis spent some time catching the other up on his family.

"Hey, you still have this thing?" Curtis asked suddenly, holding up a long blade. The handle was made of steel with silver rings at the hilt. "I figured this was long gone." He made a few slow swings with it.

"Aw, come on, you're gonna break something," Jason protested.

"I never could figure out with the point of this sport was."

"What's that supposed to mean?" Jason asked, his hands on his hips.

While studying the shiny weapon, Curtis explained. "Well, now a couple hundred years ago, I understand why it was so important to be able to use one of these things, but now? Man, with the technology we have, this is useless." He turned to face Jason. "I mean, look at you. You're a two time State champion, but what good has it done you? You're not rich or famous, and chances are, you'll never use it again."

Jason, with an exasperated look, reached out and took the sword. "You never know, I might."

Curtis shot him a doubtful look. "What, you think there's gonna be a damsel in distress? Are you going to rescue her from the evil dragon with this thing?"

He got a shrug in response. "I just might."

Still not looking convinced, Curtis went back to work cleaning the room. Jason gazed on the sword for a moment before digging its case from the pile. He hung the long pine box with the glass door on the wall. "What do you think?"

"For a decorative piece? Fine, I guess."

Both were busy for a time, and there was little talk. Curtis finally sat down on a chair and said, "I need a break."

"Sure you do," Jason teased, but he sat down as well.

"So, Jason, what do you think of the church?"

Resting his elbows on his knees, Jason said, "I'm impressed. They all seem to be very sincere and full of joy. You don't get that much in the city."

"Well, *I* noticed that the girls noticed *you*."

Jason shook his head. "I'm not going to touch that one."

"Why not? They're all great, and you could use a girlfriend."

"Curtis, don't go there again."

Sitting up, Curtis sighed loudly. "Stop living in the past, dude! You can't let one bad experience sour you on women completely!"

"I'm not sour on women," Jason insisted. "I'm just content with my life the way it is."

"Baloney!" Curtis spat. "What about Bailey? She's cute, isn't she?" He snapped his fingers. "Alana! What'd you think of Alana?"

"Very sweet," Jason answered. He looked Curtis straight in the eye. "For a friend."

Curtis frowned and slumped. His eyes strayed around the room for a while and then he glanced back at Jason. He noticed the contemplative look. "You like her, don't you?" he jumped.

Jason put his hand up. "Far from it, Curt. I was just thinking about Wednesday. She's not the type to bother anyone for herself, is she?"

"Definitely not," Curtis said with emphasis. "How'd you know?"

Jason told his friend briefly about Alana forgetting her money, and how she was content to drink water while everyone else ate, just so she would not have to borrow money.

Curtis shook his head. "Man, any of us would have been glad to help her out. I'm glad you took care of her. You see, that's just how she is. She always seems to think she's going to be a bother. She just doesn't realize how crazy we all are about her, or how wonderful she is." He pointed at Jason. "Do you realize that she makes nearly all A's in her schoolwork, but you couldn't convince her that's she's smart?"

Jason gave a short laugh, his eyes on the floor.

"Doesn't matter what we tell her, she always seems to doubt herself." Curtis gave Jason a long look. "Sound like someone else we know?" He didn't wait for an answer, and Jason didn't give one. He sat for a while, deep in thought, even when Curtis had gone back to work.

"Are you still on the paper work?" Bryan asked Alana impatiently.

"Yes, I am," she answered mildly, not looking at him.

Annoyed, Bryan spoke sharply. "You need to put that aside and count some of this money! We're getting low in fives."

"There's a bundle in the safe."

"Look at me when I'm talking to you!"

Moving slowly, Alana turned from the papers and faced him, her anger rising. "I don't need to be spoken to like a naughty child, Bryan."

"Then stop acting like one," Bryan retorted unfairly. "You forget, sometimes, who you're talking to. I'm not just a stupid associate here. I'm the assistant manager, and I have the authority to fire you if I feel you are not benefiting the company. And, right now, I don't see how you are!"

Biting her tongue, Alana did not reply. She knew he was just picking for a fight.

Bryan took the bundle of five dollar bills, unwrapped them, and took what he needed, leaving the rest in a pile on the counter. "Now, you stop fooling around and get this mess cleaned up," he ordered before he left.

Unable to move at first, Alana took a deep breath. She did not often get angry, but unfair treatment was always a sure fire way for her temper to rise.

She straightened the money that Bryan had left and for the first time considered talking to Dick about Bryan.

"But, what am I going to tell him?" she asked herself. "Will you do something about Bryan, because he's being mean to me?"

Coming to the conclusion that her problems with Bryan were for her to deal with alone, Alana tried to calm her irritation by prayer. Only then was she finally able to return to her work.

That night, she confided in her mother about the confrontation.

"It sounds to me like he's crossing the line, just a bit," Sharon observed. "I don't see why you don't talk to Dick."

Alana shrugged. "Because I just can't. He's got so much on him right now; I don't want to add my petty problems to it." She took a deep breath. "But, I do feel better, though, just being able to talk it out."

"Well, I'm glad I could help."

As Alana began to move away, the phone rang.

"Hey, Alana!" Dinah greeted.

"Yeah, what's up?" Alana could hear voices in the background.

"I'm sorry to call you so late, but I figured you'd be getting off work about now. We have a stupid question to ask you."

"Okay, shoot," Alana offered, curious.

"Was it Luke Skywalker's left or right hand that Darth Vader cut off?"

"What?" Alana laughed. "What in the world have you all been talking about?"

Dinah laughed as well. "We're at Jason's, helping him clean up. Somehow the subject got on to Star Wars, and the guys keep saying that it was the left arm. Belinda and I think it's the right. I remembered that you were a Star Wars fan, and thought you could help us. So?"

Shaking her head in amusement, Alana said, "Sorry, guys, it was the right."

Dinah immediately crowed the answer back to Curtis. Alana could hear him holler, "Well, who asked her?"

"It was your suggestion, you goof!" Jason retorted.

"Sounds like you guys are working real hard," Alana observed.

"Well, actually we did get a lot done," Dinah told her. "Until they started talking about Jedi. Now, we're not going to get any work from Curtis. He's all upset cause he's wrong."

"Thanks a lot, Alana!" he called from the background.

Alana chuckled. "Tell him no problem!"

When Alana hung the phone up, Sharon was looking at her with a raised brow.

"That was an unusual conversation."

"Tell me about it!" Alana chortled. "Those guys are nuts!"

"Jason Banks is fitting in nicely with the people of the church," the older woman observed. "He seems to be a very nice guy."

"Oh, he is," Alana agreed.

"Is there a spark of interest?" Sharon asked.

"Oh, Mom, don't go that way. I try not to think about stuff like that anymore. It just gets me disappointed. I'm glad to have Jason as a new friend, and that's it."

Sharon nodded. "I guess that's wise. No sense in counting chickens before they hatch."

Alana went upstairs for the night, but Sharon sat for a few minutes in the kitchen, mulling over her daughter's words. Surely Alana did not think that she would always be disappointed. Surely she knew that God would bring someone special into her life eventually.

Sharon was right in saying that Jason was fitting in. He made an effort to get to know the young people and even took time to play basketball with the teenage guys. He felt it was important to not only attend a church, but to be a part of it.

"I have found that a church family is essential for the times when you're facing trouble," he told Kenneth, on a visit to the parsonage.

Kenneth and Maggie, immediately liking the young cop, had invited him to the house for dinner. Jason received dinner offers from several families, specifically those with single daughters, but the pastor's offer meant more to him than many of the others.

He also found that he enjoyed being with Curtis's circle of friends. Each person was unique and had his or her own special contributions to the comradeship. Having not been a part of anything like this before, Jason was having the time of his life.

Alana had taken him by surprise when she tracked him down the next Sunday and tried to give him ten dollars.

"What's this for?" he asked.

"For paying for my meal last week," Alana explained. "I still owe you."

"Oh, no," Jason protested. "I didn't loan you the money. I gave it."

"But—"

Jason put the bill back in her hand. "Keep it. I might need you to pay for my meal someday," he said with a wink.

Dinah and Curtis wanted to arrange another outing that week, so Dinah caught Alana just before she left.

"We're going to Kansas City for a gospel group concert on Wednesday night. You interested?"

"Sure," Alana said. "I like music. Where should I meet you?"

"We'll just come by and pick you up," Curtis offered, stepping over and slipping his arm around Dinah's shoulders. "That all right?"

"Save the gas in my car? Sounds great," Alana said lightly.

Chapter Seven

Tuesday afternoon, March 25th

Alana dressed in one of her favorite outfits. It was casual, but she felt it was one of the few that played up her features nicely—a peach colored knit shirt with pale cream flowers, a knee length khaki skirt and tan colored sandals. She studied her reflection in the mirror. Her hair was pulled back in a French braid, and a few tendrils had loosed themselves and floated about her face. The green tints in her eyes seemed brighter, and her skin glowed with health.

"You look nice," Andrea told her, watching her from the doorway.

"Are you spying on me?"

"You going on a date?" Andrea asked impishly.

"No," Alana told her. "The whole group is going to a concert."

"Oh. Have fun."

Alana knew that Curtis and Dinah would be arriving soon, so she made sure she was downstairs. When the vehicle finally pulled up, though, it was Jason's truck. Audrey happened to be on the porch and watched the man approach the house.

"I thought Curtis was picking Allie up," she pointed out.

Jason smiled down on her. "He sent me over to get your sister. Is that okay?"

"I wanted to talk to him."

Jason crouched down to her level. "You did?"

"Yeah, he's my friend."

"Wow, he's pretty lucky."

"Has he ever told you about me?" Audrey was still watching him with careful eyes.

Jason turned his head and looked at her from the side of his eyes. "Has he ever told you about me?" he returned the question.

"No."

Sighing exaggeratedly, Jason said, "He's always forgetting things."

"I know." Audrey nodded seriously. "He forgets things all the time."

"We'll have to get on to him next time we see him, okay?"

Audrey grinned. "Okay."

Alana had watched the entire exchange from the door and smiled when Jason finally looked up at her. "Looks like you made a new friend."

"And a nicer friend I couldn't ask for," Jason said, winking at Audrey. "So, where *is* Curtis?"

Jason stood up, now towering over Audrey. "He and Dinah are running late, so he asked me to pick you up. They should be ready by the time we get to his place."

"Oh, okay." Alana grabbed a jacket, knowing it would be cool later.

"Bye, Jason! Bye, Allie!" Audrey called as they moved down the driveway.

Jason looked over at Alana. "Allie?" he questioned.

Alana smiled. "That's her pet name for me. She's the only one who's ever called me that."

"I see." Jason's face took on an impish gleam as he opened the passenger door. "Well, then, *Allie,* we best be on our way."

Moaning as she climbed in, Alana said, "Great, now I've got two of you!"

"So, how do you like your new job?" she asked when he climbed behind the steering wheel.

"It's great," Jason answered. "The other cops are all friendly, and my partner seems to be fun."

"That's good." That said, she felt foolish when she could not find anything else to say. She turned her head to look out the window, wishing she was a little more outgoing, like Dinah.

Jason, however, did not mind the silence, and was thinking that Alana really was a nice person. He could see that she felt a little uncomfortable riding with him, but he determined that he would make her feel at ease. *After all, she's a good friend of Curtis's.*

Curtis and Dinah were just walking to the car when Jason pulled up into Curtis's yard.

"Where's everybody else at?" Alana asked.

"Actually, we were the only ones that could make it," Jason informed. "Belinda isn't feeling good, and the others had to work, I think."

Alana was putting her hand on the door handle to get out when she heard Jason say to Curtis, "Alana can just ride with me over there."

"Sure," Curtis said easily, getting into his vehicle. "See you over there."

"That all right with you?" Jason asked.

Alana shrugged. "Sure."

It was quiet for a few minutes while the two vehicles left the small town. Then Jason asked, "So, you're going to college right now?"

"Yes," Alana answered quickly, relieved to have something to talk about. "I graduate in May with my Associate's. I start this fall working towards my bachelor's."

"What are you majoring in?"

"Education."

"Oh, really? I used to think about being a teacher, but then I thought that me and the kids would probably just kill each other."

Alana laughed. "Well, I want to teach first grade. Hopefully I'll be able to handle them."

"I don't know," Jason said slowly. "If you wind up with a class of kids like your sister, you may be in over your head. I bet she's a real livewire!"

"That describes Audrey exactly!" Alana said. "She's always talking, always thinking. Sometimes her questions throw me off. I didn't ask questions like that when I was her age!"

"She's a cutie."

"Well, you've certainly won her over today."

It struck Alana just then how easily she had fallen into conversation with Jason. Even now, with nothing more to say, she was no longer uncomfortable. His laid back attitude was certainly easy to take.

Jason sensed the change in Alana and hid a smile at her content face. She really was an interesting person to talk to once she relaxed. The rest of the trip passed by quickly with their comfortable exchange.

The concert was deemed a good one by the group as they headed back to their vehicles. Once again, Alana was riding back with Jason, so she told Curtis and Dinah goodbye.

It was a little past nine when she arrived home. Her family was still up, so Jason went in with her for a few minutes. He spent some time talking with her parents about his job. Alan had always been interested in law enforcement, and Jason willingly explained anything that Alan had questions about. Sharon found him to be a very respectful young man and was secretly glad that he had made his way to Edwardsville.

This town could use more young people like him, she thought.

Anthony was rather surprised at Jason's openness. He had not met many guys that would take time out of their day to get to know other members of his church. This cop was an exception. He even invited Anthony to play basketball with him and the other guys the next week, an invitation that Anthony promptly accepted.

Most people who did not know Andrea well suspected her of being shy and reserved. Only a few members of the church knew of the mischievous streak in her. Jason Banks took one look at her and caught on to this out instantly. He began teasing her about her petite height and within moments they were bantering back and forth like old comrades.

Audrey had already decided earlier that he was all right and now sat by him on the couch. Jason was aware of her presence and every now and then sent her a wink and a smile. Audrey would return the smile and a weak attempt at a wink.

Alana sat back and watched Jason's exchange with her family in awe. In only a few minutes, this man had completely won them over, just by simply reaching out to them and trying to know them. She had seen him do this with other families in New Hope, and had to admit that she was impressed. Jason was intent on really knowing the church members.

Jason did not stay long, aware of the late hour. Alan invited him back soon.

"Just drop in any time," he told him. "We like to have company."

Jason appreciated the invitation. "Thank you, sir. I'll keep it in mind."

"Just call me Alan, son."

Despite the lateness, Jason felt good when he arrived home. He could see just from the short time he had spent with them that the Crewes were special people, and looked forward to spending more time with them.

Thursday, March 27th

Darings' was not busy this night. There were some shoppers, but not too many. It was the kind of day Alana liked working. Only one factor kept it from being near perfect—Bryan. Each time he entered the office, he jabbed a cutting remark. He commented on how slow she was working, made fun of her boots—anything he could think of. She ignored him the best she could and found that she was still able to fairly enjoy her evening.

The front desk called her up front to check a computer, and she eagerly took the change to leave the office. After fixing the frozen screen, Alana headed back, taking her time. She let her eyes wander over the store, resting lightly on anything of interest to her. It always impressed her, the variety of items Darings' had to offer.

Keeping his hood over his head, Jack Norris scolded as his stomach grumbled yet again. He walked across the large parking lot to the sprawling store ahead. Out of money long ago, he had decided it was time to make a stop. He was wise enough to know he would not be able to rob the place, but maybe he could snatch a few items that would get him some cash on the streets.

Overhead, the sky was lit with millions of stars, but he did not notice. He stepped into the bright store, ignoring the greeter at the door. Looking around at the directive signs, he headed back to the electronics.

On duty, Jason strolled the aisles of *Darings'*. His blue and black uniform was drawing looks from customers and associates alike. The streets were quiet, which was why he was here now. He had not had much opportunity to visit the big department store and decided to take the opportunity. Standing head and shoulders above the racks, Jason spotted a familiar head across the aisle, and grinned to see what she was engrossed in.

"You never seemed the superhero type," he observed, coming up behind her and resting his elbow on the rack.

Alana started and took a step back, as if embarrassed to be seen here. "Oh, you scared me!" she scolded.

"Are you shopping, ma'am?" he drawled.

"I'm just looking," Alana said, smiling.

"So, who's your favorite?"

Alana turned back to the rack. "Well, they're all awesome, but I've always been partial to the Incredible Hulk."

"Hey, me, too!" Jason replied. "I like the TV show best, though."

"Me, too," Alana agreed. "I've always felt bad for him, you know?"

Jason sighed exaggeratedly. "Yeah, I know. The guy had to travel the world, meet all kinds of interesting new people, and get a new girl on every show. Sounds like a real pathetic case!"

Alana laughed. "You forget what happened every time he got mad."

"Well," Jason shrugged. "That's a minor detail. Actually, he's the reason I went into the police."

Raising her brows, Alana said, "A big, green monster inspired you to become a cop?"

"Well, no, not like that," Jason corrected. "I mean, I watched him every week take down bad guys. I knew I could never do it the way the superheroes did, but I could in this way."

Alana cocked her head. "That's an interesting story."

"Miss Crewe, how long are you going to waste time talking?"

Jason watched Alana stiffen as a thin, young man joined them, his face arrogant.

"You can't expect to be paid for doing nothing," Bryan went on.

Without looking at the manager, Alana told Jason, "I better get back to work. I'll see you Sunday."

"Sure. Have a good night." He gave her an encouraging smile before she left, then turned his eyes on Bryan, who was staring at him cockily. Jason held his gaze for several seconds before Bryan raised his brows in a smug look and walked away. Jason shook his head and went on his own way.

Alana was boiling as she walked towards the back. How dare Bryan belittle her like that! And in front of Jason! In her anger, she decided then and there that she would speak to Dick about Bryan's behavior. For now, she prayed for calm as she approached the Employee Only swinging doors. Just before she got to them, however, something at the corner of her eye stopped. A man in dark clothing was positioned just a few feet away from her. She paused, watching him.

Standing before a case of computer equipment, the man was acting strangely. There were discs, parts, and supplies that cost well over a hundred dollars in the case, and Alana noted that the doors had somehow been opened. Her eyes widened as the man smoothly dropped a three hundred dollar part into his pocket, glancing around cautiously.

Slipping behind a shelf, Alana kept her eye on the shoplifter and looked around for security.

They're never around when we need them! she thought agitatedly. She would have to keep her eye on the man until she spotted someone who could help.

The man slipped several more items into his large pockets, all very inconspicuously. Amazed, Alana estimated he had nearly a thousand dollars worth of merchandise. To most anyone passing, he looked as if he was just studying the case. She wasn't even sure what it was that had caught her attention. It was only because she had looked straight at him that she caught him in the act of stealing.

Finally, he straightened up, looked around again, and walked away. Alana followed him, always staying a few yards behind and out of sight. She looked around frantically for a security, a manager, anyone. The exit doors were drawing near when she at last spotted Dick Browning walking across the store. She waved to him and made the store sign for shoplifter. He nodded and quickly called on his radio for security, heading for the front as he did so, so he could cut the thief off. Alana managed to meet up with Dick.

"Can you call the cops?" Dick asked her in a whisper, his eye fixed on the man.

"There was one just in here a while ago," Alana whispered back. "I'll see if he's still here."

Hurrying, Alana went to the courtesy desk. "Did you see a tall, good looking cop just now?"

Pamela nodded. "Yeah, he left just a few seconds ago. Why?"

Alana said, "I'll tell you later," and rushed out the door.

Chapter Eight

Dick waited until the man was right up to the doors before stepping to his side. "I'm sorry, sir, could you come with me for a moment? Seems you've left something in the store."

Jack Norris paused, and then followed the man cautiously, so as not to make a scene. He stayed alert, however, for he did not like the look on the man's face. At that point, he saw a security guard heading their way, and knew instantly that he had somehow been found out. Reacting quickly, he grabbed a can off a nearby shelf and hurled it through the air. The can hit the guard square on the head, and he dropped soundlessly.

Customers screamed and gasped at the scene while Dick grabbed at Jack. Norris slammed his fist against the manager's stomach. Without waiting, Jack took off. Dick hollered after him, but he went on.

Alana could see Jason just a few yards on the other side of the entrance drive. "Jason!" she yelled, crossing the drive.

Jason turned around, puzzled.

"We need you inside," she called. "We have a shoplifter."

At that moment, Jack burst through the doors, knocking people out of the way. Alana spun around and gasped.

"Hey!" Jason shouted, quickly capturing the man's attention.

Alana froze as Norris slid to a stop, his shocked eyes falling on the cop. He glanced around furtively, clearly looking for a way out.

"Don't make any more trouble for yourself, mister," Jason advised, taking a step forward. His hand hovered just a few inches over his gun. He did not like the way this guy was acting. He wished Alana was not standing so close.

An unsuspecting car turned onto the entrance drive just then, completely oblivious of the standoff. Jack took his chance and dove across the car.

"Alana!" Jason yelled, grabbing his gun.

Jack rolled across the hood of the car, grabbed Alana, and they both went down. The car's brakes screamed as it careened to a stop. Jason went running forward when Jack rose to his feet, Alana in his chokehold. Her arm was savagely twisted behind her back.

"Freeze!" Jason had his gun up.

"Get back, cop, or I'll break her neck!"

Jason hesitated.

"Drop the gun!" Jack tightened his hold on Alana's neck. Her eyes widened slightly.

This was not the first time Jason had been put in a difficult position like this, and the feeling of frustration and helplessness were not new. However, never did it involve someone he knew and cared about. Seeing the shock and fear on Alana's face, Jason let his gun fall. He raised a restraining hand to those rushing out of the store. The driver of the car still sat in shock behind the wheel.

"Come on, mister," Jason spoke calmly. "There's no reason to react this way. Shoplifting's a crime, but it won't put you away forever."

Jack shook his head wildly, his warm breath falling on Alana's neck. "I'm getting out of here." He took a step back, forcing Alana with him.

"There's no reason to hurt her," Jason coaxed. "Just let her go."

"I don't think so!"

Jason was suddenly fighting for control. He silently prayed for calm. There was no way he was going to allow Alana to be hurt—not while he was standing here.

The thought of the man forcing her to go with him filled Alana with fear, and, surprisingly, some anger. She clenched her jaw, thinking, *He's not taking me anywhere!*

Jason saw the change on Alana's face. Her foot came up slightly. "Don't do anything rash," he warned, presumably to Norris, but his eyes were on Alana.

"Stay back!" Jack warned, twisting Alana's arm so hard she gasped in pain.

A siren cut through the air just then, and Jack's head whipped around to see police cars coming into view. Alana took advantage of his unguarded moment and slammed her booted heel into his shin. He howled in pain as his hold loosened slightly. She threw herself to the side, wrenching herself out of his arms.

Jack roared and turned on her. "Come here, you—"

"That's enough!"

Halting, Jack turned slowly to see the cop on one knee, his gun back in hand and aimed directly at Jack's chest.

"If you doubt I'll use this, just try me," Jason said, his voice cold and his eyes glittering.

Knowing he had no choice, Jack stood still but cursed loudly as the patrol cars screeched to a stop.

Officers came out of the cars, their guns also trained on the shoplifter, and two young cops quickly searched and handcuffed him. As soon as the man was covered, Jason rushed to Alana and grasped her shoulders.

"Are you all right?" he asked breathlessly.

Rubbing her neck, Alana simply nodded.

Jason gently put his hand on her neck. At her wince, he said, "You'll more than likely be pretty bruised." He put his arm around her shoulders and turned her back to the store, where customers and associates alike were pouring out.

"Are you all right, Alana?" Dick asked, his eyes worried.

"I'm fine," she assured quickly.

Dick turned to the cop next to her. "I don't know what would have happened if you wouldn't have been here. That guy was nuts!"

Sgt. Matthew Goodson stepped out of his car and approached the man being arrested. "Well, Jack Norris, looks like you're heading back to the slammer."

Jack's eyes narrowed.

"Sir, do you know this guy?" another cop asked.

"Not personally," Goodson answered. "But authorities in Nebraska have an alert out on him. Seems he skipped the state without telling his parole officer."

A rage filled Norris so that he could not see. He looked around for Alana. "I'm gonna find you, girl!" he screamed, even as the cops started pulling him towards the car. "Just wait! I'll kill you! I'll kill you!"

Jason's arms tightened around Alana's shoulders. "Get him out of here!" He turned Alana to face him. "Don't worry about him, Alana. He won't get out."

"I know," Alana said simply. She was still in sock over the sudden turn of events, and didn't know what to think.

Jason pulled her close for a quick hug, breathing a prayer of thanks that the situation had ended safely.

Appreciating his concern, Alana found that she was having trouble breathing. There were so many people standing around her, talking, asking her questions. She took advantage of his strength and leaned against him.

"Can we go back inside?" she asked Jason.

"Yeah, just one sec." He turned to Dick. "Do you have someone who can take over for her?"

"Oh, yeah, sure," Dick said quickly. "She can take the rest of the night off."

"Jason, I don't need to go home," Alana interrupted. "I just need a few minutes."

"No, Alana," Dick spoke to her. "I'm telling you to go home."

Jason started to lead her away.

"Jason, I can't just leave in the middle of my shift."

"Alana, you've just been through a traumatic experience. You're in shock and I can still feel you shaking."

"But, I don't want to be a bother—"

Jason cut her words off by stepping in front of her and looking down at her face. She had to look quite a ways up his six foot four inch frame.

"You're not a bother, Alana," he said firmly. "Stop believing you are. Dick said you could go, and I'm happy to take you home."

"Oh, but I have my car." At the look she received for that statement, Alana fell silent.

Hours later, Jason pushed his chair on its back legs, away from the desk. Back at the police station, he was filing the report on Jack Norris's arrest. He rubbed the bridge of his nose, bone weary.

Matthew Goodson sat across from him suddenly. "Our Mr. Norris is an interesting man. Do you know his history yet?"

Jason just shook his head.

"He was just released last month on parole. He was spending time for armed robbery."

His eyebrows going up, it was beginning to dawn on Jason just how fortunate they all were how the situation had gone. He shuddered to think of how tragic it would have ended if Norris would have had a gun.

"Before that," Goodson went on, "he had been in and out of prison for robbery and assault."

Jason's chair fell forward with a thump. "You're kidding."

"Nope. Every time, he managed to get back out on good behavior. But, it seems he can't stay out of trouble. Like this last time he was released. As soon as he was free, he fled the state and…"

Shaking his head, Jason finished his sentence. "And got himself right back into trouble."

"Yep," Goodson nodded. He leaned forward, his face serious. "But, that's not all. Norris has been accused and tried on several occasions for murder, but each time there was never enough evidence to convict him."

Jason sucked in a breath. Who would have known how this night had turned out?

"Didn't I hear him threaten that girl?"

Looking at the cop, Jason said slowly, "Yeah."

Goodson made a face. "I wouldn't treat that threat lightly, Jason. Better keep her safe, or Norris just might find a way to get her."

"Not if he's in jail," Jason pointed out.

Shrugging, Goodson rose to his feet. "Yeah, until the next time he gets parole."

When he was gone, Jason sat for a long moment, digesting what he had just heard. Feeling his muscles tensing, he went to prayer.

"Father, keep me calm," he whispered. "Help me to keep my head; I don't want to scare Alana. Keep her safe, Lord. Above all else, keep Alana safe."

To say Alana's family was stunned to hear what had happened was a gross understatement. Sharon, in tears, had held her daughter tightly for a long moment, and then, to Jason's surprise, embraced him as well. She thanked him for being there for Alana. It had taken a long time for Alana to convince her that she was all right, just tired. By the time everyone finally headed to their beds, they were exhausted.

In her drained state, Alana expected to fall asleep instantly, but every time she closed her eyes, she could see Jack Norris's face, screaming at her. It was after three in the morning before she finally gave up. She turned her lamp on and reached for her Bible. Psalm 91 had always been a source of comfort to her, and she let its words soak into her spirit.

"Lord, I am so grateful You were with me tonight when that man had me in his hold. I know it was Your strength that upheld me. And thank You for bringing Jason on the scene, and for keeping him safe."

She shuddered as she remembered the grip Norris had on her neck. "Don't let me live in fear, God," she murmured, sliding back under the covers. "Help me to trust You above all else. You are my shield and buckler. I am safe in You."

She turned the lamp off, and darkness filled the room once more. She held her Bible in her arms as she was finally able to drift to sleep.

The next morning was bright and sunny, the promise of spring in the air.

Sharon sent Alana out to the porch swing while she fixed breakfast. Alana was out there only a few minutes when Jason drove up.

"Are you taking it easy?" he teased, joining her on the porch.

Alana smiled. "My mom seems to think I'll fall apart."

"Well, I don't blame her." He took a seat next to her. "You've got a really nice yard here."

"Thanks. Dad works hard to keep it up. We own over twenty acres in all, and he wants to get it all cleared out and fixed up."

"I hope he won't cut all these trees down," Jason said. "Some of them look like they could be ancient."

Alana shook her head. "Oh, no. He likes them, too. Says it gives the place an air of privacy." She sighed contentedly. "I like walking through the woods on cool days. You see some interesting things. I even saw a doe and her fawn one time."

"Now that's something I didn't see in the city," Jason told her.

They fell silent at that point, taking in the big yard. Alana could sense that he was troubled. "What's wrong?"

He looked at her. "I need to talk to you about something, but I want your parents to hear, too."

"Okay," she said. "Let's go inside."

When Alan and Sharon saw the cop, they again expressed thanks for what he did in protecting Alana.

Jason shook his head as they all took seats at the kitchen table. "Not even here a month and I find myself in the middle of a standoff."

"I'm just glad you were there," Sharon told him.

"To be honest, all I did was talk. Alana's the one who took the situation in her own hands."

"I did not."

"Yes, you did," he argued. "I wouldn't have been able to get you away from him. You took care of yourself."

"The other cop cars distracted him," Alana said. "I felt him loosen his hold. Besides, if you wouldn't have had your gun, he just would have got me again."

"I wouldn't have even got my gun if you hadn't kicked him."

"Would you stop making me look like the hero here?" Alana finally asked, exasperated.

"Would you stop downplaying your part?" Jason returned.

At that moment, they became aware of Alana's parents staring at them with amused expressions on their faces. Everyone laughed.

"Okay," Jason chuckled, shaking his head wryly, "back to business."

"What's on your mind, Jason?" Alan asked. He had gotten to know Jason well in the last two weeks and thought a lot of him.

Jason clasped his hands together. "It's about Jack Norris."

"The man who was arrested last night," Sharon confirmed.

"Yes. Several heard his threat to Alana last night and there's been some concern over it."

"But, he's behind bars," Alan said. "He can't do anything from there."

Jason bowed his head in acknowledgment. "That's true, but he may have friends that would be willing to help him. And, he has a history of being in and out of prison, always managing to get parole on good behavior. If he would happen to get out again and remember last night…" He did not finish the sentence.

Sharon sat back in her chair, her face anxious. "So you think there's a real reason to worry?"

"Now, I don't want you to live in fear," Jason said quickly, directing his gaze to Alana. "But, I just want you to be aware of the threat."

Alana crossed her arms. "So, do you want me to stay behind closed doors? Go out in disguise? What are you getting at?"

He gave her a slanted look. "No, I'm not suggesting anything like that, smarty. I'm just saying be careful."

"Is he considered a dangerous man?"

The question came from Alan, and as Jason looked into the faces of Alana and her parents, he could not bring himself to tell them anything more about Jack Norris, about his history, about the suspicions surrounding him. He took a deep breath, choosing his word carefully.

"He does have a rough past, one that would cause him to be considered a menace to society." He leaned his elbows on the table. "I've already talked to your manager, Alana."

"You have?'

"Yes, he says you are not to walk outside alone. When you leave the store, you are to have a male escort, or to walk with a group, until this all passes over."

"Which could be when?" Alana pressed, clearly not pleased with this arrangement.

Jason shrugged calmly. "Could be weeks, months, even years." He spoke slowly and dramatically. "You could be doing this for the rest of your life!"

Alana reached over and slapped his arm. "You liar! I'm serious!"

With a smile, Jason answered her question. "I really don't know, Alana, but that's the plan, and I expect you to follow through with it."

Frowning, Alana said, "Sounds like a lot of trouble to me."

"To keep you safe?" Jason asked. "I would think it would be worth the trouble."

"I'm not worried about his silly threat," she argued. "People make threats all the time, but they never follow through with them."

Alan spoke up. "But, we will go along with this, just in case he's serious."

She sighed loudly. It wasn't that she didn't appreciate the help. She just hated to cause so much trouble.

"Trust me, Alana; it's no bother for anyone to help make sure you're out of harm's way."

Blinking, she stared at Jason, wondering briefly if he had read her thoughts.

Jason did not stay long after that. He left in his patrol car, waving at Alana, who had walked him to the porch. She went back inside, deep in thought. She nearly ran into her father, who promptly took the opportunity to hug her.

"What's this for?" she asked, smiling up at him.

"What, can't a man hug his own daughter without being interrogated?" he teased. He pressed a kiss to her brow. "Jason's a nice guy."

"Yes, he is," Alana agreed.

"I'm glad to know you've a got a good cop like that watching out for you."

"Not that I need to be watched."

At Alan's disapproving look, she said, "Okay, okay. No more complaining."

Chapter Nine

Jason drove back to the station, feeling satisfied with how things had gone. He knew Alana was not happy with the arrangement, but her safety was important. He admitted to himself that probably nothing would come out of all this, but he wanted to make sure. He had never expected a shoplifter to face off with him, an innocent girl in his grasp. He did not want to be caught unawares again.

Jack Norris was transported to Topeka, where there was more security. He would have a trial, but the odds were against him. In a matter of weeks, he would be back in Thomasville Prison.

The story was in the newspapers that day, spreading like wildfire. Jack Norris's picture was printed on the first page, with the news of his recent release and disappearance from Nebraska. Nothing of the sort had ever happened in Edwardsville, and everyone was shocked at the event that had transpired on the parking lot of *Darings'*. The fact that an ex-convict had made his way to their small town was rather frightening.

Alana worked to stay out of the limelight, making only a few comments about what had happened. Reporters took most of their information from witnesses, the police, and Norris's own history. Within the week, articles about his standoff and trial were circulating. The man had criminal records in several states, thus accounting for the widespread attention.

In Salt Lake City, Utah, two states away from Edwardsville, Reuban Ferraro picked up a newspaper with a large photo of Jack Norris. Reuban's dark brows rose as he read the headline. *Jack Norris Behind Bars Again.* He took some change from his pocket and paid for the paper. Settling down at an outside café, he ordered a latte and skimmed the entire article. Sipping on his coffee, he leaned back in his chair, thinking.

Business had gone good in Salt Lake. The clients that he had met with had been more than generous. Marlon would be pleased. Thus, Reuban had some extra time on his hands before he had to go on to Chicago.

Kansas is right on the way to Illinois, he mused. *Maybe I'll just pay a visit to our old friend. Seems he could use some cheering up.*

His mind made up, Reuban folded the paper and slid it into the deep pocket of his expensive pinstriped suit jacket. He picked up his suitcase and started whistling. By that evening, he planned to be driving through Colorado, his destination—Kansas.

Sunday, March 30th

Alana was thronged when she walked through the doors of the church Sunday morning. Everyone had heard about what happened Thursday and expressed their heartfelt relief that she was all right. Alana was more than a little overwhelmed and humbled by their obvious concern.

Dinah grabbed her hand when Alana was passing by, pulling her down to the seat next to her. "I could not believe what happened!" she gasped, squeezing Alana's neck. "I would have been scared to death!"

Feeling that she could let her defenses down a bit with Dinah, Alana shook her head slowly. "Dinah, you have no idea how I was shaking! I honestly thought he was going to take me with him."

Dinah bit her lip. "Don't even think that! This is so weird, though! We were just talking about stuff like this in Bible Study a couple weeks ago. Remember?"

Alana had not until that moment, and she felt chills on her arms. "That's right!" she gasped. "Who would have known that I would face a situation like that?"

"Sounds like God was preparing you for that night."

"Yes, it does," Alana agreed.

"Hello, ladies," Curtis suddenly greeted, he and Jason appearing at the pew.

"Oh, let me get out of your seat, Jason," Alana offered, preparing to move.

"There's room for both of us," Jason assured, taking the seat next to her. Curtis moved past both of them to Dinah's other side.

"Sounds like you two had an exciting week," Curtis said, motioning to both her and Jason.

Alana smiled. "I guess you could say that."

Kenneth asked Alana again if she would sing. She accepted rather reluctantly. During the opening prayer, Kenneth praised God for His protective hand on both Alana and Jason. Alana heard several quiet amens at that.

When the classes ended for the day and Alana once again made her way to the sanctuary, Dinah waved her back to sit with her. Alana felt rather strange with Jason next to her, but he just gave her a friendly wink and she soon forgot her discomfort.

When the time came for Alana to sing, her mouth went dry. She hated that she had to go through this every time she sang. Why couldn't she just sing without a panic attack?

She chose another old hymn, her father's favorite. She closed her eyes, letting herself dwell on the Heavenly Father's presence before she opened her mouth to sing.

I come to the garden alone
While the dew is still on the roses.
And the voice I hear
Falling on my ear,
The Son of God discloses.

Alana's voice rose high for the next note and she held it for several seconds.

And.... He walks with me
And He talks with me.
And He tells me I am His own.
And the joy we share
As we tarry there
None other has ever known.
He speaks and the sound of his voice
Is so sweet the birds hush their singing.
And the melody that He gave to me
Within my heart is ringing.

Alana sang the chorus for the second time, once again feeling a surge of love for her Savior. She ended the song and returned the microphone to the pastor. Eager to return to her seat, Alana smiled shyly at the enthusiastic applause of the church. She slid past Jason and sat down. She glanced up at him and raised her brows in question when she found him staring down at her, looking stunned.

"Wow," he whispered simply, bringing another smile from her. She then turned her attention to the front as the service went on, ready to put the attention behind her.

The friendship between Alana and Jason had grown stronger after the night of the standoff. The people of their church saw this, and although they expected a romance to be kindled, there was none. They seemed to genuinely enjoy each other's company, but neither sought anything more.

Curtis realized this and constantly gave Jason a hard time about it.

"If you don't care for her in any way than as a friend, what's with this sudden bond   between the two of you?" he asked Jason one day.

Jason raised a brow. "Uh, it's called friendship."

"Don't get smart with me," Curtis returned shortly. "I think you're crazy."

"Curtis, I've told you time and again, I'm not ready for a steady relationship with anyone. I think Alana's a great person, and I'm enjoying the chance to get to know her as a person, but that's as far as it gets."

On Alana's side, she was questioned by both her sister and Dinah on two different occasions. Dinah approached her after another Thursday night Bible study. "So, you and Jason seem to spend a lot of time together," she said simply.

Alana just shrugged. "He comes to the house sometimes to play basketball with Dad and Anthony. He's a good guy."

"Is that the only thing you feel for him?" Dinah asked impishly.

Slanting a look at her friend, Alana warned, "Don't go there."

"Why not?"

"Because, we're just friends. I don't want anything more."

Crossing her arms, Dinah said, "Seems like a waste to me."

"What's that supposed to mean?"

Dinah rolled her eyes exaggeratedly. "Girl, there's this good looking guy that you get along great with. He thinks a lot of you, and both of you are wasting this connection on friendship."

Alana shrugged mildly, looking down. "I don't think it's a waste. I need good friends."

Dinah suddenly felt bad for how she had sounded. "I'm sorry, Alana. I didn't mean to be snotty. If you're happy the way you are, then it's none of my business." She gave Alana a quick hug before she jogged to her car. "See you Sunday!"

Alana watched her go and gave her a weak wave. She sighed slightly as she then started her own car.

It was the very next day that Andrea caught her. "Are you and Jason considered a couple now, or what?"

The older girl threw her arms up in surrender. "What's with the interest in me and Jason?" she exclaimed. "There is nothing going on, okay?"

Andrea was surprised at her sister's vehement reaction. "Gee, I'm sorry."

Alana sat down on her bed. "No, I shouldn't have snapped at you."

"What's wrong?"

"I don't even know," Alana admitted. "Everybody seems to expect something to happen, and I'm feeling a bit uptight about it. I mean, what if it causes him to feel uncomfortable? I've come to think a lot of him, and I don't want silly comments to put a strain in our friendship."

Putting an arm around Alana's shoulders, Andrea tried to reassure her. "I wouldn't worry about that. Jason is too levelheaded to let everyone's thoughts worry him."

Alana smiled. "Thanks, sis."

On the first of April, New Hope Fellowship Church had their annual pot luck dinner to raise money for missions. Kenneth Nelson had a missionary friend down in Mexico, and the church always made an effort to support him in his work. The dinner was at the county park, and many people from the town arrived to buy a plate of home cooked food. Already there was over two hundred dollars raised.

Alana was in the midst of it all, helping where she could. She did not have much opportunity to speak to Dinah, both being busy. Even the guys were hard at work lifting heavy tubs of casseroles and cases of sodas. Feeling good about her work, Alana hoped that one day she would be able to visit a mission in Mexico.

After three o'clock, the steady flow of people finally started to slow down. The ladies cleared the tables of empty dishes and began to get ready for the next busy hour. Alana had a few minutes of free time, and she opted to take a walk through the park.

It really was a lovely area. There was a well-kept playground for children, but also attractive pavilions and benches in ideal spots throughout the park. A trail cut through the middle of it, leading into the small woods nearby. Alana liked to walk this trail whenever she had the chance.

The temperature was perfect with the sun was shining warmly above. A few fluffy clouds floated in the air, just enough to provide a few minutes of shade when needed. The trees were putting on their summer garments, and a few still had blossoms. Alana loved spring. Watching the world shake the cold winter bareness and turn green was a highlight in her year.

She was in the middle of the woods now, the trail growing thinner. She could no longer hear the chatter of the workers, but she knew where she was at. She pressed on, intent on reaching her favorite spot. She took a deep breath of the warm air, mentally thanking God that she was alive.

There was a snap behind her in the woods. Alana turned and saw nothing. She stood still, just for a moment growing nervous. She could see Jack Norris's face in her mind. Her shoulders slumped when Jason appeared out of the shadows.

"Oh, it's just you."

Jason put his hands on his hips. "Now, I like that!" he said indignantly.

Alana laughed. "Well, I didn't mean it like that. I just thought it was…someone else."

He gave her knowing look, but he did not say anything. "This is a nice trail."

"It is," Alana agreed. She resumed walking as Jason fell easily into step beside her.

They did not talk, except to comment on a bird or squirrel sharing the trail with them. When they reached the end of the path, Alana took a deep breath. "Look at that."

There was a large clearing with nicely mowed grass. A small hill was in the center of the clearing, with a sprawling gazebo perched on the top. Wildflowers were already blooming around the shelter, and the trees around it shaded the area from the direct sunlight.

"Isn't it gorgeous?" Alana murmured.

Jason had to admit that the spot was picturesque. "This is something that my mother would have liked to see."

"You've never told me about your mom, Jason."

Cocking his head, Jason stuck his hands in the pockets of his jeans. "She was a very small lady, but big in heart."

"Was?" Alana questioned softly, looking up at him. He was staring at the scene with an unreadable expression.

"Yeah," he answered, still not looking at her. "She died from cancer when I was sixteen."

"I'm sorry, Jason," she said. "I shouldn't have asked you about it."

"It doesn't bother me to talk about her," he said, finally glancing down at her with a smile.

Alana felt compelled to change the subject. "I always thought this would be a perfect spot for a wedding."

"Here?"

"Sure," she nodded. "I know of several couples who have actually rented it for their weddings, including Rachel and Tim. That's my dream someday."

"Sounds nice," he said. "For you. Guess I'm not the right person to be talking to about weddings, though. I've lost interest in them long ago."

"Why's that?" she asked, then wished she had kept her mouth shut. She turned away and fingered the collar of her denim shirt.

Jason shrugged. "I guess because I have no desire to have one of my own. Don't expect to find the one that I can't live without." He said the last comment almost to himself, once again lost in thought.

Alana did not respond.

After a moment, Jason said, "We should get back. You shouldn't have come all the way out here by yourself anyway."

"Go ahead," Alana urged. "I'm coming."

Sensing that she wanted some time to herself, Jason did not argue. He moved away, walking slowly so as not to leave her alone for too long.

Alana turned her gaze back to the lovely view. She sighed deeply, vaguely aware that her joy in the moment had diminished. She hugged herself, letting her eyes sweep the place once more before she turned away from it, not looking back as she walked back into the woods.

Chapter Ten

Anthony found Alana as soon as she made an appearance. "Alana, can I borrow twenty bucks?"

"For what?"

"Some of the guys are going to the arcade for a while and I'm broke until payday tomorrow. I promise I'll pay you back then."

Digging in her purse, Alana quipped, "You better. This is my last twenty dollars."

As Anthony took the money, he thought to ask, "Do you need money to eat on?"

"I have two dollars in my pocket. That'll buy me a plate of food."

"I thought plates were four dollars apiece."

She shook her head. "Church members get half off."

Anthony looked outraged. "I paid four dollars for mine!"

Alana laughed. "Oh, well. Consider it your contribution to the cause."

Sighing exaggeratedly, Anthony said, "Fine. I'll see you later. Thanks for the cash."

After he left, Alana proceeded to fill a Styrofoam platter with baked beans, potato salad, slaw, and a BBQ hamburger. She picked a table setting a few yards from the crowd and sat down. She said a quick prayer over her food and picked her hamburger up. It was at that moment that her eyes fell on a boy of about nine or ten. He was standing by himself, eyeing the food with a hungry look on his thin face. His clothes were worn and a bit too small.

"Did you want to buy some food?" she asked gently.

He looked surprised to be spoken to. Alana saw him lick his lips when he saw her plate. Then his face fell. "No, I don't go no money," he said honestly.

Alana set the hamburger back down, her heart melting at the child's yearning eyes. "You know what? I'm not that hungry. Would you want my plate?"

He looked skeptical.

"Really," she assured, closing the lid and holding it out to him. "It's really good."

Moving slowly, the boy reached out and took the plate, looking like he expected her to change her mind any minute. When he was finally sure that she meant what she said, he smiled, his little face lighting up. "Thanks!" He turned and ran off, clutching the plate close to him.

Alana smiled as she watched him go. "Poor thing," she murmured. She offered a quick prayer for him and his family.

Exhaling, Alana moved to get up when a plate appeared in front of her. She looked up, way up, into Jason's face. He took a seat on the other side of the table, his own food before him.

"You are determined to starve yourself, aren't you?" he asked.

She shrugged. "I couldn't let him go hungry."

"I know," he replied, his voice soft.

The admiration in his clear, blue eyes made her nervous. "I didn't do anything more than anyone else would have done around here."

"I don't know about that," he said, sticking a potato chip in his mouth.

Giving him a pointed look, Alana asked, "Would you have finished eating with him standing there watching you."

Jason had to admit that he wouldn't have been able to resist helping the boy. "But I wouldn't have been so content to go hungry for him," he returned. "You know Maggie would have given you a second plate if you would have told what happened."

"I know but I didn't—"

Jason finished the sentence for her. "Want to be a bother."

Reaching for the hamburger on the plate that Jason had bought for her, Alana shrugged again.

"So, how have you been doing this week?" Jason asked, switching the subject.

"Fine," she answered automatically.

Jason watched her. She was not making eye contact. "Have you been worrying about Jack Norris?"

"No." When he continued to watch her, she gave up. There was no sense trying to bluff him; he could see right through her. "Not much," she admitted.

"What are you worried about?"

"I don't even know," she replied, staring inside her cup. "I know he's in jail, I just…"

"It's okay to admit that you're afraid," Jason told her. "But remember that God's got his hand on you."

"Yeah, I know," she nodded.

"And I'm not going to let anything happen to you."

Alana looked up and met his gaze. Something stirred within her and she dropped her eyes. Jason fell silent as well and resumed his eating.

"I guess," Alana spoke up, almost to herself. "I'm still in shock that something like this happened to me."

Jason looked up at her. She was staring off into space, a slight frown on her brow.

"You hear about violence on the news," she went on. "But you never expect it to touch you."

"I know," Jason agreed. "Even when I was patrolling the streets, seeing everything that a cop could see, I still knew that nothing would happen to me or my loved ones."

"Exactly. It's a little scary when men like Jack Norris come into my town."

His own expression becoming pensive, Jason stirred his drink with his straw. "A few years ago I had a cousin that was involved in a school shooting."

Alana felt her brows go up.

"She was shot in the knee, but she lived," Jason informed. "The worst part of it, though, was that her best friend was killed."

"Oh, my," Alana breathed. "How awful."

"It was," Jason said. "My cousin took it hard, understandably. Shook me up pretty good, too. It was the first time I realized something bad could happen close to home. The next time I saw that was when a good friend of mine was in the middle of a standoff in front of *Darings'*."

"But, isn't it nice to know that God is just as real in those close to home situation as he is in the nationwide tragedies?"

Jason felt a smile work on his lips. "I thought I was the one teaching you this lesson."

"I guess you're a good teacher."

Topeka, Kansas
Tuesday, April 2nd
City Jail

Jack Norris stirred when a guard put a key to the lock. "You've got a visitor, Norris," the guard told him.

"Tell him to beat it," Jack spat.

71

"You might want to be nice to this guy. He looks important."

Scowling fiercely, Norris allowed himself to be cuffed and led to the visiting chambers. He sat behind a glass wall, refusing to look at the man on the other side. The visitor did not speak until the guard walked away to his post by the door.

"You're not looking too good, my friend."

At the voice, Jack's head swiveled to face him. "Reuban!" he exclaimed. "What the devil are you doing here?"

Reuban smiled at his enthusiasm. "I was sorry to hear that you had fallen into some trouble, Jack."

The prisoner's face fell. "Not as sorry as I am." He slammed his fist on the counter. "Blast it! Reuban, I was so close to freedom!"

"Calm yourself, Jack," Reuban admonished, glancing at the guard, who was watching them.

"Yeah, yeah," the irate convict muttered.

"Why in the world would you have risked everything for shoplifting?" Reuban asked. "Seems that was far below your capabilities."

"I know, but I was a little desperate. Got overconfident and acted like a fool." He ground his teeth. "It would have been fine, except for that little wretch! I'm telling you, Reuban, if I ever get out again, I'll hunt her down."

Reuban looked down at his hands. "My brother was especially upset to hear what had happened to you."

Norris sighed and ran his hands through his thick hair.

"He said to tell you he will help in any way he can. In fact, he's already working on it."

At the tone of Reuban's voice, Jack slowly turned to stare at him.

Reuban went on, his eyes fixed intently on Jack's face. "Don't you worry. We don't forget our friends."

For the first time in days, Jack Norris began to smile.

Edwardsville

Tim Johnson stirred and stretched his arm out. When he realized his wife was not in bed with him, he raised his head. "Rachel?" he called out softly. Thinking she might have gone to the nursery, Tim got up and looked for her. He padded through the house, not wanting to disturb her if she had fallen asleep somewhere else. At seven months pregnant, she often had trouble sleeping lying down and usually ended up in the recliner.

He found her in the living room, and was startling to see her kneeling on the floor.

"Honey, are you all right?"

Rachel looked up as Tim sat down on the couch next to where she was kneeling. She moved to get up, and he helped her next to him.

"What's wrong, Rachel?"

I don't know," she admitted.

"Is it the baby?"

She shook her head. "No, it's nothing like that. I just had a sudden need to pray."

Tim looked at her. "In the middle of the night?" he questioned.

"Yes," Rachel answered. "I felt as if God was urging me to pray for our church. I don't know why, but the feeling was very insistent."

Tim was silent, not sure what to say.

"You know I don't believe in premonitions," Rachel said, "but, I believe God knows something, and He is trying to prepare us for it."

Feeling a bit anxious for the safety of their baby, Tim asked, "Do you feel that it has to do with us specifically?"

"I don't know, Tim," Rachel whispered. "All I know was that I had to pray, for every family in the church. I prayed that God would uphold them in whatever is ahead for them, and that everyone else would surround them with love, prayers, and support."

Tim kissed Rachel on the head. "Then let's pray together," he suggested.

Rachel nodded. "Yes, let's."

The couple knelt on the floor and turned their hearts to prayer, petitioning God that He would keep the church family safe and sound.

Thursday, April 4th

"I have a big exam next week," Alana announced, dropping her bag on the kitchen floor.

"I'm sorry," Anthony said, not even looking at her.

"Gee, I can feel your sympathy," she teased, getting a small smile from him.

"What's it over?" Andrea asked.

"Czechoslovakia, and isn't that my blouse?"

Andrea looked down at the sky blue polo shirt. "Well, yeah, but I was going skating with the group, and you weren't here, so…"

Alana laughed. "Fine, but now I get to borrow something of yours."

"Sure," Andrea agreed easily.

Since she had to work that night, Alana went to change. A light bulb blew in her room as soon as she flipped the switch.

"Hey, where's Dad?" she called down the stairs.

"He took Mom and Audrey grocery shopping," Andrea answered.

"Anthony, can you change my bulb for me?" Alana asked.

Anthony appeared at the bottom of the steps, looking annoyed. "Can't you do it yourself?"

"You remember the last time I tried? I fell and almost broke my neck! I'm a nervous wreck on ladders."

Anthony rolled his eyes. "Just an excuse," he grumbled, moving out of her sight.

Alana knew he would not change it anytime soon and gave up. With a sigh, she turned her lamp on and changed for work.

The parking lot was crowded, so Alana knew she would be busy that night. As she passed the entrance drive, she got a sudden flashback of Jack Norris holding her by the neck. She shook her head, whispering a prayer.

"God, help me to forget that night. I still see that man in my dreams, and I don't want to live in fear. Help me to trust You."

She passed Dick on her way to the office. "Hey, Dick. Sell any pickled carrots lately?" she quipped.

Dick pulled a serious face. "Would you believe, not one person has asked for them? And we have a whole trailer full of them!"

Alana laughed. "Sure we do!"

Chapter Eleven

Friday night, April 5th

"Bryan, walk Alana out to her car," Dick directed when Alana had made an appearance at the front of the store. She had already locked up the office and was ready to head home.

"Oh, Dick, that's okay," she objected. "I can go alone."

"Don't even suggest it," Dick ordered. "You know the rules. You are to have an escort at all times. Go on, Bryan, and meet me in the stock room when you get back."

Bryan nodded respectfully, but the moment Dick was gone, he rolled his eyes and exhaled loudly.

"Come on, let's get you out of here so I can get back to work."

Alana bit her tongue as they left the store.

"This is such a waste of my time," Bryan grumbled. "I've got work to do, and here I am babysitting for someone who can't walk in the dark by herself."

"I didn't ask you to do this, Bryan," Alana protested. "Don't take it out on me. You know why Dick wants this."

"Yeah, the same reason that cop friend of yours wants it. To keep you safe!" His voice was mocking.

"They believe there is a real threat."

"Yeah, sure."

"You know what?" Alana stopped in her tracks. "Why don't you just go on back to the store? I can take it from here."

"Sure." Bryan turned and walked back to the front doors, not once looking back. Alana ground her teeth and made her way to her car. As she slid behind the wheel, she said out loud, "All right, Lord, either he goes, or I'm going to have a nervous breakdown!"

Reuban visited Jack twice more after that first visit. Each time, he continued encouraging Jack that things would get better. He was very careful with his words, always conscious of the guard standing mere yards away.

On his second visit with Jack, he noticed the man was easily distracted. "What's on your mind, Jack??"

Jack clenched his teeth. "I want that girl to pay for this, Reuban."

"What girl?"

"The girl that got me back in here! I just burn inside when I think of her out there while I'm rotting in here!"

"Don't worry about her," Reuban advised, glancing at the officer.

"I can't forget about her, Reuban," Jack insisted. "I want something done about her!"

"Seems to me that cop has something to be blamed for, as well."

Jack shrugged, acknowledging the fact. "True, but I have a feeling that if I somehow got a hold of that girl, it would hurt him plenty!"

Reuban saw the determined look on his friend's face. "All right," he finally conceded. "Let me think on it."

The very next day, he was back at the jail. As usual, he did not talk openly, but he worded his plan in a way that no one else would figure out.

"I hear there's going to be a beautiful sunset Monday evening," he said casually.

"Is that so?" Jack asked, listening carefully.

"Yeah, it's supposed to happen right at seven forty-five. I hope you'll be able to see it."

Jack nodded slowly. "What about my friend? Will she be able to see it?"

Reuban sat back, with a small smile. He cast a look around him and lowered his voice. "My brother has decided it's time to bring a feminine touch to the place again."

Jack raised his brows. "Her?"

"Why not?"

A slow smile spread across Jack's rugged face. "Now that I think of it, they would make a fine couple!"

Reuban chuckled. "That's what I thought. He's looking forward to meeting her. She'll receive his best hospitality!"

"I'll bet."

Sobering, Reuban rested his elbows on the counter. "I probably won't be able to visit you again, Jack. I hope everything works out for you. Remember what I said about that sunset, though."

Nodding, Jack nodded. "Seven forty-five," he confirmed.

With a gasp, Alana sat upright in her bed. Moonlight streamed through the window, making light patterns on her carpet. Looking anxiously around her room, she forced herself to breathe normally. She closed her eyes, and then opened them quickly, for the images from her dream still seemed too real.

Her door creaked open and her head whipped around to face it. When Andrea poked her head inside, Alana's shoulders slumped.

"Are you all right?" Andrea asked, entering. "I heard you cry out."

Alana shook her head and put a hand to her face. "Just a bad dream."

"About Jack Norris?"

Alana nodded weakly.

Andrea sat down on the bed with her sister. "He's really got you worried, hasn't he?"

"I didn't think I was, but maybe I've been more anxious over it than I thought. This dream was so…real."

Scooting next to her, Andrea said, "I was just reading Psalm 91 the other day, and it made me think of you. You know, the Psalm about protection?"

Alana nodded. She had been reading it a lot lately.

"It talks about how God will protect his people from noise-some pestilence," Andrea continued. "That's what I consider Jack Norris—just a noise—some pestilence."

Alana smiled. "That's pretty good."

Andrea put her arm around Alana's slim shoulders. "You'll be all right, Alana. God won't allow anything to happen to you."

Comforted by her younger sister's reassurance, Alana hugged her. "Thanks, sis."

"You want me to stay in here tonight?" Andrea asked. "It will be like old times when we used to share a room."

"Sure," Alana answered, moving over so Andrea would have more room.

The sisters snuggled down under the covers. They whispered softly for just a few minutes, and then the room was filled with the soft sound of their breathing.

Sunday, April 7ᵗʰ

The station was busy today. Jason was on duty, so he had to miss Sunday services, which he hated. However, he knew that he had a job to do.

"Some things you just have to do, even if you don't like them," he muttered, staring at the pile of paperwork.

"Talking to yourself, Banks?" Goodson teased.

"Yeah, I'm the only one who always agrees with me," Jason joked.

"True," Goodson agreed. "What's the latest on Jack Norris?"

"His hearing is in a week. He'll undoubtedly be convicted for shoplifting, endangering a citizen, and resisting arrest. Then, he'll be transported back to Nebraska, where he'll face more charges."

Goodson shook his head. "Seems to me there's more trouble in breaking the law than just abiding by it."

"Yeah, but those bad boys never seem to realize it."

The day flew by, and at nine o'clock Jason left for home. He found Curtis sitting on his door step.

"You're gonna have to give me a key if you're going to be out all day," Curtis said, following Jason into the living room.

"Oh, I'm sorry, I didn't realize you lived here," Jason quipped.

"Funny."

Jason sat down on the chair and stretched out his legs, groaning. "Boy, what a day."

"Now, what could have made you so busy at the station here?" Curtis questioned. "It's not like anything happened on the streets."

"Wade decided it would be a good time to do some housecleaning," Jason answered with his eyes closed. "We spent all day going through old files, packing some stuff up, and rearranging the offices. I'm beat."

"Poor baby," Curtis crooned.

"I feel the sympathy," Jason said, opening one eye. "What are you doing here? I thought you were at church."

"It's over already," Curtis shrugged. "I'm bored. Dinah went on an overnight visit to an aunt with her parents or something."

"How 'bout a movie?"

"Sure," Curtis agreed. "What have you got?"

"Superman, Incredible Hulk, Wonder Woman—"

Curtis interrupted. "Is that all you have? Superhero movies?"

"Star Wars."

"Oh, good grief!"

Alana was taking advantage of the quiet night at her house. Her parents were in their room. Audrey was sound asleep in her bed. Anthony was working on the computer and Andrea was at a last-minute sleepover with some girlfriends.

Stretched out on the recliner, Alana watched TV for a while and then opened her favorite novel. She had soft music playing and there was a tall glass of strawberry-kiwi juice at her elbow. When the phone rang, she absently reached for it, half-expecting it to be Andrea.

"Hey, Allie!"

"Jason?" Alana stammered, her mind clearing instantly.

"Yeah, it's me. What's up?"

"Oh, I'm just taking it easy," she replied. "Everyone's busy and I've got the living room to myself. I've got me a cold drink and a good book."

"I'm jealous," he complained. "I have a feeling that your company would be better than this nut that I've got over here right now."

Alana heard Curtis howl his protest, and she laughed. "What are you guys doing?"

"Well, we've got another stupid question for you."

"Okay," Alana urged, taking a sip from her juice.

"Is it Luther or Luthor?"

"Is *what* Luther or Luthor?"

"Superman's arch enemy," Jason informed. "is it Lex Luther, or Lex Luthor?"

Alana cocked her head, twirling her hair around her hair. "I think it's Luthor."

"No!" Jason groaned. "Seriously?"

"Afraid so," Alana answered, a smile on her face.

"Okay, Curtis, you were right about that one," Jason admitted. Alana heard the other man cheer in the background.

"Sorry, Jason," Alana chuckled.

"Yeah, sure," Jason drawled. "No, that's fine, Alana. Can't expect you to lie, even for me!"

"No, not even for you!" Alana agreed.

"How did church go today?"

She crossed her ankles. "Good. The lesson went really well. I'm really amazed at the girls' interest right now. I'm almost afraid I'm going to say the wrong thing and lose their attention."

"You just keep telling them the truth," Jason advised. "The Spirit will do the rest."

"You're right," Alana acceded. "I'm just good at worrying."

"There's no reason to worry. From what I hear and see, you're great with those kids. They really admire you and they know that you love them.

Because of that, they will be able to take the truth from you, even if it seems harsh to them."

Alana loved that she was able to talk about things like this with Jason. He seemed to know what she was trying to say, or understand what she was feeling.

"When did you get so smart?" she asked.

"Hey, I've always been smart!"

Once again, Curtis lifted his voice in contradiction.

"Okay, Allie, I've got to get off here and kill Curtis. Hold on just a minute."

Alana giggled as she heard the guys wrestling. She shook her head at their adolescent antics. "I never knew you guys were so juvenile," she taunted when Jason came back.

"It's not my fault," he insisted. "Curtis is a bad influence. Ouch! Nice toss, Curt. Now, put that pillow where it goes."

Alana put her book aside, getting more entertainment in hearing Jason and Curtis poking fun at each other than in her reading.

"Hey, Curtis wants to know if you want to join the rest of us for a hot dog and marshmallow roast."

"When?"

"Uh, hey, Curt! When is this supposed to be? Friday night. Are you free?"

"Sounds like fun," Alana said. "I look forward to it."

"Good, I better let you go. We've bugged you long enough. I'll see you later. Have a good week!"

"Thanks, you too." After hanging the phone up, Alana found that she no longer wanted to read. She took her glass to the kitchen and went to the desk in her room. She was feeling restless, so she knew there was no use in trying to sleep. She pulled her Bible out, the Bible that her grandmother had given to her just before she died. She hugged it to her chest, thinking of the faith of the older woman. She had been a missionary overseas for most of her life and had spent hours telling Alana of her ventures. Alana had admired her grandmother immensely, and wished she had acquired some of the woman's spirit.

With a sigh, Alana opened the Book and her eyes fell on a familiar passage.

"Trust in the Lord with all thine heart and lean not unto thine own understanding. In all your ways acknowledge him and he shall direct thy paths." She read on silently, feeling a moving deep down in her spirit.

"Okay, Lord, I've been feeling You speaking to my heart lately," she whispered. "I need to trust You, with every aspect of my life. My education, my church, my life, my future. I want to insist on things being done in my time, but that is not Your way. Help my doubt to turn into faith."

Do you know that I love you?

Alana could not say where the thought had come suddenly from, but she answered it instantly. "Yes, Lord, I know you love me."

Trust in me.

Tears welled in her eyes. She had never experienced anything like this, and she was moved beyond words. "Yes, Lord I will trust in You." Another image of Jack Norris flashed through her mind and she felt her body tense up slightly.

Trust in me.

Almost immediately, Alana relaxed. "Thank You, Father, for knowing my fears and for taking care of them for me. I know you will protect me. No matter what happens in the future, I know that You're with me. Just as You were with my grandma when she experienced danger in the mission field, I know You will stay by my side."

Alana did not know what had urged her to pray in such a manner, but she felt light, free. It was as if all anxiety she had felt about Jack Norris had evaporated. She continued whispering her praise as she climbed into bed. She drifted into a peaceful sleep, void of any troubling images.

Chapter Twelve

Monday, April 8th

Jack Norris paced the confines of his cell, his mind spinning. He had no idea what Reuban had in mind for his escape, but he had no doubt that the younger man could pull it off. Jack smiled as he remembered some of the stunts the two of them had done together. Though he had not seen Reuban or his older brother for almost two years, he considered them his closest friends. Indeed, if he had to be honest with himself, they were probably the only friends he had.

A guard brought Jack his lunch and the prisoner sat down to eat, hoping this would be his last meal before he would gain his freedom.

The Geography exam that Alana had been dreading was over and she stuffed her pencil into her bag, hoping that she had passed the difficult test.

I'll find out later this week, she told herself as she walked with quick steps to her car. She was getting out of class early so she would actually have an hour at home before she had to be at work at four.

The sun was shining brightly, and there was a faint breeze. White, wispy clouds floated in the sky, and birds were singing with all their might, filling the air with their songs.

I've always loved spring, Alana said to herself, feeling quite content with herself and the world around her.

A dark four-by-four pulled up in front of the Monroe Hotel in Topeka. Reuban Ferraro heard the motor and went to his window. He saw four men step out of the vehicle and approach the building. He nodded in satisfaction.

"Manley Elam, Charlie Hughes, Buddy White, and Duke Franklin," he murmured. His brother had sent some of his best men.

The driver's door opened then and a dark-haired man with broad shoulders and average height appeared. Reuban frowned. He should have known that Marlon would send Vic Dane, his most trusted bodyguard.

Going back to his seat, his face a study of concentration, Reuban waited for the men, still thinking of Dane.

Marlon had hired the young man several years earlier, having been impressed by his firmness of character and solid physique. Vic had quickly won Marlon's respect, and soon became his right-hand man, making him the most powerful man in their business, save the Ferraros, of course.

Leaning back in the comfortable desk chair provided in his lavish room, Reuban was facing the door when he heard the knock. At his call to enter, the five men entered, led by Vic Dane.

"Good to see you boys," Reuban greeted, directing his words to the four behind Vic. He pulled a hundred dollar bill from his wallet. "I'm sure you're hungry after your trip. Take this and get something to eat."

Manley took the money with a toothy grin. "Thanks, Mr. Ferraro," he said. "How soon you want us back here?"

"In two hours. In the meantime, I have some business to discuss with Vic, here."

The four men piled back out, eager for something to eat and a strong drink.

Reuban turned his gaze on Vic, who as staring back him mildly, his eyes hidden by dark shades.

"Vic," Reuban addressed politely.

Vic nodded slightly. "Reuban."

"How's my brother doing in my absence?"

Hooking his thumbs on his belt loops, Vic cocked his head lazily. "Seems to be handling himself all right. At the moment, he's getting ready to go on a business trip to Chihuahua."

"Really?" Reuban's brow went up. "At this time of year?"

Vic did not answer, as was his way. Reuban hid a frown and stretched his legs out in front of him, noticeably forgetting to offer Vic a seat.

"Has he told you why you're up here?"

"Of course," Vic responded calmly.

"Well, good," Reuban said. "We need to discuss our plan."

Uninvited, Vic went to the other chair in the room and sat down, crossing his ankle over his knee. He took his shades off and held them loosely in his hand. His black eyes were still fixed on Reuban. A muscular man with fierce features, his gaze could unnerve even the toughest of opponents. Reuban himself had watched more than once as Vic used his cool demeanor and piercing stare to intimidate men much taller and bigger than he.

Reuban returned the gaze, feeling rather challenged by it, which served only to irritate him. "I've decided that I am going to lead the excursion to get Jack Norris out of jail."

Vic's expression did not change, but Reuban caught a faint lift of a brow.

"It's been a while since I've seen any action, Vic, but I assure you, I can still take the best of them."

"I never said you couldn't," Vic replied, resting a hand on his black boot.

"I'll take Manley and Charlie with me tonight. I already have an idea what to do. Once that's done, I want you to take Jack to Edwardsville. Got that?"

Vic did not miss the authoritative tone in Reuban's voice.

Reuban continued. "There, Jack is going to pick up another guest. You're job is to take her back to Mexico, safe and sound."

"Another female companion for Marlon?" Vic inquired.

"As a matter of fact, she is. Marlon is looking forward to having another woman in the mansion, so make sure you get her there. I'd hate for Marlon to be upset with his best man." Reuban felt a flicker of satisfaction when he saw a muscle move in Vic's square jaw. He stood abruptly, getting pleasure at having Vic look up at him.

"We'll start moving at seven o'clock. Make sure the guys are ready. You can...rest here if you must until then."

"No thanks," Vic replied, standing now. "I'm going out. See you later." He left without another word—no explanation, no time when he would return. Reuban tightened his fist when the door closed behind Vic. He could not help but wonder what Marlon had seen in the man to put him in such an estimable position.

"Andrea, can I borrow your jean jacket?"

The teen looked up from her book. "Isn't it a bit warm for it?"

"It gets a bit chilly in the office," Alana informed. "Besides, I get off late tonight, so it's going to be cool."

"Sure," Andrea shrugged, going back to her reading.

"Thanks, sis."

"No problem."

Alana dug the jacket out of the closet, and saw that Andrea was still engrossed with the book. She left quietly, not wanting to disturb her again. She wanted to wear Andrea's high heeled boots, but she decided not to ask.

The jacket's enough for now, she decided.

In her room, Alana dressed in a knee-length stonewash denim skirt and a lacey black blouse with a v-neck. She put on her thick-soled lace-up boots and finished off the outfit with Andrea's jacket. She shrugged at her reflection.

"All right, I guess," she proclaimed, taking her purse in hand.

"You look cute, Alana," Sharon told her when she entered the kitchen.

"Thanks," Alana said. "I wasn't sure I should wear this. Do you think it makes me look like I'm trying to be a teenager?"

Sharon hid a smile, thinking that Alana looked more like an attractive young woman with a trim figure. "No, not at all."

"Good."

"Can you read this to me, Allie?"

Alana looked down at his youngest sister, who was holding a large picture book in front of her. "I can't now, kiddo, but I promise I will when I get home, okay?"

Audrey sighed exaggeratedly. "Work, work, work! That's all you do!"

"How 'bout I read you two books?" Alana suggested.

"Okay," Audrey agreed instantly and left the room, her ponytail swinging. Alana looked at her mother and they both laughed.

Anthony and Alan were in the yard, putting up a birdhouse. "That looks nice," Alana said.

"Just wait until the birds are living in it," Alan panted, holding the heavy pole up while Anthony packed some dirt around it to stabilize it.

"Can't wait. See ya!"

"Bye, hon," Alan said, a bit preoccupied.

Alana waved at them as she drove away, knowing that they could not get their hands free to wave back. She settled back in her seat, concentrating on the road. She already had in her mind what to expect for the evening, and hoped that she would be working with Stacey.

Topeka was a busy city, full of businesses, automobiles, and people. Vic Dane walked the streets, completely oblivious to what was going on around him. The time was six- fifteen. He knew Reuban would be looking for him soon, but he did not let that rush him. Vic did everything in his own time and in his own way. Perhaps that was one reason he was feeling so unsettled this night.

The relationship between Marlon Ferraro and Vic Dane was envied by all of the former man's employees. Vic had the freedom to do anything that Marlon asked of him in whatever way he chose to do so. Vic's employer bestowed upon him all privileges; there was no one, besides Marlon, of course, to whom Vic had to answer.

The only restriction that stood in their correlation was Reuban. Vic had suspected long ago that Reuban resented Vic's liberty, and displayed this by attempting to remind Vic whenever possible that Reuban answered to no one. He and his brother were equals. The bond between them was tight; Marlon would allow no one to come against Reuban, and vice versa. No one dared to oppose them.

Vic had bent the rules in winning Marlon's respect, and thus Reuban's disdain. The loss of love did not faze Vic. He thought Reuban a bit spoiled and headstrong. The fact that Reuban wanted to lead the jail break only proved this in his mind. Vic wanted to get the job done and get back to Mexico as quickly, and quietly, as he could.

At five foot ten, Vic was not a tall man, but he made up for his height in bulk. His arms were brawny, his torso tight as a drum. He could sprint at ten miles an hour nonstop for thirty minutes, and lifted over a hundred pounds of weights every day. Indeed, he cut an impressive figure, even if he did stand several inches shorter than the Ferraro brothers.

Perhaps it was more than his build that drew attention to Vic. His features were unique and bold. His head-full of raven black hair was worn slicked back off his forehead, which was highlighted by thick, straight brows. His eyes were small and piercing, blacker than the midnight sky, cutting to anyone unfortunate enough to draw his displeasure.

Vic seldom smiled, his lips usually set in a thin, straight line, easily drawn into a sneer or frown. His most striking trait, however, was his square jaw and strong chin, just a hint of the stubbornness that the man could display, albeit quietly.

It was twenty minutes until seven. Knowing that the rest of the men would have already gathered in Reuban's hotel, Vic did an about face and headed back. He did not look forward to the evening, but he was anxious to get started. The sooner the job was done, the sooner he could be back in Mexico, and away from Reuban Ferraro.

Goodson looked up when Jason entered the station. "Working the evening shift tonight, eh?" he asked. "Aw, too bad. I get off early today!"

"Don't rub it in!" Jason moaned. "One bad thing about being on the streets. These nights are killers!"

"Just wait until you get some years under your belt," Goodson promised. "Things will get better then."

"I can't wait."

It was seven thirty-five. Jack was beginning to feel antsy. He tried not to draw attention to himself by looking nervous or anxious, but his whole being craved to get out of that cell.

Sitting down on the cot, he forced himself to breathe normally, feeling himself calming. He had to be alert and ready at any time. A smile touched his wide lips. He should have known the Ferraros would come through for him. He had not been aware of Reuban being back in the states, but he was glad of it.

He slid up on the rickety bed and lay down. He let himself dwell on how sweet his freedom would be. The face of Alana Crewe came to him, but he no longer felt a burning fury to get even with her. Just thinking of her being in Marlon's custody was enough for him.

The lights suddenly flickered and went out. Jack smiled. Reuban was right on time.

Chapter Thirteen

The electricity had gone off suddenly, and mysteriously, up and down Topeka. The city had not experienced a serious blackout for some time and electricians immediately began moving to find the problem. Some businesses and homes were soon powered with generators, but for the most part, the city was in the dark. The sun had just left the sky, so it was dark enough to cause some problems.

At intersections, traffic slowed to a snail's pace, for even the lights of the traffic signals had gone out. Streetlights were dark. Stores were forced to halt business, while waiting for the power to come back on.

People wondered what had happened. There was no bad weather to cause lines to go down. Why would the power just fail for seemingly no reason?

The city was without electricity for a mere five minutes when a big explosion rocked the buildings on Third Street.

Sitting in the dark jeep, just a block from the city jail, Vic shook his head exasperatedly.

"Do it nice and quiet, Reuban," he muttered.

"What was that, boss?" Duke asked from the backseat.

"Nothing."

"Oh, goodness, is this night ever going to end?" Stacey complained.

Alana looked at the clock. "It's only eight thirty?" she asked. "Man, this night is moving slow."

"That's an understatement." Stacey shifted her position in her office chair, sitting on her feet. "So," she began, her eyes sparking with mischief. "What's going on with you and that good looking cop?"

Alana rolled her eyes to the ceiling. "Good grief! There is nothing going on! We're just friends!"

"Are you serious? After all this time?"

That got a laugh from Alana. "Stacey, I've only known the guy a few weeks. What do you mean 'after all this time'?"

Stacey shrugged. "I just figured you'd be a couple by now. Does that mean he's fair game?"

Alana knew Jason well enough to know that he would never consider dating a girl who was not a Christian, but she did not know how to tell her friend this. She seemed to change the subject. "What are you doing Sunday?"

"Nothing, why?"

"Why don't you come to church with me?" Alana invited.

"Oh, Alana," Stacey sighed, forgetting the previous topic. "You know I just can't get anything out of that."

"If you would just give it a try, Stacey, you would get more than you ever imagined!"

Stacey held up a hand. "I know. You've told me all about it. Peace that passes understanding, eternal life, a relationship with Jesus—I know all about it. I'm just not interested." She saw Alana's face fall and quickly checked herself. "Oh, I'm sorry, Alana. I didn't mean to sound so rude. I promise, one of these times, I will come to church with you. Okay?"

Alana forced a smile. "I'll hold you to that," she warned.

"That's fine. Just give me time to get it in my head and I'll go."

"I think I'll head out for a while," Jason said, standing and stretching his arms over his head.

"Head out?" his partner, Rob Phipps, questioned.

"I'm tired of sitting here," Jason explained. "I'm going to go patrol the streets."

"I hope you can handle being out there," Rob joked. "It's awfully dangerous."

"Yeah, I know."

After the explosion that had knocked a searing hole into the Topeka City jail and the neighboring store, things had gone from bad to worse on Third Street. Not only was the street without power, but now there was rubble all over the road and injuries ranging from light to moderately serious. There were no deaths, which seemed a miracle to all, for the blast had been big enough to seriously damage the two buildings.

What the civilians did not know was that Reuban had planned everything to go just the way it had. Charlie Hughes was an expert in explosives and had formed the bomb to be just big enough to make a hole in the jail and cause chaos. In the darkness, it had been fairly easy to get inside and release Jack

Norris. In fact, Reuban was wishing that his plan had not gone so well. The excitement and exhilaration he felt made him want to blast his way out of Kansas. Nothing like a good old fashioned shootout!

Sense ruled, however and he and Jack moved quietly and quickly away from the mess. Reuban and his men left Topeka on the northern road, leaving just enough of a trail to draw investigators after them. Reuban would lead the law on a merry chase towards Chicago. Meanwhile Jack Norris had found the green jeep at the spot Reuban had promised. Vic had the vehicle running, and as soon as the escapee was inside, he whipped the jeep down the street, quickly leaving the bedlam behind them. Their next destination was Edwardsville.

"Banks!" Wade suddenly barked from his office.

Jason spun around, set aback at his captain's tone. He had just come back from making rounds around Edwardsville. Rob raised his brows as Jason made his way to the office.

Wade was on the phone, sounding agitated and firm. He set the receiver down rather hard and stared at Jason. "I just got word from Topeka."

Jason frowned. "About?"

"There was a big blackout in the city. The jail was bombed."

"What?"

"It all happened two hours ago. By the time they got enough of the mess cleared away, they found Norris gone and two jailers unconscious."

Gripping the back of the chair he was standing behind, Jason felt the air being sucked from him. "Two hours ago?"

Wade nodded gravely.

"What took them so long to contact us?"

"Son, the city is in an uproar as it is. It took them some time to find out who was missing. Seems someone set the bomb, gassed a couple of guards, and got Norris out."

Jason was trying to stay calm and objective. "Any idea where they were heading?"

"There's some indication that he and his party headed north."

"Okay," Jason took a deep breath. "I need to get to *Darings'* and let Alana know."

"Don't scare her to death, Banks," Wade warned. "Just tell her of the jailbreak and make sure she gets home safely. We'll make sure she and her family are under protection during the next few days until we get this mess cleared up."

"Got it."

Jason found his car and peeled out of the parking lot, still in shock. Although all indications seemed to point to the fact that Alana was not in danger at this point, Jason felt an unexplainable urge to get to her, to see her, to know that she was safe.

He hit the gas and turned on the lights in the police car. He left the sirens off, but he wanted as few obstacles between him and *Darings'* as possible. The closer he got to the store, the more urgent he felt. The blood pounded in his ears and he felt his hands tighten around the steering wheel. Tension wrapped around him like a metal band.

"God, keep your hand on Alana," he prayed. "Let me see her before anything happens. Protect her, and help the authorities apprehend Jack before he causes harm to her or anyone else."

The short distance between the police station and the large department store seemed to be never-ending.

"Oh, I left those copies out in my car," Alana realized.

"What copies?"

"From the other day, when the copier went out. I took some papers home to copy, and I left them in the car. I'll have to go get them."

"You want to take the office keys with you?" Stacey offered.

"No, you better keep them," Alana decided.

She was nearing the front doors when she suddenly remembered she was supposed to have a male escort.

"Shoot, this is getting to be more of a pain that it's worth," she muttered. Her frustration grew to no bounds when, as she approached the courtesy desk, the only man she could see was Bryan. Her first instinct was to turn back around and forget the papers, but she could not do that. Setting her chin, she boldly approached the desk.

Bryan was leaning against the counter. He looked lazily down at her when she stopped in front of him.

"I need to go outside for a minute," she stated. "I have to get some paperwork from my car." She did not ask for his help, but she stared at him expectantly.

Raising a thin brow, Bryan shrugged. "So?"

His nonchalant attitude infuriated her. "Forget it," she muttered, spinning on her heel. She could feel his eyes on her back as she pushed through the exit doors, but he did not once offer his assistance, and she refused to ask.

"This is getting old," Duke complained.

Vic drummed his fingers on the wheel, thinking the same thing, but not saying it. Reuban had implied that Jack would have an idea of how he was to get the girl, but they had been sitting in the parking lot for over an hour, and Jack was still sitting.

Jack snarled at the man behind him. "Shut yer trap!" he snapped.

"Just what do you have in mind, Norris?" Vic inquired. "If we sit here long enough, someone is going to get suspicious, and I don't intend on being seen with you right now."

"I'll think of something," Jack promised, while Vic stared impassively out the window.

"Heads up," Charlie piped up. They all watched a cop car, with flashing lights but no siren, pull into the lot.

Vic leaned forward, his hand on the key, ready to start the ignition. "That doesn't look good."

"We better git!" Duke exclaimed.

"No, just wait!" Jack ordered as he watched the officer hurry into the store. "It's that fool cop!" he burst.

"Do you want to call this off?" Vic asked when Jack just sat motionless for a full two minutes.

"No, just wait!"

"What, do you think she's just gonna up and walk out here, by herself, in the dark?" Duke pressed, more than a little impatient.

"Like that?" Vic asked calmly, pointing out the window with his chin.

The men were stunned to see a lone figure of a girl treading through the parking lot.

"That her?"

Jack nodded at Charlie's question, grabbing for the door handle. "Oh, yeah."

Vic started the ignition. "Hold on, let's get closer before you go plunging towards her."

Turning the lights off, Jason parked the car and jumped out, noting that the parking was quiet. It did not appear to be a busy night in *Darings'*. He did not waste any time outside, but burst through the entrance doors. He looked across the vestibule and caught a glimpse of Alana standing calmly, and safely, at the courtesy desk, talking to one of the managers.

Finally able to breathe normally, Jason tilted his head back, letting his shoulders relax in relief. He ran his hand through his hair and decided then and there to find the store manager. He remembered his name was Dick.

We'll get a plan on keeping Alana safe before I tell her about Jack's escape, he thought, moving quickly through the store. *She'll feel better if she knows about it ahead of time. She wouldn't want me calling a bunch of attention to her anyway.*

Dick was fairly easy to find. The supervisor was overseeing a small group of associates rearranging a four-way shelf. He looked up and saw the uniformed policeman striding towards him with purpose.

"Hello, there, young man," he greeted, moving away from the group.

"I need to talk to you," was the first thing out of Jason's mouth. "It's really important."

Her face was flushed; she could feel it. It never seemed to matter what she did; trying to work peacefully with Bryan Wheeler was just impossible. Alana clutched her car keys, noticing how dark the parking lot was.

Maybe I shouldn't have come out here by myself, she thought, feeling uneasy. *Stop it, Alana,* she scolded. *You can't live in fear. Just get the papers and get back inside.*

She had her key ready, wishing she had not parked so far from the store. Lights flashed as a car revved up to leave. Alana hummed a tune to herself while she moved to the side so the vehicle could pass. She reached her car, and at that moment the driver turned his lights off.

"Stay calm, Alana," she whispered, feeling her heart beating faster. She put her key in the lock, only vaguely aware of the sound of a door opening behind her. Her movements became quick and agitated. *God, keep me calm.*

A hand grabbed her arm and wrenched it roughly behind her back. Alana, her head spinning with the suddenness of the action, opened her mouth to scream, but the attacker's other hand clamped over it. She clawed at him with her free hand, but his hold was vice-like.

The man turned her slightly. Her eyes widened in terror as Jack Norris's face appeared over her shoulder. She felt herself go limp as he leaned close to her.

"Good to see you again, girl!" he snarled.

She struggled then, swinging her fist at him, kicking at him with her feet. She wriggled and writhed, all the time trying to free her mouth so she could scream. If only someone would see what was going on!

A second man appeared before her, holding a white cloth in his hand. Jack moved his hand and the second man instantly shoved the cloth in Alana's face. A strong odor assailed her senses, making her lightheaded. Her knees buckled and everything went black.

Jason shifted in his seat, feeling ill at ease. It had been over five minutes since Dick had paged for Alana, and she still had not made an appearance.

"I think I'll go up front and see if I can find her," he finally said.

He got to the desk along with a red headed girl. He recognized her as a co-worker of Alana's.

"Have you seen Alana?" she was asking.

Jason felt his heart stop.

"She went to get some papers and that's been a little while ago."

Pamela cocked her head. "Well, I saw her a few minutes ago."

"Where did she go?" Jason asked, breaking into the conversation.

Pamela was surprised. "Um, outside."

"She went outside?" Jason exclaimed. "When?"

"What is it?" Stacey asked.

Feeling a sudden sense of dread, Jason spoke harshly. "When?! How long ago?"

Pamela stammered. "Uh, maybe ten minutes?"

"You didn't see her come back in?"

Pamela shook her head apologetically, sensing that something was seriously wrong.

Jason spun around to face Stacey. "Do you know what her car looks like? Where she's parked?"

Stacey nodded nervously. "A black cougar. I'll take you to it."

"Then let's go!" he ordered, taking her arm and moving her to the doors. They moved quickly through the dark lot. Stacey pointed out the car, setting alone near the end of the lot. As they neared, Jason saw the interior light was on. The front door was open, the keys still hanging from the lock. There was no Alana.

Stacey hung back as Jason rushed on. She stared at the handsome cop, her eyes filled with fear and questions. He looked ready to fall apart.

With blood pounding in his ears, Jason's eye fell on a small object on the ground next to the car. Leaning down, Jason picked up Alana's name badge with trembling hands. He knew then, without a doubt. Somehow, Jack Norris had made it to Edwardsville and had taken Alana.

His first instinct was to jump in the car and peel out of the parking lot, in a feeble attempt to catch up to them, but he knew that was foolish. A wave of frustration and fury washed over him so strong he could not hold it back. He reared back and tossed the badge with all his might, letting out an angry roar as he did.

As soon as he released the pent up emotion, the well-trained law enforcer came to the surface. He turned, took Stacey's arm, and hurried her back to the store, his mind spinning. He stopped at his car and reached in for the radio. He made a quick, brief announcement and then moved on. He knew Stacey was confused and frightened, but he did not have time to explain what was going on.

They met Dick at the front door. Jason directed his next words to Stacey. "Go on to the back. Don't say anything to anyone."

Stacey nodded dumbly and stumbled off.

Conscious of the curious stares of the employees nearby, Jason ignored them and said to Dick, "I need to see your security tapes."

"Sure, right this way." Dick led the way, somehow knowing that time was of the essence. He took Jason to a small, dimly lit room where a security guard was sitting, making entries into a log.

"Have you seen anything unusual?" Jason asked him.

The guard looked up, surprised.

"Just answer him, Pete," Dick ordered.

"Uh, no," Pete replied. "Things seem to be pretty quiet. I was just doing some extra paperwork."

Jason found the monitor that displayed the area where Alana's car was sitting. "I need this to be rewound about a half hour."

Pete moved to comply, and within seconds, the three were watching the screen intently.

"What are we looking for, boss?" Pete asked.

Dick looked to Jason for the answer.

Jason did not take his eyes off the television. "I have reason to believe that Alana was just kidnapped off the parking lot."

Sucking in his breath, Dick shook his head. "You're kidding, right?"

"I wish I was." Jason pointed at a fuzzy image. "Look there. That looks like someone walking, doesn't it?"

The figure came into plainer view. "It's Alana," Dick confirmed. "I recognize what she's wearing."

At that moment, the men watched a dark jeep pull up behind her. Jason had to clench his jaw tightly to keep from shouting at the screen. A man, who looked much like Jack Norris, snatched Alana from behind. She struggled for a moment, until a second man applied a cloth to her face and she went unconscious. The men carried her limp body to the jeep and drove away.

"Oh my Lord!" Dick breathed, his face ashen.

Jason had to bow his head to hide the emotions he was battling. Watching the abduction of his dear friend was more than he could bear. He drew in a shuddering breath and put his hand over his face. "Dear God!" he prayed, unable to say anything else.

Chapter Fourteen

Within minutes, *Darings'* was hopping with activity. Several more police cars came screaming into the parking lot, causing quite a stir among customers and associates alike. Dick added to the oddity by announcing over the PA that *Darings'* would have to be closed down immediately due to problems within the store. Several customers complained as they were led out, but the employees had no idea what was going on, and thus could say nothing to explain it.

Captain Wade also made an appearance and watched the same security tape that Jason had seen. The bristly captain lit into the security guard for his carelessness before he left the small office. He found Jason at the front of the store where Dick had just called a store meeting.

"I know you're all wondering what's going on," Dick began. He saw many head nodding, and several faces looking concerned. "I don't really know how to go about this. Captain, do you want to...?"

"Certainly," Wade said, stepping forward. "We've had an unfortunate incident here tonight. Normally I would not announce something like this unless I had more proof, but I got all the proof I needed. I'm sure you all know Alana Crewe. I'm afraid she was abducted from the lot just a few minutes ago."

Jason felt himself wince. Just hearing it from someone else's lips made it seem all too real. He heard several gasps and outcries. The face of Bryan Wheeler went suddenly pale, but Jason was in no frame of mind to pay much attention to him.

"I assure you, the Edwardsville police are already on the streets now, looking for her," Wade continued. "We will do all we can to bring her back home safely. In the meantime, I have several officers here that will be talking to each one of you tonight. We just want to know if any of you saw anything suspicious or strange, so there's no reason to be nervous about it. Your cooperation will greatly assist us in bringing the girl back."

Everyone was stunned to silence. Jason took in the white faces, the wide eyes, and turned away. He felt the captain follow him.

"Banks, I need to hear from you what you know."

Jason ran his fingers through his hair, feeling like he was in a dream. He told Wade everything that happened to him since he left the office, down to the quick prayers he had given about Alana's protection.

Wade, in a rare moment of softness, put his hand on Jason's shoulder. "There's no sense in blaming yourself over this, son."

Looking up, Jason stared at the older man, wondering how Wade had read his thoughts. "Why wouldn't there be?" he asked hoarsely.

"Because it could have happened to any of us. The timing was wrong, but that wasn't your fault. This whole endeavor was perfectly planned out."

"So, what are we doing?" Jason asked.

"I've got men out right now. I caught the last four numbers on that jeep, and there's a red alert out on it. Forces in Topeka are sending investigators down here to work with us. We'll find her, Jason."

Jason nodded numbly, knowing his senses were in shock. A sudden thought, however, made him feel almost physically ill.

"Captain, her family!"

Wade shook his head. "Someone has to tell them."

With a deep breath, Jason said, "I'll go."

The trip to the Crewe house was all to short. Alan opened the door and greeted him warmly, which cut Jason like a knife. "Good to see you, Jason! Alana's not here right now, but come on in."

His heart breaking, Jason stepped into the bright kitchen, desperately wishing he did not have to bring this family bad news.

"Hello, Jason," Sharon said warmly. "I just took some fresh cookies out of the oven. You want to join us?"

"Um, no, I can't." Jason scratched his chin absently, noting the kids were not in the room. *That's better, I suppose,* he thought.

"Are you all right, Jason?" Alan asked, getting a good look at his troubled face.

You have to tell them, Jason. "Um, no, actually I'm not."

"What is it?" Sharon asked, feeling concern now.

Jason took a deep breath, feeling a lump in his throat. "We got news that Jack Norris escaped from jail a few hours ago."

Sharon put her hand to her throat. "Does that mean Alana's in danger of him?"

"Why don't you sit down?" Jason suggested.

"Jason, what is it?" she insisted, feeling her husband's hand on her arm.

There was no easy way to say it. Though he wanted with all his heart to shield these dear people from the truth, he could not. His voice was thick as he pushed the words past his throat. "He's taken Alana."

The look on Sharon's face was one he would never forget. She went stark white and her lips moved without any words coming out.

"What do you mean?" Alan demanded. "How do you know?"

"I watched it on the security tape. There's no doubt."

Alan leaned his hands on the table and bowed his head, his whole frame shuddering. "He's taken her?" he repeated, in shock.

"We're already patrolling the streets," Jason went on, his words sounding inane.

Sharon wanted to deny it, wanted to accuse Jason of lying, but the awful reality had hit her and she knew her daughter indeed had been kidnapped. She shook her head in disbelief, putting her hands up in front of her, as if protecting herself. Without warning, she turned blazing eyes on Jason.

"Where were you? If you knew this man had escaped, why weren't you there with her? Why didn't you stop it?" He voice rose with every word until she was nearly screaming.

"Sharon!" Alan shook her. She crumpled in his arms, harsh sobs bursting from her lips. He half led, half carried her from the room, taking her to their bedroom.

Jason felt his eyes sting and ran a hand over his face. He swung a fist in the air, feeling such a load of guilt press on him that he could not stand it. He slumped to a chair and slammed his fists against the table. At that point, he felt eyes on him and looked up into the stricken face of Andrea.

"What happened?" she whispered.

Jason knew that she had already heard, but he had to tell her. He took several quick breaths before he could answer her. "Alana's been kidnapped."

Andrea braced herself against the doorframe between the kitchen and living room. "How did that happen?"

Lowering his head, Jason could only say, "Because I didn't do my job, Andie."

Andrea shook her head slowly, backing away from the troubled man. She did not say a word, but made her way to her parent's bedroom, where Sharon's cries could still be heard.

Leaning his forehead against his clasped hands, Jason prayed, his voice trembling. "God, I don't understand this. Why would You allow this to happen? Why couldn't I have gotten there just a few minutes sooner?"

Alan emerged from the back room just then, and Jason thought that he had aged considerably in just a few minutes. He joined Jason at the table, his brow creased with worry lines. "Can you tell me what happened?" he asked thickly.

Jason hesitated, but he could not refuse his request; nor could he look at him while he related the story. When he was finished, Alan sat quietly for so long that Jason feared he had forgotten that Jason was even there.

"You hear about this in other places, you know?" Alan spoke quietly, almost to himself. "You never think it will happen to your own family."

"Alan, I am so sorry," Jason spoke passionately, not sure his apology would be accepted.

"I know you are, son. I know you did all you could."

"We're already on the move, Alan. There are men at this very minute searching for both Alana and Jack Norris. We'll get her back."

Alan nodded tiredly to this.

"Is there anyone you want me to call?"

"I've already called the Nelsons."

Jason was glad to hear this. If anyone could do any good to the Crewes, it was their dear pastor and his wife.

Maggie Nelson went straight to Sharon's side when they arrived, holding the distraught woman tight in her embrace. Kenneth, his usual jovial face quite sober, sat down with Alan, saying nothing.

Audrey, fortunately, was already asleep in bed during this time. Sharon and Alan silently agreed that they would wait to tell their youngest child anything. Andrea and Anthony sat together in the living room, both still obviously in shock. After a time, Kenneth was able to draw Anthony out, and the boy opened up to his pastor, tears streaming down his young face. Andrea said nothing to anyone, though her eyes flitted every now and then to Jason.

Beginning to feel in the way, Jason spoke to Alan and headed back to the station. He felt like an old man as he walked to his car. He knew Alan and Sharon were in good hands now, but he felt helpless, useless.

Once he got in the car, he just sat for a moment behind the wheel, dully replaying the evening in his mind. It would not be long before the whole town found out about the abduction. The news would spread like wildfire, especially when the media got a hold of it.

With a deep breath, Jason pulled out his cell phone.

Curtis and Dinah were spending the evening at Belinda and Terry's and were now in the middle of an intense game of Monopoly. The phone rang and interrupted Curtis's dealing. Belinda handed the receiver to him.

"It's for you, Curtis."

"Y'ello!" Curtis greeted.

"Curtis, it's me."

"Jason?" Curtis replied, wondering why his friend had called him at Belinda's. "What's up, man? You sound like your dog has died."

"I've got bad news."

The solemnity in Jason's voice finally caught Curtis's attention and he walked a few paces from the group. "What is it?"

A long silence followed, as if Jason did not know how to proceed. "Alana has disappeared. She's been abducted by Jack Norris."

"What?!" Curtis gasped, drawing everyone's glances. "How…When?"

"Just a while ago."

Curtis felt as if he had been punched in the stomach. "I don't believe it," he murmured in a daze. He was only vaguely aware of the silence in the room.

"She's going to need your prayers, man."

Curtis nodded, knowing Jason could not see him. The turmoil in his soul matched what he heard in Jason's voice. "I'll be praying. With all my might. Does anyone else know?"

"I just left her parents' house."

"Oh, man."

"The Nelsons are over there."

Feeling agitated, Curtis rubbed the back of his neck, and looked around aimlessly. For the first time, he saw the faces of his companions and froze.

"Dinah needs to know," Jason said quietly, as if reading his thoughts. "And the others."

"I'll tell them. You all right?"

A soft snort met Curtis's ears. "Yeah, I'm fine, Curtis. It's Alana that's in trouble. Talk to you later."

"What in the world is going on?" Dinah demanded as soon as her boyfriend hung the phone up. The look on his face had her scared.

Everyone was on their feet as Curtis approached them. He put his arm around Dinah's waist, sensing that she was going to need his support.

The Edwardsville police patrolled the streets all night, sometimes even stopping traffic to investigate. Fingerprints were taken at *Darings'* though the only ones found on Alana's car were her own. Employees were questioned, but no one had seen or heard anything strange that night, so it seemed every turn was a dead end. Bryan Wheeler had admitted that he let Alana walk out to her car alone, much to Jason's anger. After his first impulse to punch the young manager's lights out, Jason left him for Dick to deal with.

If he had felt frustrated before, he was ready to pull his hair out now. There were no answers, no hints as to where Alana's abductors would have taken her. It was as if they had disappeared into thin air.

"We have to find her, Captain," he insisted, grounding his words out. "Before…something happens."

"We're doing all we can, son," Wade told him. "Some of these guys are going to be up all night working on this." He saw the exhaustion and anguish on Jason's face. "Go home, Banks."

"What? I can't go home!" Jason exclaimed. "I—"

"That's an order!" Wade barked. "You're not going to do us, or that girl, any good if you're running yourself to death. I know you were good friends with her, so this is hitting you hard. Go home, get some rest, come back in the morning and I'll fill you in on everything."

Jason opened his mouth.

"If something comes up," Wade raised his voice to sway Jason's protest, "I promise, I'll call you."

Against his better judgment, Jason left for his own apartment. Even the sight of his home made the night all the more painful. Alana had been with him when he had found the place. It just served to remind him of what was happening right now; how his night had been completely turned upside down.

There would be no sleep for him that night; he was sure of that. He changed from his uniform into sweats and a t-shirt and paced the confines of the house. His mind spun with where Alana could be, what Jack Norris would do to her, and how he could have done something differently to keep this from happening. He sent quick, half-uttered, incoherent prayers heavenward.

A knock on the door surprised him, and he opened it cautiously. Curtis stood on the porch. Without a word, he stepped through the doorway and embraced his friend. Jason gripped Curtis tightly, absently thinking as he did so that he could not have a better friend on this earth.

This was Curtis's way. Everyone knew him as a fun-loving, outgoing guy, but this was the side of him that only those closest to him were blessed with. When someone was hurting, Curtis said little, but let them know through a hug, pat on the back, or even just a listening ear, that he was there for them.

He had been there before for Jason, at the lowest point in his life. Now, when Jason was dealt yet another harsh blow, Curtis one again stood by him, supporting him. When Jason pulled away, he found his limbs trembling. Curtis closed the door while Jason stood in the middle of the living room, taking a deep breath.

"How's Dinah and everyone?" Jason asked, his voice low.

Taking a deep breath, Curtis replied, "Pretty shaken up. I think we're all still in shock." He paused. "How are you doing?"

"Curtis, I never even saw it coming."

"I know," Curtis said. "Nobody expected anything like this."

Jason shook his head. "That's not what I meant. I'm a cop. I should have been more prepared."

Curtis frowned and perched on the arm of a chair. "Jason, you're not blaming yourself, are you?"

Jason began pacing again, the events of the night crashing in on him. "Curtis, I could have stopped it!"

"How?" Curtis demanded.

"I knew he had escaped; I was heading to the store to tell Alana. I knew that Norris would be heading for her."

Curtis watched his friend helplessly, trying hard to understand. He found himself praying silently for Jason as he listened. Jason Banks had seen some tough times in his life that almost knocked him down. Curtis hated to see him like this once again.

"I saw her, Curtis," Jason said, stopping suddenly and facing the other man. "I walked in the store, saw her standing at the desk. She was safe. And you know what I did? I walked away."

"What?"

"I did." Jason, feeling overwhelmed, covered his face with his hands for a moment before continuing. "I saw her; I could have gone to her right then and kept this whole nightmare from happening. But I didn't. I left her there so I could talk to her manager." His voice rose suddenly. "Norris kidnapped her from the parking lot while I was *sitting in the office!*" He was now shouting in his emotional state.

With a wince, Curtis could see now why Jason was so upset. Of course, this catastrophe would disturb anyone, but he had sensed there was something more.

Jason was walking again, feeling a strong rage come over him. He grabbed the nearest thing he could get his hands on, which happened to be the keys he had set on the counter moments ago. He and flung them with all his might across the room. They struck a lamp and it fell with a crash to the floor.

Curtis jumped up and grabbed Jason by the shoulders. "Jason! Get a hold of yourself!"

"It's my fault, Curtis!" the cop exclaimed.

"Stop it!" Curtis yelled and shook him. "You're not going to help Alana by losing control."

The words sank in and Jason closed his eyes. He ran a hand over his face, sighing deeply. "Why didn't I just go straight to her, Curtis?" he whispered.

"I don't know, buddy," Curtis replied, dropping his hands. "But, you gotta hang in there."

Jason turned away, his shoulders slumped. He had not felt this low since just before he found Christ as a teenager.

"Jason, remember, you're not in this thing alone," Curtis reminded. "There's no reason to bear the whole burden on your shoulders. I don't understand why this happened, but God has His hand in everything. No matter where Alana is, she's not alone. He will take care of her. You gotta believe that."

Jason was comforted some, but he could not shake the feeling that had he acted differently, they would not be having this conversation at all; Alana's family would not be sitting in agony over her disappearance; Alana would not be in the hands of someone who only wanted to hurt her.

The thought sent another ripping pain through Jason's heart, as he pictured the last time he had talked to her—laughing and carefree. What was happening to her now? What would Jack Norris do to her?

Where are you, Alana?

Chapter Fifteen

Voices were mingling in the darkness, their words unintelligible. Everything was black and foggy, and her head hurt excruciatingly. Where was she? A deep breath helped to clear her mind a bit, and in that instant Jack Norris's voice cut through her semi-consciousness. With a jolt, Alana remembered Norris's sudden appearance and his rough arms surrounding her.

Alana did not move, but tried to get her bearings, her heart pounding wildly in her chest. Surely this wasn't happening! Surely this was a nightmare! The pain in her wrists, bound tightly behind her, told her all too clearly that this was no dream. Somehow Jack Norris had found her.

Oh, God, please get me out of this! she cried out inwardly. *Please don't let him kill me!*

At that point, Alana realized with a start that there were other men around, apparently in close quarters. She felt a sway and made out that she was sitting, propped up, in an automobile seat.

Where are they taking me? she asked mentally, feeling her emotions swirling in her panic.

There was a sharp jab in her hip and she gasped abruptly.

"Told you she was awake," a male voice said, laughing.

Alana's eyes flew open and she stared into the face of a man sitting very close to her. She drew back and practically fell into the lap of another one. She sat upright with a cry and looked around her wildly. She was in the back of a jeep, sandwiched between two of the roughest looking men she had ever seen.

In the front passenger seat was Jack Norris, and he turned now to face her. "Good morning, sunshine," he said gruffly, smiling maliciously.

"What are you doing with me?" Alana asked, her voice barely audible.

"Don't worry about it," Norris said abruptly and turned back around.

There was laughter all around and Alana froze when she heard yet two more voices sitting behind her. She was literally surrounded.

Oh, God, she prayed as she felt her body give in to violent trembling. *I need a miracle!*

She had lost all track of time. The vehicle she was traveling in sped down a highway—she had no idea what one. The sky was pitch black outside, with no sign of the moon or stars.

The men continued talking, their deep voices rumbling. She shrank as small as she could so as to keep from touching the men on either side of her. Jack Norris looked back at her every now and then, his malevolent grin sending chills down her back. She knew with sickening clarity that his plans for her could very well cost her life. Questions raced inside of her, but she was too fearful to ask.

Closing her eyes tightly, Alana could see the faces of her parents and siblings. Would she see them again? What were they thinking right now? For the first time since the abduction, Alana felt tears trickling down her face. The darkness of the jeep kept any of the men from noticing, for which she was grateful. As the realization sunk in that this could be her last hours, she cried.

Father, I don't understand this. I am so scared, she entreated. *If I die tonight, I know that I will wake up looking into Your face, but please, be with me. Let me feel that You are here with me. And please, please be with my family and friends! Comfort them through whatever happens.*

Her throat tightened so that it was difficult to breathe. She opened her eyes and looked at the abductors, seeing the lack of emotion on their faces. What they did to her meant nothing to them. They cared about no one but themselves. There would be no mercy from them.

Curtis did not feel comfortable leaving Jason alone, so he offered to stay the night. At first, Jason objected, but when Curtis insisted, he offered the use of his room.

"Oh, no," Curtis denied. "I'm fine in the living room, Jason. I really am. This couch is really comfortable."

Jason finally consented. He was sitting at the kitchen table, a forgotten mug of coffee before him. His mind was still so occupied with Alana's disappearance that he had trouble focusing on anything else. Curtis had to call his name three times before he even heard him.

"Why don't you go on to bed, Jase?" Curtis asked. "You're not going to be able to help Alana and do your job if you don't get any rest. You look like a zombie."

Jason sighed deeply and rubbed his eyes. "I don't know if I can do Alana any good anyway, Curt."

"What's that supposed to mean?"

Standing, Jason said only, "Nothing." He was halfway across the room when Curtis called him again. He turned slightly.

"Everything's gonna be all right, Jason."

He forced a smile. "Yeah. Sure." He gave a weak wave before stepping into his dark bedroom. He did not bother turning on a light. Sitting on his bed, he dropped his head into his hands.

"God, I don't understand," he whispered. "Why does Alana have to suffer for my blunder? Why didn't I feel the urgency to go straight to her and tell her about Norris's escape? It could have so easily been prevented! Why did I have to mess up so bad?"

Sitting up straight, Jason's eyes strayed to the window, where the millions of stars were shining like diamonds. The half-circle moon glowed like a beacon. The view did nothing for Jason's tormented spirit.

"You can pull over here."

At Norris's command, Alana felt her blood run cold. The driver pulled the jeep over to the shoulder of a one-lane road. There were fields on either side. The pitch blackness stretched on as far as the eye could see. This would be an ideal place for someone to get lost. Or to hide someone.

Ready to start screaming, Alana stiffened when the jeep was parked and Jack and the dark-headed driver stepped out. A vague light illuminated the pair as they spoke for just a moment. The driver handed Norris an envelope, and then headed back for the jeep. Norris turned and began walking alone through the fields. He did not turn to watch the jeep's exit.

Completely nonplussed, and feeling hope for the first time, Alana stared at the shrinking figure of Jack Norris as the men pulled back out onto the road. She felt her breathing accelerating.

"Are you going to let me go?" she broached.

Her answer was instantly met with laughter.

"After all that work to get ya?" the man on her left cackled.

"No, girlie," the other taunted, playing with her hair. "We've got bigger plans for you."

Pure panic began to set in. She did not feel safe in the presence of Jack Norris, but being surrounded by strangers was almost too much for her to cope with. She began struggling with the binds.

"Please, let me go!" she begged. "My family will be looking for me."

More laughter.

"Oh, please let me go!" one mocked her while the other wiped pretend tears away.

"Manley, Duke, that's enough." The driver spoke for the first time, and his quiet words carried with them a piercing authority.

"Aw, come on, Vic," Manley drawled. "You gotta admit, she's pathetic."

Vic didn't reply, but Manley and Duke both backed off. Alana took several deep breaths to calm her racing heartbeat. She winced as a sharp pain shot up her wrist.

"Take the ropes off," Vic ordered.

"Are you serious?" Duke hesitated. "She'll scratch our eyes out."

Alana found the reflection of Vic's intimidating glare fixed on her and froze.

"No, she won't," Vic then replied.

Duke reached over and cut the tight ropes and immediately blood rushed to her fingers. She bit her lip to keep from crying as her hands tingled painfully. She rubbed them in silence, still petrified over what these men would do to her now. Now, she was completely mystified. Why did Jack Norris abduct her, and then walk off and leave her?

The phone rang early in the morning, starling Jason out of a troubled sleep. He had lain in bed for hours, wide awake, before drifting into a light sleep of disturbing dreams. He kept seeing the video of Alana's abduction over and over in his mind, tormented by what he did not know.

As he sat up, holding his pounding head, he could hear Curtis's voice in the other room, talking quietly. He jumped out of bed and went to the living room, hoping beyond hope that the call would be news concerning Alana.

Curtis looked up at Jason when he entered. "I know, Dinah," he was saying, his voice gentle. "No, no news yet."

Jason turned and went back to his room. He glanced at his clock. 6:45. His eyes then fell on his uniform, which he had tossed haphazardly on the floor. He took a deep breath. He had wrestled far into the night about his next decision. There would be no more rest for him, so he dressed and told Curtis where he was going. He left while Curtis was still talking on the phone.

The sky was just beginning to light up. Alana could see the faint image of the sun just peeking over the trees in the horizon. She could also see the features of Manley and Duke more easily. Their aloof, scarred faces did nothing to calm her anxiety.

As the world around them began to brighten, Alana noticed that Manley's eyes were often skimming over her. Her skin crawled as he shifted his leg so that it was touching hers. Duke had fallen asleep hours ago and his sour breath fell on her face every few seconds. She was feeling smothered and trapped.

"You know, Vic," Manley spoke up, running his hand down Alana's arm. "She's not such a bad looker now that I can see her in the light."

There was a snort behind them. "Manley, you think every girl's a looker."

"Shut up, Charlie," Manley snapped.

"Just who do you think you are, Manley?" Charlie growled, leaning over the seat.

"You wanna find out?" Manley threatened, reaching over Alana to grab Charlie's shirt.

From the front seat, Vic cleared his throat. The men glanced in his direction and found him watching them from the review mirror. With a scowl, Charlie settled back in his seat, murmuring with his companion.

Manley turned his attention to Alana. Her heart rate accelerated as she saw the hungry look in his eyes.

"I think Reuban did a good job," he continued, even though no one seemed to be paying attention. His finger ran down Alana's face. She kept her vision straight ahead, praying furiously. She jumped when Manley slipped his arm around her waist, attempting to draw her closer.

"No," she shook her head, trying to draw away from him.

"You have a problem with me getting to know her better?" Manley asked, directing his question to Vic.

Alana's eyes nearly swallowed her face. She pushed against Manley, but the man was more than twice her size.

Vic shrugged lazily, uninterested. "Sure," he drawled.

Alana gasped as Manley instantly leaned against her, his wide mouth just inches over hers. "No!" she cried.

Vic spoke again, in the same bored tone. "I'm sure Marlon won't mind."

Manley froze, his face unsure. With a scowl and a curse, he pulled away and turned from her. Alana's chest heaved for breath; there was a horrible taste in her mouth. Her head was spinning so violently she worried she would faint.

"We're stopping at the old Farmer's warehouse in an hour," Vic announced a few minutes later.

"Why?" Charlie questioned.

"Reuban wants to see the girl before we head down."

The words caught Alana's attention. "What? Why? Where are you taking me?"

"Don't worry about it," Vic replied without looking at her. The glimpses Alana got of his face only served to intimidate her. The man looked hard, very hard. Obviously he was the leader; the other four in the vehicle toed the line with him. What was this man capable of?

In the hour that followed, the world abruptly darkened again. The sun was hidden by a curtain of clouds and rain fell in streams. Seeing the trees and plants bow their head under the weight of the moisture caused Alana's spirit to sink lower. Her eyes continued to peer out of the windows, seeking for some kind of hope for escape. There was none as long as the jeep sped down the road and she was surrounded by these men.

She had no idea who this Reuban was that Vic had spoken of, but he scared her. Why did he want to see her? Where would they take her then?

Vic drove past a small town, not stopping or even slowing down lest the girl make a scene. He passed the small buildings and headed for a deserted area. There was an old warehouse, standing three stories tall, looking quite out of place on the cracked parking lot. A cluster of trees offered the jeep an inconspicuous parking spot.

"Get her out," he ordered as he stepped out into the rain. His dark hair began dripping water into his face, but he paid little attention to it. He stared at the building, knowing Reuban was in there. He frowned to himself, thinking this was all a waste of time.

Alana's arm was seized gruffly and she was pulled from the vehicle. Her feet got tangled up and she felt herself fall headlong out. Her head smacked the pavement hard, and she saw stars.

Duke grabbed her and pulled her up. The moment she was on her feet, she took off running, with no idea where she was heading. Her head spun painfully, and her limbs shook from exhaustion and fear, but she plunged on, knowing this could very well be her last chance for escape.

In her confused state of mind, however, she had not realized just how futile her ploy was. She had only run a few steps when she felt a hand grab her by the jacket she was wearing. Before she could scream, Vic had his hand firmly over her mouth.

"That's enough," he snarled in her ear. He half walked, half carried her across the lot to the doors of the warehouse. She stiffened her limbs with every step, but despite his short stature, the man was strong and her efforts were useless.

Inside was dark, as there had been no electricity for years. It took her eyes several moments to adjust and when she could finally see, she made out a figure standing in the middle of the spacious floor, his hands behind his back. He was watching their approach.

"Vic, good to see you again." His cool voice sent shivers down Alana's spine.

Vic returned the greeting calmly. "Reuban."

The man was tall, broad, with thick, dark hair and very handsome. He smiled and stepped forward, his eyes full of Alana. Vic had walked her directly in front of Reuban and stood back, leaving her standing awkwardly between them.

This man stared at her with cold, calculating eyes. Always on his lips was the hint of a smile, as if he was enjoying her fear and pain immensely. Alana immediately sensed that this man was a cruel one.

"Miss Alana Crewe," Reuban said, looking her up and down. "I've been looking forward to meeting you. I apologize I was unable to escort you myself from Edwardsville, but please understand. I had urgent business matters to attend to. I trust your trip has been pleasant?" His voice was mocking and condescending.

"I want to go home," she told him, staring up at him with imploring eyes.

"Oh, you'll be home soon enough," Reuban assured, but she was not comforted. "I believe you'll find our humble home rather pleasant. By the way, I am Reuban Ferraro, and it's a pleasure to finally see you in person. I must say, it was well worth the wait." His face was lit with a malicious light, as if he knew something she did not.

Alana had never been around wicked men, not until Jack Norris. Now, surrounded by them, she had no idea what to do. Reuban Ferraro had an air of arrogance and spitefulness. There was a malicious, teasing glow in his dark eyes.

He finally took his eyes off her. "She's fine," he announced, as if he had been inspecting her. "Marlon will be anxious to get her. Make sure she gets there safe."

Vic did not answer. After a moment, Alana felt him take her arm again and begin leading her away. She did not resist, anxious to leave Reuban's presence.

"If you try to scream I'll knock you out," Vic threatened as they walked.

Alana believed him and stayed silent until she was back between Manley and Duke. From what she could see, there was no one to hear her anyway.

One of the men, she heard him called Buddy, moved up to the front seat with Vic, and they continued on their way. Alana's home in Edwardsville was getting further and further behind them.

Chapter Sixteen

Morning dawned in Kansas. Business went on as usual, stores opened but the town of Edwardsville was stunned. Crime had hardly ever touched the small community, save for a few shoplifters. The small population had given the place a feeling of safety, of security. Alana's abduction changed that tone overnight. Apprehension settled in as word spread. Parents watched their kids board the school buses, or drove them to school themselves. Drivers locked their car doors. The very air seemed to be different.

Even the police cars, patrolling the streets as usual, did not seem the same. There were more than usual now, and roadblocks had been set up in various areas to check vehicles. Officers could be seen in nearly every direction, questioning, investigating, searching for anything that could lead them to Alana.

The New Hope Fellowship Church was rocked to find out that one of their own was missing. As soon as the sun was up, the Crewe household began to fill up with supporters. Those who did not visit called until the walls were ringing with phone calls every few minutes.

Although reeling from the events of the night, Alan was still aware enough to deeply appreciate the care demonstrated to him by his church family. He knew Sharon would also be touched when she was able to think clearly again. She had awakened early to ask if it had all been a nightmare. When Alan tearfully told her no, she wept again. Maggie stayed by her side every minute, giving the distraught mother someone to lean on. Audrey had slept through the entire tragic night, her favorite book under her arm. Alan's heart broke at the thought of telling the little girl what happened to her big sister.

Kenneth Nelson had not wasted any time in gathering a group into the kitchen and leading in prayer for Alana's safety and return. Alan was moved to tears by the emotion in his pastor's voice, as were many others. He felt the loving arms of many brothers and sisters in Christ and heard their comforting voices. As the spiritual leader of this torn apart family, Alan found their compassion a great source of strength.

Alan called the police station at seven thirty, hoping for some kind of news. Captain Wade told him very politely that at that point there was nothing to tell him, but his men were working around the clock. Wade promised to contact the family as soon as he found anything, no matter how minute.

As he hung up the phone, Alan dropped his head. "Oh, Dear Lord," he whispered. His mind was too turbulent to be able to form a sensible prayer, but he knew his God could hear the prayer of his heart.

Turning away, Alan caught a glimpse of Curtis and Dinah pulling into the yard. Even from within the house, Alan could see that Dinah was beside herself. He knew that she had recently grown close to his daughter. This had to be hard for her.

He met them at the door with a hug for Dinah. She held tight to him, willing herself not to cry. When she pulled away she whispered, "I'm so sorry."

Alan gave her a sad smile. "Just keep praying. God can bring her home, and I'm believing He can do it today."

Dinah nodded and stepped aside for Curtis. The younger man shook Alan's hand silently, his face sober.

"Where's Jason?" Alan asked, remembering the disturbed cop.

Curtis shook his head. "He headed for work early this morning. He got in late last night, and I don't think he slept well."

Alan looked bothered. "He seemed…troubled."

"Yeah," Curtis nodded. "He'd kill me for saying this, but he's blaming himself."

"Oh, no," Alan murmured. "And after the way Sharon reacted…" His words faded.

Curtis did not ask for an explanation. He could imagine what had happened last night.

"If you talk to him, will you tell him to see me?" Alan asked.

"Certainly."

Jason walked into the station wearing jeans and a red T-shirt. He carried a black gym bag with him. The halls were bustling; everyone was busy now. He remembered how quiet things had been only the day before.

Wade looked up at him with a frown. "What's the meaning of this, Banks?" he demanded.

"I've been wrestling with this all night, Captain," he said. "Alana's abduction was a result of my carelessness. I don't see how I can be an effective cop if I'm making decisions that bring harm to others. I'm resigning."

Leaning back in his chair, Wade stared at him. "I don't believe it."

"It's true, sir."

"You're going to make a decision of this magnitude after one night?"

"Yes."

Wade shook his head. "Sorry, son, but I can't accept that. You were the cop on assignment when the girl was taken, and I expect you to get back to work investigating what happened to her."

"Captain—"

"Listen, Banks," Wade raised his voice over Jason's. "You told me what happened. I would not keep you on my force if I believed that you were careless. What happened last night was not your mistake. Maybe a misjudgment of timing, but you can't take the blame for it."

Jason took a deep breath and hooked his thumbs to his pockets. "That's not how I look at it."

"That's too bad." Wade fell silent for a moment, observing the younger man. When he spoke again, he seemed to be changing the subject. "I talked with your former supervisor a few weeks back."

Jason frowned, not knowing where this was going.

"He told me you were an excellent cop, with instincts beyond his comprehension. Made it sound like you had one of the best records on the force."

Looking away, Jason exhaled agitatedly. He was not interested in hearing about his record.

"He also told me that he tried to promote you to detective."

Jason paused, refusing to look at the captain.

"But you refused. You want to tell me why?"

With a shrug, Jason replied vaguely, "I liked working on the streets."

The chair squeaked as Wade leaned his elbows on the desk. "How 'bout the truth this time?"

Jason sunk down in the chair, sighing yet again. "I don't know," he drawled. "I wasn't ready for a change."

One of Wade's thick brows rose to the air. With his expression, he made it clear that he did not believe him. Finally he said, "I'm not going to accept your resignation."

"What?"

"Not now. I understand how you feel; believe me, I've been there, too."

Jason closed his eyes in frustration. "Captain, I don't think I would be much good to the force right now. If I let one case like this upset me, how can I concentrate on anything else?"

"You won't have to."

"Huh?" Jason's eyes came open.

"I'm assigning you to this one case. No arguing," he raised his voice when Jason opened his mouth to speak. "I mean it. I've seen your record, Banks. I know what you're capable of, even if you don't. I want you to take care of this case. I've got others investigating, of course, but I want you in on it, too. Understand?"

Jason wanted to argue, wanted to say he had no right to be a part of this after his oversight. Yet, at the same time, he wanted to do everything in his power to help Alana, to bring her safely back home, to try to make it up to her for his part in her abduction.

"All right," he breathed.

"Good." Wade pushed a file towards him. "Here's the latest info. Look it over and figure out what move you want to make next."

That very day, Pastor Nelson called a special prayer meeting of the church. The sanctuary was packed. Alana's family sat in the very front row, clinging to each other in desperation. Audrey, still unaware of the situation, had been taken downstairs with the other small children by Bailey and Christy. Kenneth stood at the pulpit, his face drawn. He began slowly.

"I think this is the most difficulty I've ever had in trying to find something to say to the church. We've had a very rude shock in our midst. Our own precious Alana has been kidnapped." He paused. Sharon's head bowed as her tears fell again.

"Times like these, I must admit, I want to ask God why. Why did He allow one so innocent to be put in danger? Why did it have to be one of my members? Why didn't He protect her? Honestly, these questions have run through my head during these very trying and troubling hours. Although I don't get a direct answer, I do know this. As hard as it is to hold on to faith, to believe that this will work out for good, we must trust God." Kenneth slapped the pulpit in time with his last words, emphasizing his point.

"Our faith in God is all we have to go on at this point," he went on. "We cannot trust in man. We need His divine intervention to protect Alana.

"Also, saints, let us rally around our members. The Crewe family, especially, need our prayers and support in such a tremendous way. Let us help Alan, Sharon, Anthony, Andrea, and little Audrey in any way we can. And, don't forget, there are others who are hurting, too—Alana's friends, people she's touched through her sweet and humble spirit."

Jason sat stock still next to Curtis as the preacher talked. He felt as if his heart was going to explode with the pain he was experiencing. On the other side of Curtis, Dinah's sniffs could be heard. Jason could see Alana's mother put her handkerchief to her mouth muffle her weeping. Tommy put his arm around Belinda when she began to cry. Tim was also supporting his pregnant wife, Rachel, as she sobbed.

To his relief, Kenneth had the congregation stand as they prayed for Alana's safety and speedy return home. Jason felt himself tense up as Kenneth prayed aloud for those who were searching for her, praying for protection and wisdom for them.

After the prayer, Kenneth spoke again, briefly. "I know this is a tragic occurrence, but let us remind ourselves that it is not over. Do not give up on seeing Alana again. I believe God can and will see her through. Do not write her off as a person of the past. She *is* a member of this church. She *is* a special part of the Crewe family. She *is* coming back to us soon, with God's help."

Agony ran through Jason's spirit as the church began to sing *In the Garden,* the last song he had heard Alana sing before she was taken.

God, I can't take this, he thought, slipping out of the pew. Trying not to draw attention to himself, he went quietly to the door and, just as quietly, let himself out.

Curtis watched him go, though he did not try to stop or follow him. When Jason was gone, Curtis bowed his head again, his brow furrowed with concern for his friends.

"We're stopping at a hotel tonight."

Alana roused at the sound of Vic Dane's voice. They had been traveling nonstop for most of the day. When they did stop at a small-town station to refuel, she was not allowed out. Her head pounded from her fall the night before, and she needed to relieve herself.

Other than her physical infirmities, she was numb. She felt no fear, no anxiety, only weariness. Her body ached from holding herself so tensely between Manley and Duke. She felt as if she was going through the day in a haze, a dream. She knew she was in shock, but she had no idea how to shake it. And she didn't want to. At least this way she was not afraid.

Now, almost midnight, they were finally stopping to rest. Alana had no idea where they were, but the plains of Kansas had long disappeared. She studied the town they were traveling through. At the welcome sign, she frowned. Even the name of the town did not ring a bell to her.

Vic let Buddy off at the front door of a small inn to rent a room for them. He then parked the jeep in the back, well out of the way and view of passersby. The men piled out, stretching and groaning as they did. Manley reached in and pulled her out of the seat. She steadied herself against the vehicle, refusing to let him assist her. When she felt sturdy again, she pulled her foot back and kicked him hard in the shin. She wasted no time in running, hearing angry curses behind her.

Once again, she did not get very far. As soon as she felt Vic close in on her, she let out a scream, halted quickly by his rough hand. She struggled against him, kicking and scratching at him. He had to literally lift her off her feet to get her back to the jeep.

Buddy appeared just then with the keys to the room, so Vic carried her to straight to the room. After Buddy unlocked the door, Vic stomped in and fairly threw her on the bed.

She shrank back, her eyes like saucers. As she took in her surroundings, it hit her that she was alone, in a hotel room, with these five strangers. Again, she felt fear rear it ugly head as she stared at the muscular man glaring down at her angrily. There was no way she could fight him if he decided to hurt her.

To her surprise, though, Vic made no move towards her. He closed the door firmly and turned to Buddy. "I've got to secure the plane. Keep an eye on her."

Just before leaving, with his back still to the men, he said, "And if I find out that any of you touch her while I'm gone, you'll answer to me before Marlon ever hears about it."

The words chilled her, even though she supposed she should have been comforted. She was relieved when none of them so much as gave her a second glance after Vic was gone. Manley settled himself at the door, effectively blocking her only chance for exit.

Buddy had chosen the room well for their purpose. On the first floor, the door opened directly to the back parking lot. It was positioned all the way to the right, so they did not have to worry about people passing by and looking through the window.

Seeing that they would not bother her, Alana took that chance to go to the restroom. She felt Manley's eyes on her, but he said nothing.

After she had relieved herself, Alana washed her hands and rinsed her face with cold water. She stared at herself in the mirror, wondering that it was the same girl who had gone to work at *Darings'* just the night before.

There were dark circles under her eyes, from the lack of sleep. Her hair hung limply in her face, the barrettes she had used to secure the front long gone. Her jacket was dirty and there was a small tear in the elbow. Alana teared up, remembering that she was wearing Andrea's jacket. How she wished she could be with her sister now!

Taking further inventory, Alana could see stains on her blouse and skirt as well. Her arms were bruised from the hold that Jack Norris had put on her. She could feel tenderness around her mouth, due to the vise-like grip of Vic Dane.

Turning away, Alana leaned against the door and slid down to the floor. "Oh, God!" she sobbed for the first time. "Please get me home! I don't want to be here! Don't let them hurt me! Please get me home to my family!" She wrapped her arms around her knees and hid her face against them, letting the tears overtake her. She wept, not caring if Vic's cronies could hear her or not.

Alana had no idea how long she had been sitting there, but she finally wiped her face and rose. She jumped when someone knocked loudly on the door.

"Hey, you, girl" Duke shouted. "Get outta there!"

Raising her head bravely, Alana opened the door. Duke scowled at her as he pushed past her into the restroom.

Not looking at any of them, Alana sat stiffly on the bed, her back ramrod straight. Buddy and Charlie were playing cards, and she could see that Manley was paying more attention to the game than to his job. Alana tried not to look obvious as she kept her eye on the man, waiting for him to step away.

Finally the moment came. Manley leaned over Buddy's cards to see Charlie's. Alana jumped off the bed and ran for the door. She flung it open but Buddy's hand appeared over her head and slammed it shut. She turned to attack him with swinging fists and open-handed slaps. Caught by surprise, it took him a moment to catch her hands and pin them to her sides.

Vic stepped in just then and saw the scene. "What's going on?" he demanded, his face fierce.

"It's not what you think, Boss," Manley spoke up. "The girl was trying to get away and Buddy was just stopping her."

Vic nodded shortly. "Get your things together," he ordered. "We're leaving."

"What?" Duke complained, having just reappeared from the bathroom.

"We can't stay here with her," Vic explained. "She'll have the whole place in an uproar. I've got the plane on the other side of town. We'll just head out tonight. Somebody will drive the jeep down later."

Manley grumbled as he picked up his few scattered belongings.

"Go on and start the jeep," Vic directed. "I'll be out in a minute."

Alana shrank back in the bed as Duke, Manley, and Charlie filed out. She watched Vic turn his angry gaze on her. Her anxiety caused her to feel lightheaded and she braced herself against the mattress to keep from going down. Fighting a strong dizzy spell, she prayed she would not faint.

Chapter Seventeen

Vic studied her intently. He noticed for the first time the flush of her cheeks and the glazed-over appearance of her eyes. Her hand shook slightly as she reached up to push her hair off her face. He motioned to Buddy.

"When was the last time she's eaten?" he asked.

Buddy shrugged. "She wouldn't take anything at our last stop, and then Manley sucked everything down."

Vic exhaled loudly. "Great, we'll starve the girl before she even gets there."

Buddy stepped closer to whisper in Vic's ear. "Hey, you know she's gonna fight when we try to get her in the plane, don't you?"

With a curt nod, Vic said, "Yeah, I'll take care of that." He slipped some bills into Buddy's hand. "Go get her something she can eat on the plane. Meet us back at the jeep."

"Gotcha."

Alana shook her head of the cobwebs and looked up, startled to see Vic standing directly before her. His face was impassive as he pressed a glass of water to her hand.

"Drink," he directed.

Her first instinct was to refuse it, but her throat was so parched that it hurt. She raised the glass to her lips, relishing the cool water. Her head pounded, and it still ached from where she fell. She drank the entire glass without stopping.

Vic took the glass from her and stepped back, leaning against the door. He crossed his arms and stared at her.

Refreshed from the water, Alana felt bold enough to speak. "Do you mind telling me what you plan on doing with me?"

"Now's not a good time."

The hours of fear, anxiety, and confusion had finally caught up to her and she was suddenly angry. Without thinking, she spouted, "So when will it be a good time? When my body is found washed up on a riverbank?"

Vic's brows went up slowly. "Aren't you jumping to conclusions a bit?"

"Jumping to conclusions?" Alana exclaimed. "Oh, forgive me if I've judged my kidnappers too harshly!"

The man's mouth twitched.

Alana wasn't finished. "I don't know what you want from me, but I can assure you, there are people looking for me and you won't get away with this."

Vic shifted his feet, leaning against the large dresser in the room. "My employer might argue with that."

"I don't care what your employer thinks," she ground out. "Even if you kill me and no one here ever knows what happens. Someday, you'll face judgment."

Crossing his arms, Vic stared at the girl, but her gaze did not waver under his dark one.

Alana took a deep breath and the world suddenly spun. She put her hand up to her head, blinking at the dots dancing before her. Her eyes grew heavy suddenly and she felt a sudden fatigue come over her that she could not fight. As blackness enveloped her, she looked up at Vic one more time, hazily noting his expressionless face.

Oh, no! she thought as she felt herself being sucked into unconsciousness. *He's drugged me!*

Vic watched Alana collapse on the bed, her breathing settling into that of a deep sleep. He stared at her a moment, thinking, *Marlon, you've got yourself a wildcat this time!*

At that moment, Buddy stepped through the door. "Hey, Boss, everything's ready."

His answer was a short nod.

Buddy noticed Alana for the first time and chuckled. "I guess that was an easy way to keep her from causing us any trouble."

"Yeah, take my bag to the jeep. I'll be there with her in just a minute."

"Sure."

Buddy grabbed the bag, but Vic stopped him at the door. Reaching inside the bag, Vic pulled out his gray trench coat. "Go on," he urged.

Wrapping Alana up in the coat, Vic took her in his arms, a bit surprised by how light she was. He peered out the door cautiously and then ventured out. Buddy was in the driver's seat so after depositing Alana once again between Manley and Duke, he settled into the passenger's seat and they were off, quickly leaving the hotel behind.

Edwardsville

"Twenty-four hours," Sharon whispered painfully, staring out the window at the midnight sky. "My girl's been gone over twenty-four hours."

All was quiet in the house. The teenagers had retired only moments before, and Audrey had been asleep for hours. In the guest room, Pastor Nelson and his wife were sleeping, unwilling to leave the Crewes as of yet.

Alan was sitting next to his wife and heard her murmuring. He put his arm around her and drew her to his chest. Once again, she cried, but he could tell that she had lost her hysteria. Although still shaken and deeply troubled, Sharon had regained her inner strength.

"What are we going to do, Alan?" she whispered. "The longer someone is missing…"

With a squeeze, Alan admonished, "Now, we can't be thinking like that, Sharon. Wherever Alana is at, God is with her."

After a long pause, she said, "I know. But I'm human and I feel that she won't be safe unless we're there to protect her."

"There's nothing we could do for her that God can't do above and beyond," Alan reminded, resting his chin on her head. He waited a few minutes until he knew that she was once again calm. He hesitated to speak again, but he felt impelled to.

"Have you seen Jason?" he asked softly. He felt her shake her head against his chest. "He's pretty upset, Sharon."

Sharon slowly pulled away, staring down at her clasped hands.

"Curtis told me that he's blaming himself for this."

Tears were flowing down Sharon's cheeks as she closed her eyes. "Oh, no."

Alan fell silent; he knew that he did not have to say anything else. Sharon would work the rest out herself.

"I reacted pretty harshly to him last night," Sharon spoke. She shook her head slowly. "How could I have said what I did? I saw the look on his face. I knew then that he felt personally responsible. Yet, I let my feelings take over and…I know I must have hurt him."

Alan brushed her hair back. "Don't be too hard on yourself," he said. "This whole situation is just a nightmare. I think we are all a little lost."

"That's no excuse," she said firmly. "Jason thinks the world of Alana; I can see that. He wouldn't have let her get hurt if his life depended on it." She turned solemn eyes to her husband.

"Will you bring that boy to me?" she asked.

Alan leaned down and kissed her brow. "I'll do my best. I'm sure he's pretty busy now, but he'll be calling soon, if I know him at all."

"Unless I scared him off," Sharon lamented.

"No," he assured. "He may be hesitant to talk to you at first, but he'll call to check on us."

Sharon nodded, relieved, and leaned her head against her husband's arm. "We need to tell Audrey," she said.

"I know," Alan nodded. "I hate the thought of it."

"But she asked about Alana today. Wanted to know where she was at. We have to tell her something, even if we don't go into detail."

"We will," Alan agreed. "First thing in the morning."

They wasted no time in doing so. As soon as Audrey had awakened and had breakfast, thoughtfully prepared by Maggie, Alan and Sharon took the little girl to their bed room to talk to her.

"How come I've been missing school?" she asked abruptly.

Alan answered her. "Well, something's happened and we wanted you close to us."

"Where's Allie?"

Alan had always been proud of Audrey's keen intelligence, but he found himself wishing now that she wasn't always so quick.

"Allie is in a little bit of trouble, Audrey," Sharon spoke up. "She needs us to be very strong and to pray for her everyday."

"When is she going to come home?"

"We don't know, honey," Alan said, "but we're praying that God will bring her home soon."

The little girl frowned. "Why can't she come home? She promised she was going to read to me."

Sharon had to close her eyes against tears as Alan continued.

"Allie is lost, right now, Audrey. She can't find her way back home."

"Does she have a map?"

Alan took a deep breath. This was so difficult! How could he explain to a seven year old that her sister had been kidnapped? "Someone was mad at her and took her away. He won't let her come home right now."

Audrey stared up at her father and then her mother. "Is he going to hurt her?"

Alan reached over and took the child on his knee. "You know what? I'm sure Allie is going to be fine. The policemen are helping us look for her, and it won't be long before they find her, I'm sure. In the meantime, we need to pray for her. God will take care of her. He's always taken care of His children, hasn't He?"

Audrey nodded slowly, her face sober. When she was sure her parents had nothing more to say, she slid off Alan's lap and left the room.

"This is so hard," Sharon cried.

Alan could not speak due to the tightness of his throat, but he agreed wholeheartedly.

By Wednesday morning, the family and friends of Alana Crewe decided that they could not sit back and do nothing. By eleven o'clock, flyers were being hung all over town. Alana's picture was already in several newspapers and her abduction had even been covered by a local news channel, along with the story of Jack Norris's escape.

All day, the people of Fellowship were raising money for a reward. When *Darings'* found out what they were doing, they pledged to double the amount raised by the church. By seven-thirty that evening, over five thousand dollars had been raised.

Alan and Sharon finally talked to the reporters, reasoning that the more they talked about their daughter, the more likely that someone would respond. The Edwardsville Gazette had the story on the front page, and soon other towns were calling for interviews.

Captain Wade Harmon also cooperated with the media, though he explained that he could not talk openly. He gave what information he felt the public needed to know in order to help bring Alana home. Quotes from Dick Browning and employees of *Darings'* were also included in the story.

One person noticeably absent from the reports was the young cop who had discovered that she had been abducted, the very one who had rescued her from Jack Norris only weeks before.

It was not an oversight on the part of the reporters, however. Indeed, they contacted Jason Banks constantly throughout Wednesday and the rest of the week, requesting interviews. He put them off, though, not willing to put himself in the public eye. He felt he did not deserve any recognition for his part of the whole situation.

Instead, he buried himself in his work. Wade had put him on the case of finding Alana, so he put his whole heart into it. He arrived at work before six on Wednesday, and did not step into his house again until three-thirty Thursday morning. He was determined to track Jack Norris and Alana down, or die trying.

He found six messages on his answering machine from journalists, and two from Curtis. It was too early to call him now; he would have to wait until morning.

He fell into his bed exhausted, but once again could not sleep soundly. He tossed and turned, his mind full of Alana. When he did sleep, he dreamed of her, alone and scared, crying out for someone to help her.

He left for work again at nine in the morning. He was on his way to Topeka jail to survey the damage and jailbreak. In his hurry, he completely forgot to call Curtis back.

Topeka, Kansas
Thursday, April 11th
City jail

The main street where the jail stood was still hectic. Men and women milled about, surveying the damage. Supervisors yelled and their employees scurried to carry out their orders. The power had been restored early Tuesday morning, but it was still chaotic. The breakout of Jack Norris was on everybody's lips, leaving a cloud of apprehension above the city. Alana Crewe's kidnapping had also filtered into the streets, which caused all the more anxiety.

The road was being restored even as Jason drove by. Blocks of asphalt were being lifted by heavy machinery and cement being poured in areas where the blast had left gaping holes. The jailhouse and next door business were also undergoing serious repair, with the jail being top priority. The prisoners had been moved to Kansas City until the cells could be securely restored.

It took a little work for Jason to get inside the jail, having to show his badge and ID to do so. Once he did, he found the commissioner and explained why he was there.

"I heard about the girl," the sheriff told him. "That's a shame. I hope you find her."

"I plan to," Jason told him. "I need to know if Jack Norris had any visitors while he was here."

"Well, you know, he wasn't the most popular guy. His attitude was plumb sour. Why, his own parole officer just telephoned him, instead of seeing him in person."

"So there was no one?"

The man frowned. "Come to think of it. There was one man who came by, visited several times in fact. Norris always seemed a little more agreeable when he left."

"Do you know who he was?"

The commissioner shook his head regretfully. "The sign in log has gotten lost in the explosion and the security cameras are all messed up. I tell you, whoever was behind this did a fine job of mangling this place up."

Frustrated, Jason sighed loudly. "So there's no way of finding out?"

"Well, the cameras are shot, but the tapes may still be in tact. Let me check it out."

Jason was left alone for a few minutes as the cop went in search of the tapes. He prayed silently, knowing that this could be a long shot, but hoping beyond hope that Norris's visitor was a link to his escape, and ultimately, Alana's disappearance.

Chapter Eighteen

At the station, Jason pulled the tapes out and watched them carefully. It took him almost two hours to track down one that had Norris's visitor. He studied the man, not recognizing him. The man was tall, broad, and walked with a confident air. Jason noticed the expensive suit, the refined manner, and even the gold watch on his right hand. Whoever this man, he was no commoner.

Jason found four other visits by the same man, on seceding days. *This guy sure took a lot of time to visit a criminal,* Jason thought.

Once he was finished with that, he took the tapes to Janice Graham, technical advisor. He explained what he needed from her.

"So, you want me to find out who this guy is just by studying his picture?" she questioned with a teasing smile.

Jason gave a small smile in return, the first since Monday night. "Think you can manage that?"

"Of course," she returned. "I am a genius, aren't I?"

Jason shook his head in bemusement. "Yes, you certainly are. That's why I brought them to you. I need to know as soon as possible, okay?"

"Sure, I'll call you when I have something."

Thousands of feet above sea level

Vic stared out the window at the miles and miles of ground below him. The plane hummed steadily as it streaked through the sky. He could hear his men murmuring softly to themselves, once again involved in a card game.

Turning slightly, Vic glanced at Alana, who was also gazing out the small glass. Awakened several hours earlier, Vic had watched her slowly take in her surroundings, her eyes finally stopping on him. He had been mildly impressed when she closed her eyes and the panic on her face slowly faded. Indeed, when she opened her eyes again and found him still watching her, her chin went up slightly and she turned away.

Now she was sitting quietly, not eating much of the sandwiches that Buddy had bought. She brushed her hair from her face, and Vic thought he saw tears on her face. At that moment, she felt his eyes on her and looked at him. She raised her brows in question. Vic did not reply but turned his attention back to the window, hiding a frown at her appearance.

Alana herself felt cold and exhausted. She wrapped the trench coat around her tightly, not caring where it had come from. There was a chill in the middle of her stomach that she could not warm. Her head was still pounding and her face felt hot. The shock of her abduction had faded somewhat, but her physical body was still responding to the sudden changes. First the fall on the head, and now being thousands of feet in the air with little food in her stomach, was taking its toll on her.

Alana was unaware of her flushed cheeks were, or her glazed eyes. She slumped in her seat, as if she had no energy to even sit up straight. Finding himself uptight, Vic was anxious to get home so that the girl would be out of hands.

Jason hurried back to Janice's working quarters after he got her call. He found her at a massive desk that held a huge computer system. She was still working when he stepped behind her.

"I think I've figured out who our mystery visitor is," she said as she pulled a picture from the video tape to the large screen. She swiveled her chair to another monitor and pushed a few buttons. Another picture appeared. This was a snapshot taken in front of a large stone building. It was obviously the same man who had visited Jack Norris in the jail.

"Who is he?" Jason asked breathlessly.

"Well," Janice read from some printouts. "His name is Reuban Romano."

"Reuban Romano," Jason repeated. "Any idea of his link to Norris?"

"Not a clue," Janice said flatly. She spoke again before Jason could react. "But, I have found some interesting info on Mr. Romano."

"What's that?"

Janice pointed to the man next to Reuban on the snapshot, who bore a striking resemblance. "This is his older brother Marlon Romano. This picture was taken two years ago in front of the Boston courthouse.

"They're the sons of very rich parents who left them their entire inheritance when they died. Seemed they owned one of the biggest oil companies in the country. Marlon took his wealth and nearly *tripled* it when he took over the company, becoming one of the wealthiest men in America, which made him very popular with the ladies." She clicked another picture onto the screen. In this one, Marlon was at a party of some kind, two young women hanging on his arms. "He was known to be very infatuated with the fairer sex."

Jason pulled a chair to sit beside Janice, curious to know where she was going with this.

"Anyway," Janice paused dramatically. "Marlon fell under fire when one of his own employees, a bookkeeper named, uh..." She studied her papers again. "Fred Jenkins went to the authorities. Apparently, Marlon was keeping faulty records. It seems that he wasn't recording big transactions and was pocketing the extra money.

"And so there was a big investigation. Marlon continued to claim his innocence. However, he began liquefying all his assets and even sold the company to someone else. The plot thickened when Fred Jenkins was found dead in an alley. When the cops went to question Marlon, he was gone."

"Gone?"

"Yep. He had taken off somewhere and hasn't been found since. He was one of the top America's Most Wanted that year, but no one has seen hide or hair of him in almost two years."

Jason shook his head. "Where does Reuban tie into all this?"

With a shrug, Janice said, "Honestly, as far as I know, he doesn't. During the investigation, there was no evidence that he was involved. He never worked directly in the oil plant, going into another line of business. Even when Marlon disappeared and he was questioned, they could never prove that he knew anything. So far, he is innocent."

Jason frowned. "But how are they tied to Jack Norris?"

"I don't really know." Janice turned to face the cop. "But, I find it strange that Reuban, who is tied to one of the most wanted criminals in the last five years of United history, is also connected to Jack Norris, another famous bad guy. And I also find it interesting that Norris escaped soon after the visits began."

Jason nodded. It was all so strange and confusing. "Where is Reuban now?"

"Funny you should ask," Janice said, skimming over a paragraph. "Soon after Marlon's disappearance, Reuban also left Boston. No one really knows where he lives anymore but he still does make appearances here and there. It's normally business related. The fact that he's shown up on a jail visit is something new."

Jason's phone rang just then and he quickly pulled it out. "Banks."

On the other line, Wade cut right to the chase. "Jack Norris has been spotted."

Gripping the phone, Jason exclaimed. "When? Where? Was Alana with him?"

"A truck driver gave him a ride through Oklahoma; thought he was just helping some guy who was down in his luck. It wasn't until last night that he found out that it was Jack Norris. He then immediately called the authorities."

"Captain, what about Alana?" Jason demanded.

"He was alone, Banks."

Jason closed his eyes tightly, his mind moving a mile a minute. If Jack Norris had been spotted in Oklahoma, then…"Where's Alana?"

"I don't know, son, but we're still working on it."

When the line was disconnected, Jason stood for a moment, trying to fight the despair coming over him. This did not look good. What had Norris done with Alana? Jason would not let himself even consider the possibilities. He had to believe that she was alive and unharmed, that God would protect her.

"You all right?"

Janice's voice cut through his reverie. "Not really, no," he said honestly. "But that's my problem." He stared at the screen at Reuban Romano's picture, trying to get his attention back on the subject at hand. "So no one knows where he is?"

"Well, he's never been accused of anything, so he's free to come and go as he pleases," Janice clarified.

"Then how in the world can I track this guy down?"

Janice printed out the picture of Reuban and Marlon Romano and handed it to Jason. "I wish I could help, but all I can say is that there have been rumors that Marlon took off for Mexico when he realized he was going to go down." She shrugged. "Maybe Reuban is there with him."

Jason thanked Janice for her help and left, still mulling over the information.

Later that afternoon he talked with Wade Harmon about the Romano brothers.

"We'll take this into consideration, but as of yet it does not have anything to do with the kidnapping," Wade reminded. "That's what we're trying to solve."

"Captain, I could care less about these guys," Jason pointed out. "I just want to know what Reuban has to do with Norris—to see if he had anything to do with Norris finding Alana."

"So, what do you plan to do about it?"

Jason thought for a moment, absently rubbing his knee as he did. He was sitting in the only other chair in the office, dressed in jeans and a black polo shirt. Since Harmon had put him on Alana's case, he had not had to put his uniform back on.

"Reuban had to stay somewhere when he was in Topeka," Jason pondered. "I'm gonna check out the hotels and see if he checked in to any of them."

Wade nodded. "Remember, Reuban has not done anything other than visit Norris. We can't accuse him."

"I just want to ask him some questions, see if maybe he knows anything. Just because he's Marlon's brother doesn't mean he's done anything wrong."

"Good," Wade nodded. "Tell me what you find."

Chihuahua, Mexico
Friday, April 12th

The air was hot and dry when the plane finally landed. Alana stared, nonplussed, at the view outside the window. Large, sprawling buildings towered high above them. Traffic was everywhere, making passage through the roads difficult. Dark headed men and women milled about. She saw women wearing loose flowing clothes in a variety of colors; some of the men were even wearing wide brimmed hats that she recognized as sombreros. The words that she heard were foreign to her, but she recognized it as Spanish.

Oh, God, I can't be in Mexico! she despaired, wondering how anyone could find her here. *What are they going to do with me?*

Vic stepped out of the plane and spoke briefly in Spanish with someone. A moment later he reached in and took Alana's arm, keeping firm hold of it as he led her to a black Cadillac with tinted windows. As soon as she was in, he sat beside her. Buddy took a seat on her other side and the car pulled away from the small airport. Taking a deep breath, Vic felt relieved to finally be back in Mexico, but he still could not shake the tension in his muscles.

The trip was long, or it seemed so to Alana. She sat still the entire time. After a while the car went through another city, smaller than Chihuahua. She heard someone say Acquiles Serdan.

It was almost an hour later when the car pulled into a wide circular drive. Vic felt more than saw the girl's body sag slightly. He could see by her face that she was overwhelmed by the size of the place.

Marlon had always prided himself in having the best, and his home certainly fell into that category. A huge, intimidating structure of three stories, the place covered fifteen hundred square feet and sat on two hundred acres of picturesque landscape. The mansion was made of white stone, and stood in stark contrast to the steel buildings they had just seen in Chihuahua, or the simpler structures in Acquiles Serdan.

The driver pulled up close to the porch, where several servants were waiting on the steps. Buddy exited the car and entered the house without a backwards glance, obviously glad to be home. Vic stood and stretched before he motioned for Alana to step out.

"Welcome home, Miss Crewe," he said lightly, watching her head go back as she took in the massive manor.

Alana had no idea what this place was, or what they were doing here. She felt more than a little intimidated by the size and power of the place and longed more than anything to see her own humble two story home.

Her body was weak, and she realized that she was not going to stand much longer. She felt as if she was on fire, and her limbs trembled violently. Her head spun as she tilted back to look at the house and she brought it down abruptly. Lights flashed before her eyes as she felt her breathing quicken.

Vic caught her just before she fell, wincing at how hot she felt, even through his shirt. He swung his arm beneath her legs and lifted her. She stiffened at first, but she was too drained to fight him. She rested her head against his shoulder and resigned herself to be carried.

The burden was no strain on his muscular arms and he moved easily and quickly through the house. He carried her up a flight of stairs and to a large room at the south wing. He laid her gently on the four poster bed, realizing as he did that she was now unconscious.

Not knowing what else to do, Vic threw a blanket over her. He stepped out the door to find an attractive, petite Mexican servant girl standing in the hall.

"Felina, I need your help," he said in Spanish.

The girl looked up at him somberly. "What is it, Senor?"

"The girl I just brought in, can you take care of her? I think she's sick."

"Si. That is what Senor Marlon asked of me before he left. I was to care for his new visitor."

Vic nodded, glancing back into the room where Alana was lying. "Okay, well, then I'll leave her in your hands." Before he moved on he said,

"Whatever you do, keep her in your sight at all times. If she causes you any trouble, let me know."

"Si, Senor."

Topeka, Kansas

"Have you seen this man?" Jason asked, pulling the picture out of his pocket. This was the fourth hotel that Jason had visited, and his patience was growing thin.

The clerk's eyes lightened. "Oh, yes."

Jason felt his heart quicken. "When?"

"Oh, a few days ago. He checked in late." The man skimmed over his roster again. "It was on a Thursday, March 30th. Wanted one of the best rooms in the place."

"Is he still here?"

"No, he checked out on Monday evening."

The day Norris escaped, Jason thought. "Can you tell me anything about him?"

"Well, he was very polite. Paid good money for the rooms. I never had any trouble with him. Why the questions?"

Jason sighed. "I need to ask him some questions about a jail escape and kidnapping."

The man's eyes widened. "Do you think he's involved?"

"I just need to talk to him," Jason said. "So, there was nothing suspicious in the time he was here."

"No…wait. He did tell me that he was going to have some friends over Monday afternoon. He gave me some extra money so that I wouldn't complain."

"Do you remember anything about these friends of his?"

Drumming his fingers on the counter, the clerk cocked his head to the side. "Well, there were five men. I saw them drive up in a dark green jeep. They asked where his room was at. They were only here a little while, and it wasn't long after that Mr. Romano checked out."

"Did you say they were driving a green jeep?" Jason asked, trying hard to stay calm.

"Yes, sir."

"I don't suppose you know the license plate."

"No, I didn't have any reason to."

Jason took a deep breath. "I appreciate your help, sir."

"If you need anything else, just let me know."

Jason's hand was shaking when he got to his car. He pulled his cell phone out and called Wade, quickly relating what he had discovered.

"Now we're getting somewhere," Wade declared. "I just got a call. Get over here so I can fill you in."

Chapter Nineteen

Edwardsville

Jason found himself back in Wade Harmon's office, his heart beating triple fast. "What is it?"

"Our girl has been spotted."

"Where?" Jason gasped.

"In a privately owned inn in Lexington, Texas."

The world spun to a stop. "Texas?"

Wade nodded, shuffling papers. "The owner of the hotel saw what she thought was a lover's quarrel out in the parking lot Wednesday night. A girl was being chased by a dark headed guy and he carried her back to the hotel."

"How do we know it was Alana?"

"The woman's sister happened to be in Kansas this week when the escape/abduction hit the news," the captain explained. "She took home one of the flyers with Alana's picture on it. The owner of the inn read the description of Alana and what she was wearing, and thought it could be the girl she had seen."

"Has anyone checked the hotel?" Jason asked breathlessly.

"Yep. They checked out later that night. Seems there were two rooms rented, under the name of Buddy White. This woman says that there were five men and a girl renting those rooms. For some reason, they didn't even stay the night."

"Five men," Jason muttered. "The clerk at the hotel said Reuban had five guys at his room Monday afternoon."

"Could be the same ones." Wade's voice was slightly skeptical.

"But why would Norris leave Alana with them?" Jason asked, not expecting an answer.

Wade settled in his chair. "This sounds too much like a puzzle to me. We have a link between five guys and Reuban Romano, and five guys and Alana, but as of yet, we don't have any of them linked to Jack Norris."

"Or do we?" Jason asked. "What about the security tape from the store?"

The two men took the time to review the tape and studied the accomplice that Norris had to help him take Alana. The second man was rather short and stout, with a wide face and narrow eyes.

"Find out who this is," Wade said, giving the tape to Jason, who promptly walked it upstairs to Janice's office.

"Can you get back to me as soon as possible?" he asked.

"Sure."

Jason sat at his desk, his eyes staring blindly at the papers before him. His brain was racing to connect all the dots.

Jack Norris had been visited in jail by Reuban Romano. Reuban had five visitors in his hotel room, driving a green jeep, which could be the same one seen in the security tape at *Darings'*.

Shortly before Norris's escape, Reuban checked out and apparently left Topeka. Jack Norris then appeared at *Darings'* where he forced Alana into the jeep. Afterwards, he was spotted in Oklahoma, alone. Meanwhile, five men and a girl, who could very well be Alana Crewe, were spotted in Texas, in rooms signed for by a Buddy White.

Jason shook his head. "What's the game Norris is playing?' he muttered. The more time passed and the more clues he dug up, the worse he felt about the whole situation. What kind of dangerous position was Alana in? Who was she traveling with now? Where were they taking her? Why would complete strangers have any desire to hold her?

Picking up the phone, Jason requested a background check on Buddy White. He also asked them to find any link between him and Marlon or Reuban Romano.

While still waiting on the call about Buddy White, Jason pulled out his cell phone. He felt guilty that he had not talked to the Crewes in a couple days, but he was also hesitant. He knew they could very well blame him for their daughter's absence. Regardless of what they thought of him, though, his conscious would not allow him to cut himself off completely. The family had become very dear to him since he had befriended Alana. He had to let them know he cared.

Alan answered the phone, and although his voice was tired, he sounded pleased to talk to the cop. He asked a few questions, and Jason told him honestly that there were several leads.

"How's the family, Alan?" he asked, once again feeling his throat tighten.

"We're hanging in there," Alan told him. "We have some rough moments, but we've got a lot of the church people helping us out. I really don't know where we'd be without them. How are you doing?"

Jason was surprised at the question. "Working hard to get Alana back where she belongs."

"I didn't ask what you were doing," Alan pointed out. "I want to know *how* you're doing. This whole thing has to be pretty hard on you, too."

Taking a deep breath, Jason felt a sudden impulse to pour his heart out to the older man, but logic refrained him. How could he unload his burdens on a man whose daughter had been kidnapped due to his mistake? "Hanging in there," he said, repeating Alan's words.

"Sharon wants to talk to you," Alan said abruptly.

"No, Alan," Jason implored. "Don't make her talk to me. I know she's pretty upset."

"She's also worried about you."

"What?"

Alan said nothing else, but Jason grimaced when he heard Sharon come on the line. "Jason?"

"Yes, ma'am," Jason answered meekly.

Sharon took a deep breath. "I owe you an apology for the way I acted towards you Monday night."

"Sharon, no," Jason cut in, devastated that she would feel any regret.

"Let me talk," she insisted. "I don't care what happened, or what you're telling yourself and everybody else. You are Alana's friend, and you did your best. I know you're working overtime to find her, and I just want to say that I'm praying for you."

Jason closed his eyes against a sudden rush of tears. He felt his defenses weakening. How could Sharon be so understanding? How could she say so calmly that she was praying for him when it was her daughter that was in the most trouble? How could she have such strength when Jason felt as if he was falling apart?

"Thank you, Sharon," he whispered. "I don't know that I deserve it, but it means a lot to me."

"Come over and see us," she said. "Having Alana's friends is like having a part of Alana here. I need to see you."

"I will," Jason promised, having to force the words from his throat. He hung up and hung his head, his heart crying out to God.

Father in Heaven, please help us all! We need Your love and mercy in such a profound way right now. This trial is too big for all of us. We can't do it without Your help.

The phone rang just then. "I got that check on White you wanted," the man said. "He's from Omaha, Nebraska. Was tried for armed robbery a few years ago, but was never convicted."

"Does he have any connection to the Romanos?"

"He used to work for Marlon Romano."

"Really?"

"Yep. Was one of Marlon's many security guards."

Jason leaned back into his chair, feeling weariness in his very bones. He had not slept more than five hours at a time since Monday, but he continued pushing himself. He felt driven to find out what had happened to Alana, to bring her home. It was the least he could do after allowing her to be caught up in this mess. At least he now had a link between one of the men and the Romanos.

Janice called just a few minutes later. "The man assisting Norris is Manley Elam."

"You know anything about him?"

"Yeah, I checked him out myself." She paused and Jason knew that she was reading over the information she had uncovered. "He's a wanted man from New Mexico. Broke out of prison with three other guys. They were tracked down, but Elam was never caught."

"What was he in prison for?"

"Sexual assault and murder."

Jason slammed the phone down. He clenched his hand into a fist. "No, God," he whispered. "She can't be in the company of Manley Elam."

Forcing himself to be calm, Jason tried to think through what he knew for sure, going over all the information he had found in the last two days. He still had no idea what Reuban had to do with Norris, but knew that there was now a distinct link between them. He knew the names of two of the men who apparently still had Alana in their custody, though that fact did nothing to comfort him. The more he found out about her abductors, the worse he felt

He thought of all that Janice had told him, his mind finally registering one comment.

...there have been rumors that Marlon took off for Mexico...

Jason's blood suddenly chilled. Alana and her captors had been seen in Texas, just north of the border from the southern country. "Oh, God, no!" he begged. "Please don't tell me that they're taking her to Mexico!"

Acquiles Serdan, Mexico

Alana stirred, disoriented as she fought for wakefulness. She stared at velvet red drapes hanging over wide windows. The massive bed she was laying in was more than a little comfortable and sprawled elegantly from one wall. The floor was tiled and waxed so that it shone like glass. Bright moonlight shone through the window, casting an eerie glow upon the room.

Slowly sitting up, Alana stared at the expansive room, wondering briefly where she was at. Just as soon as the question emerged, her memory cleared and she fell back against her pillow.

I've been kidnapped, she thought dully. *Jack Norris has abducted me and then left me with five strangers who have flown me all the way to Mexico. I'm a long way from home.*

The thought of home brought tears to her eyes. She longed to feel her mother's arms around her and to see her dad's comforting smile. She wanted to hear Andrea ask to borrow her clothes and to fight with Anthony again. She wished she could read a book with Audrey.

"Dear Jesus," she whispered, letting the tears overflow, even as her eyelids closed once again in exhaustion. "Please get me back home to my family!"

Edwardsville

Jason burst through Wade's door. "They're taking her to Mexico!" he exclaimed.

The gray haired captain was on the phone and held up his hand. Jason paced the small confines of the office, every second that passed by making him want to scream.

We've got to get to her before they take her across the border, he reasoned irrationally. *If they succeed in that, we may never find her!* He stopped and ran his hand through his hair, standing it on end.

He had no idea how frazzled he was looking these days. The lack of sleep caused dark circles to form under his eyes, and he had dropped several pounds. His patience was thin, his faith small. The easygoing, lighthearted Jason Banks had disappeared when Alana Crewe had.

"Now what is it you're going on about?" Wade asked calmly, setting the receiver down.

"Alana's kidnappers are going to take her across the border," Jason told him, setting his hands on the desk. "We've got to track them down before they do."

Wade leaned back, his face thoughtful. "What makes you so sure about this?"

"Because! Everything points to it." Jason rattled off how he had come to the conclusion that Reuban Romano was somehow linked to everything. "If he lives in Mexico with Marlon then…"

"Whoa, whoa," Wade stopped him.

Jason stared at him. "What?"

"Do you think you might be jumping to conclusions? We have no proof on any of this. It's just possibilities at this point."

"You know and I know this has to be true," Jason growled.

"Maybe so," Wade acknowledged. "But that doesn't mean we can just rush into this. Remember, jack's been spotted in Oklahoma. We have to assume he's still in that vicinity. We've got to do everything in an orderly fashion."

"An orderly fashion?" Jason's voice rose. "There's a girl that's been missing for several days who's about to disappear into *Mexico*, and you're telling me to do this in an orderly fashion?"

"Banks, calm down," Wade ordered, his brows lowering.

"I can't!" Jason snapped. "I can't believe you're just sitting there doing nothing!"

"And I can't believe you're acting so irrational!" Wade returned.

"Send someone down there," Jason pleaded.

"Send them where?" Wade demanded. "Son, if they get her across the border they are beyond our legal control."

Jason slammed his fist into the desk. "So we do nothing about it?"

Wade leaned forward in his chair, staring up at the younger man angrily. "That's not what I said, Banks. You know very well that our hands are tied in Mexico. I'll contact border control and let them know, but that's all I can do."

"That's not good enough," Jason insisted. "Send someone down to find her."

Shaking his head, Wade said, "I'm not sending anyone to Mexico. It's insane, and if you'll calm down you'd realize that."

Rage built up so strong in Jason that for a moment he was tempted to put his fist through a wall.

"But I'll tell you what I am going to do," Wade continued, his voice hard.

"What?"

"I'm sending you home for the weekend."

Jason stared at him in disbelief. "What are you talking about?"

"I mean it!" Wade barked. "You're no good to anyone in this state. You're lucky I won't take action against your behavior."

"Captain, I can't afford to be off this case for even a minute. I have to find her."

"Jason," Wade softened his tone slightly. "I understand why you're so upset. But you need to keep a clear head if you want to help that girl."

"But—"

"I'm not done," Wade interrupted. "Now you're tired and frustrated. Your mind's going into overload. You need to take a break before the strain kills you. Believe me, I've seen young men just like you completely lose it. I don't want to see the same thing happen to you."

Taking a deep breath, Jason attempted to calm down. "I'm sorry for the way I acted," he spoke slowly, staring at the floor in order to gather his wits. "Please don't send me home."

"I'm sorry, Banks," Wade told him. "But it's the best thing for you. Take two days off and let yourself work through everything. You've been so busy working that I don't think you've let yourself deal with the fact that your friend has been kidnapped."

The words stopped Jason cold. That was exactly what he had been attempting to do. He didn't think he could stand it if he dwelled on the recent events for too long. He didn't want to face the guilt that he was still fighting.

"Now," Wade was saying. "Alana's family needs your support more than they need you to work yourself to death. If any major development comes up, I'll contact you."

"Will you?" Jason pressed, knowing that he was about to lose this argument.

"Of course. In the meantime, we'll let the investigators continue working. Go home, get some rest. Got it?"

Still frustrated, Jason gave a short nod before stomping out of the room.

Chapter Twenty

Curtis was waiting for him in the living room when he got home.

"What are you doing here?" he asked bluntly.

Curtis raised a brow. "Oh, I don't know. After trying to reach you for two days I was beginning to think you had dropped off the face of the planet."

"That's not funny," Jason muttered.

"I know," Curtis admitted. "But I've been worried about you."

"I'm not the one you should be worried about, Curtis," Jason said, dropping into a chair. "Alana's the one who's in trouble."

"Yes, and believe me, I've been praying up a storm about that. But I know you. You're trying to drown yourself in your work so that you don't have to confront your feelings."

Jason frowned. "Well, you can stop worrying about that for now."

"Why?"

"Wade's ordered me to take two days off."

Curtis nodded. "Good. You need it."

"Curtis, Alana is still in the hands of men who are capable of anything," Jason responded, rising from his seat. "Anything can happen to her, and time is running out. The longer she's gone, the more chance there is of something happening to her. I've got to find her as soon as possible, and you say it's *good* that I have time off?"

"Jason, listen to yourself," Curtis said. "You're talking like you're the only one who can save her. You can't save her, Jason. You have to trust God to do that."

Jason rubbed his face tiredly. He felt as if he was sinking into a black hole, where there would be no return. His heart was torn in millions of pieces and his mind was spinning crazily. "I know, Curt," he finally admitted. "But I feel like…I'm the reason this whole thing happened. It's the least I can do for her."

"Stop it, Jason," Curtis exclaimed. "Stop blaming yourself."

"It's easy to say," the other man said softly. "You gave me advice similar to that before, remember?"

Curtis nodded. "And you took it."

"Yes, I did." He took a deep breath. "But this…I just don't know how to deal with this. This is Alana we're talking about!"

"I know," Curtis replied. He stuck his hands in his pockets. "I keep waking up hoping this whole thing was just a nightmare. Dinah has cried everyday, and Tim took Rachel to the hospital the other day because he was worried the stress would complicate her pregnancy. Alan and Sharon are both looking older than I've ever remembered. I just feel so helpless."

Jason stood silently while Curtis talked, his head bowed. "I've been in some pretty low spots in my life, Curtis," he said. "But this time, it affects someone I've come to think a lot of. She's become a very good friend recently, and we're talking about her *life*." He took a deep breath. "God help us all."

"He will," Curtis assured. "But you have to let Him work it out. Just be willing to be used and trust Him, no matter what."

Jason nodded. "That's the part I'm having trouble with right now."

Acquiles Serdan
Saturday, April 13ᵗʰ

Alana woke with a start, not sure what had awakened her. As she lay there in bed, she detected movement in the room. She opened her eyes and peered through the morning sunlight streaming in the window. She spotted a petite girl standing at the window, pulling back the drapes.

"Where am I?" Alana asked.

The girl turned and regarded Alana seriously. She was very attractive with long, dark hair and huge, soulful eyes. Her olive complexion was smooth and clear, complimenting her dark eyes well.

"Do you speak English?" Alana asked her.

"Si," she replied.

"Then where am I?' Alana asked, rather edgily.

"You are in the home of Marlon Ferraro." Her voice was heavily accented but Alana could understand her easily.

Alana frowned. Marlon Ferraro. Her mind cleared as she remembered that she had heard that name several times during her long journey. "Who are you?"

"I am Felina Gomez," she girl answered simply. "I have brought your breakfast."

"I don't want breakfast!" Alana exclaimed, throwing the covers off. "I want to go home!"

"I cannot help you there." Felina looked stern as she looked down at the captive girl.

Alana lowered her head in frustration. Her eyes fell on the long, flowing gown she was wearing. "Where are my clothes?" she demanded. She remembered vaguely that Vic Dane had had to carry her into this room and her face burned. "How'd I get into this?" she asked, the thought of him touching her making her skin crawl.

"I helped you change into it last night," Felina explained.

Relieved, Alana's eyes closed briefly. When she opened them, she saw Felina staring at her, her face unreadable.

"Why am I here?" Alana asked.

Felina turned away, her movements brisk. "You should eat your breakfast, Senorita." She left the room without another word. Alana heard the distinct sound of a key turning in the lock. She slumped back in the bed, feeling defeated. There was no one in this strange, foreign place who would help her. They were all working together to keep her from the home and family she loved.

After only a moment, Alana jumped from bed. She was not about to resign herself to her new environment. She would find a way out.

She went to the window and studied the view, staring down at the ground, two stories down. There were no balconies, no stairs, nothing she could climb down on.

Moving quickly, Alana prowled around the room. She checked every window, every door. She found a large closet and bathroom, but no possible way she could get out, except through the one door that was now locked.

What would I do if I got out anyway? she asked herself. *I have no idea where to go.*

The awareness that she was indeed trapped sobered her. She closed her eyes and took a deep breath. "Okay, God," she spoke out loud. "I don't understand why You allowed this, but I'm going to trust You to see me through it. Please give me the strength that I need to get through this. I have no idea why I'm here, but no one here is just going to let me go. I have to find a way myself. Let Your Spirit be my guide."

A few hours later, Felina brought her noon meal. She paused when she saw that Alana's plate from the morning had not been touched. "Senorita, you should eat," she admonished. "After last night, you will get sick if you don't build your strength up."

Alana was sitting in the window seat, staring outside. She did not acknowledge that she even heard Felina.

With a frown, Felina took Alana's cold breakfast and left her lunch. She cast another look at the white girl's face before she left.

Vic Dane stood on the balcony of his room, lighting a cigarette. He heard a noise and glanced through the door leading to the hall. He caught a glimpse of Felina walking by, her face looking troubled. He called to her.

"How's our guest?" he asked, speaking in Spanish.

Felina shrugged. "She's refused to eat any dinner."

With a sigh, Vic said, "She'll have to learn that the more she fights, the more difficult it's going to be on her."

Felina nodded, but said nothing.

Vic studied her for a moment and then dismissed her. He turned back to the extensive view before him. The grounds were perfectly tended to, and their beauty drew many viewers. Vic, however, was used to its splendor and no longer impressed.

Bringing the cigarette to his lips, he took a deep breath. He stared out at the perimeters around the mansion, his dark brows drawn in a frown.

Edwardsville

Jason bolted upright in the bed, his chest heaving. He swung his feet to the floor and groaned. If only he could sleep without seeing Alana in his dreams! Pulling a shirt on, he stood and went to the window, a bit surprised to see the sun already climbing in the sky. A glance at the clock told him that he had actually managed to steal almost a full night's sleep.

Curtis had left rather late the night before. Jason let himself consider everything that they had talked about, and knew that Curtis was right. He had to step back and let God take care of everything.

But as he moved about that morning, all he could think about was Alana and that he should be working to find her. The image from the security tape of her abduction kept running through his mind, as well as heart wrenching questions.

Where was she? Who had her? What were they going to do with her? Was she all right? Had she been hurt? *Was she still alive?*

That last thought was too much for him. Jason knew he was going to have to get out of this cloud of gloom, but he could not do it on his own. He grabbed his coat and headed for his car. He needed to talk, and he knew who he could talk to.

Kenneth and Maggie were both at home when he arrived. They had spent three nights at the Crewes before Sharon insisted that they would be fine on their own now. Kenneth welcomed Jason in without hesitation.

"I need to talk to you," Jason wasted no time in saying.

The men settled in the den with mugs of coffee, though Jason barely touched his. Though he started rather awkwardly, he began pouring his heart out to the pastor. He told him everything, of his guilt about Alana's disappearance, of his shutting his feelings out by working overtime, and of how he felt that he had to be the one to save her.

Kenneth listened gravely, letting the young man go uninterrupted until he was finished. Then he began by saying, "Trust is a very hard thing to learn, isn't it?"

Jason nodded miserably.

"The Bible says those that ask receive. Have you told God what you've been feeling?"

"I've tried," Jason said.

"No, don't try," Kenneth admonished. "Tell Him everything you just told me. Don't hold back. Then ask Him to help you trust Him. He will, Jason."

Licking his lips, Jason asked rather humbly. "Will you pray with me?"

"Absolutely."

The men went to their knees. Kenneth took the lead, praying once again for protection for Alana's life and her return home. Then he spent a few moments praying for Jason.

"Father, this young man has been carrying such a burden this week. He feels personally responsible, and he's having difficulty letting that go, which makes it all the more harder for him to trust in Your grace and power. I pray that You reach down into his heart and heal the hurt, let the faith that has been laying dormant for these past few days rise up once again, stronger than ever. Help Jason to surrender everything to Your hands."

Kenneth stopped and Jason knew that it was his turn. "I've been trying to do this on my own, Lord," he prayed haltingly. "And I know I can't. I need You. Alana needs You. I know I can't help her, only You can." His voice broke and he allowed himself to weep for the first time. He covered his hands with his face and continued praying, finally releasing his pent up emotions. He placed Alana in God's hands, where she belonged.

When he was finished, he felt Kenneth's arm around his shoulders, outwardly thanking God for His provision and strength. When Jason rose, though his knees felt shaky, he felt whole again. Though still concerned for Alana, he knew that he could now trust God to take care of everything.

Jason continued the day in an attitude of prayer, especially when disturbing thoughts about Alana would come to mind. Shortly after five, he was back in his car, this time heading for the Crewe home.

Though still grim, Alan and Sharon seemed to be in better spirits. They continued believing that their daughter would be found soon. They confided in Jason of how Audrey spent a lot of time in Alana's room, and that Anthony, feeling guilty for how he had treated his sister at times, had changed the light bulb like she requested a couple days before she was abducted.

They were all three sitting at the table. The kids were all gone, including Audrey who had been taken out by Dinah and Curtis for a while.

"How's Andrea?" Jason asked. "I know she's especially close to Alana."

Sharon's eyes took on a troubled look. "She's the one I'm really worried about."

Her husband agreed. "She's too quiet. I'm afraid she's bottling everything up inside, and that she might be harboring some anger over the whole situation."

With a sigh, Jason said, "I know from experience that that's not healthy."

"You look better than you have been," Sharon observed.

Jason nodded. "I finally had to get rid of the load. I couldn't handle it by myself."

"I know exactly where you're coming from," Alan said, taking Sharon's hand. "We've had to completely entrust Alana to God's care. We don't know what the future holds, but we do know that God is there, and that's all we can ask."

"Yes, it is." Jason thought for a moment. "Maybe I could talk to Andrea," he suggested.

"She thinks a lot of you," Sharon added. "She might open up to you."

"I'll try, then."

"I want to tell you something," Sharon said, her face reflective. "I appreciate you coming over here today. A lot of Alana's friends have been in and out, and I don't know what I'd do without them. But I know that Alana had come to really value her friendship with you. She spoke of you at times, saying that you always seemed to understand her, even if she couldn't explain something."

Jason smiled sadly. "I think Alana and I are a lot alike, though she's never realized it."

"Well, thank you for befriending her," Sharon went on. "She's always been shy and it's hard for her to make friends, but she seems comfortable with you."

"Thank you," Jason said. "What you've said means a lot. I value our friendship, too."

At that moment, Andrea entered the kitchen. As her parents greeted her, her eyes fell upon Jason, her face indifferent.

"Hey, Andrea," he smiled.

There was no response. She turned away and addressed her parents. "I've got to get some homework done. I'm really behind this week."

"Do you want something to eat first?"

She glanced at Jason again briefly. "No. I'll eat later." She left the room and Jason watched her leave with a sickened heart. The cold shoulder she had turned towards him was all too clear. She blamed him for the abduction. He could hear her slow steps going upstairs.

"Oh, dear," Sharon was saying. "I didn't expect her to act this way."

"That's all right, Sharon," Jason assured. "But I do think at this point I'll hold off on the talk."

"That's probably wise," Alan agreed.

"I had no idea that she was feeling this way towards you," Sharon went on. "It's probably my fault, for the way I acted at first."

"Please," Jason held up his hand. "No more blaming, okay?"

Sharon smiled sadly. "Thank you for being so understanding, Jason."

Jason reached over and squeezed the woman's hand. "You guys have become like my family in just a short amount of time. I know this is the hardest thing you've ever had to deal with. Just know that I'm praying for you."

Chapter Twenty-One

Acquilles Serdan

Alana was pacing the room like a caged animal. Felina had not made an appearance since lunch, and being closed in was driving Alana mad. The anxiety she had been fighting for days threatened to surface, and fear of the unknown had her jumping at every sound.

Why was she here? What did this Marlon want with her? Was Jack Norris coming back for her? She had a prickling assumption that her future could very well be uncertain.

Finally, at four-thirty, Felina returned. She glanced at Alana's plate, looking somewhat appeased to see that Alana had at least munched on the rolls. She looked Alana straight in the eye.

"Marlon will be home soon."

Alana felt her heart drop. What did that mean for her? "What does he want with me?" she whispered.

Felina did not look at her as she answered, but busied herself laying clothes out on the bed. "You will find out soon enough."

"No!" Alana spat. "You cannot expect me to sit here and wait. You have to tell me what's going on!"

If Alana expected Felina to grow angry, she was to be mistaken. The girl turned serious eyes on Alana, her movements growing still. Alana could not help but think that she had never seen eyes so dark. Now they seemed to resemble deep pools of sorrow.

"Senorita," she began, "Senor Ferraro is a very powerful man in these parts. Many people respect him, and it is seldom that he doesn't get what he wants."

"What does that have to do with me?" Alana asked, breathlessly.

Felina took a deep breath. Her expression softened for the first time as she faced Alana squarely. "The important thing, Senorita, is that you cannot fight Senor Marlon. Fighting him only makes him more determined to have his way."

150

Alana swallowed, her mind racing. "What are you getting at?" she whispered.

Coming slowly and softly, Felina's next words sent a chill straight to Alana's terrified heart. "Senor Ferraro has brought you here to be his female companion."

Gasping, Alana took a step backwards. "What? You can't be serious!" Her tone pleaded with Felina to admit that she was lying.

"It is true, Senorita," Felina said.

Her chest heaving, Alana looked about her frantically. "No, please," she breathed, feeling suddenly dizzy. She gripped one of the bed poles. "Oh, God, please!" she begged, closing her eyes.

Felina watched her reaction with veiled eyes. When Alana looked to her once more, Felina said, "I know this must be hard for to take in, but please heed my advice. Senor Ferraro will be much easier on you if you submit to his control. Because, like it or not, you *are* now in his control."

Alana was left alone then, and she fell to the floor in a crumpled heap. Despair welled up in her so that she could not breathe, could not think, could not even pray. All she was aware of was this faceless Marlon Ferraro who had in mind to completely destroy her.

A wildness overtook her then and she jumped to her feet. The terror that Felina's words had stirred moved her to action. She flew about the room, searching for something—anything.

She dug around in the bathroom, upsetting stacks of wash cloths and towels. Finally, in the middle drawer of the dressing table, she found a manicure set. She pulled the fingernail file out slowly.

Not thinking out a rational plan, she knelt before the door and began picking at the lock with the file. After several minutes, she heard the wonderful sound of the lock clicking. Slowly and silently, she turned the knob, barely breathing as she did so.

Still moving with caution, Alana poked her head and was surprised to see that there were no guards in the hall. There were a line of doors on her right, and a corner to her left. With a glance to the left, she began moving down the right. Holding the file tightly in her hand, she paused every few seconds to listen for someone approaching.

Alana hesitated for a moment, thinking that she might be able to get further is she went the shorter distance on the other side. She turned abruptly and ran straight into Vic Dane's broad chest.

Without hesitation, she brought the file up. Vic caught her hand easily.

She used her other hand to swing at his face, but was once again stopped. She growled and fought as he led her back into her room. She pushed against him just as he let go, stumbling as she backed away from him.

"You have to let me go!" she cried.

"I can't do that," Vic said with infuriating calm.

Alana crossed her arms in front of her, looking very vulnerable as she did. "Please, don't do this! I'll do whatever you ask, just please, help me!"

Vic stared at her. "If you try to escape again, I'll have to tie you up."

He wasn't going to help her. Alana covered her face with her hands. "Why are you doing this to me? Why me?"

"Because that's what Marlon wants," Vic answered, his hand on the doorknob. His voice was cool. "Believe me, Miss Crewe. Things will be a lot easier for you if you just resign yourself to your new surroundings."

He left without another word, the sound of the lock filling the room. Alana flung herself at the door, pounding at it with her fists. "Let me go!" she screamed, completely losing her head in the face of his indifference. "Please!"

Vic stood in the hall and listened to the pounding. He waited until he could no longer hear anything and then moved to the den. He settled down in the oversized, leather sofa gracing one wall.

If he had to be completely honest, he'd have to admit to himself that he did not like this. It wasn't that Alana was the first girl that had been held here, far from it. Marlon's lifestyle had brought a variety of young women in and out, but they were usually young Spanish girls "bought" from poor fathers, or American women Marlon lured into his home.

Resting his temple on two fingers, Vic frowned. This girl was different. Only hours before he had carried her through the house. He could still remember the light weight of her frame in his arms.

Leaning forward to rest his elbows on his knees, Vic took a deep breath. If Marlon was anything, he was determined. He had decided, for whatever reason that Vic could not comprehend, that he wanted Alana. He had staged an out-and-out kidnapping to get her. He would not let her resistance sway him. If anything, it would bring about his anger, and then there would be no way for her to fight him.

Thinking of the girl in the bedroom, Vic wondered if Marlon would get more than he bargained for this time.

Alana was lying on her bed as the sun sank into the horizon, the sky filled with a glorious array of color. The beauty was lost on her. She stared sightlessly out the window, feeling hopelessness well up in her like she had never experienced before.

The days of being kept by Vic Dane and his men had never drained her strength like this. This faceless man that Felina had told her about filled her with dread and horror. Why was this happening?

In her weakened and fearful state, she let doubts creep in that she had never given rein to before.

God, why are you allowing this? she whispered inwardly. *I thought You protected Your children. I spent my life telling other people about the way You kept Your hand on my life, never letting me be in a situation that I could not handle. Now, I found myself here, where an evil man is about to strip me of my innocence and purity and maybe my life. I lived an upright life for You, and this is how You treat me? I don't understand!*

The prayer left her exhausted and dejected. In all her life she had never gone through anything like this. How could she ever come out of it? Would God even help her? It seemed like He had completely abandoned her.

Alana knew that she was doing damage to herself, but the dread of the future had caused her to pull within herself. She did not speak, could not pray, tried not to even think. She just sat in a chair by the window and stared.

Already, it had been almost a week since she had seen her family. The plans she had made with her friends had been cruelly torn to shreds. The hard work that she had done in school was going to be lost. The honor that she had kept so diligently was about to be taken from her.

She felt no faith, no strength left in her. Tears streamed down her cheeks at the desolation she felt. She did not want to be this way, but had no idea how to fight it.

Closing her eyes, Alana made herself think of her family. They loved her, she knew they did. They would be praying for her return. She needed to keep her spirits up if she even hoped to see them again.

Her mind moved on to her pastor and his wife, to the precious families of the church, to her Sunday school class. Those sweet girls. She could not let them down.

And what about her friends? Dinah and Curtis had made her feel so warmed by their friendship, as if they loved to have her around. Alana had felt close to the others, as well. Tommy and Belinda. Tim and Rachel. Their baby would be due in just a matter of weeks now.

And Jason.

Alana's eyes came open. There was no way to describe how much Jason meant to her. He had a way of reading her, of making her feel like he understood her. He never ceased to make her feel special and appreciated. His faith and support had always uplifted her, and the gentle way he treated her made her feel like the luckiest girl in the world that she could call Jason Banks a friends.

She felts tears sting her eyes again, remembering the night that she had first encountered Jack Norris. Jason had been there for her, making sure that the man could not hurt her. He had put his arms around her, assuring her that she was safe. She wished more than anything to feel his arms once more, to know that he would protect her. She felt that she could endure anything if he was here with her.

Why could he have not been there the night I was kidnapped? she mourned.

As Alana thought of those she loved, she remembered her grandmother. An ache filled her being at the thought of the frail little lady so full of faith and fire. How would she have coped in this situation?

Alana knew how she would have handled herself. As a missionary, her grandmother experienced many hardships, some as dangerous as the one Alana found herself in now. Through it all, the woman was determined to persevere and see what God wanted her to take from her trials. If she were in this room, she would tell Alana the same thing.

"Don't give up," Alana could almost hear her voice. *"God doesn't put anything on us we can't stand. Just think, the Lord had enough faith in you that you wouldn't crumble in the face of this. Now it's your turn to have faith in him."*

"Yes, Grandma," Alana whispered, moisture clinging to her eyelashes.

The faces of her loved ones lingered in her mind as she stood and watched the sun set. "Father, I'm so sorry that I lost faith in You in these last few hours," she whispered. "I know that You will always be with me, no matter what happens. Please, keep me in this dark time. I don't want to fail You. Help me to be like my grandmother, strong, determined, and full of faith."

She walked over to the table where her untouched dinner was. An almost physical weight slipped off her shoulders and her heart. She began eating, reasoning that if she was going to get out of this place, she would have to keep her strength up.

Not long after, Felina stepped in to look in on Alana. The peaceful eyes and serene face that she encountered was not what she expected at all.

"I just wanted to check on you, Senorita," she explained, her words sounding weak even to her ears.

Alana shook her head. "Please. I'm Alana. You don't have to be so formal."

"All right." Felina nodded. She noticed then that the supper plate had been emptied.

"You speak English beautifully," Alana observed. "How did you learn it?"

"My parents wanted me to know the language," Felina informed, still rather set aback. "My father sent me to a mission where there was an American man teaching English. I was twelve at the time."

"And how old are you now?"

"Twenty."

Alana shook her head in wonder. "You've come a long way in that amount of time."

Felina found herself blushing in humility. "Thank you."

"And thank you," Alana smiled. "I know I haven't been very good to you today and I want to apologize. You're not to blame for what's happened to me these last few days. In fact, you've been nothing but kind to me."

Felina was shaken. She nodded nervously and started to exit the room. She halted abruptly and spoke again, her words sounding forced. "Senor Vic wanted me to tell you that Senor Ferraro has been delayed. He will not arrive until tomorrow afternoon sometime.

There was no denying the hopeful light in Alana's eyes. "Thank you," she said softly.

After fumbling with the key, Felina stood outside the hall, trying to clear her mind.

How could the girl be so calm? What had happened in just the short time since Felina had last seen her? And how could Alana *thank* Felina for what she had done when she was being held hostage in the mansion?

Moving on down her way, Felina frowned, confused. She had no idea what kind of woman Alana Crewe was, but she was like no one Felina had ever met.

If asked about her new mood, Alana would have had trouble explaining it herself. It wasn't that she had accepted or resigned herself to her condition, but she felt that to overcome it, she had to be positive, to keep her faith.

Felina did not seem to know what to do with Alana's new disposition. Alana felt bad that she had been so difficult towards the girl before. As a child of God, she should have been trying to get to know her, to witness to her, show God's love.

Alana somehow had the impression that Felina was rather unhappy with this situation as well. Indeed, the more Alana saw of her, the more she could see that within the depths of Felina's dark eyes were pools of sorrow and pain. The realization made her want to befriend her all the more.

"Lord, here is a girl that obviously needs You in her life," she prayed after Felina had left her. "Please, help me to forget myself and reach out to her. I don't know her story, but You do. Help me to show her that You love her and care for her."

Alana knew that she herself was in more danger than she even realized, but with her rediscovered faith, she found her heart compassionate towards the girl. Maybe by concentrating on someone else, Alana could get through her own troubles with an easier mind.

Sunday, April 14th

Vic had not heard anything from Alana's room since she had somehow managed to get out. From what he heard from Felina, she seemed to be more agreeable. For her sake, Vic hoped so. Marlon would be home early that afternoon.

Knowing that Marlon would not want to keep Alana cooped up in her room, Vic went to find Felina. He told her what he was planning, and then went to Alana's room.

She had just come from the shower when he entered, her hair still hanging damply around her shoulders.

"I was beginning to think something was wrong," he stated.

"Why?" Alana asked, drawing the robe tighter around her. She still could not stop the anxiety she felt around him.

"Things had gotten too quiet," Vic explained. "You haven't tried an escape for almost a whole day."

Alana shrugged. "Does that disappoint you?"

"Not at all. In fact, I wanted to let you know that you're gonna be able to get out of here today."

He could see her face brighten just a trace.

"Really?"

156

He nodded. "Before we go any further, let me tell you now, there are guards on virtually every foot of this place. A place likes this requires extensive security, so there's no way you could get past them."

"What makes you think I would even try?"

Vic slanted her a look. "Why do you even ask?"

Alana crossed her arms, still feeling uncomfortable standing before him in a robe that did not belong to her. "What else would you expect from me? I can't just act like this is no big deal. You've kidnapped me. Someday, you'll be found out."

His dark eyes narrowed, but he found that she returned the stare with wide-eyed directness. He twisted his mouth to the side, finding himself at a loss for words.

Alana looked away finally, wondering where she had found the boldness to say what she did. She would be lucky if she did not get herself hurt with her frankness.

"Felina will come by in a while to give you a tour of the place."

Alana lifted her head in surprise. She had expected him to grow angry and penalize her by keeping her inside.

Vic said nothing else before he left, his face still dark.

Taking a deep breath, Alana felt herself relax. There was something so intense about the man, so dangerous. Yet, at the same time, he seemed so detached, so unmoved, like he was not capable of feeling.

Afraid that someone else would enter, Alana quickly threw some clothes on. She had resigned herself to wearing some of the clothes that she had discovered in the closet. Her own outfit was yet to be brought back from the wash.

She pulled on a loose fitting cream colored blouse. The sleeves nearly covered her hands to the fingertips and hung past her hips, but she did not mind. The more of herself that was hidden, the more protected she felt.

Chapter Twenty-Two

Edwardsville

The Fellowship church was packed to the brim Sunday morning. People Jason had never seen before were filing through the doors, looking for a place to sit. He was glad he had decided to come early.

Sitting beside him, Curtis expressed the same thought. "Boy, if I'd been any later, I'd be standing."

"I guess this whole thing has shaken the town up pretty hard," Jason observed.

Curtis nodded. "Understandable." He was relieved with how normal Jason was acting now. Of course, no one was normal these days anymore, but he had been genuinely concerned for his friend. Jason looked much better today than when he had talked to him Friday night.

The Crewes were in their usual pew, but Alana's spot was noticeably empty. Jason noticed Dinah gazing in that direction with moist eyes.

"You all right?" he asked, leaning over Curtis.

Dinah shrugged. "How can I be all right when my friend is who knows where? But I'll make it."

Jason could see the pain and worry still evident on the faces around him. His heart grew heavy over this burden that the church had unexpectedly been given. As the service went on, he prayed that God would draw near to them and be the strength that each person needed.

Acquiles Serdan

Felina seemed hesitantly pleased to be able to lead Alana about the house. She spent a little time on the floor where Alana stayed, but she did not go through every door. Alana felt as if she had been liberated when they walked down the stairs, but she could see at once that Vic's words were true. There were men everywhere, mostly Spanish but all were rough-looking. They cast curious glances her way. She unconsciously tensed.

"Do not worry, Senorita," Felina assured. "These men are under Marlon's payroll. They will not harm you."

Though Alana smiled and nodded in recognition, she did not feel comforted. In fact, the more she heard Marlon's name, the more she wondered what kind of power he had over his people.

Felina led Alana to a large sitting room. "Normally, servants and hired hands are not to be here, but as I am your guide, I am allowed right now. Have a seat."

Alana perched on an elegant chair with exquisite wood arm rests. "Nice."

"Senor Marlon had that shipped all the way from Spain."

"Seems you know a lot about this place," Alana observed, not looking at Felina.

That girl's movements stilled. "Yes, I've lived here for a while."

"Have you always worked for Marlon?"

Felina did not answer right away. "No. I worked on my father's ranch until I was seventeen."

Alana became conscious then that Felina looked agitated. "Are you okay, Felina?"

"Yes," she nodded. "I'm fine."

Someone stepped to the doorway just then, and Alana felt more than see Felina stiffen. Alana recognized the man as Manley Elam, one of her kidnappers.

Manley glowered at the girls. "What are you doing in here?" he demanded.

"I am sorry, Senor," Felina apologized, standing abruptly. She reached down and grasped Alana's hand. "We will leave."

Felina did not look up as she and Alana filed past the man. Alana reacted to Felina's discomfort with a racing pulse. She glanced back at one point to see Manley still staring at them, his intent expression sending chills down her spine.

"Senorita," Felina spoke as they moved up the stairs again. "What I said about Marlon's men is true for all of them but that one. Manley Elam is a dangerous man. Whatever you do, stay as far from him as you can."

Felina's warning scared Alana. She thought back to the times that Manley had stared at her while traveling in the jeep. His eyes would rake over her as if he was mentally stripping her of her clothes. It made her feel exposed and humiliated. She would take Felina's advice to heart. At all costs, she would avoid Manley Elam.

Alana was to have lunch that day in the dining room. The table alone would have taken up every inch of space in her kitchen. In this room, however, it was dwarfed by a huge china cabinet that stood over eight feet tall and ten feet wide.

Wondering how anyone could feel comfortable in such lavish settings, Alana approached the table, eyeing the empty chairs. Would anyone be joining her? And who?

Felina was busy setting the table. "Just take any seat, Alana," she offered.

"Will you be sitting with me?"

"Well, I normally don't." Felina saw the vulnerability in Alana's face. After a moment's hesitation, she said, "I suppose I can today, though."

Alana smiled in relief. "Thanks."

Upon hearing voices in the dining room, Vic paused before entering. He slowly pushed the door open wide enough to see Felina sitting with Alana, both eating and talking quietly.

Alana looked much more at ease than he had last seen her. He knew that to enter would cause her to immediately close up and be on the defensive.

Vic watched the pair for a moment longer, his brows raising just a pinch when both girls actually smiled at something said. It had been a long time since he had seen a smile grace Felina's face, and he had never seen Alana smile. The sight held his attention for a moment. Then he stepped back and went on down the hall, leaving them alone.

"You did not eat any dinner," Felina caught him a while later.

"I grabbed something from the kitchen," he said.

"Is anything wrong?" she asked. "I know I shouldn't have been in the dining room, but—"

Vic put his hand up "That doesn't bother me, Felina, whatever makes Alana's transition smoother."

Felina nodded.

"She, um, seems to be taking everything better," he observed flatly.

"Yes," Felina agreed, her dark eyes shadowing. "I really don't understand it. There's something about her that's…different."

Vic did not respond, and Felina seemed embarrassed by her remark. She excused herself and left him alone to ponder her words.

He knew what she meant. In the beginning he had had the opportunity to see her resistance to the situation. She had fought him every step of the way, at times growing nearly hysterical in her need to be freed of him. Now, she seemed calm, serene. Though he knew she was still scared, as was obvious from the way she looked at him if he passed her way, she seemed stronger now, more resigned.

No, that wasn't it either. Vic had a feeling that Alana would still try to flee if given the chance. Maybe she was just acting this way to get them off their guard. The moment they turned their backs, she would run.

Vic frowned. Why was he dwelling on this? Alana was not his problem. He only had to make sure that she stayed here and was treated respectfully until Marlon returned. Then Alana Crewe would be Marlon's problem.

Vic was in the den when Marlon's butler announced that Marlon had arrived. Grabbing the tan blazer that was lying nearby, Vic pulled it on over his black woven shirt and went out to meet his employer.

The limousine pulled up near the steps and Marlon Ferraro stepped out, wearing black shades and a blue tailored suit. He tilted his head back and sighed at the sight of his elaborate home. "Home, sweet home," he exulted. He grinned as Vic appeared at the stairs. "Good to see you again, Vic."

Alana had watched the sleek limo pull up in the driveway from her window. The man who had stepped out was tall and dressed finely. She licked dry lips as he disappeared from view. Marlon Ferraro was home.

Vic nodded shortly to Marlon. "How was the trip?"

As the two men moved through the doors of the mansion, Marlon described his business excursion. "Long and tiring, but most satisfying."

They settled down in the den, a maid quickly bringing refreshments. Vic gave the woman a short nod as he took his glass. "I was actually surprised you took off down there."

Taking a deep drink before answering, Marlon crossed his ankle over his knee. "To be frank, I was surprised to get the call."

"So what was it all about?"

"Well," Marlon paused. He loved drawing it out as long as he could, but he had forgotten that such tactics never roused Vic. The man sat, staring at him impassively. Making a face, Marlon went on. "Our clients in Chicago have a big order and they wanted to discuss the particulars."

Vic cocked his head. "I thought Reuban was headed for Chicago. Why didn't they just wait for him?"

"They sent a contact to El Salto with some prototypes of what they want." He stopped and whistled softly. "Let me tell you, Vic. They've got a tall order this time. Ought to bring in a pretty good bundle this time."

Vic did not respond, but he could not help but think that the Ferraros were really not in need of another "good bundle."

"I told them that Reuban would be meeting them shortly, if he hasn't already. I explained that he got held up on some other business." Marlon's mouth twisted into a cocky grin.

Vic snorted.

"So, Vic," Marlon stretched his legs out and smiled. "What's my new girl like?"

Slanting a look at the man before him, Vic pulled out a pack of cigarettes. "Do you really want to know?"

"Why, is she dirt ugly?"

"I wouldn't say that," Vic answered.

Before waiting for any more, Marlon summoned his maid. "Would you do me a favor and bring my new houseguest down?"

"Si, Senor," she answered with a curtsy.

"Now, what was you saying, Vic?" Marlon asked. "Am I going to be satisfied?"

"I think you're going to find her more trouble than she's worth."

Marlon's brows lifted slightly. "Why's that?"

Drawing a deep breath from the cigarette, Vic narrowed his eyes at the floor. "I've lost count of how many times she's tried to make a run for it. I suspect she's going to be next to impossible to conform to your criteria. She's stubborn as an old mule and she'll fight every step."

Resting his elbows on his knees, Marlon looked more intrigued than concerned. "She must have given you a hard time."

Vic shrugged. "I handled her fine, if that's what you're asking. But she's a strange one, very opinionated."

"I hope you know, Vic, that you've unintentionally challenged me," Marlon said with a smile. "I've never met a girl yet that I couldn't win over, in one way or another. But, I won't rush her. She'll have plenty of time to familiarize herself with the place before I expect anything more from her."

Vic couldn't help but feel skeptical.

"Don't look so concerned, Vic," Marlon chuckled. "This isn't the first time, you know."

"True," Vic acknowledged. "But you've never kidnapped a girl from the states. She's going to have investigators searching high and low for her."

"Vic, come on," Marlon drawled. "Don't tell me a mere girl has caused you to lose confidence in me."

The maid stepped in the room just then, alone. She looked worried as she looked at Marlon. "Senor, the Senorita," she spoke haltingly in broken English. "She will not come."

Marlon looked at Vic with raised brows. "Well, it seems you were right about our girl."

"I warned you."

"Well," Marlon slapped his legs as he stood. "There's no time like the present to show her who's in charge."

"What happened to not rushing it?" Vic inquired.

Marlon paused and looked down at the sitting man. "Vic, I'm not going to force her to bed." He gave a wink before leaving.

A frown appeared on Vic's thin lips. He stared at the floor with unseeing eyes, unable to shake the unsettled feeling in his stomach.

Alana moved quietly about in her room. She was dressed in her own clothes again, drawing a little comfort from that much familiarity.

Her nerves were drawn so tight she felt ready to snap. Marlon's maid had attempted to take her downstairs to meet him, but she had adamantly refused. The maid had gone so far as to take Alana's arm and force her out the door, but Alana, being younger and stronger, was able to wrench herself free. Frustrated, the maid had left, muttering Spanish words under her breath.

The doorknob turned again and Alana expected to see the maid return. She gasped when the tall man she had seen out the window graced the doorway instead. He leaned against the doorjamb and regarded her with clear, blue eyes. His good looks did nothing for Alana.

"I have been told about your attractiveness," he said, his voice rich and smooth. "But I can see now that they were grossly unstated. You are a sight for sore eyes."

Alana did not answer. Her breath came in short gasps in her apprehension and her eyes never left the man.

"I was disappointed that you refused to join me." Marlon Ferraro moved into the room and she automatically backed up. "Oh, Miss Crewe," he spoke softly. "I don't know what anyone has told you, but get rid of everything that you're thinking. I don't mean you any harm." He walked towards her until she had backed up against the wall. He stopped just a few feet from her.

"I apologize for the crude way I was forced to use to bring you here, but I hope you will let me make it up to you." He waved a hand. "As you can see, I lack for nothing. You will have everything your heart desires while here, and you will be treated as a queen." His eyes looked her up and down. "It's been a long time since I've had a lady grace my place. I look forward to getting to know you."

Alana cast her eyes around the room, hoping for a way to escape the man's presence. The way his eyes raked over her sent chills up her spine. Under his smile was a cruel, calculating soul who was used to getting what he wanted. And right now, for whatever reason, he wanted her.

"There's no need to panic," he went on soothingly. "I won't rush you. I know these things take time. I am a patient man. Over the next few days and weeks, we will be spending a lot of time together, but I won't force you to do anything that you're uncomfortable with." His eyes suddenly narrowed. "So long as you're cooperative."

His mouth turned up once again, and in a smile meant to be comforting and appealing, he managed to terrify the girl before him. He stepped backwards and deposited a package on the bed. "I tell you what; you can stay in here, if you wish, until dinner. Then I'd like you to join me in the dining room." He motioned towards the box. "Inside there is a dress I bought just for the lady of the house." His eyes glittered. "I'd really like to see you in it." Then he was gone.

Alana released the pent up breath she had been holding, even as tears came to her eyes. She had never experienced such trepidation. A longing for home rose in her, sweeping over her like a tidal wave. Marlon's taunting face crowded her mind again, and she could not stop the shaking that overcame her body.

Marlon found Felina standing in the hall outside Alana's room. "Miss Felina," he greeted. "You're looking as lovely as ever."

Felina gave a small nod in acknowledgement, her eyes dropping to the floor.

He approached her slowly. "I'm sure you're glad to have another girl in the place," he said, resting his hand on her waist. "I encourage you to befriend her. She'll need you to help her feel more at ease. Besides, it will do my heart wonders to see my two girls becoming friends.

"Now," his tone grew brisk and businesslike. "I've given Alana a little gift that I would like to see at dinner. Please assist her in any way you can. I'm sure you'll know how to handle it."

He smiled down at her and chucked her chin before moving on down the hall.

Felina's eyes darkened as the man disappeared around the corner. She glanced at the door leading to Alana's room. A soft sigh escaped her lips, even as desolation and guilt plagued her soul.

There was no stopping Marlon Ferraro when his mind was made up. She knew that as well as anyone.

Chapter Twenty-Three

"I will *not* put this on," Alana ground out, standing at the foot of the bed with her arms stiffly at her side.

Felina answered from behind her, her voice tired. "You must, Alana. It is the dress that Senor Marlon chose for this occasion."

Alana spun around. "This thing is indecent!" she snapped. "I have never in my entire life put on anything like this, and I don't intend to start now, no matter whose house I'm in!"

Felina only stared at her, her eyes dark orbs of misery. "You must. If you don't, the consequences will be terrible."

Alana stilled her movements, taking in Felina's pained expression. The realization that suddenly swept over her left her weak and heartbroken as she stared at the girl who had become her only friend in this place.

"Marlon has done this to you, hasn't he?" Alana whispered, wondering how she could have been so blind. "That's why you know so much about him."

Felina dropped her head.

"Oh, Felina," Alana sighed, tears dimming her eyes. "I'm so sorry. I never even thought. Were you kidnapped, too?"

"No," Felina shook her head, glancing toward the door. "My father owed him a debt. Senor Marlon offered to drop the debt in exchange for me."

"Your father sold you to Marlon?"

"He had no choice, Alana," Felina insisted. "Please, do not put blame on my father. He had a wife and five more children at home. They could not survive without him. I understood that."

Alana wanted to weep. She stood and paced agitatedly, her heart sending fragments of prayers heavenward.

"I am truly sorry, Alana. I wish I could shield you from what is to come, but there is no fighting it. Marlon will win. You must put the dress on."

Alana shook her head. "No, I won't."

With a small sigh, Felina said, "If you don't, he will put it on you."

166

Alana gasped, her hand going to her throat. "You're not serious!"

"I'm afraid so, Alana."

She stared wildly at the dress lying on her bed. She would rather die than wear it, but to have this man physically force it on her? That would be unbearable.

Feeling her resolve crumbling, Alana's lips quivered as she gathered the bundle of red and white silk and carried it to the bathroom. She slipped it on, feeling practically naked even with it on.

The dress settled snugly, very snugly, over her waist and hips and ended just above the floor. A slit opened up in the side, going all the way to the top of her thigh. It was sleeveless, with thin straps tying over her shoulders. The back dropped low down her back. She was grateful for the length of her hair.

But there was absolutely nothing Alana could do about the front. She twisted and turned, but no matter how it lay, the bodice dipped way down, revealing far much more than she was comfortable with.

"I can't do this, Felina!" she called through the bathroom door.

"I have something that might help," Felina answered.

Alana peeked around the door, not willing to be seen by even Felina.

That girl held out thin, colorful scarf. "Maybe he will not notice if you wear this with it. It matches the dress very well."

"Thank you, Felina!" Alana whispered, in near tears as she wrapped it around her.

The energy that Marlon was feeling fairly radiated. He paced the dining room restlessly, pausing at times to check the door where Alana was to make her appearance. That he was enjoying having another female guest was obvious.

Already seated, Vic watched his boss with veiled eyes. Marlon was in fine form tonight. Dressed in a black blazer over a red shirt, his silver-tipped hair was perfectly in place, and his clear eyes twinkled in good humor.

Taking a deep breath, Vic turned his attention back to the table. Knowing what kind of man Marlon was, he could not help but wonder how long the stubborn girl upstairs could uphold beneath his determination.

Alana stared at herself in the mirror as Felina prepared her hair. Even with the scarf she felt as if she was doing something wrong. But, what was a girl to do when in circumstances like these? Alana had no choice. It was to get dressed, or be dressed. Resign herself to the situation, or be completely broken down and destroyed.

Alana closed her eyes, feeling her body begin to tremble. *Oh, dear Lord!* she cried. *I need You like I've never needed you before. Please, let me feel that You're with me. I need Your comfort. Be my pillar of support. I have nothing else on which to lean.*

Felina finished pining Alana's curled hair up and stepped back. Though she obviously felt no joy in saying so, she complimented Alana.

"You really do look lovely with your hair like that, Alana."

Hating the way her back was exposed now, Alana could not bring herself to thank her, but Felina did not seem to mind.

"Let's go. Marlon is waiting in the sitting room."

With wooden feet, Alana followed Felina. At the doorway, she stopped abruptly. With almost tingling clarity, she felt a rush of love wash over her so that she gasped.

"Are you all right, Alana?" Felina asked, taking Alana's arm.

Alana could not speak, so overjoyed was she to know that her desperate prayer had been heard. Tears stung her eyes as the moment passed. *Thank You, Lord! Oh, thank You!*

"Alana?"

Finally looking at Felina, Alana realized how she must have looked. Felina was staring at her with acute concern. "Don't worry, Felina," she assured. "I'm fine. I'll be all right."

"Ah," Marlon smiled when Alana, with Felina beside her, stepped into the dining room. "Here's the guest of honor. Don't you look lovely? I'm glad to see the dress I chose fit you so well."

Alana stood still as Marlon advanced. He gently took her arm. "Come. Join us for a celebration feast. I told Cook to prepare something special."

Moving awkwardly to her seat, Alana's eyes fell on Vic. He returned the look briefly before reaching for his glass.

Studying the table before her, Alana almost did not notice the pressure of Marlon's hand as he pulled a chair out for her.

"Here," he offered. "Sit by me. We can talk."

If you think I'm going to talk to the likes of you, you're crazy! Alana thought, feeling anger bubbling inside her. How arrogant this man must be! To kidnap her from her home, hold her captive for his own pleasures, and to expect her to appreciate his hospitality was unimaginable!

Sitting down in the cushioned chair, Alana felt Marlon's hand rest lightly on her shoulder. Her spine was so rigid her back hurt. Marlon moved on to his chair at the head of the table. Vic was sitting across from her, at Marlon's left.

The table was already loaded with food and drink. Fancy dishes of tortillas and enchiladas were spread out before her, and a bowl of soup was sitting at her plate. A tall goblet of a sparkling liquid was set in front of her by the maid.

Alana's lips went dry at the sight of the drink. The fluid bubbled slightly and was foamy at the top. *I can't drink this,* she thought, worried.

Vic was watching her as she studied the glass. "Anything wrong" he asked lightly, suspecting her problem. He watched her take a deep breath as her chin went up.

"I can't drink this," she said, her voice soft but firm.

"Why not?" Marlon asked.

"I do not drink alcoholic beverages," she answered, staring him straight in the eye.

His brows rose. "Is that so? Not even for a celebration dinner?"

"No," Alana replied quickly.

"Well, I don't think that's a problem. Maria." He called the maid. "Bring my guest a sparkling water." He looked at Alana. "Will that be okay?"

Alana nodded slightly. The goblet was taken from her sight, replaced shortly by a glass of sparkling water. She felt a small measure of comfort that she had been able to take control of that situation at least.

Vic was impressed with how calm she had stayed, while determined to have her way.

The meal went on with no more dilemmas. Fortunately, Marlon did not expect Alana to talk much, which was good, because she stayed silent through the entire meal. Her stomach was so tight that she had difficulty eating, but she forced the food down her throat, knowing she would need the sustenance in the days to come.

Marlon talked business with Vic throughout the meal, in words that Alana could not understand. They spoke of places and names that were foreign to her, and she didn't care to try to decipher them. All she wanted was to escape and go back to her own room.

No, that wasn't she wanted. What she really wanted was to go home, to Edwardsville. She wanted her family and friends to surround her with their loving arms. She wanted to hear Jason tell her that everything was going to be all right.

Alana reached for her glass, hoping the water would appease the lump that had suddenly appeared in her throat.

Monday, April 15th
Edwardsville

Jason walked through the halls of the police station early in the morning, feeling as if he was finally ready to work without falling apart. He returned several greetings from fellow cops, including his partner Rob Phipps.

"How you doing, man?" he asked.

"A lot better, thanks for asking."

Rob shook his head. "You had me worried there for a while. I would have hated to see you lose your mind over this."

"Well," Jason began, "I still intend to do everything I can to bring her home. Not knowing where Alana is just about kills me. But I've realized that I've got to let God be God in this. I can't do His job."

Rob looked a little puzzled, but he slapped Jason's back. "Glad to have you back."

Jason found his captain next, who studied him critically.

"I see you're looking much better," he observed.

Jason nodded. "I got rid of some heavy baggage."

"Whatever it takes."

Taking a seat, Jason asked, "Any new developments?"

Wade scratched his head. "I know you're going to hate to hear this, but no one has come any closer to finding where she might be. It's like that girl and her abductors just disappeared off the face of the earth."

Licking his lips, Jason said, "You're right, I don't want to hear that. But, I really do think that we're wasting our time looking for her in this country."

"We've already gone over that," Wade said with a warning look. "We did find out that Norris may have been the one behind a robbery in Des Moines, Iowa after he disappeared from Nebraska. A small jewelry store owner lost a bunch of money and got a whack on the head."

"Seems Norris has been keeping himself busy these days," Jason muttered.

"Yeah. And we've got to figure out where he's at now."

Jason opened his mouth and closed it. He slid to the edge of his seat and asked, "Captain, is there no way we can go across the border to do some investigating? I mean—"

"Banks," Wade interrupted. "As much as I'd like to check that out, the fact is if she's in Mexico, chances are slim we'll ever find her. That's a big, unfamiliar country down there. Not to mention, our people could get themselves in trouble if they're caught investigating in a country where we have no control."

"I know," Jason sighed, "but I can't shake this feeling."

"I'm sorry, but the best shot we have at this point is to find Jack Norris. All evidence points out that he may still be in the States. His story is spreading throughout the country, as is Alana's. Maybe someone will know something."

Jason was glad to hear that the escape/abduction was gaining more media attention. The more Alana's picture was out there, the more chance of someone seeing her and recognizing her. At this point, that was all he could hope for.

After the young officer had left, Wade sat for a long time at his desk, his face contemplative. His gaze fell on the papers before him—Alana's file. He sat back in his chair, deep in thought.

"So, what have you come to tell me, Jason?" Alan asked later that evening.

"Huh?"

Alan smiled. Sharon was in their room taking a much needed nap. Jason was glad to have found him alone. "When you came in, I knew something was on your mind. Can you share it?"

He was not sure how to start it. "There's no way to prove this, so I don't want you to overreact."

"Son," Alan said tiredly, "I've had a daughter kidnapped. There's nothing you can say that can be worse than that."

"I can't give you all the details," Jason said. "But, I've discovered some facts that point out that Alana's abduction may be more than just that."

"What do you mean?"

"Norris apparently has some friends that are involved with this," Jason informed. "Although we can't know for sure, I believe that they've...taken Alana south of the border."

"You mean to Mexico?"

Jason nodded.

The older man took a deep breath. "That's rather troubling. How are we going to find her if that's true?"

"Don't worry," Jason assured. "I don't care if I have to go to Mexico myself. I won't stop looking for her."

Alan studied him for a moment with discerning eyes. "Somehow that doesn't surprise me."

Jason found himself wanting to squirm under Alan's gaze. He glanced away.

"Do you believe she's in danger?"

The question stilled him.

"I want to know the truth, Jason."

Jason forced himself to look Alana's father in the eye. "She's in the company of some dangerous men, but that doesn't necessarily mean they'll harm her."

Alan rubbed his jaw. "Then why do they still have her?"

"I wish I could answer that."

Fiddling with the place mat before him, Alan began talking. "I love all my children the same," he said, almost melancholy. "But each of them has something special about them. Alana always had a heart full of love. Sharon used to talk about her sensitive heart, worrying that she would get hurt by this harsh life."

Jason was staring at the floor, his elbows on his knees. As Alan talked, he could see Alana in his mind's eye, her smile sincere and her manner gentle. The times he shared with her came to him—times that had been full of joy and friendship, but now were only painful memories. He felt his heart being crushed little by little as Alan continued.

"I was always protective of Alana," Alan was saying. "Andrea always seemed confident, like she could take the world by the tail. Alana was more fragile. She was afraid to push, afraid to assume too much. It never mattered how much I told her she was special and beautiful, I don't think she ever believed me. Why she couldn't see that for herself, I'll never know."

There were tears in Jason's eyes now, and he looked up at the ceiling, blinking furiously to clear his vision.

"Fathers are always supposed to protect their daughters," Alan mulled. "I've tried so hard to be strong for my family, but the truth is I feel like I'm dying inside." His voice shook. "My little girl is somewhere, scared, alone, and maybe hurt and I can't do anything for her."

He broke down then, dropping his face on his arms. Jason immediately moved next to him, putting his arms around the weeping man. He did not say anything, but just let Alan cry, wiping his own tears. He prayed silently the entire time.

Finally, Alan raised his head, rubbing his hands over the face. He took a deep breath. "Thank you, Jason," he said.

"I didn't do anything, Alan," Jason said.

"You let me talk and cry," Alan explained. "And you listened. That means more than I can ever say. I feel ready to be the strength of my family again."

"I glad I could help," Jason told him sincerely.

Chapter Twenty-Four

"We just got some more news," Wade told Jason the next day.

Jason looked up, his heart beating. "What is it?"

"Norris's parole officer was found dead this morning in Nebraska."

With a deep breath, Jason shook his head. "This is just getting stranger and stranger."

"It is," Wade agreed, staring intently at the cop. "The only thing they know is that someone broke into his house, strangled him, and then stole his car. Someone spotted the car shortly after, leaving the state. It was heading south, but that could be any state south of Nebraska."

Jason ran his hands through his hair. "Captain, I know you're getting tired of hearing this, but—"

"I have a feeling I know what you're about to say," Wade said.

"Well, you're probably right," Jason admitted. "We have to do something to find Alana. I can't sit around here, wondering where she's at."

Wade began moving papers around on his desk, his movements agitated. "I'm not going over this again."

"Captain, let me go down," Jason requested. "I won't go investigating. I just want to find Alana."

"Jason! That's enough!" Wade barked.

Jason had not expected Wade to get so angry. "Captain, listen to me!"

"We are not going down there to find Marlon! If he's there, he's out of our hands, you understand?"

"I'm not interested in finding Marlon!" Jason exclaimed. "I am interested in getting her out of there, if she's down there."

"Well, I am not going to tell you to go down there," Wade insisted. "End of story."

Jason was frustrated now. The captain was not even trying to listen to him. "Captain."

"That's it!" Wade shouted, standing to his feet. Jason was set aback at his reaction. "I'm sick and tired of hearing about Mexico! I thought when you came back that you'd be ready to work, but I can see you're not."

"But—"

"I'm not done!" Wade reached for the phone. "I'm pulling you off the case."

"No!" Jason shook his head. "I don't want—"

"I don't care what you want!" Wade snarled.

Jason could not believe Wade was acting like this, completely unreasonable and irrational. "All right," he conceded, "I won't bring this up again."

"That's right," Wade nodded and took his seat again, punching some numbers on his phone. "Because you won't be working for the next month. I'm ordering you a leave of absence."

"What!"

"And that's final!" Wade shouted. "You're out of here for thirty days! And if I see your face before then, I'll suspend you. Now, I want you out of here today! I've had it with you. You've got a month off to get your head on straight. What you do with that time is for you to decide. I don't want to hear about it."

Wade completely ignored Jason's argument, turning his attention completely to the phone. Jason stared at the top of his head for a moment, shaking his head in angry bewilderment. What was the man's problem? How could he pull Jason off the case? Alana needed him!

Seeing that Wade was not going to talk any more to him, Jason left the room. He did not speak to anyone as he walked out of the station, got in his car, and drove home, barely holding his anger in check.

That night, Jason was still confused over Wade's sudden anger. He prayed about it, thinking that maybe he still had some surrendering to do.

"I thought I had given everything to You, Lord," he prayed. "But, maybe I'm still fighting the need to find her myself. Why couldn't I just have let it go? Now I've let Alana down. How can I do anything for her if I can't even work on her case?"

More frustrated now than ever, he picked up the phone and dialed Curtis's number.

"Hey, buddy," Curtis greeted. "How are you doing?"

"Well, I could be better, to be honest," Jason replied.

"Any news on Alana?"

"No. But I've been pulled off the case."

"What?" Curtis exclaimed. "Why?"

Jason shook his head, still wondering. "To be honest, I really don't know."

"What happened exactly?"

"Well," Jason began. "I have a strong hunch that Alana's kidnappers may have fled to Mexico with her."

"Oh, man, that can't be good," Curtis murmured.

"No, it's not." Jason paused to take a deep breath. The anxiety he had been fighting was threatening him again. "That's why I've been pushing Wade to send someone to look for her, but he refused, because of the law."

"That's tough," Curtis admitted.

"I know, but all I want to do is find Alana. When I suggested that, he blew up."

Curtis sounded as confused as Jason felt. "Well, what did he say exactly?"

Jason spoke almost absently now, concentrating on everything that was said. "If he sees my face in the next thirty days, he'll suspend me. Said I've got a month off to decide what I want to do with my time, and he doesn't want to hear it."

"Why would he say something like that?"

Jason suddenly stopped in his tracks. "No way," he murmured.

"What?" Curtis demanded.

"Um, nothing. Hey, I just thought of something I need to do. Can I call you back?"

Curtis agreed. "Sure. Is everything okay?"

"Yeah. Talk to you later."

Jason hung up and stood in the living room, replaying the scene in his mind. He could see Wade staring at him with thoughtful eyes. He could still hear Wade's words echoing in his ear, especially his last ones.

"You've got a month off...What you do with that time is for you to decide...I don't want to hear about it."

Jason closed his eyes. "God, if I'm overreacting, please stop me right now. I don't want to try to take control of the situation again. I already know that I can't help Alana without You. But, I'm willing to do anything to bring her home where she belongs. If Wade was sending me a message, please let me get it right."

"What you do with that time is for you to decide."

If Jason expected to feel doubt about his sudden assumption, he was wrong. He suddenly felt sure in his spirit that he was on the right track. He licked his lips, very aware that his next step would be the biggest he had ever taken. He had no idea what the future held, but he did know this. He was going to Mexico to find Alana.

176

"I know it sounds hard to believe, but I think my captain was sending me a hidden message."

"What kind of message?" Kenneth asked him.

Jason had headed straight to the pastor's house after his discovery. He wanted the older man's insight and prayers.

"Wade can not legally allow me to cross the border on an investigation. We have no jurisdiction down there. However, he cannot stop me from going in my own time. He gave me a month off, on the spot. He covered it up with this pretend argument, so as not to raise suspicion. I think he was telling me to go."

Kenneth shook his head in uncertainty. "I don't know your captain, so it's hard for me to make any kind of judgment."

Jason was sitting with him in the living room. Maggie was seated next to her husband.

"Are you really sure that's what he's saying?" Maggie asked. "Maybe you should take this slow."

"I don't have time to take things slow," Jason said. "And I've never been surer of anything."

"What do you plan to do?" Kenneth questioned. "Mexico is a big country."

"I know," Jason acknowledged. "To tell the truth, I have no idea what I'm supposed to do exactly. But, I can't sit here idly waiting for someone else to do something. Alana has to be found before something happens."

Kenneth leaned forward, fixing his wise eyes on Jason. "I want to ask you an important question, Jason, and I hope you don't take this the wrong way."

Jason nodded.

"You're not making this decision based on your feelings, are you? Is this your way of making up for the mistake you think you made? Are you trying to rid yourself of guilt you might still be feeling? Because if you're going for that reason only, you won't be able to think clearly, and you may wind up making the situation for Alana even worse."

Jason sat back in his seat, seriously considering the question. He let himself search his heart. Was he doing this for the right reason?

"I know this seems sudden," he began, "but I really have a peace about this. I don't know what the future holds, but I believe that God is allowing me to be used to somehow help Alana."

Sitting back in his chair, Kenneth took a deep breath and studied him.

"Well," he finally spoke. "In that case, I know someone who might be able to help you."

"Who's that?"

"A friend of mine is a missionary down there. He's located somewhere around Chihuahua. Now, chances are slim that he would happen to be in the same place as Alana, but I know he'll be willing to do what he can."

"I'd appreciate any help I can get," Jason told him. "I know once I leave the states I won't be able to count on much."

"You'll be alone," Maggie stated the obvious. Her weathered face was lined with worry. "Seems an awful lot to take on by yourself."

"I won't be alone," Jason reminded her with a small smile.

"Jason," Kenneth got his attention. "I know that you're going to have to be very, very careful, but if you ever need to get a hold of someone up here, feel free to call us. You can let us know how things are progressing, so we can know how to pray. We'll keep your information private, except what you tell us to pass on."

"Actually, that would ease my mind a lot," Jason said. "I want Alana's family to know what's going on, but I think that would come a lot easier from you, than by my phone call. Wade's already told me I'm not to contact him. That way if I'm caught, his hands are clean."

"Oh, it sounds so dangerous," Maggie breathed. She pointed a finger at him. "You better be careful, young man!"

Jason held his hands up in surrender. "Yes, ma'am!" he chuckled, feeling lighter than he had in days.

She eyed him shrewdly. "It seems like you're taking a pretty dramatic measure just for a friend."

Jason found her gaze a bit disconcerting. "Alana's a special person. She belongs home. As a friend, I just want to do what I can to ensure that she gets back here." He shrugged awkwardly.

"Well," Maggie nodded, her face still reflective, "if everyone had friends like you, this world would be in much better shape."

Maggie's words stuck with Jason for the rest of the night. He did not consider himself any more a special friend than anyone. He just happened to be in the position to help her. He was only doing this to get her back to her family, friends, and church. He would do the same for Curtis.

Acquiles Serdan

Tuesday night, Alana lay in bed, sleep far from her. The last two days had been torture, though she had to admit that Marlon had not done anything to her other than to expect her to join him for meals. After what Felina had told her, she was still afraid to say no.

Alana knew that at this point, Marlon was busy with whatever kind of business he was in. He was on the phone a lot, and often shut himself and some of his men up in his office for hours at a time. Alana had also overheard that his brother, Reuban, was soon to be home. The fact did not please Alana at all. In fact, just the thought of the man with the cold, blue eyes arriving made it difficult for her to breathe.

Being surrounded by so many men, all criminals, made Alana feel very small. She had to fight hopelessness that she would ever get out of this place.

Life in Edwardsville had been so good, so simple. Spending Friday nights around the dinner table with her family seemed like a thing of the past now. Sunday morning services were just a memory. She would give anything to be able sit in her pew, listen to Pastor Kenneth preach a godly message from the word. Why, she would even relish the chance to experience nerves at the thought of singing before the congregation!

Had it only been little more than a week since she had been home? Was it only a few days ago that she had arrived at this mansion? It seemed that she had lived a lifetime since she had first laid eyes on Jack Norris, Vic Dane, and Marlon Ferraro. Yet, she had only been in their captivity for a mere eight days.

Staring at the moon from her bed, Alana sighed deeply. She was in Mexico; her family and friends far away in Edwardsville, Kansas. There was next to no chance that anyone could find her way down here. How would she ever get home?

Edwardsville

Wade Harmon walked into his house and tiredly pulled his blazer off. He settled down heavily in a chair, worn out from the long night he had worked. It wasn't until the early morning hours that he had been able to get away.

Pulling Jason off his assignment had caused a barrage of extra work. He had had to face an onslaught of questions from Jason's fellow workers, and the officer now in charge was not as competent. If all worked out as Wade hoped, however, it would not be long before he could put a close on the case.

Wade started when the phone rang at his elbow. "Who in the world?" he muttered.

"Captain, it's me."

Wade could not stop the smile that spread out on his lips. "I thought I told you I didn't want to hear from you."

Jason cleared his throat. "I was assuming you meant at the station."

"Very perceptive," Wade granted. "I was hoping you'd be sharp enough to catch the hint."

"A very subtle hint," Jason said. "I just called to let you know that I'm taking your advice."

"Hmm, somehow that doesn't surprise me."

"I know that we won't be able to talk after this," Jason said, "for obvious reasons. But, just in case you're interested, Kenneth Nelson's phone number is in the book."

"Who in the world is he?" Wade asked with a frown.

"My pastor," Jason answered. "We'll be keeping in touch. If you ever have something you want to pass along…"

"I got the message," Wade nodded.

"Okay, good."

There was a brief silence. "I better go," Jason said. "Thanks for the time off, Captain."

"I hope everything works out," Wade said sincerely. "I'll keep up with things on this side."

Chapter Twenty-Five

After getting off the phone with Wade, Jason spent the rest of the night in prayer. Early Wednesday morning, he went to see Alan and Sharon. They were shocked to hear his announcement.

"You're just taking off for Mexico?" Sharon exclaimed.

"Yes, I am," Jason answered calmly. "I've already got the traveling details worked out. I already have a passport, and a plane ticket for a nonstop flight to Mexico."

"That's crazy!" Alan blurted.

"I know," Jason admitted, "but I feel like that's what I should do. The sooner I go, the sooner I can try to find her. Wasting time here is not going to do her any good. I'm leaving early tomorrow."

Anthony was present as well, and he stared at Jason in shock. "I can't believe you'd do that."

Jason reached over and softly slapped the boy's leg. "You guys have become like my family. It tears me up that Alana is not here. I would do anything for her. For you."

Sharon was in tears. "This was too much to hope for," she murmured. "I know the authorities are doing everything they can, but I would feel so better just knowing that someone, especially you, was actually out looking for her. This means so much."

Alan was overcome as well, so much so that he could not speak.

The emotion in the room moved Jason. He felt a painful stirring in his heart, missing Alana so much it hurt.

Audrey entered the room, breaking the spell. She had a book under her arm. She gave Jason a sober look.

"Did you know my sister's lost?" she asked.

Jason swallowed and held his arms out. She willingly went to them and he settled her on his lap. "Yes, I did know that," he told her. "It hurts, doesn't it?"

Audrey nodded. "She was supposed to read this book to me when she got home."

"Well, I'm sure she will as soon as she gets home."

Staring up at him, Audrey asked, "Do you think she'll find her way back?"

Jason had never had such a conversation with a child, and he had to speak carefully. "We have to pray and believe she will, Audrey."

"Can you go find her?"

Closing his eyes, Jason drew her in a tight hug, kissing the top of her head. He could see Alan putting his arm around his wife.

"I'm doing all I can to find her, Audrey," Jason answered.

She seemed comforted with that. She settled back against his chest and opened the book, slowly going over the pages.

The goodbyes Jason gave before leaving the Crewes had brought about an emotional encounter between him and Andrea. She had caught him at his truck just before he drove off. He rolled the window down and watched her approach, noting her red rimmed eyes.

"Hey, Andie."

She stood uneasily, her hands moving self-consciously. "I heard everything," she finally stated.

Jason nodded. "Did you?"

"I never expected you to…" She closed her trembling lips. "I've been awful to you."

"We've all been under a lot of pressure, Andrea," he said softly. "It brought out characteristics in me I know were not good."

"I know, but—I blamed you for Alana being kidnapped."

"I know you did."

Andrea's face clouded up. "I couldn't help myself. All I could think about was my sister being hurt, and I've convinced myself that I'll never see her alive again. I don't know what I'd do if—"

She could not finish her sentence, due to the sobs overcoming her. Jason quickly stepped out of the truck and pulled her to him, letting her cry against him.

"Shhh," he soothed. "It's all right, Andie, to let yourself feel everything you've been feeling. I've been having my battles as well. We're human. But, we've got to let God take care of us and Alana. He's the only one who really can."

Andrea nodded as she stood back. She looked up at him. "Thank you, Jason, and I really am sorry for the way I've been treating you."

He squeezed her shoulder. "Don't worry about it."

She tried to smile through her tears, but it ended up wobbly and crooked. "Alana really is fortunate to a have a friend like you to care so much about her."

"Alana has a lot of friends that care for her," Jason said. He gave the teen another hug before climbing back in his truck. She stood and watched him leave, giving him a last wave before he disappeared around a curve.

Acquiles Serdan

"I'm going into town to meet my brother," Marlon told Vic during lunch. It was just the two of them at the dining room table. Knowing he had business to discuss, he had allowed Alana to have her meal in her room. In the days to come she would not be doing that as much, so he did not mind her doing so now.

"Are you?" Vic asked, spooning some chili into his mouth.

"Yeah, it's been months since I've seen him," Marlon went on. "I miss him. We'll probably eat dinner out."

Vic did not respond to this.

"So, if you don't mind, you'll have to keep an eye on my princess for a few hours."

Eyeing his employer, Vic reached for his glass. "I should ask for a raise," he muttered.

Marlon chuckled. "If this order from Chicago turns out well, you just might get one."

A few hours later, Marlon was true to his word. He left in the long limo to meet his brother. Vic could see the anticipation on his face at seeing Reuban again. Vic, however, was not so excited. Reuban never hid the fact that he resented Vic's place in Marlon's life. Vic could not help but dread what the next few days would bring.

One good thing had come out of the past two days. Alana felt that she was gradually drawing Felina out. Beneath her trained demeanor, Alana suspected there was a shy, insecure girl and was determined to offer her friendship, even in these unusual circumstances.

Felina seemed to be drawn to Alana, which made it easier. Maybe it was the shared situation that the two girls were in that created the strange bond. Indeed, the Mexican girl, while trying to keep a professional front, seemed to be starved for female companionship. Alana had caught glimpses of other women working in the mansion, but they seemed to be much older than Felina. She often sought Alana out, though she tried to act as if she had found her on accident.

Alana had been pleasantly surprised to learn that Felina had wanted to be a teacher, just like she did.

"That's great," Alana exulted. "I've always wanted to teach first grade."

"What age is that?" Felina questioned. She was taking a break from her work and the two young women were enjoying each other's company for a while.

"It's the grade that six and seven year olds are in."

Felina smiled. "Such a sweet age."

"Yes. I have a sister that just turned seven." Alana's face grew pensive. "She has always been very inquisitive. She probably drives her teachers crazy."

"I have a brother that is five now," Felina said.

They were walking through the halls of the manor. By now, Alana knew the layout of the first floor, and most of the second. She continued to memorize everything she saw; she wanted to know every exit, every possible way out. Sometime soon, she planned to escape this place.

Vic took his outer shirt off and un-tucked the sleeveless one he was wearing. He had told Felina earlier that he would be in the gym for a while. Though Alana had not caused any trouble for some time, he still felt leery about leaving them on their own for too long.

This was the one place he felt he could release any pent up tension or stress. Lifting weights or sparring with the muscle bag always helped him to clear his mind and put things back in the proper perspective. There were times he could spend over three hours in this room, which very well explained his bulging biceps and rock hard abdomen. Indeed, his solid physique kept him from being challenged much at all.

"You ever find it interesting that our names are so similar?" Alana asked abruptly.

Felina laughed, a merry sound when it occurred. "Come to think of it, that is strange."

"Alana and Felina," Alana mused. "Like we were meant to be friends."

With a somber smile, Felina said, "For which I am grateful. I know that you have a very good reason to hate me for what's happened to you. The fact that you've shown such grace is beyond me."

184

"I never have a good reason to hate anyone," Alana stated. "Besides, you have nothing to do with my kidnapping. That fault lies exclusively with the men who were involved."

Felina did not respond.

They entered the large library. Alana, in other conditions, would have been thrilled to visit this place. Wall to wall shelves lined the room and several sitting chairs were nestled around the massive fireplace.

"You know, you're free to read any book that you would like," Felina told her.

Alana smiled, but shook her head. They moved on to the drawing room. It was twice as big as the library and had a lot of floor space.

Alana's eyes lit on the several fencing sets that were hanging up on the walls. "Impressive swords."

"Senor Marlon takes great pride in his ability to fence. I am sure you will witness this during your stay. He loves to show off, and his duels can become pretty intense."

"I always liked swords," Alana said. "In the old books and movies it was always so romantic to see a knight rescue a princess with his sword." She sighed dramatically. "It was enough to sweep me off my feet."

"Well, you're in the right place to be swept off your feet, my dear."

Both girls spun around, startled. Alana gasped at the sight of Manley Elam standing in the doorway, leering hungrily at her.

Alana instinctively took a step backwards, glancing about the room. Manley was blocking the only exit.

"Senor Elam, we were just leaving," Felina said abruptly.

"Not yet," Manley shook his head, his eyes still full of Alana. "I have something I want first."

Alana felt her heart jump to her throat. As chance would have it, she was trapped by a wall on one side and a display of trophies on the other. Manley was slowly but surely approaching.

"Senor, please," Felina beseeched. "You know that Marlon would not be pleased!"

It did not stop Manley's advancement. "He'll never know," he growled.

Alana backed up as far as she could, her blood running cold at the lust in his eyes. *Oh, Jesus, please help me!* she cried out silently.

She knew she would have to try to run past him if there was any hope of getting away. She dashed to the side of him, almost clearing him before he grabbed her wrist with lightning speed.

"Let go!" she cried, hitting him with her other hand.

Manley only drew her closer and let his lips touch her face.

"No!"

"Senor, don't!" Felina pulled at his arm. "Let her go!"

Manley turned and backhanded her with such force that she was knocked off her feet. "You've had your turn, girl!" he spat. "Now you're old news." He turned menacing eyes to Alana. "I want something fresher!"

Alana kicked at his legs, but with one, swift move, he knocked her feet out from under her. She fell backwards on the floor. Her eyes were wide with fear as she inched away from him.

"I've had my eye on you, girl," he said, standing over her, "now I'm gonna get what I want!"

Alana screamed as he dropped down on her, nearly crushing her. He smothered her scream with his lips, and she could smell the alcohol on his breath. She felt her shirt rip and wrenched her face away to cry out again.

Suddenly his weight was lifted off her and she watched as he was thrown across the room. In shock, she stared at Vic, his face black with rage. His eyes were shooting sparks and the muscles in his back tensed as he stalked over to where Manley lay moaning. With hardly any effort, Vic lifted Manley's burly form and slammed it against the nearest wall.

"I really ought to rip you limb from limb right here and now!" Vic snarled in Manley's face. Vic's shirt was damp and his bare arms glistened with perspiration.

"Come on, Boss!" Manley whined, his voice breathless.

Vic raised Manley off his feet and beat him against the wall again, knocking the breath from him. "Don't talk, Elam!" he snapped. "I want you out of my face, and out of this room, now. You understand?"

Manley nodded quickly.

"And if I see you standing within fifty feet of these girls again, don't think I won't do something about it, and you know what I'm capable of, you loser! Now, get!"

Vic shoved Manley so hard that the latter man lost his footing and fell heavily on his face. Vic grabbed his shirt and jerked him to his feet, giving him another push. Manley half ran, half stumbled out of the room.

Turning back to where Alana was still laying on the floor, Vic reached down for her. He paused at the look of terror she directed towards him. He hesitated just an instant before he took her arm, helping her firmly, but gently, to her feet. He did not miss the way she drew back from him.

Looking at Felina, who was now standing at his side, her face white, Vic asked, "You all right?"

"Si, Senor. Muchas Gracias."

"Take her back to her room and get her calm," he ordered, completely disregarding the thanks she had given him. He watched Felina lead Alana away, her arm around Alana's waist. He could still see Alana's trembling from where he stood.

"Oh, your arm. It is cut."

Alana dazedly turned her head towards Felina. That girl was sitting beside her on the bed, looking completely distraught.

"I'll go get something to take care of it," Felina said. She squeezed Alana's before she went.

Alana felt her legs still shaking. She had honestly thought that Manley Elam would have his way with her, that he would take away her decency and purity. She closed her eyes, still trying to compose herself. She felt suddenly sick, repulsed that she had been handled so roughly. She wanted to scream, cry, kick at the line of events that had put her in the place to be attacked so savagely. Instead, she forced herself to praise God for delivering her.

"Thank You, Lord," she whispered, "for keeping me from being hurt worse. It was horrible, but it could have so much worse. Thank You for stopping him."

She remembered that it was Vic who had intervened, but she could not bring herself to thank God for his part. She had seen in that moment just what Vic Dane was capable of, and it frightened her. What could he do to her if she ever caused him to be that angry? He could kill her without even trying.

Alana shook her head. She was safe now. As much as she feared Vic, he had kept Manley's attack from getting any worse. She had to allow him that much at least.

The room was dark even with the drapes pulled back, but Vic did not turn on the light. He stalked to the large chest of drawers and pulled out some clean clothes, his movements quick and agitated.

He had not expected the surge of rage when he witnessed what Manley was doing to Alana, and it bothered him. He would not have allowed Manley to continue in any case, but the way he had dealt with the situation was not the norm for him. He seldom lost his temper.

Vic sighed and ran his hands through his dark, thick hair, thinking already that Marlon could not get home soon enough. He was not accustomed to being watch guard for any of Marlon's girls, and the job was getting to be more than Vic had bargained. At least for this one particular girl.

What was it about her that set him so on edge? She barely spoke to him, and from the way she looked at him earlier, he knew now that she was terrified of him. He frowned. He had never anticipated the arrival of one young woman to disrupt his world the way this one had.

Tired of the mental monologue, Vic grabbed his things and headed for the shower, hoping the water could clear his mind as well as wash his tired body.

Chapter Twenty-Six

The brutal encounter with Manley Elam left Alana skittish about leaving her room the rest of the day. She moved about restlessly, seeing the face of the man leaning over her every time she closed her eyes.

Climbing up on her bed, Alana leaned against the headboard, her arms wrapped around her legs. Trying to shut out the danger she had been facing, she let herself dwell on her family.

Tomorrow would make nine days. Nine days since she had been snatched off the parking lot of *Darings'*. Nine days since she had felt the hug of her father or the hand of her mother.

What was going on at home? How was her family dealing with her absence? Were they able to keep faith that they would all be reunited? Or had they lost hope? How close were the authorities to finding her location? Would they ever find her now that she was no longer even in the United States?

The thought reminded her of Jason. As a cop, she was sure that he was trying to find her. How long would he continue? How hard would he work? Would she ever see him again?

Alana rested her face on her knees, feeling the tears soak through her clothes. She missed him terribly at that moment. Maybe it was being surrounded by men with no thought of any decency toward her that made her more appreciate the man that Jason was. She wished she had the chance to tell him how he had touched her life through his friendship.

Alana lifted her face and set her chin on her knee. Her view of the near future was bleak. She did not know exactly what would become of her, but she knew one thing for certain. Her life would never be the same. The simple life she had enjoyed in Edwardsville was like a far off dream now.

At precisely nine o'clock, Felina knocked. "Are you okay?" she asked.

Alana shrugged. "Define okay."

Felina came in and sat on the bed, an act she would not have considered a few short days ago. "I'm sorry."

189

"Why?" Alana frowned. "It's not your fault. You told me about him."

Felina licked her lips. "But, I should have explained more fully. I knew what he was capable of."

Alana stared at her new friend, seeing the shame and misery etched clearly on the dark face. "He's done it to you, hasn't he?"

Felina took a deep breath and nodded. "Yes."

"Why haven't you told anyone?" Alana exclaimed.

"Because he threatened to hurt my family," Felina explained. "And I knew he would."

Alana leaned back against the headboard, feeling suddenly more helpless than she ever had. Felina had fallen quiet.

"Felina, how can you allow yourself to be kept here? After everything that's happened, why don't you leave?"

Looking down, Felina replied in a soft voice. "I was trapped, Alana, the same way you are now. After Marlon…grew tired of me, he was not willing to let me go completely, so he offered me a position with his staff."

"And you accepted?" Alana asked incredulously. "Why?"

Dark eyes lifted to find Alana's. "Because I had no choice."

Turning away in frustration, Alana closed her eyes. She felt the bed move as Felina stood and left her. Tears welled up. Felina was completely resigned to her condition. There was no hope or desire to attempt to leave. All her failed attempts had left her desolate and timid.

Alana's fists tightened. She would not allow herself to become like that. At all costs, she would find a way out of this prison and get away from Marlon Ferraro and his men.

It was late when Marlon and Reuban arrived back home. Both were red-faced and laughing loudly, the lingering effects of their time spent in town. All were retired to their beds for the night, but the brothers, in their drunkenness, stumbled through the halls loudly, chuckling at each other's clumsiness and calling out to the other.

Finally, all grew quiet. Alana waited an hour, just to be sure. She had been afraid that Marlon would come to her room in his drunken state, but he had not. Now she could carry out her plan.

The bundle she had put together earlier came out from under her bed. She had tiptoed to the kitchen just a while together, after the cook had finished her chores. She stuffed whatever foods she could find into a small pack she had discovered. Tortilla chips made up the bulk of her provisions, but she took what she could. She filled a bottle with cold water.

Sticking her head out the door, Alana made sure the hall was empty before she emerged. She was dressed in a loose-fitting Mexican dress, figuring it to be less confining than her jean skirt and jacket. Those were wrapped up in her bag.

Moving soundlessly down the steps, Alana peered through the darkness, trying to catch any kind of movement. Remembering Vic's words about Marlon's guards, she kept close to the wall.

Feeling breathless with the excitement of her success so far, she paused before the double doors in the foyer. She looked all around, and caught sight of no one. The rooms were still and dark in the late hour.

Biting her lip, she reached for the doorknob. Not knowing what she would find outside, she inched the door open little by little. The wide porch and curving steps were empty.

I'm going to do it! she thought as she closed the door behind her and tread lightly down the steps. *I'm going to get away!*

She had no idea what she would do once she was free from this mansion, but she knew that she had to get away from Marlon before he decided to make her his.

The moon favored her this night. Clear moonlight lit her path as she stole away. Running on silent feet, she left the house behind her and headed down the long driveway that led to the town Acquiles Serdan—and to freedom.

A soft knock on Vic's door made him stir. He was having difficulty getting to sleep as it was, and the interruption did not make him happy. When the knock sounded again, he rose and pulled his robe on, his movements agitated. He opened the door with a fierce frown.

"What?" he demanded. He stopped abruptly when Felina's finger went to her lips. "What's wrong?" he whispered.

"Alana is gone," she answered. She cast a glance nervously towards Marlon's door. "She is not in her room, and I'm afraid she might have gotten out of the house."

"Oh, good grief," Vic muttered. He closed the door briefly as he pulled on jeans and a shirt. Felina was still standing where he left her.

"Don't say anything," he told her. "Keep it quiet. I'll try to get her back before anyone wakes up. If someone misses her, you don't know anything."

Felina nodded. "Please find her, Senor," she said. "She'll get lost out there and it is dangerous for someone who doesn't know their way."

"I know," Vic replied as he slipped past her.

He made his way to the Marlon's elaborate stable. He could have taken his motorcycle, but he did not want to wake anyone in the house. If Marlon knew that Alana had escaped, what she experienced with Manley would be nothing compared to what Marlon would do.

Vic did not waste time with a saddle but grabbed the lead rope of a spirited stallion and jumped up bareback. "Come on, boy," he murmured, urging the horse to leave the barn at a fast trot. "We've got a runaway filly to catch."

The horse tossed his head and snorted. Vic glanced up at the mansion, hoping the noise would not awaken anyone. He caught a glimpse of Felina looking at him through the window.

He had no idea which direction Alana would have gone. If she took to the woods, there was no telling where she was. Hoping that was not the case, he headed down the road. *Maybe she's hoping to get to the town,* he thought.

When he was a safe distance from the house, he let the horse speed to a gallop. The darkness made it hard to see, but the road was lit by the moonlight. He was beginning to get tense after fifteen minutes of running without any sign of Alana. Had he taken the wrong direction?

A blurry image appeared a ways up the road. Vic kept his eye on the apparition. It began to take shape as he neared. When he saw the figure look back at him and then take off at a full run, he kicked the horse's sides. "Gotcha."

Alana dropped the pack she was carrying on and plunged on, not looking back. Vic overtook her easily. Leaning down from the horse, he wrapped his strong arm around her and swung her up in front on him. She fought him the whole time. With his attention on the girl in his arms, he dropped the lead rope and the horse slowed to a stop, whinnying softly.

"Let me go!" Alana shrieked, trying to free herself from his grip.

Vic pinned her against him, holding her wrists in one hand. "I'm doing you a favor, girl," he said calmly.

"A favor!" Alana cried. She tried to pull her hands free, but to no avail. "By taking me back to that prison! I won't go back!" She wriggled and writhed violently in his arms.

"Listen!" Vic barked. Alana started and stared up at him. His jaw was set, his narrowed eyes fixed on her face. "Believe me, Alana; you would not have gotten away. Marlon has got people under his thumb all over Acquiles. They would have reported you instantly."

Alana opened her mouth to retort, but he cut her off.

"He would have had you back by midmorning, at the latest."

"I don't care," Alana whispered. "I'll do it again."

"Alana," Vic's tone was exasperated. "If Marlon catches you in an escape, your encounter with Manley Elam will seem like playtime."

Seeing that Vic was serious, Alana's features paled. She pulled her gaze from him and stared out at the dark woods around them.

"Now, no one knows you're gone," Vic told her. "There's no reason they have to know, if we can get back to the estate without anyone waking. You'll have to keep quiet and cooperate, though. Got it?"

After a long moment, Alana nodded.

"Good." Vic released his tight grasp and gathered the lead rope. He turned the horse's head to the opposite direction, pushing him in an easy canter. He stopped briefly to pick up Alana's bundle that she had dropped.

The darkness hid the tears that Alana was fighting. The feel of Vic's arms around her made her feel imprisoned, yet strange. Though she wanted to hate him for bringing her back to the manor, she knew that he was actually protecting her from Marlon's wrath. Why would he? Was he not Marlon's most trusted and loyal bodyguard?

Vic, meanwhile, was focusing his attention on getting Alana back to the house safely. He knew that dawn was approaching soon, and Marlon was an early riser. Vic could only hope that Marlon's late night would cause him to sleep in this day.

The mansion came into view, bathed in the soft light of the moon. Its splendor was undeniable, but Alana turned her face from it. She felt the muscles in Vic's arms as he turned the horse towards the stables. She wondered why he did not take her to the house first.

Vic drove the horse straight to its stall. He slid off its back easily, grabbing some hay from a nearby bale. The horse went willingly to its stall. Alana grabbed the mane nervously as it moved.

Vic reached up and put his hands on her waist, pulling her off to stand by him. As he did, he caught a glimpse of tears standing in her eyes. His movements slowed slightly. He cleared his throat. "It's just going to be harder on you if you continue to fight, Alana."

She did not answer. Vic closed the stall door and took her arm. He led her out of the barn and towards the mansion. She stumbled slightly on the steps, and he caught her before she fell on her face. His arm lingered around her waist as she regained her footing.

"All right?" he whispered.

"No, I'm not all right," she returned. "But there's nothing I can do about it, is there?"

Vic had no reply for this. He had never met a girl who could make him speechless the way this one did. The disconcerting doubts she brought out in him made him uncomfortable.

Fortunately, the place was still as they went through the halls. It seemed Alana's turbulent escape and capture had disturbed no one but Vic.

That was not true. Alana found Felina in her room and the girl looked completely distraught. Forgetting herself, Felina threw her arms around Alana's neck. "I thought Marlon would find you and hurt you!" she exclaimed quietly.

Alana hugged her in return, regretting the way she had left without any thought for her only friend here. "I'm sorry, Felina," she told her. "I didn't mean to scare you."

Vic stood at the doorway and watched the scene, keeping his thoughts off his face. When he saw that Alana would settle down for the night, he turned to leave.

"Vic," she called to him, surprising him. He turned with an uplifted brow.

"Thank you," she said softly.

The other brow joined its partner. "For what?"

"For keeping Marlon from finding out." Alana's eyes were on the floor, but Vic could see that she meant her words.

"You're welcome," he answered, unable to think of anything else.

"Oh, Senorita," Felina breathed when he was gone. "Please do not leave me like that again!"

Alana forced a smile. "I won't," she said.

"Really?" Felina questioned.

"I promise," Alana nodded. The Mexican girl sighed in relief. She may have not been so relieved if she could have read Alana's thoughts. *I won't leave you, Felina, because next time I get away, you're going to be right with me!*

Chapter Twenty-Seven

Chihuahua, Mexico
Thursday, April 18ᵗʰ

Jason walked the street of Chihuahua, trying to blend in with the crowd. Dark-headed men, women, and children scurried about around him. He was amazed at the diversity of the city. There were many businessmen and women, dressed in stylish suits. Other people were dressed poorly. Still others were wearing loose clothing to protect them from the heat of the sun. There were a few Americans mingled throughout the populated streets. Spanish words floated around him.

Taking a deep breath, Jason felt a measure of comfort in knowing that he was at last here. He really had no idea what his next step would be, but knew that God would direct his steps.

Bringing the strap of his single bag over his head, he settled the pack at his hip, always cautious of thieves and muggers. It would not do to get robbed while here.

Somehow, Kenneth had managed to raise money for Jason's cause without telling anyone Jason's intention. When Kenneth gave him the money in a fat envelope, he told him, "You're going to need all you can get. I'll do all I can to make sure you have what you need."

Jason was thankful for the money, especially now, since he had to find a motel or boarding house. Not caring about quality, Jason wanted only a place that he could stay in cheaply for as long as he needed. He did not plan on spending much time in the room anyway. He was here to find Alana, and he would spend every waking hour doing just that. Chances are, he would not even be staying in Chihuahua. There was no telling where Alana's captors could be.

God, help me to stay on track, he prayed. *Keep me under Your sheltering wing and lead me to where Alana is. Keep her safe, Lord, until I can get to her. Give me a place to start.*

Acquiles Serdan

Alana sat at the breakfast table, silent as always. She would much have preferred to eat in her room, but Marlon would have none of it. Indeed, just the look on Felina's face when Alana had suggested it made her drop the idea.

Vic had been true to his word, and Marlon was none the wiser about her escapade the night before. Vic had barely even glanced at her all morning. In fact, he was quieter than usual.

That could have been due to the fact that Reuban had joined them for breakfast. He spent much of the time talking about future business and his recent trip. Alana did not pay much attention to him. She had other things to worry about.

Marlon was scaring her. He seemed much more attentive this morning than usual. He kept turning to her, giving her sickeningly sweet smiles. Once he rested his hand on her arm, but she quickly pulled away. He did not seem upset, but shook his head at her like an exasperating youngster. It made her ill.

As soon as breakfast was over, she retreated back to her room, where she was spending all her time these days. She did not want to run into Marlon any more than she wished to see Manley Elam again.

She tried to pray for endurance, but her prayers were choppy and made little sense. *I need my Bible,* she thought. It hit her that she had not been able to even touch a Bible for well over a week. An intense desire to lose herself in God's Word came over her. She felt like a thirsty man in a desert. Her fingers itched to hold the book in her hands.

I can still have the Scriptures, she thought suddenly. She remembered the times she had tried to instill in her Sunday school class the importance of memorizing portions of the Bible. She felt tears sting her eyes. Even without holding the actual book, she could hold the word in her heart.

Settling herself in the chair by the window, she began pulling Scriptures from her memory that she had filed away.

"With God, nothing is impossible." She paused at that, finding this one verse so comforting to her right now. "Nothing is impossible for You," she whispered. "I am so glad of that. I would really not have a chance without You. I know that I am in Mexico, alone, but You still are in control and can take care of me."

She moved on, verses coming back to her that she had long forgotten. She stopped to ponder on a few, praying, confessing, and claiming the words. She spent the entire morning in this way, and before she knew it, it was time to join Marlon again for lunch. She stood, feeling stronger now.

Marlon met her at the dining room door. He smiled down at her. "Did I tell you that you look lovely today, Miss Crewe?"

Only twice, she said mentally. She said nothing outwardly, though.

Reuban sent her a cool smile as Marlon led her to her seat. Something about Marlon's brother set her on edge. While Marlon certainly was dangerous to her, he had proven to be professional and patient. She sensed a temperamental spirit within the younger Ferraro.

Halfway through the meal, there was a moment of silence. Alana looked around briefly and raised her chin in determination. "May I ask you something?"

Marlon was surprised but covered it well. "Why certainly, my dear."

She inwardly recoiled at the endearment, but pressed on. "Since I am going to be here for some time, I wonder if I might make a request."

More than a little pleased to know that his guest was resigning herself to her new dwelling, Marlon nodded. "Of course."

"Will you bring me a Bible?" Alana asked boldly. "In English?"

Marlon faltered for a moment, casting a look at Reuban and then Vic. Vic was staring at Alana as if she had grown a second head, but Reuban looked annoyed.

"A Bible?" Marlon repeated.

"Surely that won't be a problem?" Alana asked. "They're not expensive."

"Well, of course not, but," Marlon stammered. Alana felt a thrill in seeing him so flustered.

Recovering his bearings, Marlon said, "If a Bible would make you feel more at home, then of course you'll have one."

"Marlon!" Reuban spoke up.

"Come, come, Reuban," Marlon admonished. "Let the girl have her Bible. It won't matter any to us." He turned to Alana. "I'll have one for you by the end of this week."

Alana nodded serenely, but she felt such joy that her hand trembled slightly. She looked across the table to see Vic still observing her. He nodded slightly to her, as if impressed.

After the meal, Alana stood to go back to her room. She was startled when Marlon joined her.

"Can I walk you to your room, miss?" he asked, his eyes lit with a teasing light.

No! Stay away from me! Alana wanted to shout, but she did nothing. Marlon chatted about nothing important as they ascended the stairs. He seemed content to just be near her.

At her door, Alana turned towards him, not willing to open the door for fear he would enter with her. Marlon towered over her, his face softening. He wrapped his arms around her before she could react. She put her hands against his chest to put some distance between them, her heart beating like a drum.

"Alana, you make my life complete," he murmured. "I am so glad to have you here."

Alana stiffened when his head dropped, but he only rested his cheek against hers. When he turned his face towards her she tried to push away.

"No, Marlon!" she whispered. "Please."

Marlon paused and looked down at her fearful face. "How long have you been here, Alana?" he asked. "You should know by now that I mean you no harm. I wish you wouldn't resist me this way." He smiled, his eyes glimmering. "I promise you won't be disappointed."

Alana gave a great shove and managed to step away from his arms. "I will never want what you have to give," she said firmly. "I will not give in to you."

Instead of growing angry, Marlon merely reached out and touched her face with his hand. "You are certainly beautiful when you are angry." He dropped his hand and stepped away. "You will find out soon enough."

Alana went to her room, infuriated. Marlon Ferraro was a man who thought he could run the world any way he pleased and not have to face consequences, and that included what he did with women in his possession.

Edwardsville

"Honey, what is it?" Alan asked, having just come into the kitchen. He had watched Sharon hang the phone up, a peculiar look on her face.

Sharon looked up at him. "That was Humanity magazine. They want do a story about Alana's abduction."

Alan immediately began shaking his head. "I don't want my daughter's story exploited and her picture—"

"Alan, you're not thinking this through," Sharon interrupted.

Alan stopped and looked at his wife.

Sharon licked her lips, her face a study of concentration. "I don't want Alana's story to appear in tabloids, but Humanity is not a tabloid. It's the most popular news magazine in the country. Alan, the more Alana's story is told, the more people will see her picture. It could help someone find her."

Still looking concerned, Alan nodded. "You're right. I wasn't thinking. But, let's agree now not to say anything about Jason, all right?"

Sharon instantly complied. "Of course. I don't want to get in his way of finding her."

Acquiles Serdan
Friday, April 19ᵗʰ

"I don't want you to spend all of your time in your bedroom."
Marlon's words from the night before still echoed in Alana's ears. That was the very thing she wanted to do, but she heard his voice once again.

"How is a man to see his lovely lady if she's in her room?" He'd asked. *"Why, I'd have to spend half the day in your room just to get to know you."*

She had caught his meaning. It was after supper and Marlon had once again escorted her to her room, though he did not try to touch her again. But, the promise in his eyes told her that she would no longer find protection in her room.

She stood at her window, feeling petrified. If she left the safety of this room, what would happen? Would Marlon force her into his own room? Would he catch her unsuspecting somewhere else? Why was he putting her through this mental torture?

Closing her eyes, Alana once again went over the verses that brought her the most comfort. Even if she felt alone and scared, she knew her God was with her, and that was really all she needed.

The sound of a car motor interrupted her. She saw the limousine pulling away from the mansion. Would she be so fortunate to have Marlon gone for the day?

Her door opened behind her and she whirled around, her hand going to her throat.

"It's all right, Alana. It's just me," Felina assured.

A huge sigh burst through Alana's lips.

"I just wanted to check on you," Felina explained. "It's been a while since we've talked."

"Was that Marlon that just left?"

Felina nodded. "He and Reuban had some business at their office in Chihuahua."

"Good." She had not even thought of the possibility of Reuban going with him. "That man scares me," she said out loud.

"Marlon?"

"No," Alana shook her head. "Well, he does, but I was speaking about Reuban. He seems so…dangerous."

Felina settled on the edge of the bed. Alana joined her. "Alana, Reuban does have a very hot temper," Felina confirmed. "But I've learned that if you stay out of his way, you will have nothing to fear from him. He does not bother with things that are not his concern. But, he is not more dangerous than Marlon." Her dark eyes stared straight into Alana's pensive face. "Marlon covers a cruel man under his professionalism."

Alana could see that Felina was very serious. She knew more about Marlon than Alana ever hoped to know.

"Marlon is not below doing anything, Alana," Felina went on. "You must remember this, and be careful. Reuban's quick temper is nothing in the light of Marlon's anger when he is crossed."

Alana licked her lips and turned to better face Felina. "Marlon Ferraro has no right to hold people here against their will. He has no right to take what does not belong to him, and that includes a girl's purity."

"I know that, Senorita, but—"

"Listen to me, Felina," Alana cut in. "I appreciate what you're telling me. You have been a real friend to me in all this."

Felina dropped her head, touched at Alana's compliment.

"But Marlon's way of life will not last."

"What do you mean?" Felina raised her head.

"God judges everyone on this earth, Felina, and soon Marlon will stand before Him. Even if he gets away with everything on this earth, God will make him pay for his sins."

Felina looked frightened. "How do you know this?"

"Because that's the God I serve," Alana answered. "It's written in the Bible. Every act that we do is recorded. The only way we can erase them is if we confess them before the Lord and change our ways. He can take the worst person and accept them as His child, but they must be covered by the blood of Jesus."

Alana did not know how she had gotten on this subject, but she could tell by Felina's face that her words were affecting the girl. "Marlon is supposed to be bringing me a Bible," she went on. "Can you read English?"

"Yes."

"I won't force you to, but anytime you want to read my Bible, feel free to do so. Everything written in it is for our benefit, so we will know how to reach God."

"But, I know God, Alana," Felina said, her voice shaking. "I was raised in a very religious home."

Alana chose her words carefully. "To really be saved, one has to understand the plan of salvation. Jesus gave his blood on Calvary so anyone who had ever committed a sin, which is everyone on this earth, can come to him and be saved. If one has not done this, they are not a child of God."

Felina stood, her movements quick and agitated. "I must get back to work. If you need anything just let me know."

"Felina," Alana called just before the girl left. "I hope you are not angry at me, because I would never intentionally hurt you."

Seeing the sincerity on Alana's face, Felina gave her a shaky, but reassuring smile. "I know, Senorita. I am not angry at you. I just don't understand everything you are saying."

After she was gone, Alana was drawn to her knees. She realized that God had opened a door for her to witness to the girl and prayed that in the days to come she would know the words to say to convince Felina that she needed to surrender to the Lord.

Chapter Twenty-Eight

Curtis had confronted Jason when he found out he was leaving for Mexico.

"Why are you doing this?" he asked.

At that very moment, Jason was packing his bag, so he could not deny what Curtis was talking about. "I'm going to find Alana."

"I know, Jason, but Mexico?" Curtis shook his head. "I don't understand."

Jason stood and faced the other man. "I have reason to believe that she's been taken down there, and I really feel led to go down and look for her." He shrugged. "It's as simple as that."

"So, you're going all the way down there, possibly risking your life, just to help a friend?"

"Yeah." Jason resumed his packing.

Curtis crossed his arms. "I can't help but think there's more to it, Jase."

"Like what?"

"Come on, man!" Curtis exclaimed. "I don't know why you can't just face the fact. You have feelings for Alana."

"Curtis, stop," Jason warned, stuffing a change of clothes into his bag. "This is about getting Alana home where she belongs. Stop making this into more than it is. I feel the same way about Alana as I do about you."

He obviously had not convinced Curtis, and it was proven with Curtis's last words just before they parted.

"If you find that girl, Jason, you're going to find that it's going to be very hard to continue denying your real feelings," Curtis had cautioned. "It's time to stop running from the past and take another chance."

Jason had shaken Curtis's advice off as that of an overly concerned friend. He appreciated Curtis's words, but knew they were not exactly accurate.

Now, he stood at the window of his motel room, staring down at the bustling business of the large city. Alana's face crowded his mind, and he felt his chest constrict. "Please, God," he whispered. "Help me find her before it's too late."

Acquiles Serdan

"Felina, have you ever tried to escape?" Alana asked the Mexican girl later that day.

Taking her time to answer, Felina swallowed. "Yes, Alana, and I did not get far."

"What happened?"

Felina shook her head. "You do not want to know."

Alana took a deep breath. "Do you think you could escape if you had help?"

"No, Alana— "

Alana cut her off. "How can you let yourself be trapped here for the rest of your life, Felina?" she demanded. "You do not belong to Marlon, you belong to God. He does not will for you to be held captive in such a degrading way."

"You promised you would not try to escape, Alana," Felina reminded, growing fearful at Alana's talk.

"I won't." If Felina felt comfort at Alana's words, it was shattered by the next words. "Not without you."

"No!" Felina gasped. "I won't!"

"Felina, we can work together!"

"Alana!" Felina raised her voice abruptly. "Do not bring it up again. I will not try to escape. I have seen and endured the consequences of such a feeble attempt."

Alana knew she was going to have to let it go for now. Felina left her alone then, murmuring something about getting back to work. Alana lifted her chin resolutely. She would not give up so easily. Somehow, even if it took weeks, she would convince Felina that they simply had to leave this place!

It was hours later that the limo arrived back at the Ferraro mansion. Alana was in the library when she heard their voices in the hall. Unwilling to meet either of the brothers, she stayed where she was, trying to lose herself in *Treasure Island.* To her dismay, however, Marlon tracked her down.

"There you are, my little bookworm!" he crooned. He swaggered in and pulled an ottoman over in front of the easy chair where she was sitting. "Presenting…" he announced, laying a wrapped package on her lap. "Your Holy Bible, madam," he said teasingly.

Alana touched the package almost reverently. She forced herself to say thank you.

"I'm glad to see that my gift pleases you so much."

Biting her tongue against any remark on the contrary, Alana just concentrated on unwrapping the Book. Feeling a bit bold, she looked up at him. "If you ever want to read it, you're free to."

Marlon looked surprised and amused. "Thanks for the offer, my sweet, but no thanks."

"You might find it interesting," she said.

"Alana, there are far more things to occupy my time than reading an outdated book like this."

"What about facing God's judgment?"

Now he laughed outright. "God's judgment? Goodness, I have a real religious fanatic living under my roof! How interesting."

"I don't know much about you," Alana went on, marveling at her own nerve, "but I know that what you're doing is wrong. Soon, God is going to bring you to a stop. Why don't you change before that happens?"

Marlon sobered. "Listen, honey, I got the book for you, read it as much as you like, but don't start bugging me about it. Got it?"

Alana nodded promptly. She had caught the impatient glint in his eye.

"Now, if you are ever interested in anything else," Marlon's voice had dropped suddenly, "I am all yours."

"No," Alana shook her head.

Marlon reached out and held her hands in his. "You might as well give up, Alana," he said softly. "Whether you come to me, or I come to you, you will know me. And you will love me."

Chihuahua

Jason's first priority was to find Kenneth's friend—the missionary that the church had been supporting for years. The mission was on the edge of the city, the last building on Manchez Street. Jason had little trouble finding the place.

The young Mexican girl that answered the door led him into a large sitting room. She told him to in broken English to make himself comfortable while she found the missionary, who was in the back working with some carpenters. Jason could not relax, however, and paced the room until the man showed up.

When Martin Jacobs entered, he shook Jason's hand firmly, his manner welcoming and reassuring. Lines marked his face and his thick brown hair was streaked with gray. Although Martin looked to only be in his mid to late thirties, Jason could sense a lifetime of wisdom and experience in the man. Joy fairly shone from his eyes.

"Maria told me your name, but I'm afraid I've already forgotten it," he said apologetically.

"That's all right," Jason assured. "It's Jason Banks. I'm a friend of Kenneth Nelson."

"Oh, really?" Martin brightened. "How wonderful? How is he doing? Last time I talked to him his church was thriving."

"He's doing well," Jason responded. "His church has been growing and it's got some really good people." He swallowed slightly, feeling his anxiety returning. "However, the church has been through a real bad time, lately, which is why I'm here."

Martin looked surprised, but did not hesitate to invite Jason to sit down where they could talk. He turned his chair to face the younger man. "What is it? Something I can help with?"

"I'm hoping. I had half expected Kenneth to contact you before now."

"He may have," Martin told him, grimacing. "We've been experiencing some vandalism around the place here lately. We've had windows smashed, phone lines cut, and garbage strung out just in the last two weeks. My phone's been out for almost a week now, and I'm afraid we're not at the top of the list for the phone company. Seems that the majority is not happy with what we're doing here for God."

"That's a shame," Jason murmured, wondering how he would have endured the past days without the Lord.

"I'm sorry for rambling on," Martin said. "Go on."

"No, you're fine. You see, a member of the church was recently kidnapped. From my investigation, I believe she's in the custody of wanted men who have been hiding out in Mexico. My last lead makes me think that they have already brought her across the border. Therefore, my captain can't do anything else from the states, so I've come here looking for her on my own."

Jason stopped and took a breath, just realizing how fast he had been talking. His heart felt wrung out as he sat, shoulders slumped, in Martin's chair.

"Oh, my," Martin breathed. "How awful. What do you want me to do?"

"I don't expect you to get involved with my search and investigation, but Kenneth told me I could come to you for help."

"I'll do whatever you need me to do," Martin promised, his jaw set. "Believe me, it would not be the first time I have been in a precarious position. What can I do?"

Jason leaned forward in anticipation, feeling heartened. "Do you know of anyone by the name of Romano? Marlon and Reuban Romano, to be specific."

Martin sat for a long moment, his brows drawn low in concentration. "Can't say that I do at the moment."

Jason bit his lip, frowning. "I was so set on coming here," he spoke out loud to himself. "Now that I'm here, I'm not sure what I should do."

"Don't worry, son," Martin comforted. "God will go before you." He paused, staring at the young man. "Was this girl special to you?"

"Yes," Jason answered immediately. He glanced up quickly. "As a friend."

Martin nodded. "I see."

Chapter Twenty-Nine

Martin promised to make some phone calls and let Jason know if he found anything. Jason made his way back to the hotel, praying as he went. He tried not to dwell on the overwhelming job before him. How was he to find Alana and her abductors in this vast country? For all he knew, they could be hundreds of miles in any direction from where he was. How was he to even begin looking?

"All right, God," he muttered, sticking his hands in his pockets. "I'm here. This is what I felt led to do. I have no idea what to do next, so I'm going to need Your guidance like never before. Give me a direction, a lead to go on. Help me to find Alana as soon as possible. Help me get her out of here and back home."

Acquiles Serdan

"You may want to be careful with that girl," Reuban warned his brother.

Marlon looked up from he was sprawled on the sofa, reading the newspaper. "What's that?"

Reuban sat down in the stuffed chair. "Alana."

"What about her?"

"Her abduction is causing quite a stir in the states. From what I've heard, her story is spreading like wildfire. Her picture is pasted on every magazine and news bulletin from Kansas to Texas to even Florida."

Folding the paper calmly, Marlon pursed his lips. "That's up north. We're down here."

"True," Reuban nodded. "But there's a lot of business between the US and Mexico. I'm just saying you better be careful."

Scratching his head, Marlon frowned thoughtfully. "You may be right. I'll have to give it some thought. Thanks for the warning, but I don't think I'm willing to give her up just yet."

Reuban shrugged. "That's up to you. I just don't understand why you're being so patient with her. She's challenging you too much."

A slow smile stretched across Marlon's lips. "That's half the fun, bro. When the time comes for me to show her who really is in charge, she'll realize that her bravado was for nothing."

Alana soaked up the words from the Bible that Marlon had brought back for her. As soon as she could, she had taken the book up to her room and pored over her favorite verses, especially those that promised protection and grace. She felt her spirit lifting as she read, and thanked God continually for His word.

She read over Job's story, remembering the lessons she had been teaching her teens about his trials. Here was a man who had suffered more than anyone in this world, yet he never lost faith in God. Then there was Esther, the great lady her Bible study group had been studying. In the face of danger and death, she stayed strong and courageous. Their stories did more to encourage Alana than anything else.

Reading far into the night, Alana fell asleep with the Book in her hands. The next morning she found it resting on the mattress and reached for it, turning through its pages once almost reverently. She picked it up again off and on throughout the day, and when she joined her captors for lunch, she felt more serene than she had for a long time.

If Marlon noticed a change in her, he did not say. Reuban kept him busy with talk of their business, though Alana still had no idea what exactly the brothers did—besides kidnap girls and hold them hostage. The Ferraros talked in hushed tones at their corner, only looking away to eat their food.

Vic was quiet, not as interested as they obviously were. He had noticed something about Alana, though he could not put his finger on it. He stabbed the bacon on his plate with more force than he needed and the utensil scraped across the ceramic dish. He winced at the grating sound and stuck the meat in his mouth, his movements agitated. He was suddenly in a sour mood, and he did not even know why. All he wanted to do was get away from the table and get some air.

Marlon received a phone call just after the meal and he and Reuban shut themselves up in the large office at the end of the hall. Vic had disappeared somewhere and Alana was alone. She wandered the halls, really noticing for the first time the interior design of the mansion. Had she visited a place like this under any other conditions, she would have loved the magnificence of it. Now, though, she only saw it as a large prison.

Seeing sunlight on the carpet ahead, Alana hastened her step. Her first thought was that maybe she could find an unguarded porch and slip away. As she neared, she could see that the light was coming from a veranda set off the side of the house. This was why she had never noticed it before. She stepped cautiously out on the wide veranda. Her face instantly fell as she saw the screen wrapped securely around the porch.

"Looking for a way to escape again?"

Alana turned to see Vic observing her from his seat on the rail. "Would it do any good?" she asked.

Vic shook his head. "No." He was leaning against the wall of the mansion, his legs stretched out before him on the wide banister.

Not willing to go back in for the risk of running into Marlon, Alana wandered to the wrought iron bench sitting on the porch. Vic watched her a moment before putting a cigarette to his lips. He held the pack out to her. "Cigarette?" he offered, his face slightly amused.

"No, thank you," Alana returned, her words clipped.

"Good choice," Vic said as he lit his own. "It's a bad habit, and I seem to be doing it more and more lately."

"I wouldn't think bad habits would bother you," she said.

Vic grinned at her, a rare act for him. "Hey, I know I'm a far cry from a saint, but I'm not a monster, either, you know."

Alana shrugged. "Sometimes, I'm not so sure."

Vic had no answer for that, and the way Alana was watching him intently unnerved him. "I do my job," he told her. "I may not like every part of it, but that's life."

It was the most personal thing he had said to her. "If you don't like it, why do it?" she pressed.

"Because it's my job," he said again.

"That makes no sense," she frowned. "A man like you could have gotten a job anywhere, doing anything. Instead, you're wasting your life away working for a man that's going to land you in jail."

A wry smile lifted a corner of his lips. "Now you sound like my grandmother."

His comment set her aback. "Forgive me for asking, but is that a good thing?"

Vic regarded her for a moment. "You would think so."

"Why is that?"

He bent one knee and rested his arm on it. "She was a very religious person. And very stubborn. Something tells me you two would have gotten along great."

Alana was surprised. Of all people, she would not have expected Vic Dane to have any religious background.

"You're wondering how she had a grandson like me?" Vic asked, reading her expression accurately.

"Well, I…" she stammered.

He shook his head. "Don't worry. But don't blame her for what I am." He paused a moment, his face growing pensive. "She actually raised me and my sister both. Our parents died when we were kids."

"Where is she now?" Alana asked.

Vic lifted dark eyes to hers. "Dead. My sister ran off and I've not seen her for years. I ended up joining the Mexican army just to keep from starving. After I left that, I was looking for work when I met Marlon. He offered me a job. It wasn't any worse than some of the things I had seen in the army. So I took it. And I haven't regretted it since."

Vic wondered about his last words. Indeed he hadn't had any negative thought about his occupation. All anyone ever did was look at for himself. Why was he any different? Now, though, he wasn't so sure. He also wondered what it was about Alana that had caused him to give out so much information. There were very few people associated with him that had any idea about his history.

Alana felt uncomfortable. She was a bit surprised that he had shared so much with her, but she had never thought about the kind of past this man could have to bring him to the place that he was in today. "What was your grandmother like?" she asked, hoping she did not seem pushy.

Vic leaned his head back against the stone wall. "There was no one that she would not stand up against. She was as feisty as an old gal could get." He turned to look at her. "You'll never meet a woman with more mixed blood than her. She had grandparents in her past that were Mexican, Indian, Japanese, Italian, and even Greek."

Alana's brows rose. With that kind of background, it was no wonder that Vic was of such unique physical appearance. His hair was as black as a crow's wing, his eyes piercing, and his jaw square. He was as dark as the Mexicans, yet set apart from them somehow.

Alana averted her gaze, feeling rather foolish for the way she had been studying him.

Not noticing, he went on. "She used to tell us that we could be proud of our heritage." He snorted slightly. "My own mother was of French and German blood, so you could say I'm a real mixed breed."

"Wow," Alana breathed, fascinated. "I always wanted to know where my ancestry was."

Vic started to say something up, but he glanced up and cut off abruptly as Marlon and Reuban joined them on the veranda.

"There you two are," Marlon greeted lightly. "I was beginning to think you had run off together."

"Right," Vic snorted, bringing the cigarette to his lips. His face was closed off again.

Alana had not realized just how relaxed she had become sitting on the porch until the brothers made their appearance. Automatically, she stiffened, becoming so tense she could not think straight.

"We need to talk business," Reuban said, taking a seat in a chair across from Vic.

"I'll leave you alone," Alana said quickly, rising to her feet.

"No, no, no," Marlon argued, pushing her back to her seat and sitting next to her. "I don't mind if you sit in on our discussion."

He was sitting so close that his knee was pressed against hers. She couldn't move to put any space between him, sandwiched as she was between him and the arm of the bench.

Reuban jumped right into the business at hand. "We've gotten word that some of our associates are giving their supervisors trouble at the plant. Seems some of our men have got it in their heads that they're gonna play the saint and refuse to work any more."

"These are the same men who tried to run off on us last year," Marlon put in, he stretched his arm along the back of the bench.

"We can't afford to have them get word to the authorities. There's too much riding on this next order. Our contacts in Chicago are expecting their merchandise in a month, and they're paying a pretty penny for it. I say we need to eliminate these guys before they cause more damage than can be easily repaired."

Alana stared at the man, wondering if he was actually suggesting what she thought.

Vic swung his feet off the rail, shifting his position so that he was facing the Ferraros. "I don't think we should."

Reuban scoffed. "How come I knew you were going to buck against that?"

"What's your idea, Vic?" Marlon asked.

Tossing his cigarette away, Vic said, "If we cut our numbers, it's just going to make it harder for us to fill this order. And from what I hear, our very wealthy Chicago clients would not like a setback." Alana thought she caught just a hint of mockery in his voice.

"True," Marlon acknowledged.

"Then what are you suggesting, Vic?" Reuban ground out.

"What if the Ferraro brothers themselves made a trip to the location where they're working?" Vic asked. "Maybe a pep talk would do them some good."

Marlon nodded. "I like it." He turned to Alana. "Don't you, my dear?" His hand had moved over to rest on her leg.

"And what about the next time they buck against authority?" Reuban asked. "Are we going to run down there every time?"

Marlon's eyes were still on Alana. "Let's not cross that bridge until we come to it, brother."

Seeing that Marlon was sold on Vic's proposal, Reuban frowned and stood. "I've got some things to do in town," he said. "See you later tonight, Marlon."

"Sure, Reuban."

Vic waited until the younger man was gone. "That means he's gonna come home drunk again."

Marlon looked up at his best man. "Oh, don't be so hard on him, Vic. He's young. Let him take advantage of it. In the mean time, we need to plan this trip down south."

"When would you like to go?"

Cocking his handsome head, Marlon said, "Let's plan to take off next week. Can you make the arrangements?"

Vic shrugged. "Sure."

Turning his attention back to the silent girl beside him, Marlon smiled. "We just might take my beautiful guest down there as well."

"What?" Vic questioned, his tone doubtful.

"Why not?" Marlon asked, tracing his finger down her cheek. "I think she'd enjoy the trip. Wouldn't you, my sweet?"

Alana's throat was so tight she couldn't speak if she wanted to. Her skin crawled at his touch.

"Okay, whatever," Vic responded, pushing off the rail. "I'll talk to you later."

Alana cast a pleading look in Vic's direction, but he didn't seem to notice. Marlon merely grunted at his departure.

"Alana, dear, you're going to love going with me," he crooned, leaning into her slightly. "My men down there will treat you like their queen, giving you your every desire."

"I'd rather stay here," she croaked.

"Oh, no," Marlon murmured, dropping his outstretched arm around her shoulders. His other hand rested on her stomach as he pulled her into his embrace. "I couldn't bear the thought of leaving you behind." He lowered his head and caressed her neck with his lips as his hand caressed her side.

Alana tried to pull away from him, but he only drew her tighter against him. "There's no need to resist, my dear," he whispered, his eyes smoldering with desire. "I would never hurt you."

Feeling panic rise up in her throat, Alana knew that she could not get away form him now if he decided to have his way with her. "Marlon, please," she whispered, still struggling.

Marlon grinned suddenly. "Is that how you feel?" he asked. He dropped his head suddenly, covering her lips with his own. His hand caught her jaw just as she tried to turn her head from his kiss.

She could feel his weight leaning against her, his hand sliding down her back. Her mind screamed at her to stop him, but she was powerless against him. There was no way to escape his hold.

Chapter Thirty

A deafening crash filled the air just then, and Marlon jumped up, Alana forgotten. "What the devil?" he exclaimed, rushing inside.

Alana sat still for a few seconds, trying to catch her breath. Her legs felt weak as she forced herself to stand. She had to leave this place before he came searching for her again.

As she stepped in the doorway of the drawing room, she saw Marlon and Vic staring down at a broken vase.

"How did it happen?" Marlon was demanding.

Vic shrugged.

"Vic! That's an expensive vase!" Marlon exclaimed. "Imported from Spain."

"I bumped into it." Vic's voice was flat.

Marlon stared at Vic as if he had lost his mind. Pointing at the tall, skinny table it had been resting on only moments before, he said, "It was standing in the middle of the room! Surely you're not blind!"

"It was in my way."

Alana did not wait any longer. She could hear Marlon's ranting as she slipped past them and hurried up the stairs to her room. She knew she was not exactly safe there either, but Marlon had not made an attempt to come here as of yet.

Taking a deep breath, Alana tilted her head back. "I'm not sure exactly how that happened, but thank you, Lord, for Vic's clumsiness!"

Marlon was testy and frowning as he made his way to his room later that evening. Being very finicky about the appearance of the mansion, he was not at all pleased at the loss of the vase that Vic had broken. He was even more disgruntled at Vic's lack of concern over the matter. Oh, he offered to pay for it, but that was not the point.

To add to Marlon's frustration, when he stepped back out on the veranda, he found Alana gone. He had cursed softly when he realized that she had slipped away and hidden herself in her room. The temptation to break through her door and force her to succumb to him was overwhelming, but he considered himself a gentleman. He honestly thought that he could win Alana over in time, and waited for her to want him.

He caught a glimpse of his butler and called him. "Send Felina to my room," he demanded briskly.

Closing the door to his room, Marlon ran his hands through his hair, muttering under his breath. "I'm not sure how much a man can take," he mumbled. A soft knock interrupted his ranting. "Come in!"

Felina entered, her face solemn. She already had her nightgown on when she was summoned, but hadn't bothered dressing again. She knew what Marlon would want. It did not matter how she was dressed.

"Come on over, Felina," Marlon called, his voice softer. He sat down on a chair, his hand reaching out to her.

Felina moved on silent feet to stand before him. He smiled up into her face. "I haven't had a chance to talk to you in a while," he said. "I hope Alana has not been causing you trouble."

"No, Senor," Felina answered.

"Seems she's taking longer to adjust than I thought she would," Marlon contemplated. His hand reached up to cup her cheek. "A man gets lonely, you know?"

"Si, Senor," Felina answered automatically.

"You will always hold a special place in my heart, my dear Felina, no matter what happens," Marlon whispered.

Felina did not reply, nor did she move, not even when she felt Marlon's hands on her back. He pulled her into his arms, his lips caressing her smooth cheeks. On instinct, her hands rested stiffly on his shoulders.

"Very special," he murmured. He brought her face to his, covering her lips with his own. Felina felt him draw her tight against him, his lips now on her neck. He swept her up in his arms, still kissing her fervently, and carried her to the bed. She did not fight him. There was no use in fighting.

Saturday, April 20th

Alana woke late the next morning, still feeling tired after a restless night. She had stayed up far into the night, scared to death that Marlon would come looking for her. When she did manage to sleep, she dreamt of Marlon's hands on her body and the kiss he forced on her. She knew that she was running out of time. Marlon would eventually grow impatient and force her to be with him.

"Dear Lord," she whispered, tears forming in her eyes. "I know You've protected me until now, and I thank You." A knot formed in her throat, making it difficult for her to speak, but she forced the words out. "I'm asking you now to extend Your hand of protection. Please help me get away from this place before it's too late!"

Letting herself dwell on the awesome power and mercy of her heavenly Father, Alana slid out of bed and dressed for the day. She knew that Marlon would be looking for her, and she did not want him to have a reason to come to her room.

A soft knock met her ears and she froze. Praying silently, she called out, "Come in."

Felina appeared in the doorway, her face large and solemn.

"Good morning," Alana greeted.

Felina did not answer but moved into the room, making sure to close the door firmly behind her. She walked over to the window, a few feet from Alana. Her eyes darted around the room for a moment before settling on the floor.

"Felina, what's wrong?" Alana asked, sensing something different from the girl.

Felina raised her head, but did not look at Alana. "I thought that I could survive here," she began. "If I stayed out of his way, did my duty like everyone else, that the nightmare would end, that he wouldn't...touch me anymore."

Alana stifled a gasp. "What happened, Felina?"

For the first time, she looked up at Alana, and Alana was struck by the torture deep in the dark eyes. "I am tired of that man using me, Alana," she whispered. "I am so tired of being forced to share his bed. I want it to stop."

Alana's heart broke. She reached out and pulled the girl to her, trying not to sob. "I'm so sorry, Felina," she murmured. She heard Felina sniffling. "I wish you had never been put in this awful place." She pulled away. "This is my fault. If he had had his way with me, he would not have forced you again."

"Don't think such a thing, Alana," Felina ordered. "I won't hear of it."

Alana let go of her, feeling helplessness wash over her. "If only there was something I could do," she said softly.

Felina grew still and caught Alana's gaze. "There is. If we do it together."

"What?" Alana questioned, feeling her heart jump. "Are you saying what I think you're saying?"

Felina bit her lip, her brow wrinkling in her anxiousness. "I don't have much hope in our getting away from here, Alana, but anything has to be better than what I have to endure in Marlon Ferraro's arms. And I don't want you to face it, either."

Alana gripped Felina's hand. "We'll make a plan," she said. "We'll make sure we make it. Together."

Nodding shortly, Felina returned Alana's squeeze. "Together."

Sunday, April 21st

Alana went to her knees about her escape. She prayed fervently that she would not do anything foolish that would bring Felina to harm. She was so anxious to get her friend from Marlon's hold that her own danger seemed unimportant. Her heart yearned to see Felina turn her life, broken and scarred as it was, to the heavenly Father, who could make something beautiful out of her life again.

The girls spent as much time together as they could, planning and devising. At times it seemed hopeless. No matter how they thought to connive or strategize, they always found holes in their plans that would keep them from succeeding. Alana was determined to find a way, though she could tell that Felina was losing hope. Through it all, Alana continued talking to Felina about God, encouraging her to trust Him to take care of them. She tried to keep her own faith up, for Felina's sake as well as her own.

Alana wandered the halls of the mansion, her mind going a mile a minute. Felina was busy in the kitchen. They had agreed to meet again at two o'clock. Alana hoped that they could come up with something soon.

The sunlight beckoned to her from a window at the northern end of the house. She had not been able to be outside in so long. Padding to the window, Alana rested her arms on the sill and looked out.

This was a part of Marlon's massive yard that she had not seen yet. Tucked away behind the house was a large swimming pool and a tennis court. Rows upon rows of perfectly trimmed trees stretched for miles from the house. Small flowering bushes lined the gravel walkways. Alana had to admit that it was a picturesque view.

Movement at the edge of the window caught her eye. She saw Vic, alone, doing some kind of workout. He wore only black pants and the muscles on his arms rippled as he performed a series of punches and kicks in the air. Alana could not help but be captivated at his quick, graceful moves.

She felt someone at her back and somehow knew it was Marlon. Although her heart immediately jumped to her throat, she tried to stay calm.

"Pretty impressive, isn't he?" he asked, motioning towards Vic.

Alana acknowledged that he was with a quick shake of her head.

"Vic is the star of my employees," Marlon said. "I've had a lot of men working for me, but none with the abilities, intelligence, and talent that Vic has. I found him almost four years ago. He was penniless, and just a little bit desperate, but don't tell him I told you that."

Alana kept her gaze on Vic, but listened intently to what Marlon was saying.

"Watched him take on a guy twice his size and I offered him a job on the spot. I've never regretted it. You see, I'm not too good with a gun and I like to have men around me that can shoot. Reuban's good, but I never had the patience to work on my skill. Vic, though, not only can shoot, but he can use his hands and feet, too. I figure that I could use his talents to keep my adversaries from shooting at me." He paused. "I know Reuban doesn't care for him. Says Vic is too soft. And, if I have to be honest, Vic's not like the other men. He questions my orders at times, usually coming up with another plan. Drives Reuban crazy, but Vic's alternatives usually work, so I let him get by with it. He'll harden up over time."

Alana found herself hoping not.

Marlon caught her intense look and frowned. "You sure seem to enjoy watching him," he said, suddenly resenting the interest she was showing in his best man.

She shrugged, turning away from the window. "I like martial arts."

"Do you?" Marlon suddenly grinned. "Well, then I know something you might enjoy just as much."

An hour later, Alana was hustled into the drawing room, where Duke was taking down the display of swords. "What's going on?" Alana asked Vic, who was standing a few feet away.

"Marlon and Charlie are getting ready to duel," he answered blandly.

"Duel?"

Marlon entered the room. She could see that he had changed from his black blazer into loose fitting pants and shirt. Charlie was on his heels, dressed similar.

"Come on, boss, can't this wait 'til later?" he was complaining.

"Stop whining, Charlie," Marlon snapped. "I haven't had the chance to play with the swords lately, so just get over it."

He selected a blade and took position. He pointed the saber at Alana and winked. Charlie, looking none too pleased, took his own weapon and faced Marlon.

Vic had to refrain from sighing. Alana was sitting on the couch, looking ready to snap. Vic suspected that Marlon was wanting to show off his sword fighting abilities to Alana. *So, someone's going to get hurt just so Marlon can prove a point,* he thought tiredly.

The two men went at it, their swords clashing. Alana gasped at the aggression displayed by both men. They were not holding back. *They're going to kill each other!* she thought. Her hand went to her throat when Marlon swung his blade at Charlie's head, narrowly missing it. What kind of man was he?

Suddenly, in a very skilled move, Marlon sidestepped a sweep from Charlie and slashed the other man's side. Charlie howled and Marlon made another move to flip Charlie's sword from his hand. There was instant applause.

"Good match, Charlie," he said with a grin.

Charlie stood holding his side, blood dripping from his fingers. "Yeah, thanks," he muttered.

"Duke, go get him patched up," Marlon ordered as he made his way to where a white faced Alana was sitting. He grinned. "Well, m'lady, I may not be able to shoot straight, but I can swing a sword. What'd you think?"

"You could have killed him!" she exclaimed.

"Nah." He waved a hand in dismissal. "I know when to pull back. I've never killed anyone without meaning to." Alana's wide eyed look seemed to please him. "You didn't think Vic Dane was the only one with talent around here, did you?"

Vic's face darkened slightly. "Are you done, Marlon?" he asked abruptly.

Marlon looked surprised. "Oh, yeah."

"Fine." Vic turned and walked away, his shoulders rigid.

"Gee, what did I say?" Marlon muttered.

Reuban had overheard the entire exchange and frowned darkly at Vic's retreating back.

Chapter Thirty-One

Alana fled to her room, still shaken. Now, more than ever, she was determined that she had to leave this place. True, Marlon had not killed Charlie, but she had watched the fight; she had seen what he was capable of. Marlon could have killed the other man easily.

"Oh, Lord, get me out of here," she prayed for the umpteenth time.

Later that day Alana and Felina met again to plan their escape. They talked for hours and seemed to be coming up with a workable plan when Marlon called Alana to his office. She went there with leaden steps, her heart filled with dread.

"We're going to the south, my sweet," he told Alana. "Sometime tomorrow. I'm looking forward to having you along."

Alana had to fight the panic she felt. "I don't want to be a bother," she stammered, trying to come up with a reason for why she should stay.

"No, no," Marlon insisted. "I want you to come. It'll be a good time for us to get more acquainted."

Hiding her distaste for the man, Alana had no reply. A thought came to her and she acted without thinking it through. "May Felina join us?"

Marlon cocked his head, thinking. "Hmm, yes, it might be kind of nice having her with us as well. You two get along quite well, don't you?"

Alana gave a short nod. "Yes, I think a lot of her. She's more than just a house servant." She didn't know where the last comment came from, but she was glad she said it. It was true. Felina was a person of worth, not a piece of property like Marlon thought.

"Well, I'm glad for the both of you," was all that Marlon said.

Marlon called for Felina so that he could give both of them his plans. "We're going by car," he explained. "It's rather a scenic drive, and Reuban doesn't like flying. Don't tell him I said that, or he'll have me for breakfast!" He chuckled as he talked.

Alana was sitting in a stuffed chair in the office. Felina, seated across from her, looked ready to snap with the strain she was feeling.

"So, we'll start late tomorrow afternoon, probably three o'clock," Marlon went on, oblivious to their tension. "I have a few last minute details to take care of in Chihuahua before we go. We'll probably stay the night there. I don't often make it to Chihuahua very often, so I'm looking forward to staying there for a while before we head any further. Vic will be going with us, as well as the rest of my team. You'll be familiar with them all. From Chihuahua, we'll go further south. My plant is not far from El Salto. The last town before we get to it is San Marquez."

The statement brought no comfort to Alana. Indeed, as Marlon talked, her stomach churned. She cried out to God that He would help her and Felina get a chance to break away before it was too late. If they went too far south, there would be no way for them to find their way to safety. From what she had heard, Marlon's plant was practically located in the middle of a forest, near the mountains.

Marlon rambled on for another twenty minutes before he dismissed them, his excitement causing him to fairly tremble. After they left him, Felina faced Alana, her face pale. "Alana, we can't do this!"

"Yes, we can," Alana replied firmly.

"How?"

Licking her lips, Alana thought for a moment. "Our first stop is Marlon's office in Chihuahua. Marlon said he has some business to attend to there. It's a big city. We'll wait until late that night and slip out. It shouldn't be too hard for us to find a place to hide in the streets."

"It sounds too risky."

Alana couldn't deny the feebleness of her idea, but it was all she could. They had no time to come up with anything else. "God will be with us," she said, setting her chin. "We'll be fine."

Chihuahua

"I'm afraid I haven't been able to come up with anything else as of yet, but I promise I'll keep trying."

Jason sighed in frustration, his feeling not directed at Martin, who was sitting across from him. "I haven't been able to come up with anything either," he muttered. "I feel like a lost cause. What am I supposed to do? Show her picture everywhere?"

Martin fingered the coffee mug in front of him, his expression troubled.

He had hoped to be able to give the cop some good news, and felt terrible that he couldn't. Jason looked more worried now than he had when Martin had first met him.

"Her family is back in the states, waiting for me to be able to do something for Alana," Jason went on. "How can I tell them that I don't even know why I came down here?"

"You're doing your best," Martin reminded. "And remember, you're not doing it alone. Let God lead you. Don't try to do it on your own."

The reminder was good for him. Jason nodded at the older man. "That's what I've been trying to do since this whole thing started."

"It's hard not to try to take things in your hand, especially if it's someone you really care about."

His throat feeling tight, Jason could see Alana's face in his mind. How he longed to see her again! The desire to hold her in his arms was so strong that he could not think of anything else. He was not himself anymore, all due to the absence of a particular young woman from his life.

"We'll get through this, Jason," Martin encouraged.

Jason thanked God silently for the missionary. In just the short time he had come to know him, he felt that he had gained a friend. Martin's wise council was what he needed with the absence of his pastor and friends right now.

"The good news is that I've had my phone hooked up again," Martin told him.

Jason did not seem to hear him. "The longer it takes," he murmured, "the harder it is to find someone."

"That's true," Martin admitted. "But, don't lose heart. Go home and get your Bible. Read it until you feel better. In all my years down here, I've had some rough times, and in those times I grab my Bible. Sometimes I read for hours at a time until I feel that my God is bigger than my problems. It'll work the same way for you. Find a verse and claim it as your own. When you feel yourself getting low again, think of your verse."

Jason took the older man's advice when he went back to his hotel. He pulled his worn Bible from his pack. Settling down on the bed, he opened the Book and read. He lost track of the time as he lost himself in the word. Passages of God's mercy and grace called to him. He began reading out loud, letting the words soak in. At times tears blurred his vision, but as he continued reading, he felt release. Martin was right. It was just what he had needed to keep him on the right track.

Monday, April 22nd

The phone rang in the room, waking Jason up from sleep. He had no idea how long he been sleeping, and felt disoriented for a moment while reaching for the receiver.

"What was the last name of these two men you're looking for?"

Rubbing his eyes, Jason tried to focus on Martin's question. "Romano," he mumbled, staring at the clock. Was it eight-thirty already?

"Hmm," Martin's murmur met his ear.

"Why?" Jason asked, reaching for his shirt.

"I thought of a pair of guys that have an office here in the City. I don't know why I didn't think of them before. The older brother's name is Marlon."

Jason stilled his movements. "Does he have a young brother?"

"Yeah, but I don't know if I've ever got his name. The problem is, their last name is Ferraro, not Romano."

Biting his lip, Jason's mind spun. He did not want to jump to conclusions. The chances were pretty slim that these were the guys he was looking for. "Where's their office?"

Marlon gave him directions. "It won't be hard to find. The Ferraros are pretty known around here, some of the richest businessmen."

Jason thanked the man and hung up, praying that he was going in the right direction this time.

It was unbearably hot in the jeep. Alana fanned herself with her hand, wishing she had more room to stretch. She was crammed in the back seat with Felina and Buddy White, who was snoring loudly in her right ear. Alana was glad when the jeep stopped and Marlon and Vic stepped out. A few minutes later, Marlon opened the door and escorted her up a few steps into a tall, red stone building.

"This is my temporary home," Marlon explained. "I hate staying in hotels, so I keep this house for when I have to stay in Chihuahua. What do you think?'

"Nice," Alana answered, not really caring what the place looked like. She was more interested in studying the layout. The main door was facing the street and the house was set in a quiet area, just south of the city. There was not a lot of activity here, but there *were* plenty of scraggly bushes and buildings. These would cast dark shadows in the evening, perfect for staying out of sight when she and Felina tried to slip out of the house later.

Marlon showed Alana to her room, stating that his room was right across the hall. Felina's room was next door to Alana's.

Everything's looking good so far, she thought to herself.

After a while, Marlon told Alana, "Reuban, Vic, and I have to go to the office to pack a few things up. We'll be back later tonight."

Alana nodded, trying to appear calm, even as her pulse raced. Maybe her chance to run would come sooner than later. She stiffened when he bent down and kissed her lightly across the lips.

"I'll see you tonight," he whispered, a frightening glint in his eye. "Don't you be trying to get away from me, because you know it won't work."

Alana's heart quickened. She was relieved when he left without another word.

Vic stood watching as freight was loaded into Marlon's jeep by Mexican associates. The boxes contained supplies for the plant down south. Vic shifted his weight as the men worked, growing restless.

Marlon and Reuban were inside, still making plans and doing some last-minute paperwork. With a deep breath, Vic turned his gaze to the street, watching cars pass and people go about their business. His attention was drawn to a man on the other side of the street who was watching the activity in front of the office intently. Vic observed the onlooker inconspicuously. When the Mexican man in charge of the loading went to talk to the Ferraros, Vic slipped away.

It had taken longer than Martin thought for Jason to find the office. By the time he had, the sun was high in the sky and scorching hot. Debating what to do next, Jason had stood on the opposite side of the street, wondering what move he should make. His first instinct was to go in there and demand they return Alana, but common sense overruled. There was no actual evidence that these were the men he was even looking for.

Just when he had decided to at least go inside, a dark jeep pulled up in front. Jason watched as Spanish men poured from the office, and boxes and crates were loaded into the jeep. His view of the door was blocked by the jeep and he could not see who entered or exited the office. The only man he got a good look at was a rather short, broad man with dark hair, who was apparently overlooking the loading. He did not look at all familiar to Jason.

Sighing, Jason stepped back a bit more into the shadows, thinking that this was getting him nowhere. Deciding to move down the sidewalk a little, he figured he would try to get a good look at the men. It was a long shot, but all he could do at this point.

Feeling the hair on his neck tingling, Jason was suddenly aware of someone standing behind him. Forcing himself to act casual, he glanced over his shoulder and found a man staring at him, his black gaze unnervingly piercing. It was the same man who had just moments before had been standing in front of the office.

"Is there a reason you find the doings of the Ferraros so interesting?" the broad shouldered man asked him, his voice soft but there was a hint of steel that Jason did not miss.

Shrugging nonchalantly, Jason replied lazily. "I thought everyone around here was interested in what the Ferraros are doing."

Vic narrowed his eyes at him, finding the tall man hard to read. Light blue eyes stared unflinchingly back at Vic. "For future reference," he spoke low, "you may want move on." He leaned forward slightly. "The Ferraros don't like nosy people."

Jason waited a long moment before nodding slowly. "I'll keep that in mind."

Vic backed off slowly after another long look. Jason did not move until the man was gone, then exhaled deeply. He looked back at the jeep to see the man climb in and drive off. In the strange confrontation, Jason had missed his chance to get a look at the Ferraros.

It was dark now. The sun had set less than an hour ago, and Marlon still had not returned.

"Okay, God," Alana whispered, standing at her window. "Show me what to do now."

She had been heartened at the few men that Marlon had left behind here. She guessed that he felt comfortable that she would not try to escape from here. Her mind moved quickly as she went in search of Felina. The girl was sitting alone in her room.

"Are you ready?" Alana asked.

Felina's eyes widened. "Now?"

"Yes, we won't have a better chance than this. There's a side door off the main hall that leads outside. We can slip out there."

"What about the others?"

"I think Marlon is feeling pretty comfortable with me right now," Alana told her. "He doesn't think I'll run, especially in a strange place like this. There are not very men here and I think we can slip past them."

Taking a deep breath, Felina nodded, still looking unsure. She trusted

Alana, though, and followed.

Alana grasped Felina's hand. "Let's go."

Moving as quietly and quickly as they could, the girls slipped down the stairs. They halted at one point with their backs pressed against the wall when Manley stepped into view. He soon left and they went on.

Apparently, the guards were immersed in cards, not overly concerned with the two girls who were supposed to be upstairs. Alana and Felina would have to creep right past the open door to get to the side door—the side door that would lead outside and to freedom. Putting a finger up to her lips, Alana motioned for Felina to go first.

Her face stark white, Felina slowly and silently made her way past the door. Alana feared that she would take too much time in passing and would be spotted, but Felina made it safely to the other side. Alana quickly followed, holding her breath and listening for the sound of angry shouts and running feet. There were none.

Getting the door open without making any noise was going to be tricky. Alana worked with the door handle inch by inch, sweat trickling down her back. With every second that passed, her nerves drew tighter and tighter. Once the handle was turned, she began working the door open. At that moment, a dog started barking across the street. She took advantage of the extra noise and pulled the door open.

The girls slipped out into the dusky street. Alana carefully pulled the door to again, reached for Felina's hand, and led her into the shadows. Both were panting with exertion. So far, everything was going well. If only they could put some distance between themselves and Marlon's townhouse. Then they could take to the shadows. The city was big. Surely they could hide from Marlon and his men in such a large area.

"What do you mean they're gone?" Marlon growled, a white light in his eye.

Buddy hesitated before going on. "We found their rooms empty just a little while ago."

"How long ago?" Reuban asked.

"Less than an hour."

Marlon's lips came up in an angry snarl. "I want you all out on the streets, and you had better come back with them. There's no telling how long they've been out there."

Buddy nodded, anxious to escape Marlon's rage. "Yes, sir."

Chapter Thirty-Two

It seemed like hours had passed. Alana and Felina had no idea where they were going, except that they wanted to get as far from Marlon as they could. The night was quiet; few people were out. They stayed away from streetlights as much as they could. Alana was just beginning to hope that their plan had worked when she heard a vehicle approaching.

"Felina, in here," she urged, pulling Felina to the shadows between two shops. They watched Marlon's jeep drive by slowly, Buddy White at the wheel. Alana could hear Felina's sharp breath intake.

"It's okay, Felina," she assured. "Let's keep going."

They went on a bit further, but another jeep cut across in front of them. Alana also spotted Manley Elam on foot across the street. They had not gotten as far as she had hoped. If the men were scouring the area, it would not be long before they spotted the two girls.

"Let's split up," she suggested.

"What?" Felina gasped.

"They'll find us faster if we stay together. We have more of a chance of getting away going alone. You can do it, Felina."

Felina was shaking in terror, but she nodded shortly. "I will pray that you escape," she told her.

Alana was moved. "And I will pray for you," she whispered, touching Felina's arm.

Alana moved away from her friend, in the direction they had just come from. She could see Felina's form fleeing into the shadows. "Lord, please help her," Alana whispered.

The sky was black as tar, the air hot and dry, even though the sun had been gone for a few hours. Jason strolled silently, not really paying attention to what was around him. His mind was full of Alana.

Where was she? It had been several days since he had come here looking for her. He knew that he was going to have to be patient and take things slow, but not knowing where she could be just about killed him.

He still planned on checking out the Ferraro office. Something about the activity that he had witnessed earlier stuck with him. He had no idea what they were doing, but their bodyguard had sure seemed displeased to find Jason watching them. Maybe they had something to hide. Was it Alana?

He paused and looked up at the sky, the moon just a sliver. With a deep sigh, he turned to go on. Only two steps later he was nearly floored by a small figure that crashed into him. On reflex, his hands went out and gripped the shoulders.

There was a small cry from the girl in his grasp. Her wide, dark eyes peered at him from beneath her shawl, and he could see that she was terrified.

"Please, let me go!" she begged. "They'll catch me! Don't let them find me!"

Her voice was trembling, and she was rambling in her fear.

"Calm down, no one is going to hurt you," Jason soothed. "What's wrong?"

The girl looked over her shoulder. "They're coming! They're going to find me and kill me!" She was on the verge of hysteria.

Jason squinted his eyes in the direction she was looking. The darkness made it hard to see, but he could barely detect a group moving in their direction. The sound of their agitated voices fell on his ear.

"Here, come over here," he said quickly, moving her to a side door of a closed business. He stood her in the doorway, and then leaned against the wall before her, effectively blocking her view from anyone in the street.

About five or six men emerged from the darkness, several of them cursing loudly. A couple glanced at Jason, but for the most part, he was ignored. He watched them go down the street; they were obviously looking for someone, and they certainly did not seem to have reasonable intentions. When they had disappeared, he turned back to the frightened girl.

"They're gone."

She shook her head, her face white even in the darkness. "They'll be back. They'll find me. And then Heaven help me if they do!"

Jason could hear more voices in the distance. He had no idea what to do, but he could not leave this girl out here if she was in danger of some kind. "Why are they after you?"

"Because I escaped."

Taking a deep breath, Jason made a quick decision. He took his coat off and handed it to her. "Put this around you, and hide your face. I'll take you someplace where they can't find you."

"Oh, Gracias, Senor," she breathed, taking his jacket.

"Just hurry. I hear more voices coming."

When she was sufficiently covered, Jason put his arm around her and led her from the alley. He made sure not to walk in the light of the street lamps, but moved quickly to his hotel room. He was relieved that the clerk was not at his counter, so as not to face curious questions.

Taking the girl to his room, Jason offered her a chair. He went to the window and looked down at the street. He could still see men moving about. *How did I get into this?* he wondered. He was here to find Alana. He could not afford to get tied up in something else that could take time out of his search. He had barely escaped trouble with the confrontation earlier that day with the Ferraros' watch dog. And now this.

He needed some answers. He turned and leaned against the wall, staring at the girl. She seemed to be in shock now.

"Can you tell me your name?" he asked softly.

She looked up at him dumbly. "Felina. Felina Gomez."

"Felina, why were you running?"

Felina began breathing rapidly, her fear overtaking her. "I have been trapped for too long. I cannot go back to that house. I can't! Not after I've gotten so close to getting away." She clasped her hands together.

"You're safe now. How did you escape?"

"I couldn't do it alone," she went on, still sounding breathless. "We went together. But we got separated. I don't know what happened to her."

She was still not making any sense. Jason could see that she was very much upset and scared. He let her talk, hoping that by releasing her turbulent thoughts, she would calm down.

"It was her idea, and I was the one to get away." Felina shook her head. "I don't know what happened to her. She was just behind me. She turned off of Manchez Street, and I went on First." She paused and bit her lip, completely forgetting where she was. "Oh, Alana, I hope you've made it to safety!" she whispered.

Jason jumped to attention. "What did you say?" he demanded, his voice harsh.

Felina stared up at him, startled. His fierce expression alarmed her. What if he was not as he seemed? How did she know that he did not work for Marlon in some way? She had just given Alana away!

The fact made her lose what little strength she had left. "Oh, no!" she cried, coming to her feet. "Please, don't take me back to Marlon, please!"

Marlon. The man he was searching for! Jason shook his head abruptly and stepped forward. "Felina—"

"I'll go back on my own!" Felina continued. She backed up, her hands before her in defense. "Just don't hurt me! And don't hurt Alana! Please!"

Jason realized how threatening he must have appeared. Even though his whole being screamed for him to demand Felina to tell what she knew, he knew he had to assure her first that she was safe.

"I don't work for Marlon," he said, working to keep his voice calm. "I would never hurt you or Alana. I am a friend of Alana's from Kansas. I came down here looking for her. I'm her friend."

Felina stared at him wildly. "A friend?"

Jason nodded, his face beseeching. "How do you know her?"

She was still unsure. "How can I be sure you are telling me the truth?"

Trying to be patient, Jason strained his brain to come up with a way to convince Felina. "I'm a cop. Jason Banks?"

Felina's face suddenly relaxed. "Jason. She has told me about you."

He had to fight the sudden desire to cry. Alana was still alive! "What can you tell me?"

Felina sat down, still feeling weak. "We escaped Marlon together. She had convinced me to come with her. We left his town house, where we were all staying tonight. The men were getting louder, so we knew they were getting close. She suggested we separate so that it would harder to find both of us. I told her I would pray she escaped, and she said she would do the same for me." Her face crumpled.

"Where did you see her last, Felina?" Jason asked.

"Turning on Manchez Street. Just a little while ago."

Manchez Street! Just a little while ago! "Felina, stay here! Don't let anyone come in until you hear me. Okay?"

Felina nodded. "Please find her, Senor. I fear for her safety if Marlon catches her again."

Jason left without a word, his heart in his throat. The blood pounded in his ears as he thundered down the sidewalk in the direction of Manchez Street. She was just a little ways away! *Please, God! Let me find her before they do!*

Alana panted for breath as she ducked behind a dumpster. Vic and his men had been just a little ways behind her. She waited until she heard their footsteps again before she went a little further in the alley. On the other end, she could see another street. If she could only get there!

There was a crash behind her and she stifled a gasp. Manley Elam was peering into the darkness. After a moment, he and Duke walked in, shining their flashlights back and forth.

Her pulse racing, Alana knew she would have to make a run for it. They would find her if she stayed where she was. Jumping up, she bolted for the other end.

"There she is!" Manley roared taking off after her.

Alana whimpered as she ran, mustering as much speed as she could. She was only a few yards from the opening when Reuban suddenly blocked her way. Sliding to a stop, she wailed, "No!"

The expression of outrage on Reuban's face sent a chill down her spine. He reached out and grabbed her by the hair, pulling her head back unnaturally. She cried out in his hold.

"I don't know why I shouldn't just kill you right here!" he snarled, his eyes wide. "You've caused us way too much trouble."

Alana clutched at his hands, but his hold only tightened, making her wince in pain.

Vic appeared from the darkness, his dark eyes taking in the sight. Sounding rather bored, he said, "Let's let Marlon do that himself, Reuban."

That man growled and let go. Alana fell to her knees, feeling as if her scalp had been pulled from the roots. Reuban reached down and grabbed her arm, roughly pulling her to her feet. "Let's go!" he snapped, his fingers digging into her elbow. "And no noise, either, or your precious friend will get twice what you get when we catch her!"

Alana didn't make a sound as she was forced to go with Reuban. Tears streamed down her face, though, as she thought of how close she had come to freedom. She could only hope that Felina would not be caught.

"You take her back to the house," Reuban snapped to Vic after Alana was safely in the jeep. "I'm gonna look around for the other one. I'll walk back in a little while." He sent her a scathing look. "I'm rather eager to see how Marlon handles this one."

Vic only nodded and climbed behind the wheel. He was anxious to get Alana back to the house and away from Reuban's hot temper.

Jason was only two blocks away when he heard a strangled scream cut through the night air. He bolted in that direction. The sound of a car revving up met his ears and he rounded a bend just as a green jeep drove away from Manchez Street. Jason searched the area frantically. He called for Alana, no longer caring who might hear him.

"She was just here!" he moaned, exhaustion and despair bringing him to his knees. He looked upward. "Oh, God. I was so close!"

Marlon was coldly silent as Alana was led back through the town house and straight to his bedroom. He pushed her inside, turned to say something in Spanish to the maid, then closed the door.

Alana was not prepared for the savage, backhanded slap across the face. The force of the hit was so strong that it literally knocked her onto the bed. A scream escaped her lips as he leapt on top of her, grabbing her by the throat with one hand as he straddled her. His iron-like grip cut off her airway and he leaned over her, a cold fire blazing in his eyes.

"You disappoint me, Alana," he ground out. "You've cost me valuable time and now your friend will be facing a very harsh punishment, thanks to your influence. I hope you're happy with the choices that you've made. Let's just hope *she* can live with it!"

Alana gagged for air and felt the world darkening. He let go of her neck and pushed himself off the bed, still eyeing her cruelly. "We'll settle this later. I can promise you that."

The man left, slamming the door behind him. Alana touched her bruised neck, her throat feeling as if it was going to cave in. There was a sudden flashback in her mind of Jason Banks, right after Jack Norris had attacked her outside of *Darings'*. Concerned that she had been hurt, Jason's touch on her neck had been so gentle, so soft.

"Oh, God!" she sobbed hoarsely. "I need him here!" As she lay there in pain, she knew that it was not for his protection that she wished for him to be at her side. She needed his calm assurance, his endearing smile, his gentle touch.

"I wish he could find me!" she whispered painstakingly, rolling in a fetal position. "I wish he could save me!"

Chapter Thirty-Three

As soon as Jason was sure that Alana was not in the area, he called Martin on his cell phone. The man agreed to come to his hotel room at once. Jason needed his support. After coming so close to finding Alana, he wanted to beat the air at missing her. He rushed back to the hotel room. It took a few minutes for him to convince the girl that it was him knocking. When he entered the room, he was desperate for some answers.

"Is she all right?" he had to know.

Felina bit her lip. "She is strong," she said. "A survivor. As of yet, no harm had come to her. But I fear what Marlon will do to her if he finds her."

"Marlon?" Jason repeated. "Marlon Romano?"

She shook her head. "No, Marlon Ferraro."

This was the very man Martin had told him about earlier. The man that Jason had tried to get a glimpse of in front of their office building. Jason took a calming breath, his whole body trembling with the emotions that he was trying so hard to contain. "Does he have a brother named Reuban?"

"Yes."

Jason stood up abruptly and turned from her, his back rigid in tension.

He had been right. Marlon Romano was behind her abduction, linked somehow with Jack Norris, who at the moment seemed to have dropped from the picture. *I should have known that someone with such a criminal record would change his name.* "What does Marlon want with her?" he asked.

The silence spoke volumes and Jason clenched his fists, still keeping his back to her, trying hard not to frighten her. He was relieved at the knock on his door, signifying Martin's arrival.

Felina, however, looked alarmed.

"Don't worry," Jason assured her. "It's a friend."

Martin entered in, glancing at the girl inside, and then focusing his attention on Jason.

"She knows Alana. They tried to escape from Marlon just a while ago," Jason informed, his jaw clenched. "I looked for Alana, but there was no sign of her."

Martin widened his eyes. Then he took a deep breath and spoke to Felina in Spanish. She relaxed and rattled off a long sentence in reply.

"What did she say?" Jason asked.

"This Marlon is not staying in town long. He's apparently on a business trip and had intended on taking the girls with him. They're heading south."

"Oh, no," Jason breathed.

"Near the western border," Felina said in English. "Marlon runs a plant down there and he was going to visit it."

"Do you know exactly where it is?" Jason demanded.

Felina shook her head regretfully. "I'm sorry, Senor. I've never been there."

Fighting hard hold his emotions in check, Jason grabbed a chair and set it by Felina. He took a seat across from her on the bed. Martin stood in the background, quiet, but there if they needed him.

Jason took a deep breath. "I need to know everything," he said almost afraid of what he was about to find out. "From the moment you met her."

Felina took a deep breath and licked her lips. "I met Alana less than two weeks ago. Even then, I knew there was something very different about her..."

Jason knew that he had to get Felina out of the hotel, but he had no idea where to take her. From what Felina told him, this Marlon had many friends in the area, and there was no telling who he could trust.

Thank you, Lord, he prayed then and there, feeling like he was on emotional overload. He wanted to cry, laugh, and yell all at the same time. *Thank you for allowing Felina to run into me. At least there's one girl out of Marlon's hold. Now, help me find Alana and get her away from him before he hurts her. Show me what to do now.*

Jason turned around and studied the Mexican girl, who was looking more exhausted by the minute. "Martin has a mission that he said you can stay at for the night," he told her, making a quick decision. "You'll be safe there."

Reuban scoured the street for a sign of a feminine figure trying to flee. He stomped up the sidewalk, back to the area where they had found Alana. Maybe Felina was still in the area.

He paused when he detected movement, his eyes peering in the dark. He saw a silhouette, but it was too large and broad to be Felina. Watching the shadow suspiciously, Reuban saw that it was a man. "Probably some drunk stumbling over his own feet," he muttered. He soon found this not to be the case, though, when the man stood up and began walking steadily.

Something made Reuban follow him, even though he was sure he was wasting time. The stranger, still shrouded in darkness pulled out a cell phone and talked excitedly for a moment before picking up speed. Reuban traced his steps to the hotel, and then waited. A few minutes later another man arrived, parking his beat up Volvo next to the hotel. He looked agitated as he mounted the few steps. Then all was still.

Growing impatient, Reuban frowned and wondered why he had followed the man to begin with. "Forget it," he muttered, tossing a rock to the ground. At that moment, the two men reappeared, this time with a third person. This one was small and covered with a jacket of some kind so he couldn't see the face.

Reuban watched them all enter the Volvo, casting anxious looks all around. The older man took his seat behind the wheel and drove off, leaving only the tall one behind. That man watched them leave, then slowly disappeared back into the building.

Stepping out of the shadows, Reuban cocked his jaw, thinking. *Looks like our little Felina got herself some help.*

Tuesday, April 23rd

She must have fallen asleep through her tears. Stirring and fighting against the darkness, Alana tried to figure out why her neck was hurting. Her attempt to escape and Marlon's violent reaction came to her rudely and her eyes popped open. She stifled a gasp as her gaze fell on Marlon, sleeping soundly beside her.

Her heart pounding against her ribs, Alana turned her head slowly, trying to figure out how she could get out of the bedroom before he awakened. She licked dry lips as she studied the door, measuring how many steps she could make on tiptoe. She was repulsed at the idea that she had shared a bed with this man. Apparently he had joined her after she had fallen asleep.

The mattress moved just then and she felt an arm close around her. Her head swiveled back to see his eyes resting on hers thoughtfully.

"Good morning, my sweet," he greeted.

"Morning," Alana returned breathlessly, making a move to get up.

"No, I don't think so," Marlon denied, tightening his hold on her. She stiffened as he settled her closer to him. "Our little escapade last night has disrupted my plans," he went on, as calmly as if he was talking about the weather. "I had so hoped that you would come to realize that I mean you no harm. If you only did as I wanted, you could live in peace. Felina had been content the way she was, until you filled her head with nonsense. Poor thing is a hopeless cause, now."

Alana's heart sank as she thought of the penalty her friend must have faced. Marlon would have surely killed her. It was all her fault. Why had she talked the frightened girl into trying to flee this man?

Marlon rose up on one elbow, leaning over her threateningly. "I've decided, that since you had no more respect for my consideration, I cannot allow you to be in charge anymore."

Alana's eyes widened in fear.

"I'm not waiting for you to come to your senses," Marlon said, his voice low, his hand sliding up her arm. He dropped his head and swiftly cut off her call for help with his forceful kiss.

Jason met with Martin early that morning and asked about Felina.

"She's been very quiet," Martin told him. "She looks like she's been crying, too. I think she's feeling guilty that she couldn't help you more."

Feeling responsible for her now, Jason went in search of her. He found the girl sitting by herself outside the back door of the mission. Her eyes did look suspiciously red. Jason grabbed a chair and pulled it close to hers. "How are you this morning?" he asked.

Felina pursed her lips. "Trying to figure out why I was rescued while Alana had to be caught."

Jason bent his head, trying to come up with an answer. "We don't always know why things happen the way they do," he said thoughtfully. "We just have to trust God to be in control."

"She talked about God a lot."

Jason could not stop the smile that touched his lips as he remembered the love Alana had for the Lord. "That doesn't surprise me," he murmured, thankful that that much, at least, had not changed.

"Her prayers worked."

"Hmm?" Jason looked up.

Felina sighed, her expression sad. "I told her I would pray she escaped. She said she would do the same. Her prayers worked. Mine did not."

Jason spoke slowly, collecting his thoughts. "Maybe He answered hers for a reason. He has a purpose for getting you out of there before her. I don't know what. That's only for you to figure out, with God's help."

Her face crumpled. "But I don't deserve another chance."

"None of us do," Jason replied. "He loves us enough to give us another chance anyway."

Felina fell apart then, burying her face in her hands and sobbing. Jason moved his chair closer and put his arm around her, pulling her into a gentle embrace. It was true that he had only known her for a few hours, but their intense link with Alana made that seem unimportant. All that mattered now was that Felina needed to know that God loved her.

The morning had passed by in a flurry of activity. Marlon had decided to leave earlier than he had originally planned, partially because of the incident the night before. He was anxious to get Alana away from the city. He barked out orders in rapid succession, not waiting to see if they were followed. Shortly before six o'clock, they were back on the road, heading south.

Alana sat, once again, in the back seat with Buddy White, but this time she was lacking Felina's presence by her side. Alana's heart ached for the girl, feeling guilt weighing down on her for talking Felina into trying to escape. Why hadn't Alana learned from all of her prior failed attempts that to try again would only bring trouble?

I'm sorry, Felina, Alana mourned, believing with all her heart that Marlon had found the girl and done away with her. *I only hope you had time to find God before...*

Leaning weakly against the window, Alana felt bruised and battered in spirit, body, and mind. She was not the same girl she had been in Kansas. Her innocence had been shattered. Her dignity stripped. Her faith sorely tested. Marlon had taken it all from her. She knew now how Felina had felt. She was a possession, a plaything for Marlon—nothing more.

Shutting her eyes against the memories of earlier that morning, Alana tried to pray but found she could not. Her soul was drained and hurting. Indeed, it would take a long time for her to heal now, if she ever could.

Chapter Thirty-Four

It wasn't until seven that morning before Martin tracked down the location of Marlon Ferraro's townhouse. He insisted on accompanying Jason, though the cop was adamantly against it.

"I don't know what's going to happen," Jason explained.

"Exactly, you need someone to watch your back."

Against his better judgment, Jason finally acceded. They drove within a block of the house, Jason's heart squeezing in his chest all the while. He prayed fervently, even desperately, that this would be the end of his search, that he would find Alana.

The place was quiet, too quiet. There were no vehicles around, no movement. Jason prowled around the area looking for some evidence that there was life inside. He was sorely tempted to break in with his pistol and demand that Alana be returned to him.

"Let me knock," Martin suggested. "I'll pretend I'm gathering donations for the mission."

Ready to try anything, Jason acceded, following Martin closely.

The missionary rapped loudly and waited, his head cocked as he listened for any noise within. A tall, bid-boned Mexican woman answered. "*Si?*" she asked, staring down at them suspiciously.

"Yes, Senor Ferraro?" Martin requested.

"He is not here," she returned in heavily accented English. "He is away on business trip."

Jason felt his insides squeezing.

"Is there anyone I can speak with?" Martin inquired. "It's very important."

Shaking her dark head, the woman answered, "No, Senor. Only hired staff is here. Anyone you would wish to speak to is with Senor Ferraro."

"Does that include Alana Crewe?" Jason blurted.

"I do not know, Senor." The woman did not wait any longer, but shut the door in their faces, anxious to be left alone.

Jason gritted his teeth and descended the steps.

"Jason," Martin called. "We'll find her."

"How? If Marlon's already taken her down south, there's no telling where she is!"

Martin had no reply, and Jason turned away, closing his eyes in frustration. Once again, he had hit a brick wall.

The vehicle turned a corner and Alana felt her heart rate pick up at the large building they were approaching. The sprawling *Darings'* supermarket stood before her like a beacon.

"Now, there's no use in trying to get away in here," Marlon was saying. "Half the employees know me personally, not to mention the manager's a good friend of mine. Besides, my men will be standing at every exit, so don't even think about it."

Alana nodded absently, not really hearing him. In her mind, she was reviewing everything she knew about *Darings'* business and the stores they had opened in other countries. She now knew where she was in Mexico, as there was only one store in the country at the moment.

The group entered the building, and Alana could instantly see the similarities between her store in Edwardsville and this Mexican store. The only difference was the employees. Most greeted Marlon heartily, anxious to please the wealthy man. Others looked from afar, too intimidated to approach.

Marlon and Vic immediately busied themselves with buying supplies for their trip down south. Reuban had disappeared to another part of the store, and Alana could not see any of Marlon's men. While Marlon's back was turned, she slipped away quietly, her mind moving quickly.

She did not head for the exit doors. Marlon's men would be on top of her in an instant if she did. That would only bring her more pain and heartache. Instead, she found a manager in the grocery area. Lifting her chin slightly, she tried to make herself appear confident and sure of herself, even though she was shaking inside.

"English?" she inquired.

"*Si,* Senorita," the dark man smiled. "What is you need?"

Alana crossed her arms and pursed her lips. "I'm looking for something that I was sure your store would have, but I can't seem to find it."

"What is that, ma'am?"

Alana swallowed. "Pickled carrots."

The man blanched slightly. "Um, pickled carrots?"

Rolling her eyes exaggeratedly, Alana said, "Yes! I need some by next week, and I want to know why you don't have any!"

"Well, ma'am, to be honest, we don't carry that product."

With a loud sigh, Alana muttered, "I knew it was too much to hope that you would. However," she raised her voice. "I do happen to know that *Darings'* is supposed to do everything in their power to please their customers. Correct?"

"*Si,* Senorita." The manager was beginning to look nervous.

"Well, I happen to know of only one store that carries pickled carrots," Alana explained, making herself sound more than a little irritated. "I want you to call that store, speak to the manager himself, no one else." She stared at the man before her. "He's the only one that I've ever dealt with before now about this product. He will know what you're talking about."

Nodding his dark head, the man asked, "What do you want me to call him for, ma'am?"

"Good grief, man!" Alana spat. "*Darings'* stores contact each other all over the country if they need a product that they are out of at the moment. I want you to call the store in Edwardsville, Kansas, speak to the manager, Dick Browning," she pronounced his name pointedly, "and order a case of pickled carrots."

"The Kansas store?" he squeaked.

"Yes!" Alana exclaimed. She stepped closer to him, narrowing her eyes. "And when I come back next week, I better hear that you've made the call. I happen to be in the company of one Marlon Ferraro, and I would hate to see him displeased with the service I receive."

The manager nodded, his eyes wide. It was clear he knew the man.

"I am sure you want to keep your job. Correct?"

"*Si,* Senorita. I will call now."

"Good," Alana smiled victoriously. "I want a case by next week. Don't forget." Her tone became stern and her gaze hardened. She turned on her heel and walked away. She could hear the man rambling in Spanish behind her.

With her heart pounding, Alana dashed to the stationary aisle. She picked up a book and pretended to be looking through it. Closing her eyes tightly, she took a deep breath, hoping that her ploy would work.

"Alana!" Marlon's outraged voice made her jump. "What do you think you're doing?"

Alana looked up at his angry face. Vic was standing behind him. "I lost you somewhere," she said haltingly. "So I came over here to look at the books until you found me. I never could have found my way through this store. I'd have gotten lost for sure."

Marlon's face seemed to relax, but he still looked suspicious.

"I wasn't trying to run, Marlon," Alana added. "I know it wouldn't have done any good."

This won a smile. "No, it wouldn't have," he agreed. He took her hand and entwined his fingers through hers. "I'm glad to see that you've finally realized that." He led her away, leaving Vic behind them, his eyes narrowed thoughtfully.

Edwardsville

"Dick, there's a call for you," Pamela called the manager. "It's from the store in Mexico," she added, looking bewildered.

"Mexico?" Dick repeated as he took the phone. "This is different."

The man on the other side spoke with a thick accent, and sounded flustered.

"Senor, I am sorry to have bothered you in your work," he said, "but I had a very important customer who is in need of a product that we don't carry. She wanted me to call and order the product from you."

"Okay, sure." Holding the receiver between his ear and shoulder, Dick grabbed a pad of paper and pen. "What is it?"

"Well, she said she wanted a case of…pickled carrots."

Dick grabbed the receiver before it fell. "She wanted what?" he practically yelled. Pamela started, staring at him in bewilderment for his tone.

The man sounded startled as well. "I am sorry for the trouble, Senor," he stammered. "But she insisted, and I feared for my job, and—"

"No," Dick interrupted. "Who was she?"

"I do not know her name."

"What did she look like?" Dick pressed. "Tell me!"

"Well, she was young, and-and, um, I don't know, Senor!" he cried. "I did not talk to her for long. Do you have the product?"

"No, it doesn't exist, but—"

"Then I am sorry for the trouble." The sound of a click met Dick's ears.

"No, don't hang up!" Dick shouted. He did not care who was around him. Customers and associates alike were staring at him.

"Dick, what's wrong?" Pamela whispered.

Dick slammed the phone down. He ran his hands through his hair. "I don't believe this!" he murmured.

"What?"

Dick finally looked at her. "I think I just got a message from Alana."

"What?" Pamela exclaimed.

With a short nod, Dick began walking away. "I've got to call Captain Wade."

Chihuahua

Martin left the room to answer a call. Jason sat with head bowed, praying silently as he waited for Martin to return. Alana was in Mexico. He knew this for a fact, but he was no longer sure what part of Mexico she was in. Felina had no idea where this plant was that Marlon was taking her to. So here Jason sat, maybe hours from where Alana was, and unable to do a thing.

"Hey, Jason!" Martin called from the other room.

"Yeah?" Jason asked, looking up blearily.

"I just got a call from Kenneth," Martin said as he made an appearance.

Jason sat up. "You did? About what?"

Martin sounded out of breath as he talked, his hands moving animatedly. "Alana just snuck a message to the store she worked at in Kansas."

Standing to his feet, Jason gasped. "She what?"

"It's true. I don't understand it all, but it was some kind of joke between her and her manager. She somehow finagled someone from the Mexican store to call Kansas about it." Martin's face was lit with a wide smile with the wonder of it all.

"The Mexican store?" Jason repeated.

Martin nodded with a smile. "Yes, in Los Diablos."

Jason let his head fall back as a huge sigh burst through his lips. "Thank You, Lord," he whispered, feeling his throat tighten in his emotion. "Thank You for letting me know that she's still all right for now. And thank You for giving me a direction."

Alana had no idea if her idea would actually work. All she could do was hope that her message would get to Dick in Kansas. She didn't know what the authorities in the States could do if they knew she was in Mexico, but at least they would have a clue where to start. If the message even got to Dick and if he figured out where it came from. And if the message wasn't too late.

Marlon seemed none the wiser about her secret, for which she was thankful. She figured he thought she had finally resigned herself to not being able to escape his grasp. In addition, he was determined to reach El Salto, soon, and thus was preoccupied.

The ride to San Marquez was long and tiring. With every passing mile, Alana knew her chances of escape were growing dimmer and dimmer. There had been a time that the thought would have filled her with dread and fear, but those feelings were old to her now. She had never thought one could get used to being in constant danger, but that's how she felt now. Her worst fears had been realized. Marlon took what he wanted from her. The only other thing he could do to her now was take her life.

Maybe that wouldn't be so bad, she thought dully. *At least this nightmare would be over.*

As soon as she thought of it, though, she disregarded it. She wanted to see her family again. She had dreams and goals she still hoped to fulfill. More than that, she still felt that God was in control and He was walking ahead of her, smoothing every wrinkle in the path.

Staring out the window at the passing trees, Alana felt her spirit quicken within her. It did not matter how she felt or what Marlon did to her. She would never give up. Until her last breath, she would fight to get away from him, to be free again.

Free. She would forever understand the true meaning of the word now. To be free from Marlon, from his cruel ways—that was her goal now. It was more than that, though, she realized. While she was held captive in body, her spirit was still free. Marlon could not take that from her. Her heavenly Father held her in his hands at all time, and no one, not Marlon, Reuban, or even Jack Norris, could take her from God's grasp.

Alana closed her eyes, her body slowly relaxing against the seat. This fact comforted her more than anything. God hadn't changed. He never would. That truth was so soothing in the midst of a scary world.

She had changed, though. Sitting back, still watching the landscape go by, Alana contemplated the changes. She remembered the conversation she had had with her Bible study group those long few weeks ago. The topic of assault had been brought up. The girls had wondered what they would do in a situation such as that. Alana no longer wondered. Even in the face of danger, she fought to survive.

She had learned a new dependence on God, like none she had ever known. Not knowing if she was ever going to get back home caused her to lean on

Him completely, realizing that He was all she had. He was all she needed.

Not all the changes were good, she knew. Even though she tried to stay positive, at times she grew very pessimistic about ever getting free. Indeed, it would take a miracle. How many times had she tried to escape? And how many times had she failed? It would have to be God that would get her out of this. No one back home could come after her.

Perhaps the most devastating change had been just recently. Marlon had taken away her purity, for which she had been cherishing very carefully until the day she was ever to marry. How could she ever ask someone to take her as she was now, used goods? Another man had touched her, used her, and made her feel worthless and cheap. Her innocence and naivety had been shattered. How could she ever relish the touch of a man again after Marlon's cruel hands?

Her mind took her back to a conversation she had had with Jason. It was at the park, during their fundraiser for the Mexican missions. Alana had shown Jason the gazebo she would like to be married at someday. The memory of that day was painful to her now. She would not have that wedding. She couldn't do that to someone she loved.

Maybe Jason was right in not wanting to marry, she thought bitterly, tears clogging her throat. *At least you wouldn't have to worry about causing yourself or anyone else to be in pain.*

The hurt in her own heart made her thoughts seem like a mocking lie.

Chapter Thirty-Five

"I'm getting hungry."

Vic cast a glance to his employer, sitting in the passenger's seat. "We can stop for a bite," he suggested.

Marlon grinned. "I take it you could use a break as well."

With a shrug, Vic said only, "Wouldn't hurt."

Less than thirty minutes later, Vic pulled into a small tavern in a small town called Pedros. Loud music and laughter poured from the windows. "This looks like Reuban's kind of place," he muttered.

"Too bad Reuban's missing out," Marlon remarked. "I hope he gets his business, whatever it was, taken care of and catch up with us." Reuban had for some reason decided to stay in Chihuahua for the time being.

Vic couldn't say he wished the same thing, so he wisely stayed silent.

Martin went back with Jason to his hotel so they could go over their next step. Both were feeling positive now, as if God himself was laying out the path before. "I'm really starting to feel like this is all going to work out," Jason confided as he put the key in the lock and opened the door. He stopped short, Martin nearly running into him.

"Whoa," Martin breathed, staring at the destroyed room. "Who could have done this?"

Jason licked his lips, trying to stay calm. "Someone knows I'm here," he said.

"But how?"

Trying to think, Jason ran his fingers through his hair. "I don't know. I've not been asking questions or anything." He stopped and snapped his fingers. "Felina. Somehow someone's found out that I helped her get away the other night."

"So this is a warning."

"We have to get Felina away from here," Jason breathed, staring at the torn apart room.

"You're right," Martin agreed. "I had no idea that they had their eye on you."

Jason sighed, biting his lip. He could only hope that his presence was not causing harm to Alana.

Leading the small caravan to the door of the cafe, Alana's elbow firmly in hand, Marlon spoke to Buddy. "You take Alana in and find us a good table. I'll join you as soon as I can."

"Sure, boss."

Buddy and Duke led Alana to a small table in a dark corner of the bar. Alana felt her stomach tighten at the smell of the place, as well as the coarse voices filling the smoky building.

Marlon and Vic had moved away to make a phone call, disappearing from view around a corner. It seemed Marlon always had a call to make or something to do. It was clear that he put a lot of investment into his business, whatever it was.

Alana sat stiffly in a hard backed chair while Buddy ordered drinks for them all. Alana did not touch hers, but Duke drank his greedily. When he was done, he wiped his mouth and asked if Alana was going to drink hers. She slid it over to him, eager to get the mug away from her. He gulped it down without so much as a thank you.

There was a singer on a makeshift stage, prancing back and forth and singing in Spanish. Alana could not make out the words, but felt her face grow hot at the catcalls the singer was receiving from the patrons. The girl stepped off the stage with a seductive smile and was immediately swept up into the arms of a grinning man with a thick mustache. The two walked off, their arms wrapped around each other and laughing together.

"Hey, let's get her up there!" Duke suggested.

Horrified, Alana began shaking her head even as Buddy said, "I don't know. The boss may not like it."

"We won't let anything happen to her. Maybe she'll give us more entertainment than the others." He grabbed Alana's elbow and pulled her to her feet.

"No, I can't sing!" she gasped as he roughly led her to the stage.

He ignored her and spoke to the manager. The manager ushered her on the stage, his face eager for some entertainment. He called to the crowd, speaking words that Alana could not understand. She felt her knees shaking as he turned and handed the microphone to her, an eager grin on his face.

"No, I can't!" she tried to back out of it, but felt Duke's grip on her elbow. "You sing, girl!" he growled.

She had no choice. She had to sing, whether she wanted to or not. Her throat dried up and her stomach did flip flops. Alana closed her eyes in resignation, trying hard to come up with a song. She raised the microphone and sang the first words that came to her mind. *"Wise men say only fools rush in, but I can't help falling in love with you."* Her voice was shaking and cracking. As the men hollered at her, she took a deep, shuddering breath and tried again, stronger this time. *"Shall I say, 'twould it be a sin, if I can't help falling in love with you."*

Keeping her eyes closed, Alana let the song take her away from the rough and dirty bar. She was not aware of how quiet it had gotten, focused only on losing herself in the words and getting off this stage as soon as possible.

"Like a river flows, surely to the sea, darling, so adored, some things are meant to be. Take my hand; take my whole life, too. For I can't help falling in love with you."

As her voice faded with the last note, the place erupted in applause. She opened her eyes with a start. She tried to hand the microphone over, but the manager pushed it back towards her and motioned for her to sing again. She looked over to where Buddy and Duke was sitting, but they merely returned her look.

They're no help, she thought dryly. *All right, fine. If you want me to sing, I'll sing. But I'll sing the way I want to sing.*

Once again she began to sing, the words flowing through her freely, with little effort.

Oh, Lord, my God, when I in awesome wonder
Consider all the works thy hand has made.
I see the stars, I hear the rolling thunder.
Thy power throughout the universe displayed.

Then sings my soul! My savior God to Thee.
How great Thou art. How great Thou art.
Then sings my soul! My savior God to Thee.
How great Thou art. How great Thou art.

As she sang, she became very aware of a presence other than the customers. Chills rose on her arms as she felt her Lord drawing very near to her. This being an experience she had never had before, she let her emotions loose with the song, singing her praise to her heavenly father with more feeling than she had ever done before.

Jason and Martin hurried back to the mission, determined not to waste any more time. Jason quickly explained the seriousness of the situation to the girl, watching her face go from puzzled to concerned to fearful in just a few seconds.

He was just about to assure her that she would be all right when she spoke and completely surprised him with the direction of her thoughts.

"I did not mean for you to be in danger," she told him. "I am sorry that they are watching you."

"No, no, no," Jason said quickly, grasping her hand in his. "I'm not worried about that in the least. It's you I'm concerned about. Now that Marlon's lost you, he's going to more than determined to get you back, and I don't want that to happen."

Felina ducked her head, a frown still on her face.

"Felina, think about it. God made it happen that we bumped into each other. As a result, you've become a Christian and are already growing in faith. I don't think He intends you to go right back into the ring of fire."

"But what about you? And Alana?" she asked, raising her gaze.

Jason gave her a reassuring smile. "The same God that takes care of you will be with us. Just keep us in your prayers."

Finally, she took a deep breath and nodded. "All right," she agreed. "I will do as you ask."

Marlon hung the phone up. "I look for this trip to be very successful," he told Vic. They turned and headed back to the bar. As they neared, they heard someone singing.

"That's a nice voice," Marlon remarked.

They entered the bar just as Alana ended the song. Marlon's face turned black with anger. As everyone in the room stood and clapped, he marched to the front and pulled her off the stage.

"What do you think you're doing?" he demanded.

"Duke insisted I sing," she answered meekly.

Marlon turned blazing eyes on Duke. "How much of an idiot are you?" he spat. "Don't you realize this girl's picture is on every front page in the States? If someone spots her here, they could trace her to me!"

248

"Sorry, boss, I didn't think—"

"Yeah, well we'll have this out later on," he promised, leading the way from the bar.

Vic stood where Marlon had left him, staring at Alana. She caught his eye briefly before Marlon pulled her away. Vic eyed the stage where she had just been. He turned to follow his employer, wondering once again just what kind of girl this Alana Crewe was.

Just outside the mission, a sleek black Firebird sat in the shadows, its motor running idly. A few yards away behind an old, rotting, wooden barrel, Reuban sat waiting. Only a few minutes ago he had watched the tall man and his older friend hurry from the hotel. Careful to keep his distance, he had followed them back to this rinky dink shack of only a few rooms. He waited patiently.

It was several minutes before the men appeared again, this time a petite, attractive Mexican girl walking between them.

"Ha, gotcha," Reuban muttered, pulling his pistol of the glove compartment. Resting the barrel on his arm, he aimed the gun at the trio, waited the space of a heartbeat, and fired.

The gunshot met Jason's ears even as he felt the bullet graze past his shoulder.

"Get down!" he yelled, pulling Felina down behind a parked car. He could see Martin scrambling for cover. Jason sat with his back to the car, keeping himself and Felina out of sight. Felina was gasping beside him, clutching her cloak around her with white knuckles.

There was another shot fired, the bullet scattering dust near where Martin was sitting.

"Martin?" Jason yelled, pulling his handgun from his belt.

"I'm fine!"

His heart racing, Jason turned and peered carefully through the car's windows in the direction the shots were coming from. He saw a dark head appear and heard another blast. Jason ducked briefly, then raised his gun and fired two successive shots.

We've got to get to the car, he thought. There was no telling how many were with the gunman; it would do no good to get surrounded by unseen attackers.

Looking to where Martin was hiding, Jason could see a clear path between the man and their rental car. "Martin, can you get to the car?" he asked.

Martin took a quick look and nodded. "I can make it."

"Go when I say," Jason directed. He rose up on his knees and began firing rapidly. "Go!"

With a mad dash, Martin slid into the car. As soon as he was safe, Jason dropped down under a rain of answering bullets. Martin got the passenger door opened and climbed inside. Jason heard the motor start.

"Felina, get ready to run," he ordered.

She crouched down on her hands and feet. Jason rose up again and she flew towards the back door, clambering inside before their attacker could react.

Jason shifted his position. Martin reached across the seat and opened the driver's door. Clutching his gun close to him, Jason dove out from hiding and rolled, firing his gun mid-roll. The gunman fired a shot close to Jason's head. Just as he jumped into the driver's seat, Jason felt a stinging sensation in his shoulder. "Everyone stay down!" he commanded as he shifted the car into drive.

Reuban cursed as the car peeled out of the mission's parking lot, scattering gravel as it went. He stood up and fired at the car, watching in satisfaction as two windows exploded. He watched the vehicle speed away from him. With another confident smile, Reuban pulled his cell phone out.

"Manley, they're heading north. They should meet up with you in about ten minutes."

Chapter Thirty-Six

"Is everyone all right?" Jason asked as he carefully turned onto the main highway.

"Shaken up, but fine," Martin replied with a shake of his head. He saw Jason reach up and touch his shoulder. "Goodness! Are you hurt?"

"Nah, I think it's just a graze," Jason assured.

"That's an experience I never expected to have," Martin breathed.

"Yeah, sorry to get you messed up in this," Jason apologized.

"Hey, I got into this of my own free will." He glanced over his shoulder, through the shattered back window. "I just hope the mission won't be bothered."

They were in the busy part of the city now. Traffic was all around them, this being the lunch hour. Jason maneuvered the car into the traffic, keeping his eye on the street signs at all times. He was still getting used to the Spanish street signs.

"You sure Felina will be safe up here?" he asked Martin.

"No doubt," Martin said. "I have a friend that runs a shelter. Fortunately, the shelter sets right across the street from the police station. She'll be fine."

Jason slanted a look over at him. "I'm kind of worried about you now, too."

Martin returned the look. "Why's that?"

"Whoever it was that was shooting at us had to have gotten a good look at you. In addition, he knows you're involved with getting Felina out of here. I'm afraid they may come back for you."

"I'll be fine."

Shaking his head, Jason said, "It's more than just you. If they know you're involved with the mission, they may bring harm to it to get to you."

This caught Martin's attention. He grimaced. "There are a lot of people that need the mission to keep going," he murmured.

"Exactly," Jason agreed. "So, maybe for the time being, you should stay with Felina. Until this thing clears up."

"And how long will that take?" Martin asked with a pointed look.

Jason had no answer.

With a nod, Martin said, "That's what I thought."

The road was getting thick with automobiles, taking Jason's immediate attention, even though he was not through discussing it. Cars, trucks, and jeeps were moving all about him, keeping him on the alert at all times. In the midst of this traffic flow, his gaze was drawn to a black car that pulled out of a side street and pulled up close to Jason's back bumper.

Jason felt his muscles tense, even as his senses went on high alert. He made a quick right turn, and clenched his jaw when the car instantly followed. "I think we've got company," he said out loud.

"How do you know?" Martin asked.

"Just a gut feeling. Felina, stay down back there. Don't let them see you."

"Si, Jason," Felina answered breathlessly, crouching down in the seat.

Pushing the accelerator down, Jason picked up some speed, noting that the car kept up with him. *They want a chase, they'll get a chase,* he thought, tightening his grip on the wheel.

"Hang on, guys, this may get wild," he warned.

Martin quickly put his seat belt on.

Drawing on all the training and experience he had had patrolling the streets of Kansas City, Jason's instincts overtook him. He slammed the accelerator to the floor and heard the squeal of tires. "Lord, keep everyone around me safe," he prayed automatically, as he always did when involved with a police chase. He didn't want any innocent drivers or pedestrians harmed.

The driver of the black car roared behind them. Jason weaved in and out between motorists, trying to lose their pursuer. There was some space put between them as he expertly maneuvered the small car. Letting his instincts control, Jason relied more on his reflexes than his reasoning. His shoulders were straight and rigid, his eyes on the road and the mirrors at all times. Lips set in a stern line, Jason was acutely aware of every move and turn of the black car. It was critical to lose this chaser, whoever it was, before they arrived in Chihuahua. They couldn't afford to let them know where Felina was going to be staying.

Seeing an open space, Jason abruptly cut the wheel, feeling the car's weight tip to one side. He held his breath as the car settled down again and flew down the congested street. Looking in the rearview mirror, Jason could see the pursuer trying to make the same turn. "Here we go again, guys!" he called, making another L-turn to the left. The car disappeared from view and he quickly made several more turns. He was determined that the car would lose his trail.

He was nearing the edge of the city now; the signs directed him to exit off the highway and make a sharp right turn. He did all this while still keeping his speed up. There was no sign of the black car.

"Did we lose them?" Martin asked.

"Let's pray so."

"Who do you think that was?"

Glancing over his shoulder at Felina, still huddled in the seat, Jason said, "My guess it's some of Marlon's men who've figured out we've got Felina. They may even know that I'm after Alana next."

"They must be pretty determined to keep her."

Jason narrowed his eyes. "Well, I'm sorry to disappoint them."

They finally reached El Salto. The motel that Marlon stopped at for the night was large and spacious. He claimed it was the last nice spot before they reached San Marquez.

"You see, the further we go in this direction, the more uncivilized the area is." He went on to explain that the plant was located at the southern end of the Sierra Madres Mountains. The hills had once been mined a few years earlier and were now mottled with caves and tunnels. "My plant is smack dab in the middle of the woods and hills," he ended with.

Alana swallowed her aversion for the thought. What would she do once they arrived down there? There would be no place for her to run. She was even more distressed when Marlon announced that he had only rented one room for the two of them.

"I want my own room," she spoke out loud in front of the clerk.

"That's not necessary," Marlon said quickly, taking her arm and moving away.

"Marlon—" Her words were cut off with a gasp when his fingers dug into her elbow.

"That's enough, Alana!" he snapped. "Don't cause a scene. Why you still think you have a chance to fight is beyond me. Learn when you've been beaten."

The look in Marlon's eye stopped Alana cold. Marlon saw this and led her calmly from the lobby into their hotel room.

Wednesday, April 24th

Jason squinted and opened his eyes, for the moment disoriented. He was in a room he did not recognize. Sitting up in bed, the events of the previous day filing through his mind, Jason reached for his shirt. As always, his thoughts turned to prayer. "Lord, help me find Alana."

He had delivered Felina safely to the shelter Martin had told him about. While there, Jason convinced Martin to stay there for a while as well, just to be on the safe side.

"I'll do it for the sake of the mission and everyone there," Martin finally decided. "But, I must admit, I wish I could go on with you to find your friend."

"I appreciate it," Jason had told him. "But it would be easier for all concerned if I go alone. Marlon already knows I'm following them."

"I know, you're right," Marlon admitted. "But I'll be praying for you."

Martin had insisted that Jason spend the night at the shelter. "Make it harder for that black car to find your trail," he said. "And, get a fresh start in the morning to wherever you're going."

But where was he going?

Leaving his room, Jason went to the sitting room, where Martin was already up, reading the paper. "Good morning," the older man greeted. "How'd you sleep?"

"Pretty good," Jason answered honestly. "Just trying to figure out my next step."

Felina joined them a moment later and, after a few minutes of small talk, Jason asked her, "Do you know anything about the location of this plant?"

She shrugged regretfully. "Only that it is in a well-hidden location. Surrounded by woods, I believe. Marlon—"

"Jason!"

Startled, Jason looked sharply at Martin, who had interrupted. "What?"

In shock, Martin pointed to a picture in the newspaper he was going through. "Isn't this Alana?"

Jason grabbed the paper and stared. It was her! She looked thinner and worn, but it was his Alana! The first glimpse he had of her since her abduction. "Where was this taken at?" he asked, suddenly overcome.

Martin quickly translated the article. "Apparently they stopped for a drink and she was put on stage. The place was waiting for a joke, but she blew them away with a song done by Elvis Presley. They encored her and she then sang "How great Thou art." The second song was an even bigger hit than the first.

It talks about the emotion she put into her song, giving everyone goose bumps."

"She's still alive," Jason breathed.

"Yes, and this shot was taken southeast from here, in a town called Pedros. Should take you about two hours from here to get there."

"And then what?"

Martin asked for a map and the two of them studied it for a long time. "Here, look," Martin pointed out. "They started in Chihuahua. After that, she sent a message to her manager from the store in Los Diablos. Then, her picture appeared in the paper for Pedros, right here." His forefinger touched the place on the map.

"They're traveling in a southeastern direction," Jason said.

"That's the way it looks. After El Salto, towns and cities start getting a bit thin. One of the small towns in that direction is San Marquez. It's right by a big wooded area, which would be the perfect place for a hidden plant to be located."

"How long would it take me to get there?"

"If you drove straight through, very carefully, maybe four hours."

Jason nodded. "All right. That's where I'm headed. Will you call Kenneth Nelson and explain the latest developments? Tell him to be careful what he tells the Crewes. I don't want to raise false hopes."

"I'll do that," Martin agreed. "Let's pray before you go."

Felina joined them in prayer. They stood in the center of the room, holding hands, while Martin led them. His voice rose and fell in its intensity as he beseeched God to put His hand upon Jason in his quest for Alana. The three felt a strong sense of kinship as they released one another.

"I wish you Godspeed, Senor Jason," Felina said, her eyes suspiciously moist.

"No, not senor," Jason corrected. "I'm a friend, and all my friends call me Jason."

"I am pleased to have you as my friend," she said. "You are every bit as precious to me as Alana."

Jason gave her a brotherly hug before he left. Martin shook his hand solidly. "It's hard to believe I just met you a matter of days ago," he said with a smile. "I feel like I've known you for years."

"I can't thank you enough for the help."

Martin made a face. "That's what friends are for. I pray you find her. I believe you will."

255

"I hope so."

"Don't hope. Believe."

"That's getting harder to do all the time," Jason admitted.

"It does get hard," Martin agreed. "But that's when God really expects it from us. It's then that He will really be able to move."

Jason tilted his head. "I'll keep that in mind."

San Marquez

San Marquez was the last stop before arriving at the plant. Marlon assured Alana that he had comfortable living quarters at the plant, but he needed to make a stop here first.

Alana followed Marlon numbly. Vic was just a few steps away, always on the alert. Alana knew there was no use in trying to run away anymore. Even if she was to get away from Marlon, where would she go? It seemed Marlon knew people in every place they stopped. If she asked for help from the wrong person, she would instantly be carted off to Marlon's.

Vic was aware of Alana's feeling of defeat, and found himself fighting self-reproach. This was none of his doing. He worked for Marlon. It was up to Marlon what happened to Alana. Even as he gave himself the lecture, though, he could not help but mentally grimace at the look of weariness he saw in Alana's face. It was as if she had completely given up and the thought left him quite unsettled.

"I'm going to take Alana on to the plant," Marlon told Vic. "Reuban is supposed to meet us here. You stay here and wait for him."

Thinking that Reuban was a big boy and could find them by himself, Vic only nodded and watched Marlon leave, Alana in tow. He knew it might take Reuban some time, so he went for some lunch.

Chapter Thirty-Seven

Still going in a straight line southeast, Jason arrived at San Marquez tired, hot, and dusty. He sat in the car for a moment, just studying the small town. Then, with a tired sigh, he stepped out. He pulled his cap lower on his head, noting absently that he need a hair cut. In all that had happened in the last two weeks, his dark hair had grown shaggy.

Shaking the mundane thoughts from his mind, Jason locked the doors to the rental and entered a small inn. He had no idea how long he would be staying.

Sitting by a large window in the café, Vic could see everything that moved on the streets. A few people moved about, none looking suspicious. It wasn't until a tall, dark-headed young man, wearing a blue ball cap, walked by that he snapped to attention.

"I've seen him before."

He waited until the man entered the inn across the road, then quickly left the restaurant and followed.

He could hear voices in the lobby as he stood outside the door, out of sight. The white man did not know much Spanish and the clerk knew even less English. It took several minutes before they could make themselves understood. And by then, Vic knew everything he needed to know.

"We're being tracked," he told Marlon a couple hours later when he and Reuban arrived at the plantation.

"Tracked? By who?"

Vic crossed his arms. "I think it's the young cop who's been involved with Alana's case since the beginning." Even as he talked, he had a strange feeling that he was doing something wrong.

Reuban stared at him askance. "Banks? That's impossible! We just chased him from Chihuahua only yesterday."

"What?" Marlon asked.

Vic turned to Reuban. "You ran him out of Chihuahua?"

"Yeah." Reuban quickly described the shootout outside the mission. "He had Felina."

"Felina?" Marlon questioned.

Now Vic was surprised. "Seems the guy is getting around. I don't know what happened in Chihuahua, but it was Jason Banks that checked into the hotel in town."

"I don't believe the persistence of that guy," Reuban muttered.

Marlon stood up abruptly. "Okay, that's enough. I have no idea what either of you are talking about. Care to fill me in?"

"The cop that took Jack Norris in the first time he ran into Alana is following us," Reuban explained. "And apparently he's not taking a hint."

Pursing his lips, Marlon took a seat again. "Alana must be pretty special to him for him to come all the way down here after her."

"Yeah, well I hope she's worth it," Reuban said.

Vic shifted his weight uncomfortably.

"Well, we'll have to keep our eyes open and a close watch on Alana. After all this I'm not about to lose her now."

"How 'bout I take a few men to pay a visit at the hotel?" Reuban suggested.

"Don't do anything rash," Marlon advised. "I don't want San Marquez authorities following us here. We can't afford it."

"How did he even know we were here?" Reuban wondered.

"The man's a cop," Vic reminded. "And evidently a good one."

Marlon's eyes glittered. "Let him nose around. The second he shows his face around here he'll have me to answer to."

Alana had been more than a little dismayed at the place that Marlon had taken her to. The cluster of long, low buildings and miles of barbed wire fencing was surrounded by thick, dark woods. They had had to leave their vehicles behind and continue on ATVs. This place certainly was not meant to be found.

Dirty Mexican men, and a few American ones, were meandering about on the place when the travelers broke through the thickly growing trees. Alana watched as the onlookers grew excited at their approach. It was obvious they were surprised at Marlon's arrival.

Marlon, a smooth as could be, stepped off the vehicle and spoke to the men in Spanish. Alana could see the apprehensive looks on the faces of the listeners. After a moment, Marlon continued on his way. Buddy motioned for Alana to precede him.

Feeling her skin crawl under the curious gazes of the men, Alana hugged herself as she followed a few steps behind Marlon. There was something so dark, so sinister about this place, though she couldn't put her finger on it. She was sure she was about to see just what kind of man Marlon Ferraro was.

The house that Marlon entered was two stories, a proud structure with tan paint and green trim. Trimmed bushes lined the walls and even wildflowers dared to poke their heads up occasionally. It would have been a very charming spot had it been at any other location than this.

"Looks like they've been keeping the place up pretty well," Marlon remarked. He turned to Alana and smiled, putting his hands on her shoulders. "I'm glad you're here. I think you'll be pretty comfortable."

Alana had to physically refrain herself from shuddering at his touch. She did resist him when he pressed a kiss to her brow.

"You're room is adjoined to mine, for convenience's sake," he whispered in her ear. "After breakfast tomorrow I have to take a tour of the plant. I want you right by my side."

Oh, boy. Alana could think of a million things she'd rather do than go back out there under the gaze of those intimidating men.

"Okay, I'm here. Now what?"

Jason was sitting on his bed, staring out the small window. This place certainly would not win any awards for charm. The room was small, fourteen feet by fourteen feet. The bed was small and lumpy, and a closet size bathroom sat in a corner.

"But I'm here to find Alana, that's what matters," he reminded himself, trying to come up with his next step.

From the vague clues he had received from Alana's appearances in Pedros and Los Diablos, he had guessed that the Ferraros were traveling in a straight south-eastern direction. Unfortunately, it was only a guess. He had no idea if he was anywhere near Alana, but had felt compelled to stop here for the night.

He was feeling anxious. Alana was still alive. Felina had known her. Dick had received a message from her. The gossip column of the Mexican newspaper had printed her picture. He had yet to lay eyes on her. And that fact made him ache to find her and, surprisingly, hold her.

"Overall, Lord, give me direction," he prayed. "Don't let my emotions get in the way and cause me to bring harm to Alana."

Keep in mind that God knows exactly where Alana is. Martin's words just before their separation came drifting back to his mind. *Keep your mind wholly on the Lord, and He will lead you to her. You won't have to search for her.*

Jason nodded slowly. He knew Martin was right. In his heart he felt that he was supposed to be in San Marquez. He just had no idea why.

"I'm going to San Marquez," Reuban told Vic the next day.

"What for?"

Reuban rolled his eye. "I'm going for that Banks creep. Do you want in on it?"

Surprisingly, Vic was undecided. He found himself unwilling for the cop to find Alana, because once he did, Alana would be gone and Marlon would go on the warpath. The thought of joining Reuban, however, on his visit with Banks did not appeal to him in the least.

"Earth to Vic!" Reuban's rude voice cut into his thoughts.

Vic shook his head slightly. "No, I think I'll stay here," he decided on the spur of the moment.

"Suit yourself," Reuban mumbled.

Vic frowned at himself after Reuban was gone. He had no time to investigate his feelings, however, as Marlon stepped out of the house, heading for the plant. He had Alana's hand in his, and she looked as stiff as a board. Vic hesitated a moment and then joined them.

"Just the man I was wanting," Marlon greeted him. "I'm about to see the progress of the Chicago order. I want you there with me."

Vic nodded silently. He could see that the employees were watching their approach with keen interest. Especially Alana's. Their dark eyes watched her, scrutinizing her figure hungrily. Irritated, Vic stepped closer to her and gave the men a dark glare. They backed off then, obviously not willing to draw his anger.

Although she did not acknowledge it, Alana was aware of Vic's presence at her side. Strangely, she was comforted by it.

An hour later, Alana stretched out on her bed, still overwhelmed by what she had seen at the plant.

Marlon was running a black market weapons factory. He explained the business to her in great detail. At the moment, there were prominent gangsters in Chicago that were waiting for a very large order from him. The order consisted of nothing but high-tech rifles and pistols. Alana was horrified at the thought of watching these weapons being built that were someday to be used by gangsters in the states to hurt and kill people. He was using the country's struggling economy to lure desperate men into working for him for scant wages.

"My men have been bucking against authority here lately," he had told her at one point. "I have a feeling this speech will calm things down." He gave her a cold smile before he stood up on a platform.

"Gentlemen," he called, speaking in English. There was a Spanish interpreter nearby for those who could not understand English.

"I must commend you on the quality of your work so far," he began. "These weapons are some of the finest I've seen, and I'm sure you'll be paid graciously for a job well done.

"However," his voice hardened. "I'm disappointed with what I have been hearing from your supervisors. They tell me that some of you have been resisting their orders, trying to stir up trouble in your midst, and working slowly just to make a point. Let me tell you now, I will not put up with such behavior."

Alana stared at him as he talked. There was such a menacing sound to his words that she felt a chill.

"You men signed up for this job and I expect you to finish it. For whatever reason you are wanting to quit now, put it out of your mind. You are to stay until my work is complete. After this order is complete, we will discuss your termination. If you were to cause problems beforehand, it would only bring you trouble. I'm sure you would not want wives or children to suffer for your stupid choices."

It went on until Alana was nearly sick. Marlon was literally threatening his workers' families and by the looks on their faces, she could see that they believed him. These men not only worked for him in assembling black market guns, but they feared him as well.

She was more than a little relieved when Marlon ended his speech and led her out. He talked animatedly, as if what he had just done was of no importance to him. If he noticed that he was not receiving a reply, he did not show it. He seemed content that his show of force and threat was enough to keep his operation going full force until his Chicago clients could receive what they wanted.

Jason had gone to the café across the street for dinner. He was still waiting for direction, but knew he couldn't starve himself as he waited. Afterwards, he took a stroll, enjoying the somewhat cool air.

San Marquez was a rather small town. The people were quiet, but not unfriendly. Some cast curious gazes his way, but none approached him, which, for the moment, was what Jason wanted.

The last time he had taken a walk like was the night he had come so close to finding Alana, when Felina had run into him. He wondered how Felina was doing now.

She had looked so scared when Jason left her and Martin with Martin's friend. She only expressed concern for him and Alana, however, not herself.

"You will be careful?" she asked.

"Definitely," Jason smiled. He glanced over to Martin. "You make sure this guy takes care of you, all right?"

"I'll do that," Martin answered. "I'll pray you find Alana soon and we can all go back to our normal lives."

"Amen to that," Felina piped in, bringing about smiles in the men.

"Amen to that," Jason murmured now, his hands stuck deep in his pockets. He longed so much for the way things used to be.

He thought of all he knew about Alana.

Her sweet spirit, the way she gave of herself without asking for anything in return, those somewhat vulnerable expressions she had when she doubted herself, the love she had for her God, family, church, friends, that winning smile that could take one's breath away—Jason stopped, feeling his chest tighten again. All these qualities and dozens more, made up the Alana Crewe he knew.

Though he had fought it before, he realized now that Alana had changed him. As soon as she was gone from his life, he felt a void so large that it could only be filled by her return.

Keeping his eye on the ground as he walked, it took a while for Jason to notice the voices ahead. When he did, he stopped short. Reuban Ferraro was outside the hotel with a small group of men. Jason felt his heart jump as he stepped behind a telephone pole.

They were standing to the side of the building, out of sight from anyone who stepped outside. Jason watched them warily. They were joined by another man who had been inside.

"He's not here," he told Reuban.

Reuban swore and looked around him. He looked plain outraged.

"What now?" another asked him.

Reuban glared at him. "I'm not missing Marlon's party tonight. You stay here and wait for him, Manley."

Manley glowered. "Why should I be the one to stay?"

Standing up straight, Reuban narrowed his eyes. "You want to face Marlon if this Banks guys ever tracks Alana down?"

Jason's breath caught in his throat.

Reuban continued. "You know how obsessed he is with the girl. You tell him you don't want to stay."

Although he looked none the happy, Manley finally conceded with a wave of his hand.

Reuban led his cronies away from the hotel to a sleek Firebird. Jason quickly memorized the license plate number. The Ferraro drove off, a cloud of dust in his wake. Jason's car was parked directly in front of the hotel, in plain sight of Manley.

Watching the car as long as he could, Jason noted that it turned west out of town. *I have to get rid of this guy,* he thought, leaving his post to creep in the shadows.

Chapter Thirty-Eight

Manley crossed his arms and waited silently, stewing as he did. Marlon had promised a break from the work that night with drinks and music. Manley had been looking forward to it, but was now stuck here to guard and watch out for this Banks guy.

Still brooding, he missed the soft footsteps creeping up behind him. It wasn't until Jason was right on top of him that Manley realized he was being observed. Acting quickly, Jason wrapped his forearm around the man's stocky neck. Manley sputtered and gasped for a moment before reaching up and ramming his fingers in Jason's eyes. The cop grunted and released him.

Turning to face his attacker, Manley swung a meaty fist, which Jason ducked. Jason stayed poised on his toes until he had a chance to kick the man's leg. Manley grabbed his leg with a cry. Jason stepped in and brought his fist down on Manley's face. Manley slid to the ground, his eyes glazing over. With another deep breath, Jason punched again, meeting Manley flush in the nose. Manley flopped backwards, out cold.

Jason had no time to do anything with the man. Fishing his keys out of his pocket as he ran, Jason jumped into his car and tore down the street. He turned on the same road he had watched Reuban turn on only moments before. Jason could only hope that he was not too far behind to catch up.

The speech that Marlon had given hours before seemed to have the effect he had wanted. By that night, some of the supervisors were giving him positive reports. Already their work had developed more speed and fewer problems.

"I'll probably stick around for a couple days anyway," he told Vic. "I want to make sure everything continues smoothly. Besides, with everything heating up north with Alana's story, I don't want anyone spotting her."

"What about Banks?" Vic could not help but ask.

"What about him?" Marlon questioned. "He'd have to be a fool to come after her here. Believe me, Vic. I'm not worried about him."

Vic did not respond. A servant girl stepped into the room just then and announced a visitor.

Marlon frowned. "What kind of visitor?" he asked abruptly.

Vic rubbed his face, strangely bemused by Marlon's alarm. For someone who had been boasting only seconds before, he was sure fretting over an unexpected visitor.

Jack Norris appeared, a tired but pleased smile on his face.

"Jack!" Marlon greeted, brightening. "You're the last person I was expecting."

His amusement gone, Vic felt his muscles tensing. "How did you find us?"

"Vic, you forget," Marlon answered. "Jack used to be my best man, back before I found you. Jack knows all about our operation."

Norris sent a condescending look in Vic's direction, who was feeling more on edge with his arrival.

"So, my friend, what brings you here?" Marlon asked.

"Things were getting a bit tight in the States," Jack said. "I needed some breathing room."

"Well, you're most welcome here."

Standing off to himself, Vic did not feel the same hospitality his employer had.

Marlon put his arm around his friend and pulled him further in the room. "I've been wanting to see you anyway, Jack," he said. "I wanted to let you know that I appreciate your crossing paths with my Alana."

Jack raised a brow. "You've been satisfied?"

"More than satisfied."

Vic shifted his feet, disgusted. He wanted to leave, but felt he would draw questions now—questions that he could not answer.

Marlon offered Jack a seat and poured him a glass of wine. "Alana has proven to be more than a little entertaining with her spirit, hasn't she, Vic?"

Having to clear his throat, Vic responded gruffly. "She certainly has."

"I'm afraid Reuban's been growing impatient with her stubbornness, but I find it an interesting change from what I've dealt with before. I'd have to say now, though, I've got her fire toned down some."

Vic couldn't take anymore. "Marlon, I think I'll go check on the plant."

"Sure, Vic," Marlon dismissed him.

Jack cast Marlon a knowing look. "Acting a bit strange, isn't he?"

Marlon waved his hand in dismissal. "Vic's always strange."

"Whatever," Jack shrugged. "I'm glad to hear that you've had better luck with the girl than I did."

Sitting across from the convict, Marlon cocked his head. "I'm sure you'll find her much easier to handle now."

"You mean she's here?"

Marlon grinned. "I couldn't bear to leave her behind."

Jack raised his brows. "That's a first."

"I tell you what." Marlon leaned forward, resting his elbows. "I'm throwing a party tonight. Just to break the monotony. I'm pretty sure Alana will prefer to stay in her room. She's real fussy about things like that. Since the two of you have some history together, how 'bout you pay her visit tonight?"

"You wouldn't mind?"

"For you? Not a bit. You need a diversion after everything that you've been going through. And I'm sure you'd like to repay her for the trouble she's caused you."

Norris sat back. "I must say, Marlon, you're a generous man." He raised his glass. "I appreciate the offer."

Marlon lifted his own beverage in reply. "I'm sure you'll be satisfied."

Jason had no sight of the car as he drove, but as there were no places to turn off, he went on. He was beginning to get worried when he almost missed a vague trail going deep into the woods. He slowed down, studying the path. It was wide enough for a vehicle, and the marks looked fresh.

"Here goes nothing," he breathed, going onto the road.

The woods grew thicker, limbs scratching against the car with nerve grating noise. Jason was brought up short when he found the empty Firebird a quarter mile down. Looking ahead, he could see why. There was no driving anything through this brush. There were several other vehicles setting there, including a familiar looking green jeep.

Not wanting to leave the rental to be found, Jason backed out of the secretive parking lot and went further down the road, parking the car off the shoulder in an inconspicuous spot. Then he turned, his heart pounding the entire time, and jogged back into the woods, following a hard to see path worn into the dirt.

"Lord, let this be a breakthrough," he panted as he went. "Let me find Alana."

The rowdy noises from down the hall were getting louder by the moment. From what Alana could tell, the liquor was flowing freely and the men were having a good time. She sat in her room, alone, trying to ignore what was going on outside. Indeed, the events of the day had her so troubled she could not sleep even if she wanted to. This place was so frightening, so dangerous that she found herself wishing she was back at Marlon's mansion.

Rolling over her side, Alana gazed out the window. How time had flown, yet dragged at the same time. From what she could figure, she had been away from home for two weeks, yet it felt like literal months, or even years since she had seen her beloved family and friends.

The door opened slowly just then, but she did not move. Suspecting it was Marlon, she hoped to evade his advances by convincing him she was asleep. She could hear slow, heavy footsteps padding across the carpeted floor. Her brows pursed in puzzlement. It did not sound like Marlon.

"Wake up, girl!" someone growled, poking savagely at her back. She gasped and sat upright, the moonlight from the window falling square on the ugly face of Jack Norris.

"Never thought you'd see me again, did ya?" he slurred, his eyes rid-rimmed.

Pure terror clawed at Alana's throat as he stood over her. She looked behind him at the open door, but there was no way she could get past him.

"No, you're not getting away this time," he snarled. "Your pretty boy cop ain't here to rescue you. You're mine tonight!" He reached out and grabbed her shoulders, pushing her back into the bed.

Jason crept carefully to the edge of the woods. There was a clearing up ahead, lined with barbed wire fences. He could barely see in the darkness the forms of several buildings inside the fence. Several figures moved about. There was light streaming from the windows in the big house.

This has got to be it, he thought, having nothing to rely on but his speculation. This place was well hidden from anyone not looking for it. It would be the perfect place to hide something—or someone.

Alana screamed and fought against Jack, but he dropped his heavy body on top of hers, his hot breath falling on her neck. She felt his lips on her as she struggled. "No! Get off me!" she cried, raking his face with her fingernails. He roared and smacked her across the face before covering her lips with his. Alana turned her face from his and cried out again as he tore the front of her gown. She could feel his rough hands on her back.

Reaching out blindly towards the nightstand, Alana felt her fingers close around the metal base of the lamp she had turned off only moments before. Without a moment's thought, she raised it up and smashed it as hard as she could over his head. He instantly went limp, blood gushing from an open wound. She gasped for breath, recovering from the moment. With a groan, she slowly pushed the big man off her. He fell to the floor like a rag doll.

Alana scrambled off the bed, still eyeing the unconscious man warily. He was so still. Scattered glass lay on the bed and floor where she had broke the lamp. She felt her fingers pricking from the glass that had cut them. Blood stained the sheets bright red, as well as pool the floor where he lay.

"Oh, God," she whispered, her mind spinning. She stared at Jack's chest, waiting to see some movement. There was none. His face was frozen in an expression of surprise.

"He's not dead," she whispered shakily, stepping closer to him. Her torn gown hung haphazardly off her shoulder. "He can't be."

Slowly stretching her hand out, Alana searched his bloody neck for a pulse. She stepped back in horror when she found none and wiped her hand on her ruined gown. "Oh, God, I've killed him!"

Spinning around in confusion for several minutes, her mind in shock, she tried to form a plan. If Marlon found Jack Norris, lying dead on her floor, he was sure to kill her. The thought filled her with panic. "I've get to get out of here!" she whimpered.

Her limbs shaking violently, Alana grabbed a long-sleeved blouse to pull on over her the gown. Not even thinking to grab shoes, she yanked the door open and peeked up and down the hall. The party was still going on a few doors down. So far, Jack's presence had not been missed.

"Help me, Father!" she whispered as she fled, barefoot, to the door. There was no one guarding it, as everyone was enjoying themselves in the party room. She slipped outside and ran to the woods, not knowing where she was going, but she did know one thing. She had to get far from here.

Gasping for breath, Alana was stopped short by the searing pain in her side. She rested her hands on her legs, leaning over and taking in deep gulps of breath. When she felt the pain subside, she ran again, heedless of the rocks and sticks cutting into her feet.

The woods were dark and fearsome, many of the trees standing straighter and taller than any she had seen at home. The moon kept hiding behind thick clouds, making it difficult to see. She was forced to stop again as she waited for the clouds to pass the moon. When once again the soft light was before her, she saw the dim outline of a building ahead. She went towards it.

It was nothing more than a shack, perhaps a hideout for old bandits. At the moment, she didn't care what it had been, as long as it was empty. She could not continue for very much longer. Her side screamed at her to stop, her lungs were burning, and her feet felt cut to shreds.

She peered in a cracked window to ensure that the place was abandoned. Working the door open took several minutes and she froze every time the rusty hinges squeaked. At long last the door swung open and she entered inside the dark building.

Alana crept silently to the far corner of the minute shack. A shaft of moonlight shone through a hole in the shack's dirty window. She leaned against the corner and slid down to a sitting position, trying to breathe normally.

She knew it would not be long before Marlon and his men would find her. It would only be a matter of time. He always found her.

Alana put her hand over her mouth and shut her eyes tight, willing herself to not cry. Tears came unbidden, though, as she sat there, listening for the sound of footsteps. Once Marlon found Jack Norris, he would be hunting for her.

There was no describing the utter despair that swept over her.

Chapter Thirty-Nine

Jason moved quietly through the woods, not sure what he was doing. He knew now where the plant was located, but had no idea what to do about it. He couldn't march in there alone and get Alana out safely.

The sky was dark, with clouds covering the moon at times. He would have to stop for the night. Knowing that he could not make himself leave the woods, he decided to camp out somewhere. Spotting a wooden structure up ahead, he changed directions. It looked like an old deserted cabin. Maybe he could sleep there for the night while he thought of his next course of action.

All seemed quiet, but he moved cautiously anyway. He knew that the factory was little over a mile away. There was no telling how many men Marlon may have on guard. Creeping to the door, he listened intently. There was nothing. Finally sure that he was alone, Jason opened the door.

Alana spun around with a scream when the door opened. At the sight of the masculine silhouette in the doorway, she fell apart. She had been found.

"Please, don't," she cried, backing up against the wall. "Please, God, I can't go back!"

The light from the moon was behind the man, keeping her from seeing his face. He stood still and stared at her, not making a move or sound. She fell to the ground, shaking and sobbing.

Feeling like he was in a dream, Jason could not speak or move. He stared at the frightened girl before him, wondering if she was real. Was he delirious? Was it a trick of the moonlight? Could Alana really be right in front of him after all this time and searching?

Still moving as if in slow motion, Jason fell on his knees before her, longing to reach out to her and comfort her. She cried out and tried to shrink in the corner, away from his touch, hiding her face against her drawn up knees. Finally, he murmured hoarsely, "Allie?"

At the sound of her nickname, used by only two people on earth, Alana grew still. She lifted her face. The moonlight illuminated the man's face so that she could make out the familiar features. "Jason?" she gasped.

His throat suddenly tight, Jason nodded. "It's me, Alana."

With a cry, Alana flung herself in his arms. Jason crushed her to him, feeling tears on his own face as she cried against him. He buried his face in her hair, still unable to believe that he had found her. As he held her tightly in his arms, unwilling to let go for even a moment, his heart welled up with praise that God had led him to this cabin.

Jason turned his face towards the window. Clouds had once again filled the sky, covering the moon and stars. It was deathly still outside. Alana was at his side, her head resting against his chest in sleep. He looked down at her, his arm tightening slightly around her. He had never before experienced such exuberant emotion like he was now. The only moment that topped this was when he had received Christ as his Savior. Having this precious girl back in his arms was more than he had imagined.

It had taken quite some time to calm her down. He had left her in the cabin for a short time while he surveyed the area surrounding it. Once he was sure that no one was nearby, he joined her. She had rushed to him and clung to him, terrified of being separated now that they had found each other.

His mind moved to the conversation they had shared just before she had fallen asleep.

"Did they hurt you, Alana?" he asked, his eyes on her drawn face. The rosy, glowing girl he had known was no where to be found. In her place was this woman with thin, pale cheeks and slight frame. Yet from her eyes shone a serenity and faith that assured him that Alana might still be whole.

At the question, though, she dropped her eyes, unwilling to answer.

"Allie?" He was leaning against the wall, as there were no chairs in the abandoned shack. Alana was sitting on a block of wood that he had found just outside the door.

She looked up, hazel eyes looking deep into his blue ones. "I was abducted and held captive, Jason," she said quietly. "One can't expect to go through that without any pain. I don't want to dwell on the past, but face what's ahead."

He smiled softly, even as his heart ached for what she must have gone through. "Like getting home?" he asked.

Once again, she looked troubled.

"What is it?"

"Jason," she began, her voice uptight. "Marlon is a very powerful man and he's not going to just let me go without a fight. He will have his men searching every inch of this place until he finds me. Especially when he finds..." her voice trailed.

"Alana—"

She cut him off, her eyes growing wide. "Jason, we can't trust anyone. He has people everywhere that support him. He'll find me, and when he does—"

This time Jason interrupted. He knelt in front of her and took her hands. "Alana, listen to me." He waited until she was looking at him. "I'm not going to let Marlon hurt you again. We'll find a way out of here, with the Lord's help. If Marlon finds us, he'll have to get through me to lay hands on you again."

He seemed so confidant, so sure, so determined, that Alana's fears were appeased for the time being. She knew that the days ahead would not be easy, but she felt that she could face anything with Jason at her side.

"Come here." He pulled her up on her feet and led her to the corner of the cabin. He slid down until he was sitting down, inviting Alana to sit beside him. She did so, allowing him to wrap her in his arms without hesitation.

Now Jason stared down at her peaceful face, still wondering what pain she could be hiding behind her eyes. He knew that they could not stay here long. It was not safe. He planned on waking her up late into the night, but he had a feeling that she needed this uninterrupted rest for now.

He brushed her hair from her face, tucking it behind her ear. His hand lingered on her cheek for a moment. Still overwhelmed by the fact that she was safe with him, he rested his cheek on her head. A few heartbeats later, he had joined her in sleep.

Alana had not realized just how much she had longed for Jason Banks until he had found her at the shack. He had come to her thoughts many times over the last two weeks, but the heartache was not something she expected. Feeling his strong arms around her was more than she could have ever hoped for. The reality that he had actually left home searching for her had yet to hit her. For now, she was still in shock. Jason had found her. He was taking her away from Marlon and his cruelty.

He had wakened her late in the night, apologizing as he did.

"We want to put as many miles between us and the plant as we can," he

272

told her, helping her to her feet. "Darkness will be our best cover."

She smiled sleepily up at him. "As long as I'm with you, I don't mind anything anymore."

She had no idea how Jason's heart constricted within him at her words. He merely smiled, touched her cheek lightly, and then took her hand. "Let's go."

They hiked through the woods, staying as quiet as they possibly could. Both of them kept their ears attuned to any unusual noises. Now that she was with Jason, Alana's biggest fear was that Marlon would find them, find her again. She could not go back.

"My car's just outside the woods, down the road a little ways," Jason told her. "If we can get to it, we'll have a better chance of getting away."

Alana nodded, already praying that they would find the car.

Time had been Alana's friend after Jack's attack. Marlon had not looked for his friend for almost two hours, thinking that Jack was merely enjoying his way with Alana. Finally, he went to Alana's room. Finding Jack lying dead on her floor was the last thing he had expected.

"Vic!" he roared, his nostrils flaring in rage.

Vic, not much for social gatherings, had been spending the evening in his room. He heard Marlon's call and found him just inside Alana's room. "What happened?" he demanded, seeing Jack's body.

"That's what I'd like to know," Marlon said, his voice suddenly dropping. "Where's Alana?"

"I haven't seen her," Vic answered.

Marlon turned and stalked away. "Have someone take care of him," he barked. He found his brother a few minutes later and told him what happened.

"Dead?" Reuban repeated, stunned. "You mean to tell me Alana killed Jack?"

"That's what it looks like."

"She's gotta pay for that, Marlon."

Marlon sneered at him. "You're not telling me anything I don't know."

Reuban wisely held his tongue. He had seen Marlon's anger before. When roused, it was best to stay out of his way.

For the next hour, Marlon had his men tearing the house and grounds apart, looking for her. "Where is she?" Marlon snarled. No one had the nerve to answer him, and most tried to avoid him.

Marlon did not notice. He was seeing red. Alana had pushed her limit now. It was more than Jack's death. Marlon wondered what it was that had driven him to keeping her so long, after all the trouble she had caused. Her absence now was driving him wild with anger.

"All right," he snapped. "I want every available man out in the woods. Do *not,"* he spat the word out, "come back without her."

While they were preparing to leave, Manley stumbled into the house, his face black and blue.

"What happened to you?" Marlon required of him.

"That cop," Manley answered, painstakingly due to a swollen lip.

"Where is he?" Reuban demanded.

For the first time, Manley noticed the Ferraros' anger and hesitated.

"Better speak up, Manley," Vic warned. "They're in no mood for games."

Slumping his shoulders, Manley answered in a defeated tone. "I don't know."

While Reuban cursed loudly, Marlon stepped forward and backhanded Manley across the face. "You pathetic little loser!" he spat.

Manley straightened up and clenched his fists, glaring at Marlon. Marlon saw this and stopped. "Go ahead," he urged coldly. "I need a diversion."

After a long moment, Manley turned away.

"Do you think Banks helped Alana escape?" Buddy asked. "That could be how Jack ended up dead."

"I don't know," Marlon muttered. "But I want them both found and brought to me. Alive."

Marlon himself joined the search, as did Reuban and Vic. Vic suspected that Marlon wanted to be on hand as soon as they found her so that he did not have to wait to punish her. Vic wasn't sure he wanted to be around if Marlon did get his hands on her.

Reuban immediately headed for the parking lot in the wood. All seemed normal until he noticed a different set of tracks. He called Marlon on the radio. "Somebody's been to the lot."

"Find out where they went," Marlon ordered.

"You got it."

"Almost there," Jason encouraged. "Just over this hill, I think."

Alana panted for breath, wildly hoping that they were actually going to make it.

Jason slowed down as they neared the road. He looked around carefully before allowing Alana to follow him. Alana saw the dark red rental setting just a few yards away.

"Let's go," Jason said.

Jason had just opened the door for Alana when there was a loud bang and the window shattered. "Get in!" he shouted, pulling his gun out.

Reuban Ferraro was in the black Firebird, quickly advancing on them. Jason fired rapidly while he made his way to the driver's seat. Reuban had no choice but the stop the car amidst the rain of bullets. Still using the pistol, Jason opened the door and jumped in the car.

"Come on, car, let's go," he said out loud, putting the key in the ignition. He twisted around and shot three more times out of the already demolished rear window. Then he shifted in drive, hit the gas, and sped down the dirt road.

"He's following!" Alana cried, her heart in her throat.

"Don't worry," Jason told her, his eyes never leaving the road. "He won't get far."

Marlon got another call on his radio. "What?" he shouted.

"Banks and Alana just got away," Reuban's voice cracked across the walkie talkie. "I was heading them off, but my tires have been slashed."

Vic watched as Marlon tried to control himself. Unable to do so, Marlon roared and smashed his radio against a tree.

"We are going to find them," Marlon promised. "And we are going to do it soon."

"We did it," Jason said with a smile, reaching over and taking Alana's hand. "We're on our way."

Alana nodded, still breathless. Even as she rejoiced wildly over this victory, in her heart she felt wary. As much as she wanted it to be, she had a troubling sense that it wasn't over yet.

Chapter Forty

Marlon took his best men and took off in the direction that Reuban last saw the rental. Reuban, feeling more than a little testy at being bested by the cop, went with them. As did Vic.

In the years Vic had worked for Marlon, he had rarely seen him this angry. Ranting and raving, Marlon's eyes were nearly white in his fury and anyone who dared speak against him got a severe tongue lashing. He was a live wire, fairly sparking with suppressed energy.

"When I find her—this is it," he growled to Vic. Vic had no reply, to which Marlon hissed, "Well, she's asked for it! All this time, I've done nothing but good for her, and this is how she treats me. So help me, if she gets to the authorities with information about the plant, I'll kill her! That's what I'll do. You had better find her, Vic, before I do, or I may kill her on sight."

"I hear you, Marlon," Vic assured. "I'll track her down."

"I know you will, Vic," Marlon said, calming for a brief moment. "I know you and Reuban have had your issues, but I've never regretted hiring you."

Vic gave a short nod, not knowing exactly what to say.

Marlon gave him a smack on the back, and looked away. A moment later, still stewing, he again exploded at the incompetence of his men.

"How's my family?" Alana asked, not long after they had left Reuban behind.

Jason glanced over at her, seeing the extreme longing in her eyes. "Holding up and missing you. Your family is strong, Alana. Most others would have fallen apart under the pressure of these last two weeks, but not your parents. They have a lot of support from the church."

Alana swallowed away tears. "I miss them so much."

Feeling her pain, Jason squeezed her hand. "I can't tell you how much I've missed you." Sensing her head turning in his direction, he added, "We've all missed you. Terribly."

Gripping his hand with both of hers, Alana fought her emotions. "All I want to do now is go home and forget this ever happened. Even though I know I never will."

Jason was troubled by her words and the tone she spoke them in. It was obvious she was still in deep pain over the past two weeks. He wanted to comfort her more than anything. "I tell you what. As soon as we put some space between us and them goons back there, we'll get a call in to your folks."

"Really?" Alana brightened.

"I'm sure they would love to hear your voice. I wish I had my cell phone so you could call now, but it got left in the hotel room after it was ransacked."

"Your hotel room got ransacked?"

Jason grimaced. "It was no big deal. I think Marlon was just upset that I helped Felina escape."

Alana gasped and grabbed his arm. "Felina? You know Felina? She's all right?"

A bit surprised at her exuberant reaction, Jason hurried to ease her mind. "Yes, Felina is fine. I found her the night you two tried to escape. Marlon can't hurt her anymore."

Alana covered her face and took a deep, trembling breath. "I thought she was dead. I was sure I had caused her death."

"As of yesterday, she was as alive as either of us, and newly accepted into the family of God."

Staring at him, Alana was afraid to ask. "You mean…?"

Jason nodded. "Two days ago. Your witness played a huge role in that, I might add."

"Oh, thank you, Jesus," Alana breathed.

Jason was touched by the obvious concern Alana had for her friend. But, then again, he shouldn't have been surprised. That was just the kind of girl she was.

Throughout the conversation, Jason had been keeping an eye on the road behind him. As of yet, he saw no sign of any vehicles following. His gaze fell to the gauges of the car.

"Uh, oh," he murmured.

"What?" Alana asked quickly, her heart stopping.

"Looks like this little car is not as good with gas mileage as I had hoped. We're gonna have to stop for gas in San Marquez."

"But they'll find us," she said.

"We'll make it quick. I'll get us enough gas to get going and get outta there."

Still worried, Alana nodded and sat back. She wished she could be as confident as Jason sounded. She would not have thought this if she could have read Jason's mind. The thought of stopping made his stomach tighten, but he had no choice. He prayed they would have time to do what they needed to do before Marlon showed up.

After another hour, they arrived at San Marquez. Jason parked his car to the side of a small store, by the gas pumps. Alana stayed in the car while he filled up. Wanting get everything done as quickly as possible, Jason had to restrain a groan when the trigger on the pump was stuck. It took several minutes of working with it to get it to start pumping. By then sweat had appeared on Jason's brow. He kept casting looks down the road, noticing Alana doing the same.

When he felt there was enough gas to last them a while, Jason moved to the store. He motioned Alana to join him. If, by chance, Marlon was to arrive while he was inside, Jason did not want to be separated from her. The store was small and quiet, with only a few customers moving about. The storekeeper was a tall, thin man in his late forties, maybe. His eyes never left the pair. It unnerved Alana.

"Grab you some clothes," Jason whispered as he waited for the line at the counter to go down. He glanced out the window again. As he did, he spotted a payphone at he wall. The storekeeper was still busy, so Jason stepped quickly to the phone.

Edwardsville

"I'll get it, Maggie!" Kenneth called when the phone rang.

"Kenneth, it's me."

The older man gasped and found a chair. "Jason! It seems like forever since I've talked to you. What's going on? Have you found Alana?"

Suddenly overcome, Jason said hoarsely, "Yes, sir. She's right here with me. Safe and sound."

"Oh, thank you, Jesus!" Kenneth breathed, suddenly weak.

Alana stood in line, clutching the cheapest articles of clothing she could find. Her nerves were stretched thin as she tried not to appear conspicuous. The way the storekeeper kept eyeing her made her on edge. She looked back to see Jason talking on the phone. *Please, hurry,* she silently implored the customers in front of her. Once again, she looked out the window. A familiar looking green jeep had just pulled up outside the store.

Jason noticed Alana dash out of the line, her face stark white. He whipped around and widened his eyes at the sight of the jeep. "Kenneth, I can't explain it, but I've got to go. We're gonna need your prayers in a big way to get Alana back across the border."

"You got it!" Kenneth promised even as he heard what sounded like the other receiver falling. His heart pounding, he called to his wife. "Maggie, we gotta pray, and we gotta pray now!"

Jason dropped the phone. Alana was no where to be seen. Obviously she had panicked and hid somewhere. His mind screaming at him to do something, Jason left the window and went further into the store.

Alana was crouched behind a flower display, trying hard not to cry. What was she going to do? Where was Jason? Moving carefully and silently, Alana raised up to see the phone hanging from the cord and Marlon Ferraro darken the doorway. Stifling a scream, she dropped down again. She spotted a door just a few feet away. Maybe it leads outside. Gathering all her strength, she moved in that direction. She had taken only a step when she heard Vic's voice. "That's far enough, Alana."

Her gaze flew up, straight into Vic Dane's indifferent face. She felt her resolve crumbling then. "No," she whispered. Just then Alana saw Jason, positioned behind a row of shirts, creeping up behind Vic. Just before he reached him, however, Reuban appeared and put a gun to his back.

"Don't move," Reuban growled.

Marlon stepped in front of Alana. "Your first mistake was running, which you seem to do a lot of. You made it worse by somehow meeting up with your friend here." His cold glare touched Jason for just an instant. "And your last mistake was coming here. Jose is a very loyal friend of mine. There was no escaping this. Don't you know?" He leaned forward and spoke into her ear. "There's nowhere for you to turn."

It took all of Jason's restraint not to hit the man. The anguished look on Alana's face was almost too much.

With a move of his head, Marlon motioned for them to move. Vic kept his hand on Alana's arm; Reuban had the barrel of his gun still planted firmly in Jason's back.

"Thanks for the call, Jose," Marlon said, tossing the storekeeper an envelope. "This is for the trouble."

"You are welcome, Senor," Jose said with a wide smile.

Edwardsville

"Alan, what's wrong?" Sharon asked.

Alan looked at her for a long moment, trying to gather his thoughts. He went to her and put his hands on her shoulders. "That was a call from Kenneth."

Sharon's eyes widened. "Has he heard from Jason?"

"He has. Alana's with him."

Sharon covered her mouth with her hands and cried. "Thank you, God, thank you! My baby's safe!"

Alan hesitated.

"What?" she asked.

He took a deep breath. "Kenneth couldn't go into great detail, but he believes that they may both be in some trouble now. I don't think it's going to be easy for Jason to bring her back. Alana's not safe yet."

Sharon wiped her tears. "I know," she admitted. She crumpled up again as she tried to speak. "But just knowing she's with someone who cares for her is such a comfort. As long as he's able, he won't allow anyone to hurt her. At least there's some hope. We just have to pray. Keep praying. I can't lose my daughter now, not after being so close."

Acquilles Serdan

The ride back to the plant was a long one. Alana was sandwiched between Vic and Buddy, feeling like she was falling apart inside. She knew Marlon would not let this escape, or Jack's death, go. What would he do to them, especially Jason? Jason had been taken to another vehicle and Alana had no idea how he was faring.

Vic rode beside her silently, deep in his own thoughts. The scowl on his face was enough to keep anyone from speaking to him. When they arrived at the plant, he planned to retire early. Alana was Marlon's responsibility. He had no interest in seeing how the evening would turn out.

However, when Marlon led the entourage into the house, Vic found himself following. Marlon took them all to a large room at the back of the house, facing the woods. There were only a few pieces of furniture about, all resting against the walls, leaving the floor open and spacious.

Alana and Jason were pushed to the center. Jason stood before Alana like a protective warrior. His eyes took in everything about the room—the large windows, the open floor, the large chandelier directly over them, the display of fencing sabers hanging on the wall. He felt Alana reach out and take hold of the back of his shirt, holding it tight.

"I must say, Mr. Banks, you've led us on a merry chase. Too bad we're on opposite sides. I don't suppose I could convince you to work for me?"

"Not a chance," Jason growled.

"Too bad," Marlon shrugged, looking very calm despite the rage that was lurking behind his eyes. "You're a very efficient. If it had not been for Vic's tracking and Jose's call, you may have actually gotten away."

Alana's eyes turned to Vic, standing by himself, watching the entire exchange. Feeling a wave of despair and disappointment, she buried her face in Jason's shirt.

Vic hardened his heart against the hurt he saw on her face. He looked up into the piercing gaze of the cop. Their eyes locked for a long moment, neither willing to be the first to look away.

Marlon finally broke the moment. "I don't know what you thought you were doing, young man, but it's obvious you had no idea who it was you were coming up against. I pity you for that. I really do."

This was the first time Jason stood face to face with Marlon, and he could instantly sense the cold nature. There was no remorse, no heart. Marlon was not below doing anything to bring hurt on those who opposed him. Instead of fear, Jason felt boldness. He spoke without thinking.

"I pity *you*, Marlon Romano."

Marlon's eyes narrowed slightly even as Reuban stood upright. "Romano? What makes you call me that?"

"I'm an efficient cop, remember?"

Amused now, Marlon shook his head. "You've got guts, that's for sure. Now, why do you pity me? Especially in your position."

Jason set his jaw. "I pity you the day your actions finally become your undoing. God's judgment will catch up to you."

Instead of angering, Jason's words made Marlon laugh. "My, my," he chuckled. "You and Alana make quite a pair. No wonder you came after her. I'm sure you've been missing your precious girl." He moved his hand and Buddy stepped forward to pull Alana away. Jason instantly reacted with a swift kick to Buddy's knee.

He heard the click of a gun and looked up to see Reuban holding one at his chest. "I recommend you calming yourself down, Banks."

Gritting his teeth, Jason stood still while a limping Buddy led Alana to a nearby chair.

"Now," Marlon spoke, crossing an ankle over his knee. "What have you to say for yourself?"

Jason stared at him. "Only that you took what didn't belong to you and I came back for it. You would be better off to just let us go before more trouble comes to you."

"I don't know where you get your big talk," Marlon said, shaking his head. "Look around you, man. What do you think I'm going to do? Slap your wrist and let you go? I can't do that. I'm not that patient, you see."

Alana sat upright on the chair, hardly breathing. Her silent prayers were short and unfinished, desperate pleas for God's intervention.

Raising his head high, Jason looked straight into Marlon's eyes. "How 'bout a deal, then?"

Marlon looked at Jason askance. "You actually think I'm going to make a deal with you?"

Jason shrugged, making himself appear confident. "Only if you're sure you can win."

His brows going in the air, Marlon smiled. "Don't you think you're in a strange position to be acting so high and mighty?"

Jason pulled a face. "You're probably right. You wouldn't want to risk losing us anyway."

Looking impatient, Marlon asked, "Okay, what kind of deal?"

Jason motioned to the crisscrossed blades hanging in a display on the wall. "You know how to use those?"

"Jason, no!" Alana gasped, standing, and taking a step.

Buddy grabbed her by the arm and pulled her back, forcing her to sit down again. "You shut your trap," he snarled. "You've already caused enough trouble."

Alana shook her head. She had seen what Marlon could do with a sword. Apprehension filled her being.

A slow smile had appeared on Marlon's face. "Do I know how to use them?" He glanced at Reuban, who was also smiling. "Yeah, I can use them, a little. Is that the deal you want to make?"

Jason nodded, his eyes never leaving Marlon's face. He figured out fairly quickly that Marlon was arrogant and knew that the man would not pass up what he thought was a chance to prove his superiority. "Sure. If I win, you let us go. If you win, we're yours." Everything in him screamed at him to shut up, but something urged him to speak on.

Marlon shrugged with an exaggerated sigh. "All right. If that's what you really want to do."

"I have only two conditions."

Crossing his arms, Marlon asked, "What's that?"

"We duel at nine o'clock tonight, and we do it in here."

"Well, I wouldn't dream of doing it anyplace else, but why nine?"

With a casual shrug, Jason said, "I do better at night. That doesn't concern you, does it?"

A glint in his eye, Marlon grinned. "No. Not at all. Give you a little time to dwell on your stupid choice."

Alana stood to her feet again as she watched Marlon's men put their hands on Jason.

"No!" she cried, taking a step forward. She was quickly halted by Vic's arm.

"It's okay, Alana," Jason told her as he was forcefully led from the room. He cast her one more steady look before he was gone from her view.

Vic then took Alana's arm and quickly, but firmly, led her away. She resisted, thinking of what could happen to Jason.

"Let me go, Vic!" she demanded, pulling at his fingers with her free hand. "They'll kill him!"

"They won't kill him before the duel, Alana," Vic said calmly, taking her to an empty room on the first floor.

"How do you know that?" she snapped.

"Because Marlon loves to put on a show. He'll fight the man before he does anything else."

"Vic, please help us!" she begged, her wide eyes looking beseechingly up into his stern face. "You're not like Marlon, Vic, I know you're not. Can't you do something?"

Vic held his breath, caught by her pleading gaze. "No, Alana," he answered, pushing the words through stiff lips.

"Why?" Alana gasped as he opened a door and stepped through it with her.

"Because I won't."

Alana pushed away from him just as he let go. "Why can't you make a decision for yourself instead of following that man?" she cried, her eyes filling. "Why can't you do something for someone else? You know I don't belong here!"

Vic froze, gritting his teeth. Her face was too much for him. His eyes never left her features, thinner now but no less stunning than when he had first met her. Her strong character shone through, even in times of difficulty. Even now, when her rescuer was in danger and she begged him to do something, Vic could detect an inner strength radiating from her, a strength that was completely foreign to him.

"I know," he whispered through a sigh. Alana froze when he lifted a hand. His knuckles softly touched her cheek. "You don't belong here."

His hand fell and he left without another word, his shoulders looking as if there was a two hundred pound weight on them.

Alana stood stock still after he was gone, wondering what the look in his eyes had meant.

Chapter Forty-One

Jason paced the confines of his room. It was almost nine. He knew that he was taking a big chance here, and he was also more than certain that Marlon would not hold to his word if Jason won. Yet, he still felt at peace that he was doing the right thing.

Stopping in the center of the room, Jason closed his eyes and took a deep breath. He pictured himself at prior competitions, how he had managed to get the upper hand. He meditated on success. It was in this way that he had won his two State Championships.

When he was done with that, Jason turned his mind to prayer. "Lord, you know the situation that Alana and I are in. Every other time I've picked up a sword was in sport, in play. This is life or death. I need you to guide my every move, my every stroke. Help me to stay clearheaded and alert. Help me to know what I have to do to get Alana out of here."

He heard someone at the door. There was no more time for prayers or preparation. He had a quick memory of Curtis, standing in his living room, holding Jason's old sword.

"What, you think there's gonna be a damsel in distress? Are you going to rescue her from the evil dragon with this thing?"

Jason took a deep breath as he was led from the room. *I'm going out to slay your dragon, Alana.*

Alana was led to the courtroom by Reuban's steely grip. He took her to a corner of the room and pushed her into a chair.

"Now, don't get up," he ordered. "You stay right there and watch what an idiot your heroic boyfriend turns out to be."

Alana nodded dumbly, her hands buried in her clothes. She had been given fresh clothes earlier, for which she was thankful at least. The torn gown was in even worse shape after her flight through the woods.

The men were taking their places throughout the room. Alana watched someone take down the swords. She clenched her hands together so tightly that she knew she was sure to have bruises. "Oh, Lord, please," she whispered. "Don't let Jason get hurt!"

Jason entered the room just then, escorted by Vic Dane and Manley Elam. Jason sought her eyes and gave her a long, searching look. She sensed he was trying to tell her to trust him. She gave him a short nod.

The swords were presented and selected. The two men face each other and raised the weapons. Jason stood stock still, determined not to make the first move. As Marlon seemed to be of the same mind, they stood for what seemed like an eternity as everyone sat in tense silence, waiting for the duel to begin.

Finally, Marlon grew impatient and made the first swing. Jason blocked it easily and stood back. They went round and round in like manner—Marlon on the offense and Jason on the defense.

As soon as he could see Marlon slowing down just a bit, Jason attacked. His jab was blocked and he instantly saw that Marlon was still full of suppressed energy. This could be a long fight.

The room was silent, save for the clash of the blades, as Marlon and Jason circled round one another. Reuban stood straight and poised, his expression one of surprised disgust. It was clear that none had expected Marlon's opponent to exhibit such skill with the sword.

The muscles in Jason's arm were screaming at him, and he could see that Marlon was flagging as well. That fact alone made Marlon's eyes light up with fury, and Jason knew he was going to have to act fast.

Marlon struck at him and Jason sidestepped the stroke. He took advantage of Marlon's unguarded moment to bring his sword down in a sweeping move on Marlon's blade. The sword went flying out of Marlon's grasp.

Jason brought his foot up to shove it in Marlon's gut and send him flying backwards. Not pausing for a second, he turned and sent his saber flying into the ornate chandelier hanging from the center of the ceiling. The light fell to the floor with a deafening crash and everything went black.

In the midst of the screaming and cursing, Alana felt a gentle yet firm hand on her arm. Without question, somehow knowing it was Jason, she let herself be led quickly from the room.

A light was brought into the room and Marlon screamed in rage. He turned wild eyes on the seat where Alana had been sitting only to find it empty. "Find them!" he roared.

Vic observed the shattered chandelier, his face pensive. Jason's sword was lodged within the broken pieces of glass. It had been thrown in just the right move to cause the large light to fall.

Casting a look through the windows into the dark world outside, Vic thought that the man they were dealing with had turned out to be more than Marlon had reckoned with.

Zigzagging between the thickly growing trees, Jason and Alana went deep into the forest, where the moonlight could barely filter through the low hanging branches above them. Roots stuck out of the ground in hazardous places. It seemed that no matter how far or fast they went, they heard the voices right behind them. They came across the barbed wire fence that surrounded the plant and quickly climbed through it.

We're not going to make it! Alana mentally cried. *Oh, God help us!*

Jason was doing his own praying as he led Alana along. After all the searching he had done the past weeks, he was not about to lose her now. He just had no idea how he was going to get her away.

Vic was at Marlon's side, witnessing his employer's almost insane wrath. Driven by obsession, Marlon's only goal was to get Alana back. The cop was an obstacle that had to be removed.

Vic had not been prepared for the unsettled emotion he was experiencing at seeing Alana and the cop. They way Banks had dropped everything to get Alana to safety stuck with him. He had to know how dangerous it would be to cross Marlon Ferraro a.k.a. Marlon Romano. What had caused him to do it?

Keeping his automatic weapon close to his side, Vic brushed past the prickly branches clawing at his face. In the midst of his turbulent thoughts, he kept his eyes open for where Alana and her rescuer might be hiding. He was Marlon's best man; Marlon had never shied from saying so. It would not take long for Vic to track them down in the woods.

They spoke not a word as they ran, moving like shadows in the night air. Alana's heart was pounding in terror. She could hear the men not far behind them, searching for them, and Marlon's outraged voice. She feared for their lives if they were to be caught again. What would they do to her? What would they do to Jason?

God, help us, please! was her repeated prayer as they ran.

Jumping over broken limbs, rocks, and dips in the ground, Jason kept his hold on Alana's hand, helping her along. His jaw was tightly clenched and his senses were on high alert. He was not going to let Alana fall into the hands of these men again.

At times the voices of their pursuers seemed far in the distant; other times it sounded as if they were right on top of them. It was at these times that they ran the hardest, trying with all their might to keep from being heard or seen. When able, Jason slowed their pace, mainly for Alana's sake. He did not want her collapsing from sheer exhaustion.

It had been quiet for several minutes now. Jason had Alana's hand tight in his own. When she was not using her free hand to shield herself from the sun or low hanging branches, she clung to his arm. Her very being shook in her desperation to get to safety. She wanted the nightmare to be over. She wanted to go to her family where she was safe.

Jason looked down at her and noticed her pale face. "Hang in there, Allie," he whispered. "We're gonna make it."

Alana nodded silently.

Jason squeezed her hand slightly as they walked. He had not heard or seen any sign of their hunters for some time and dared to hope that they were leaving them behind. All he wanted to do was get Alana out of these woods and on her way home.

"Up here," Jason panted, motioning towards a small cliff. He boosted Alana up and climbed up behind her. They continued running, Jason directing their steps where it would be hard to track them. Piles of leaves lay before them as well as broken limbs, jagged stones, and hard-packed dirt. It would take an expert tracker to be able to follow them.

If only there weren't so many following them. The room had been full of Marlon's men, at least a dozen of them. They were all now spread out behind them, searching for them. And most had mechanical guns in their hands. Jason, especially without his pistol, could hold up against them for long.

The sun set in the midst of a blaze of color-orange, purple, red, and blue. The moon rose high in the sky, millions of stars surrounding it. Huge puffy clouds drifted about, occasionally hiding the light of the moon, but never for long. Dampness hung in the air, making it harder to breathe. All was still— too still. Not so much as a bird called in the black darkness. The shadows of the ancient trees hung creepily over all that cowered before them.

It was late, almost ten. Jason and Alana had fled until they could not run anymore. At that point, Jason knew that all he could do was find a place to hide for a few hours. From the silence that he was hearing, he could only hope that, for now, they had lost their pursuers.

It was too much to hope for another abandoned shack. He had to settle for a deep cleft in a hill. It was rather cozy and hidden, but did not offer much protection from two-legged prowlers.

Still feeling it was too risky to start a fire, Jason gave Alana his jacket to keep her warm. He was worried about her. Her face was pasty white, and every time he touched her, he could feel her trembling slightly. In short, she was terrified of being caught.

"I still can't believe I've found you," he said, trying to get her mind off their present situation. "It was only by the grace of God that I did. If I had not run into Felina…"

"I'm so glad she's all right," Alana exulted again. "She's suffered so much at the hands of Marlon."

Seeing her emotion, Jason knelt down next to her. "She was mostly worried about you when I couldn't find you that night."

Alana bowed her head and wiped her eyes.

Jason continued, almost absently. "I went back to Manchez Street, hoping I'd find you, but apparently they already had. I was so close."

Looking up at him, Alana saw his pained expression. "Jason," she murmured, putting her hand on his arm, "You haven't been blaming yourself for all this, have you?"

Startled, Jason's eyes met hers. "The night you were kidnapped, I knew Jack Norris had escaped," he said lowly. "Instead of going to you then, I went to talk to your manager." He choked up. "I let you down."

Alana shook her head. "No. I know you better than that. You acted on your best instincts. We can't look back and wish things had gone differently." She dropped her gaze. "It's too late for that. I don't know where I'd be, Jason, if you hadn't found me." Swallowing, she kept her gaze on the floor. "I've killed someone, Jason."

Blinking, Jason stared at her, wondering if he heard her right. "What?"

Tears streaming down her face, she explained. "In all the time I've been with Marlon, I've never seen Jack Norris. Until last night."

Jason felt his fists tighten. He had never seen such turmoil on a person and he had to fight the hatred he was feeling towards Marlon for the agony he had put Alana through.

"Last night, he came to my room," she went on falteringly. "I couldn't…" She shook her head slightly, not wanting to relive the moment. "I grabbed a lamp that was setting nearby and…I just wanted to get away from him. I didn't think it would kill him."

Shutting his eye against the tormenting images in his mind, Jason pulled her against him, holding her tight. She wrapped her arms around his waist and clung to him almost desperately, breaking his heart as she did.

After a long moment, he said, "You did what you had to do, Allie. You're not at fault."

"But—"

"But nothing. Jack Norris has lived in life in dark sin, taking what he wanted with no thought of consequences. As long as he lived that lifestyle, God's judgment was going to find him. You are not to blame for his death. You acted in self-defense. In God's sight, you're innocent."

She cried then, sobbing against his chest. He let her cry. She began to talk, her words stumbling over themselves, halted by her sobs.

"I knew Marlon would kill me, so I ran. I didn't stop for anything, not even shoes." This explained to Jason the way she had been dressed when he found her. "I just ran, knowing that he would find me again, and when he did…"

"But he didn't," Jason reminded, giving her a squeeze. "I did."

Unable to control herself, Alana leaned back and pounded her fists against Jason's chest. "Why couldn't you have found me sooner? Marlon will never let me go!"

Jason was startled by the sudden outburst, but not surprised. He knew she had been holding too much in. He took hold of her hands and cupped her face with his other hand. "Alana! It's all right! I'm so sorry that you've had to go through so much, but don't lose faith now. God is still in control."

Her face cleared. "I'm sorry, Jason," she cried. "I didn't mean—"

"I know you didn't," he soothed. "I have no idea what kind of nightmare you've gone through, but know this. I'm here for you. No matter what."

His gaze deepened as he said this and Alana felt suddenly drawn. Their eyes locked on one another for a long moment before she finally broke it, pulling her hands back and looking away.

Jason had no idea what had happened, but he pushed it aside. Now was not the time for complicated emotions to cloud his reasoning. Now was the time to find a way to get Alana out of Mexico and back to Edwardsville, where she belonged.

Chapter Forty-Two

While Alana slept, Jason kept watch, feeling himself tense at every sound in the woods. His gaze kept straying to Alana, sleeping peacefully a few feet away. She was thinner now. Her face was marked with weariness and an inner hurt. Bruises and scratches were on her arms and legs. The very sight of them made Jason burn within.

What had she gone through? What damage had Jack Norris and Marlon Romano done to her? How much had she had to change against her will? Would she ever be the same?

Jason knew the answer to the last question. Too much had happened to allow Alana to be the same innocent, carefree girl he had known. She had seen too much, experienced more than he could imagine. Yes, he had rescued her, in a sense, but the Alana Crewe he had known in Edwardsville, Kansas was no more. The thought made him want to weep.

Overwhelmed by emotion, Jason rubbed his hand over his face. He could feel himself getting uptight. Just the sight of Alana moved him unexpectedly.

"Lord, help me, please," he whispered, shutting his eyes tightly. "Don't let me do anything rash. Finding Alana has made me emotional. I don't want to get carried away. This is not the time, not that any time is a good time. Alana is a dear friend, one that's in very serious danger right now. Help me to focus on getting her home, nothing else."

Looking on her once again, Jason sighed deeply. He felt more tired than he had ever felt. How was he supposed to get her home? They were in these woods, unfamiliar to either of them, still pursued by Marlon and his men. Alana was convinced that Marlon would not let her go. Jason was now doubting his move to run to the woods. How was he supposed to get out now?

Even as he berated himself, Jason knew that there was not much he could have done. He had had no other place to go. He could only hope now that, with the miles of trees, he and Alana could keep themselves out of sight until they could find a way to get out of Marlon's reach.

Where that help is going to come from is another story altogether, he thought grimly. Even as his gaze gently caressed Alana's face, he knew that he would get Alana home. Even if he had to die doing it.

They were on the move again early the next morning. The sun had yet to make an appearance and a chill hung in the air. Still listening for sounds of their pursuers, Jason kept them at a hurried but not rushed pace. He had not heard anything unusual since early the evening before. Maybe they had actually lost them. He prayed it was so.

They had not eaten since the day before. Jason wondered how their strength would endure. With his gun confiscated the day before, he did not even have a way to catch small game. They found berries and edible plants, but that would not suffice them for very long.

Once again evening fell. There were no natural shelters around, so Jason risked a small campfire. It had been over twenty-four hours since they took their flight.

"What are we going to do now?" Alana asked as they sat close to the fire.

Jason knew there was no sense trying to hide the truth from her. "Honestly, I'm not sure. I don't know my way around these woods. But, don't worry. We'll find a way."

"I'm not worried now," Alana spoke softly, staring into the fire.

A silence fell then, strangely reassuring despite their insecure position. They found comfort in each other's presence.

"I wish my parents could know that I'm okay," she murmured.

"They'll know soon enough. In fact, when you get home, you're more than likely to get mobbed. First by family, then by friends, Dinah and Curtis to be specific. I think Dinah's about to go nuts without you around." He could feel Alana's eyes on him a he talked; very intent was she to hear about those she loved.

"Dinah's been taking care of your Sunday school while you've been gone," he went on. "I think she was scared to death at first. But, your kids seem to connect with her pretty good. There's one thing for sure, though."

"What?" Alana asked when he didn't say anything.

He looked at her. "They love you to death. You have no idea how your life has been touching them, including Breanna. Dinah said she's finally accepted Christ into her heart."

Alana closed her eyes in relief, feeling joy for the first time in weeks.

"She'd been asking a lot of questions about God," Jason added. "She's really shaken up about your abduction and I think it got her thinking about life beyond this earth."

"It's amazing how God can move in strange ways," Alana said. "I would have never asked for this to happen to me, but He's using it for good. Felina first, and now Breanna. It makes this whole ordeal worth it in a way."

Jason watched her, amazed and rather humbled. "You know, Allie," he said, "I think you're pretty special."

Alana smiled and looked down at the fire.

The next morning was just as still, but Jason felt unsettled, as if he was missing something. Was it possible that they had actually managed to lose the men? Surely Marlon had not given up just yet.

"Where do you suppose they are?" Alana asked, as if reading his thoughts.

"I don't know," he said grimly. "I have to admit I don't—" He paused abruptly and put his finger to his lips. "There's someone over there," he mouthed. Alana felt her blood freeze.

Moving silently, Jason took Alana to cluster of bushes. "Get in here, and stay here, until I come back."

Alana nodded.

"Here." Jason handed her a knife from his boot. Marlon's men had missed it when searching him. "Use this if you have to."

Her eyes wide, Alana once again nodded.

Dropping a kiss on her forehead, Jason left her there, cautiously moving towards where he thought he heard movement.

Crawling over a small cleft, Jason looked down to see Reuban standing by himself. The younger Romano looked distracted and annoyed, as he gazed around him. He pulled his radio out. "I don't see anything," he spoke into it.

"Keep looking!" Marlon's voice came over it.

Reuban scowled and pocketed the radio. "If I get my hands on the girl, I'll…"

Now he was passing below where Jason was laying. Jason pulled his feet underneath him, ready to jump. As soon as Reuban was underneath him, he leapt on top of him. Reuban gave a startled shout before he rolled and came face to face with Jason Banks.

"That was a fool move, Banks," he sneered.

"I've never been known for smart ones," Jason shrugged. He sprang at him, driving his head into Reuban's gut. Reuban fell flat on his back and Jason straddled him. Clasping his fists together, Jason raised them up and brought them with a sickening thud against Reuban's head. The man went out cold.

Moving quickly, Jason rolled Reuban on his stomach and bound his hands as well as he could with his belt. He brought Reuban's feet up under his hands, and then pulled his gun out.

"Sleep tight," he muttered as he left him, hoping that his clumsy binding would hold the man long enough for him and Alana to leave the area.

"What happened?" Alana asked when Jason pulled her from the bushes.

"I ran into Reuban. Hopefully he'll be out of our way for a little while, but we've got to get out of here."

They went north at a hurried pace, Jason listening for sound of anyone discovering Reuban's plight.

A twig snapped just then and Jason stopped short. Vic Dane stepped out of the trees, his steely gaze fixed on the pair. Jason automatically stepped in front of Alana, his hand dropping to where the gun was stuck in his belt.

"Vic!" Alana gasped.

The man stared silently for a moment, fingering the trigger on his gun. His very stance conveyed his strength and intention. "Looks like I intercepted your escape once again," he addressed Alana, but his gaze was on Jason.

"Vic, please," Alana pleaded.

"Marlon is waiting for you. He's growing tired with your antics."

"You know what's going to happen if I go back to Marlon," Alana told him, moving away from Jason slightly.

Jason stayed completely still, intently studying the dark face of the man before them, ready to act if he had to. He had no idea what was going on, but sensed there was an unseen struggle going on.

"Vic, you're a better man that this," Alana continued. "Don't do this."

"It's my job, Alana," Vic reminded, his voice a growl. "It's what I do."

"And you hate every part of it," Alana said. "You know you do."

Vic did not respond, but his brows drew low as he glared at her. Jason tensed, waiting for Vic to do something.

"Please," Alana tried again, taking another step toward him. "Please help us."

Her plea was met with stony silence and she feared that she had lost him. He raised his gun up slightly, his face a thundercloud. He paused and cocked his head slightly, listening. His face changed abruptly and he shouted, "Look out!" He jumped forward, falling into both of them, knocking them all to the ground. He threw his body over Alana as a loud explosion sounded just a few feet from them.

"They're using grenades. Let's go!" he ordered, getting to his feet and pulling her to her feet. Without hesitating, he took off running, pulling her after him.

"Jason!" Alana called, looking behind her. She could see nothing through the dust and smoke hanging in the air except for broken limbs and jagged tree branches. Jason was nowhere to be seen. "Jason! Where's Jason?" she called out to Vic.

That man did not answer, but his expression grew grim as he led her deeper into the woods.

"I can't leave without him!" Alana tried to pull her hand away. "Vic!"

Vic stopped and faced her. "Alana! We can't do anything for him right now. He can take care of himself. If you go back, you won't get out."

"But what if he's hurt?" she asked tearfully.

"Then he's gonna want you as far from here as you can get," Vic answered, beginning to move again at a rapid pace.

Wanting to fight with all her might, Alana followed him without resistance. She cast another look over her shoulder, while sending a prayer that Jason had somehow managed to slip away under the cloud of smoke.

Another grenade went off to their right. Vic pulled her in his arms and turned his back to the flying debris. She could hear him grunt as he was struck with tiny, sharp particles. When the air had cleared again they went on. The ground rumbled every few minutes with explosions and the dust was filming Alana's throat, making it difficult to breathe. Her legs were starting to feel like jelly, but still she went on.

In all this, all she could think of was that she had left Jason behind, after all he had done for her. How could she? What kind of friend was she? Thus, with every step that she ran, with every new bomb, she felt her heart being wrung tighter and tighter in pain and guilt.

She could hardly breathe as Vic hurried her through the woods. Branches slapped at her, leaving scratches and welts on her arms and face. Thorns ripped into her legs until blood trickled down. She stumbled at times, but Vic's steady hand was always there, keeping her from falling.

Vic suddenly stopped and Alana stared up him, confused. "Why are we stopping?" she whispered.

Putting his finger to his lips, Vic listened intently. Someone was following, and he was catching up fast. There was no way he could outrun the man with Alana. And there was no way he take her back to Marlon. He had made his choice. "You need to go on, I'll stay here."

"What?" she gasped.

"We won't be able to outrun them," Vic insisted, giving her a push. "Get going. I'll hold them off."

"I can't leave you," she said, still remembering how she had lost Jason. "What will happen?"

"I don't know," Vic admitted. "But it's time for this to end. Get going."

Her heart suddenly full, Alana turned and laid her hand on his sleeve. She looked up at him with wide eyes. "Thank you, Vic," she said simply, her voice thick.

Vic hesitated for a moment, staring down at her, looking somewhat distraught. She turned then and disappeared into the woods. He closed his eyes and exhaled deeply, a myriad of emotions in him.

"I always knew Marlon was making a mistake, trusting you."

At the sound of Reuban's voice, Vic froze. Almost in slow motion, he faced the man behind him. "She slipped out of my hands," he said, his lie sounding feeble even to his own ears.

"Oh, come on, Vic," Reuban scoffed, approaching him. "There's no way you, of all people, can convince me that you can't keep track of a little girl. You've had no trouble up to now."

Staying calm, Vic did not answer, but regarded Reuban with dark eyes.

The younger man looked a bit rough. His clothes and hair had grass and leaves in them and his face was marked by a large, black bruise. He did not seem to notice his own appearance. A cruel smile lit Reuban's features. "No, your heart just got too soft, Vic. And that was your first mistake. I've been waiting for this chance for a long, long time. It's time my brother know that his best man is not who he thinks he is."

Vic's eyes dropped slightly to Reuban's belt. He was heartened to see that in the chase, Reuban had somehow lost his gun. Staying cool regardless of the hatred boiling in Reuban's eyes, he said, "Go ahead, then. If you can."

Reuban's eyes narrowed at the challenge. The two men squared off, their poses tense and ready. Vic knew that this was not a fight he could just walk away from, as if it never happened. Reuban would settle for nothing less than victory.

Alana flew through the brush that tried to clutch her clothes and slow her down. She could hear voices behind her; Manley and Buddy were right on her. She knew they couldn't see her, but it would only be a matter of time before they could.

Feeling panic well up in her, she forced herself to speed up, even though her heart felt ready to explode. A cluster of large rocks, sitting in the middle of the woods, beckoned to her. She longed to sit down and rest on one, but she had no time.

As she passed them, an arm shot out and grabbed her around the waist, pulling her tightly against a broad chest. She opened her mouth to scream, but the man's hand quickly clamped over it. She struggled wildly for a moment before a familiar voice fell on her ear.

"Shhh, Alana, it's me!"

Slumping against Jason in profound relief, Alana could not stop the tears from welling up in her eyes. Jason held her tight and still while Manley and his followers passed. They all seemed too preoccupied by their hunger and discomfort to really concentrate on the search. They walked by the rocks with barely a glance.

Jason let go of Alana's mouth, but kept his arm around her. He held up a silencing finger as they stood. "Let's go," he mouthed, going in a different direction than Manley had gone.

After a few minutes, he asked her, "What happened to Vic?"

"He stayed behind," Alana answered, her face troubled. She glanced behind her, as if hoping to see him appear. "He let me go and stayed to hold them off."

Jason noticed her worry, his eyes resting on her thoughtfully for a moment. "Vic can handle himself," he said, finally.

Alana nodded, but it didn't erase the frown on her forehead.

Reuban spun his body around and kicked high in the air. Vic easily dodged the kick and swung his fist in a roundhouse, a move that Reuban effectively blocked. Vic then spun and drove his elbow into Reuban's torso, feeling a small amount of pleasure at the grunt of pain from his opponent.

Reuban recovered quickly, however, and slammed his knee into Vic's back. It knocked the breath from the man, and Reuban quickly followed up with several hard fists. Dropping to the ground, Vic swung his leg out and swept Reuban's feet out from under him.

The brawl went on for several long minutes in similar fashion. Each man matched the other's moves in skill and power. Both were breathing heavily, but knew that to stop would mean defeat and even death.

Reuban was driven by the hatred and jealousy he had felt for Vic since he had known him. His cold blooded nature had reasoned that it was time to be rid of him. Vic' betrayal of Marlon was only the last draw in Reuban's fiery vengeance.

In one last move, Vic did a back kick and caught Reuban square in the gut. He did not stop there, but continued knocking Reuban back with a rock hard fist or flying boot. Reuban's eyes suddenly glazed over and he had difficulty standing. Vic took a quick breath and leapt into the air, spinning completely in the air and kicking Reuban in the face with such force that it literally knocked him off his feet.

Vic stood over the man, panting heavily. Reuban groaned and stared up at Vic with dull eyes. "So, now what, Vic?" he slurred, his bloody mouth drawn up in a sneer. "You know you're gonna have to kill me, because I'm not gonna let you live after this."

Standing up straight, Vic took a deep breath. Before he had a chance to say anything, he heard someone step behind him. He swirled around to face Marlon, whose gun was in hand.

Marlon's blue eyes were glittering, and there was a small smile resting on his lips. "Reuban always said you weren't trustworthy, Vic Dane, but I had no reason to believe it."

Reuban struggled to his feet, his own expression lit with a cruel glow.

Seeing the murderous look on Marlon's face, Vic felt his heart sink slightly. His boss's eyes narrowed and the smile disappeared. "Until now." He raised the gun to Vic's chest and fired twice.

Chapter Forty-Three

The sound of gunshots stopped Alana in her tracks. Jason paused as well, frowning into the woods behind him.

"Oh, no," Alana breathed. "That was Vic. I know it was."

Jason reached out and put his hand on her arm. "We can't know that for sure," he said, though he did not believe his words.

"No," Alana said, shaking her head. "He let me go, Jason. They'll kill him for it." She started to head back, but Jason stopped her.

"Alana, we can't go back."

"But, Vic!" she protested, her eyes beseeching. "We can't leave him here!"

"As much as I hate to, Allie, we have no choice," he insisted. "There's nothing we can do for him."

Men's voice rose in the air, sounding riled up.

"Come on, Alana," Jason directed, pulling her with him.

Alana cast one more look behind her. The thought of Vic suffering for her filled her with such sorrow that tears streamed down her face as they ran.

Marlon's men seemed to be closing in behind them. Whatever happened with the gunshots, it seemed to have put fire into their pursuit. Jason was beginning to lose hope that that they would be able to run for much longer. His feet felt like blocks of wood and Alana looked ready to drop.

"God…" he panted. "Show me…a way…out of here."

His chest was burning with every breath that he drew in and Alana was gasping beside him. Their pace was steadily slowing and they would be overtaken at this rate in little time.

A strange light caught Jason's eye and he peered through the woods. There seemed to be openness about them, giving the sun room to shine through.

"Let's go this way," he advised.

Alana only nodded and followed his lead.

After a few minutes, Jason thought he heard the sound of water. A little while later, they came to the edge of the woods and looked down a small cliff into a wide river, about twenty feet below them. The water looked a little rough, but not wild.

"Can you swim?" he asked Alana, his eyes on the river.

Alana stared down at it as well, knowing from Marlon's earlier explanation of the land that she was looking at the Mezquital River. "Yes," she finally answered.

Faintly they could hear the men following their trail. They were running out of time.

"When you come up, go to the shore and wait for me," Jason said, glancing back into the woods. The voices were getting louder. "Be careful," he cautioned, putting his hands on her shoulders."

"You too," Alana returned, her face anxious.

"We'll be all right," he assured her. He stared down at her, wanting to say more but he held back. "I'll find you."

Alana nodded quickly. They could hear the men crashing through the woods now so they hesitated no more. They turned to face the river, gripped each other's hand tightly, and jumped into the swiftly flowing river.

Jason came up, sputtering and gasping. With long, strong strokes, he swam to the nearest shore and climbed up. From what he could tell, the water had carried him a ways downriver. Looking around him, he called out, "Alana!" only the river answered.

"Alana!" He peered over at the far side of the shore. Maybe she had ended up over there and was waiting for him. "Where are you?"

Feeling his heart quicken, he walked the bank, still calling her name, every second feeling like an hour. How far could the river have carried her? Praying that he had not made a mistake in having them jump the cliff, Jason searched the shore frantically. Finally, he spotted a patch of white some yards downriver, on his side. "Alana!" he called, running to where she was laying, facedown on the bank.

"Allie!" He turned her over, alarm piercing him at her white face. "Honey! Wake up." She had been swept on the shore, apparently losing consciousness. There was no movement under her chest.

"No, God," he ground out, laying her flat on the ground. "I can't lose her now."

Putting his lips over hers, Jason breathed into her mouth. "Come on,

Allie," he demanded, pumping her chest. He did this a few more times, panic rising with every breath he gave her. "Breathe!"

She coughed suddenly and he slumped with relief. "Thank you, God," he prayed as he helped her to sit up so she could breath. He wrapped her in his arms. "Thank God you're okay."

Alana clung to him, still coughing from the amount of water she had inhaled. She was wet and cold, but all she could feel at that moment was Jason's strong embrace.

Jason took the opportunity to fill his canteen with water from the river, not knowing when they would find more. He was feeling fairly safe from Marlon's men now, but he still proceeded cautiously. The sun was going down soon and Alana was shivering with cold. He had to find some kind of shelter for the night. He did not even notice his own pain and exhaustion in light of Alana's state.

After walking for almost two miles, he discovered a cave cut out of a small mountain. He checked it out first, to be sure it was safe, then built a small fire for Alana to warm herself by. It was only after they had rested and warmed a bit that he felt a searing pain in his leg.

Alana heard him grunt. "What's wrong?" she asked.

"Oh, it's nothing," Jason said lamely.

"Don't give me that," Alana said sternly. "Let me see."

Jason tried to put it off. "No, I'm fine."

Alana's face grew hard. "That's why you're grimacing. Sit down."

More amused than anything by Alana's stubbornness, Jason limped to the cave wall and sat down on the ground. He pulled his pants leg up and Alana gasped at the gaping cut on his lower leg. "How did this happen?" she asked, kneeling before him.

"Must have done it when I dove in the water," Jason answered, gritting his teeth.

"We have to wrap it up or it will get infected," Alana said. She pulled at her long Mexican skirt. With all the rips and tears she had inflicted upon it recently, it was easy to tear off a wide strip off the bottom of it.

"Alana, you don't have to—"

"Yes, I do." She took the canteen in hand. "First, we'll have to clean it."

"Don't use too much," he cautioned. "We'll need it later."

"You need it now."

"Did anyone ever tell you you're impossible to argue with?" he said lightly.

She gave him a small smile in reply.

Jason sat, gritting his teeth, while Alana tried her best to gently clean his wound. He had cut a deep gash that had bled profusely without him even knowing about it. While she cleaned it, it began bleeding again and she applied pressure to it until it stopped. Now she was attempting to wrap it, her hands gentle and soft.

Closing his eyes, Jason hoped that the wound not slow him down in getting Alana back to safety. He looked up at Alana, who was intent on wrapping his leg.

"How'd things get so switched?" he asked, with a hollow chuckle. "I'm supposed to be taking care of you, not the other way around."

Alana smiled slightly, and then frowned. Jason saw her expression grow anxious.

"Hey, I was just kidding, Allie," he assured.

Alana sniffed, her eyes looking suspiciously moist. "We have to depend on each other if we have any hope of getting away, Jason," she whispered, not looking at him.

"Don't worry," he said, lightly. "We're gonna get out of this."

Wiping tears with her hand, Alana took a shaky breath. "I'm so sorry I got you into this mess, Jason. You'd be perfectly fine if it wasn't for me."

"Whoa, whoa, whoa!" Jason interrupted, reaching for her hand. "I don't want to hear any talk like that. No one forced me into this. I came on my own free will. There is absolutely no reason for you to blame yourself."

Alana nodded, trying to compose herself.

"Besides, I had nothing else to do at the time," Jason quipped, trying to lighten the mood.

It worked. A smile broke through Alana's troubled face and she shook her head at him. She finished bandaging his leg and sat back. "It's a sloppy job, but at least it's protected for now."

Jason winced as he pulled his pants leg back over the cut. "You did fine."

"You know, there's still something I don't understand."

Jason looked at Alana to see that she had grown sober again, her face a mask of concentration. She turned her questioning eyes on him.

"Why did you come in the first place?" she asked. "I mean, I can never express how glad I am that you came after me, but what made you go through all this trouble, just for me?"

Staring at her upturned face, Jason felt a myriad of emotions. *Because I love you.* The words flew through his mind, but he did not speak them.

Instead, he leaned forward and rested his hand against her neck, his thumb caressing her cheek. "Because I could not bear the thought of you being anywhere but home, where you belong," he answered, his voice suddenly hoarse. He wanted to say more, but he didn't.

Her gaze deepened. "I don't know where I'd be, Jason, if you hadn't. Thank you."

His leg was burning like fire, but for the moment he did not notice. All he could see was Alana's huge hazel eyes, and feel her soft skin beneath his hand. Not able to stop himself, he drew her closer and covered her lips with his own. He thought his heart was going to explode with what he felt at that moment. He framed her face with both hands and kissed her, their dark, gloomy surroundings forgotten.

Alana responded to the electrifying kiss for an all-too-short moment and then abruptly pulled away. "Jason, I'm sorry, I can't," she said breathlessly, her own heart breaking inside her. She lowered her gaze, unable to face his own.

Though he felt bereft at her sudden withdrawal, Jason wanted to erase the distraught look on her face. "Hey, it's okay, Alana," he whispered, his hand resting on her shoulder for a moment. He lowered his head so that she was forced to look at him. "I mean it. It's okay." He forced himself to look normal again. Her saw her face relax.

"I'm sorry," she whispered again.

"Don't be," he said, giving her a smile.

After an awkward moment, he painstakingly rose to his feet. Alana watched him limp across the cave floor. "Stay here," he directed. "I'm gonna check and make sure everything is still quiet."

When he was gone, Alana covered her face with her hands and wept. "Oh, God!" she cried. "I never realized how much I've come to love him, but I do! I wish it wasn't so, because I could never ask him to lower his standards to what I've become."

Feeling grief well up in her so strong that she could not breathe, Alana tried to muffle her sobs with her hand. In all that she had been through recently, she had never felt anguish as painful as this.

It was quiet outside. Only the birds could be heard. Jason took a deep breath of the night air, closing his eyes in pain. Curtis was right. He had fallen in love with Alana, although he had denied it the whole time. Now he feared that he had ruined their friendship with a foolish, unguarded moment. How would Alana feel around him now?

"I'm in pain right now, God," he spoke out loud. "I have Alana back, but I'm afraid she's still so far away. Her heart doesn't belong to me."

When Jason returned inside the cave, he found Alana curled up against the wall, sleeping. His heart constricted as he watched her peaceful face. He took his outer shirt off and covered her with it, knowing it would get cool during the night. Then he moved to the other side, stretched out on the hard floor, and tried to get some sleep.

Chapter Forty-Four

"Tell me about home."

Jason could not say what it was exactly that had awakened him earlier, but he could not get back to sleep. He sat up by himself until Alana woke a little while later and spoke to him for the first time. He sensed that she needed something safe to talk about.

"What do you want to know?"

Alana thought about it. It had seemed so long since she had seen her family. "Everything."

Jason leaned back on the wall. "Everyone was pretty shook up after you disappeared. The church has been supporting your family since the beginning, and everyone has faith that they'll see you again. Your story has been in every newspaper and magazine across the country, trying to get as much coverage as possible."

"Really?" Alana was amazed.

"Did you expect anything different?"

She shrugged. "I didn't know what to expect."

Jason watched her sit up, his shirt wrapped tightly around her shoulders. "Curtis and Dinah are nearly beside themselves, worrying about you."

Alana's lips trembled. "I've never met anyone I like as much as those two. They're just so special."

"They are," Jason agreed. "Curtis has been a good friend of mine for a long time."

With a smile, Alana quipped, "I bet he has some stories about you."

Jason nodded, his face pensive. "He does. Has he ever told you about the year we met?"

Alana shook her head.

"We were both seventeen, eighteen years old. My home life was not the best, and I was a mess. I got into trouble a lot in school, and got labeled as a bad kid. I hung around a rough bunch, and none of the decent kids gave me the time of day. Except for Curtis. He reached out to me when no one else did."

305

"That sounds like him," Alana observed.

"Mm hmm. As I spent more time with him, I realized there was something different about him. He had his problems, sure, but he never seemed to worry, and he was always cheerful. I wanted that, but I didn't know how to get it."

Alana listened, drawn by the story of her friends' history. She appreciated getting to know more about both Curtis and Jason.

"I quit hanging around the rough bunch, but my life just went downhill. My mother died right at the end of my senior year, my father up and married some rich gal, and I felt in the way."

He fell silent for a moment, gathering his thoughts. "Curtis kept witnessing to me, but I was convinced that I couldn't do it. I couldn't be a Christian. A few years later I was at the end of my rope. I had an engagement that went sour. She ran off with another guy." He quickly glanced at Alana, as if he hadn't meant to reveal that much. Alana only encouraged him with an understanding smile, so he went on.

"I literally hit rock bottom. I was convinced I had nothing going for me. I called Curtis up, told him I was going to end everything, and hung up."

Alana's eyebrows rose. She had never expected such a painful admittance from Jason.

He smiled then, still staring off into space. "But, I sold Curtis too short. He called me right back and told me not to move until he got there. Something in his voice made me listen. When he got to my place, he found me on the couch with a bottle of pills in my hand."

"What did he say?" Alana asked.

"You know, I can't even remember exactly. All I know was that he was there when I needed him, and it was at that time that he led me to the Lord. And he's been watching out for me ever since."

"Who, Curtis or God?" Alana asked with a smile.

Jason gave a soft chuckle. "Both."

"Well, thank the Lord that Curtis was there."

"I do everyday."

Alana stretched her legs out. "So was it at that point that you decided to join the police force?"

"Soon after, yes," Jason nodded. "I found a good position in Kansas City and held on to it until I moved to Edwardsville a couple of months ago."

"What made you decide to move?"

Jason cocked his head. "A little bit of pressure, I think," he admitted. "My captain wanted to promote me to detective."

Alana frowned. "And that's a bad thing?"

"I felt like it was at the time," he said. "I refused the position."

"Why? If you don't mind my asking," she added quickly, thinking that she might be getting too personal.

"No, I don't mind." He gave her a long look. "But, before I answer I want to give a little insight about you."

"Me?" Alana asked, confused.

Jason narrowed his eyes thoughtfully. "If you were to describe yourself to someone else, you would say something like this: 'An all right person, but nothing special.'"

Alana stared at him.

"You compare yourself to other girls, such as Dinah, your sister, Belinda, and find yourself lacking. You never want to bother anyone else because you don't feel you're worth the trouble and people are going to be annoyed by you. Your skills, intelligence, and appearance are average, but could be better. Overall, you know you don't measure up to other young women around you."

Alana looked away, uncomfortable with how close Jason was to the truth. It was like he had literally read her thoughts at times.

"You're wondering how I know all this?"

"Yes," she answered him softly.

He smiled grimly. "Because I know the signs real well. Girls aren't the only ones who go through times of serious insecurities."

Turning her gaze back on him, Alana stared at him.

"From the time I was a kid, I always I couldn't be anything spectacular. My parents loved me, I know, but they didn't see how I was struggling. I was constantly failing, or so I thought. When the girl I thought I was going to spend the rest of my life with decided I wasn't good enough, it was the last draw. I knew I would never succeed at anything." He paused and rubbed his face, the memories from his past lingering in his eyes. "Fortunately, God came on the scene at that point."

"I didn't take the detective position because I still struggle with what I may or may not be able to do. I've always had this fear that I wouldn't be capable of doing the job. I was afraid I would make a mistake and someone would have to pay for it. I thought I had done it with you when you were kidnapped."

Tears came to Alana's eyes and she tried to blink them away.

"I never felt I was good enough to do anything but what I was already comfortable doing," he went on. "Captain Wade found out about the promotion and put me in charge of your case, against my better judgment."

"And you found me," Alana spoke.

"With a lot of help," he reminded.

"But you did it," she insisted. "Maybe that's what this was all about, Jason. Maybe God was showing you what you were capable of."

Jason's heart nearly broke. Here this girl was, having gone through unspeakable horrors, telling him that she may have played a part in helping *him*. "I think there's more to it than that," he said hoarsely. "What about you? You've proven yourself to be more than what you thought were. Felina's told me how you fought to survive. There's more to you than you give yourself credit for."

Alana dropped her gaze, feeling something stir in her at his words. She would never have asked for any of this to happen to her, but since it had, she knew he was right. She was coming out of it stronger than she had entered.

"Thanks, Jason," she said softly.

He smiled at her. "Right back at you, babe," he quipped. "I'm beginning to think we're good for each other."

He caught the pained expression on her face and wished he could cut his tongue out. "You're a good friend," he added clumsily.

"So are you," she returned. After a long moment, she lay back down and rolled over, her face turned away from him.

Jason rubbed his face tiredly and sighed long and deep.

Alana wondered if it was ever going to end—the constant running and fear, the ever present pain that she carried with her now. The pain was from oh, so many sources. It was from knowing that she would never be the girl she had once been. Too much had happened. She had suffered too much.

Vic was constantly on her mind, hurting her with every memory. Although she thrilled that he had stepped out of Marlon's shadow to help her, she grieved because she was sure it cost him his life. She was fairly sure he had never let God save him. Now it was too late. He had died saving her. It was a wound she would bear to the grave.

She missed her family so much it hurt. She caressed every face in her mind, longing to see them. Even Anthony's abruptness would be welcome after the abuse she had endured. She so wanted to wrap her arms around Audrey and enjoy her sweet innocence, something she had lost recently.

The other source of pain came from Jason. His presence, though so welcome, was like a knife in her heart. He had saved her life, most certainly. His steady friendship had kept her going. Even before the abduction, Jason had played a very important part in her life. He understood her so well.

Maybe it was because, like he said earlier, they had experienced the same insecurities, the same self-consciousness.

But now....now she knew that she could never love anyone the way she did Jason. He could never be replaced. That fact alone hurt her deeply, because she felt that she could never have him, even if he wanted her. She was no good to him now.

The next morning, Alana was quieter than usual. Jason saw the strain on her face and knew he had to say something to ease the tension.

"Hey, listen, Alana," he began falteringly. "Don't worry about what happened last night."

Alana blushed and dropped her gaze.

"Seriously," he went on. "I know you've been through a lot, and I don't want you to feel obligated or anything. That was...just a crazy thing that happened. Just forget about it. I just wanted you to know that upfront. Nothing's changed."

Brushing her hair back from her face, Alana thought *No, everything's changed. I can't forget about that kiss. It's been haunting me all night.* She spoke none of her thoughts out loud, though, and said only, "Thank you."

There was a different sadness about Alana now. Jason sensed it. He suspected it had something to do with the man they had crossed paths with earlier. Jason had seen the way Vic had thrown himself over Alana, protecting her. Afterwards, he had let her go, which Alana was sure led up to the gunshots a little later. What kind of relationship had they had?

Troubled over the thought, Jason left his worries at the foot at the cross, knowing that it would do no good to dwell on them. He knew he was at a very vulnerable place in his life at that point. Having Alana so near was torture. Being rejected was not something he wanted to go through again.

He knew Alana was growing weary, in body and soul. The last few weeks of her life had been nothing short of a nightmare. A person could only endure so much without being scarred for life. She needed to be surrounded by her family and friends again, to be given a chance to heal, to feel something good.

With the battles he was fighting himself, Jason knew he was no good to her. He was constantly forcing himself to hold back. All he wanted to do was hold her, cherish her, love her. But she didn't need that from him. All she wanted was friendship and safety.

And that's what I'll give her, he decided. *Her heart's been though too much. I won't add my own hurt to it. She needs a friend now. That's all.*

"How could they have gotten away from me twice?" Marlon ranted.

Reuban stood nearby, chewing on a straw. "He's good."

Turning blazing eyes on his brother, Marlon snarled. "But he's one against all of us? How could you let him get the jump on you?"

Throwing the straw down, Reuban glared at him. "Don't even go there, Marlon. This is the same man that bested you in the duel. There's more to him than meets the eyes. Besides that, he's after something he really wants, and that's the same thing you want—Alana. That girl has messed you up."

"What's that supposed to mean?"

"It means, there was a time you would not have put up with a girl this long," Reuban said testily. "She give you just a little trouble and you'd pack her up and sell her to the South Americas. What's with this one?"

Marlon turned away, seeing red in his rage. "The reason doesn't matter. The fact is, she was mine."

"Whatever," Reuban mumbled. "I'll warn you now, Marlon, if I see her again, I'll kill her on sight. I won't wait for your permission. We have too much at stake if either of them gets to the authorities."

Marlon snorted. "You might want to hang on to your gun then," he said, tossing a handgun to him. "You let Banks take off with yours. Would have made things a lot easier for you with Vic if you'd had your gun."

Reuban shrugged. "You handled it fine."

Shaking his head in disgust, Marlon said, "Don't know what got into that guy. Threw everything away to play the hero."

"Come on, Marlon, don't you get it?" Reuban asked, sticking his gun in his belt. "Vic was pathetic. How could you not have seen all this time? You couldn't get him to do any of your dirty work, not like Jack Norris. I don't know why you hired him in the first place."

"Because he was good."

"But not good enough," Reuban pointed out. "Have you never seen the way he looked at Alana?

"Yeah," Marlon answered, surprised Reuban.

"Then why didn't you do anything about it?"

"I knew he wouldn't do anything about it. Alana's always been a bit afraid of the man, but a little fascinated, too. Who can blame her? He was dark, handsome, mysterious, and a little dangerous."

With a grunt, Reuban waved his hand. "Please, don't make me sick."

"Anyway, I didn't have to worry about any harm coming to her with Vic around. I used his little infatuation for my benefit."

"Until it got you burned in the end," Reuban put in.

Marlon laughed. "Reuban, I'm not the idiot you must think I am. I always knew Vic would outgrow his usefulness. I just took advantage of it while I could."

"Oh." Reuban made a face. "Well, I'm sorry I underestimated you."

Chapter Forty-Five

The still morning was broken by voices in the distance. Jason got Alana up and they were on the move, ducking beneath low hanging branches, their feet growing weary of the constant walking. They walked the whole day with no idea how far behind them Marlon was. Now that Jason had Reuban's pistol, he was able to shoot small game to roast over their campfire. He could see Alana flinch every time he shot the gun, looking behind them, afraid the shot would bring Marlon on the run. Jason had no choice, though. They had to eat to live.

Soon dusk fell again, enveloping them in the black woods. Still Jason went on, determined to put some space between them and the Romanos.

"How do we know that they're not going to catch up to us eventually, anyway?"

Jason stared at Alana. "What?"

Alana shrugged, her face emotionless. "I'm tired of this, Jason."

"So, what do you want to do?"

"Let them have me."

Jason's brows rose to his hairline. "Are you serious?"

"We both know that they're going to find us eventually. I don't want you to end up dead for me. Like Vic."

The name catching his attention, Jason stopped and looked down at her face. "Do you want to talk?"

"What's the point?"

Her lack of fight frightened him. "Alana, you can't give up now. There's too many people counting on you getting back home."

There were sudden tears in her eyes. "Like this? Useless baggage?"

He gripped her shoulders, his voice growing thick. "That's not what you are, Alana," he said.

She broke away from him. "Than what am I?" she asked. "A piece of property for Marlon. A piece of property that got Vic killed and likely you, too. It's not worth it. Not anymore."

"What about Felina?" Jason asked. "Was she worth it?"

Alana turned away, crossing her arms. She couldn't explain what had come over her, except that she wanted to give up. She really believed that Marlon would find her again, and this time he would kill Jason on sight. He would not give them another chance to escape.

Jason took a step towards her. "Alana, there are people at home that love you more than anything. They need you to want to get back to them."

"I don't want to go back like this," she said with a half sob. "I want to go back to the way I used to be. I want to stop remembering."

His fists clenched, Jason stood like stone, once again wanting to get a hold of Marlon. What had he done to his Alana?

"I feel like lying down and dying," she breathed. "I'm no good to anyone anymore."

"That's not true," he rasped.

"Look at me!" she exclaimed. "What do you see? I'm trash, worthless, a piece of property!"

Jason could not take anymore. He grabbed her shoulders and pulled her to him, covering her lips soundly with his, letting her feel all that he felt. She resisted at first, but her own emotions won over. She gripped his arms, returning the kiss with as much fervor as she could. Jason's arms went around her waist, drawing her closer, making her feel more cherished than she had ever felt.

When they finally broke away, Jason stared down at her, still in his arms. "You'll never be worthless in my eyes, Alana Crewe," he said, his voice thick.

"Well, isn't this a sweet moment."

Jason spun around and stared as Reuban Romano stepped into sight. Jason put his arm protectively around Alana.

Reuban sneered and leaned against a large tree trunk, a light weapon in his hands. "There's no getting out now, Banks."

Other men made their appearance, their guns aimed directly at the couple. The last one to step out was none other than Marlon. "I'm tired of the game, Alana," he said, his dark eyes fixed on her. "No more running." He stepped forward.

"You're not taking her back," Jason said.

Marlon's brows rose. "I'm not?"

"Over my dead body."

With a shrug, Marlon raised his gun. "That can be arranged."

"No!" Alana cried.

"Marlon!"

The voice cut through the air, stopping Marlon in his tracks. Whirling around, Jason forgotten for the moment, Marlon watched Vic Dane approach him from the woods.

"Vic!" Alana exclaimed.

The man was limping, holding his side as he walked. His face was pale, but set. "It's over, Marlon."

Before Marlon could react, there was the sound of many guns clicking. Over two dozen Mexican men, in police uniforms, encircled him. One, the captain obviously, spoke to him in Spanish.

Red hot rage welled up in Reuban, and in his anger, the one person he wanted to hurt was Alana, the one responsible for this. With a roar, he lifted his gun towards her, not caring who was around.

Moving quickly despite the pain, Vic brought his own gun up and fired. His bullet pierced Reuban's chest and Reuban stood for a few seconds in shock before falling face first.

"Reuban!" Marlon wailed, dropping to his knees beside his brother. "You've killed him!"

It was like a cork unplugged. Marlon's men began firing wildly, and the Mexican authorities answered with gunfire of their own. It lasted for only a few minutes before the criminals surrendered, several, including Manley Elam and Duke Franklin, lying dead on the ground. During it all, Marlon stayed by his brother, not once thinking of trying to escape or get out of this new turn of events. All he could think of was what Alana had told him long ago. *Someday, God's going to bring you to a stop.*

In the midst of the shooting, Jason had pulled Alana to safety behind a wide tree, and held her there until the shooting stopped. He peered out carefully until the captain called to him. Then he helped Alana to her feet. She was trembling almost violently.

"It's okay, Allie," he said breathlessly. "It's over."

"Over?" Alana repeated dumbly.

Jason nodded. "Marlon can't hurt you anymore."

Covering her face with her hands, Alana leaned against Jason, who promptly wrapped his arms around her again. She didn't cry. She didn't know how to feel. It wasn't until the captain approached and spoke to them that the truth sank in.

"You, senor and senorita," he said, "are free now."

The words erupted a stream of tears from Alana. The captain looked at Jason, puzzled.

"Trust me," Jason assured, feeling like crying himself. "She's glad."

Vic Dane had been left for dead by the Romanos, who were in too much of a hurry to find Jason and Alana to make sure he was dead. Unlike Jason, Vic had known exactly where he was, so as soon as he was able, he drug himself out of the woods, losing a lot of blood as he did. He found a Mexican couple off the road who helped tend to his wounds. Not willing to stay there long, not while the search was still going on in the woods, Vic convinced the man to drive him to San Marquez, where he went straight to the authorities, telling them everything. He then led them to where Marlon and his men were, who had just tracked down Jason and Alana.

Now, he sat in the police station, trying not to grimace with the pain he was feeling. Marlon's bullets had pierced his side and grazed his neck, leaving a deep crease. His body was weary and painful, but he hardly noticed.

A broken Marlon was behind bars, as were the others. Reuban was dead. Alana was free. He knew there would be some consequences for his own part in everything, as well. He knew about the weapons plant, which was being disintegrated as he sat there. He helped kidnap Alana. And he knew that Marlon was a wanted man in America for embezzlement and murder. He was at fault as much as anyone.

Jason and Alana were in a room with the captain, giving as much information as they knew. The authorities had already promised free passage for them to return to the states. It would not be long before Alana would be gone, back to her home.

Vic closed his eyes and sighed deeply, wincing as he did. He had a lot to answer for, but he felt most regretful for his part in bringing harm to that girl. As he sat there, he could not help but remember the strength that she had displayed, strength borne from her deep faith in God.

Like my grandmother, he thought. For the first time in years, he found himself wishing that he could have had that kind of faith. Now it was too late for him.

The door opened and Jason and Alana stepped out, both looking completely exhausted. Vic's eyes rested on Jason for a moment, who was always barely a step from Alana. It was Alana, though, that arrested his attention. She took one look at him and went to him. Jason wisely held back, giving them some room, though he watched warily. Vic slowly stood, his side

315

feeling like it was on fire.

"Are you all right?" she asked.

He shrugged. "I'll live. Marlon was never a good shot anyway."

"That's not what I meant," she said.

He caught the meaning in her eyes and averted his gaze, staring out the window. "I never saw it ending like this," he muttered.

"It doesn't have to be an end, Vic," Alana said. "Let it be a beginning."

He shook his head, a sad smile on his lips. "I'm past that, Alana. I've done too much."

"No, you haven't," she said firmly. "God loves you and He's willing to forgive. Just as I have."

Frowning, he looked at her. "How can you even say that? After all that we've put you through?"

She swallowed. "I'm not saying that it wasn't hard. There were times I wanted to die. I'm human. It's only by God's grace that I'm saying all this to you now. Don't be fooled into thinking you can never ask Him to help you. He's only a prayer away."

There was a long pause. Alana prayed silently that he would take her words seriously.

"I've never met anyone like you, Alana," he said finally, so soft that she barely heard him.

She smiled slightly. "I could say the same thing about you."

He shook his head. "Don't even compare me to you."

Seeing the deep regret in his dark eyes, Alana was moved. She put her hand on his arm. "Regardless of how you feel right now, I know what kind of man you are. In the end, you turned things around and made the right decision. There's still some good in you. Just let God in."

His face looked stricken. He reached up and touched her cheek. "I wish things would have been different," he whispered.

Alana stood still, wishing there was something she could do to erase the pain from his eyes.

Vic saw an officer step into the room and knew their time was up. "Goodbye, Alana."

"Goodbye," she answered, her throat tight. "I'll pray that you realize that it's not too late for you."

He hesitated a moment, then slowly put his hand on the back of her head and pressed a long kiss to her brow. "I'm sorry." He turned away and went with the officer. Alana did not watch him leave.

Vic passed before Jason and paused. He did not meet his gaze when he spoke. "I never wanted to hurt her."

Staring at the man, seeing the inner turmoil he was going through, Jason could not feel anger, only pity. "I know." He put his hand out. Vic stared at it for a moment before hesitantly taking it.

"Take care of yourself," Jason urged soberly.

Vic nodded and moved away. "You too."

Alana felt Jason's presence at her side and reached for his hand, needing his support.

"Are you ready to go home?" he asked, watching her face.

Sniffling, Alana nodded. She was so ready.

It was quiet on the plane. Alana had slept for the first hour, but now sat, staring out the window, her hands clutched tightly in her lap. Jason wanted to comfort her, but after she reached for him in the police station, she seemed to refrain from touching him. It was as if she had put a wall between them.

"That's a pretty sight, isn't it?" he asked, motioning to the puffy clouds just on the other side of the window. "Ever think you'd be riding in a plane?"

"I did once," she answered.

"Really? When?"

She sighed. "When I was being taken to Mexico."

Jason winced. "I'm sorry, Alana."

With a smile, she said, "It's not your fault."

"Allie, it's going to be okay."

It hurt her every time he used her nickname. She wanted to throw herself in his arms, but knew she shouldn't. "I know. I feel like I've disappointed you."

"How could you disappoint me?" he asked.

She didn't answer, so he did, his voice low.

"Because there can't be anything between us?"

Feeling a flood of sorrow at his spoken words, she forced herself to nod, wanting to beat herself as she did. What was she doing?

Jason's suspicions had been correct. He had gathered, from the emotional goodbye with Vic at the station, that there was more to her grief than met the eye. "It's all right, Alana," he assured, dying as he did so. "I'm fine with that."

She looked up at him. He gave her a reassuring smile and a wink. He seemed to be fine, like he said. How could he be so fine when she felt like falling apart? Because he did not feel the same way she did.

But the kiss? What about the kiss? The question came to her.

It was nothing. He got caught up in the moment, she insisted mentally. *Trying to make a point.* No, it was obvious that the kiss had not meant the same thing to him as it did her. Her cheeks burned slightly at how fervently she had returned the kiss.

Outwardly, though, she merely returned his smile, making herself look relieved. "I'm glad," she said inanely.

Both fell silent, deep in their own thoughts, and both anxious for this flight to end.

Chapter Forty-Six

Tuesday April 30th
Edwardsville

The town of Edwardsville was beside itself the closer it came for Alana Crewe's plane to land. Her homecoming had become a big event and hundreds of people were gathered at the airport to get a glimpse of the girl who had been missing for exactly three weeks. Reporters, cameramen, and the police were everywhere.

In the very front, were the Crewe family, surrounded by close friends and church members. Sharon gripped her husband's hand as she scanned the skies.

"It won't be long," Alan encouraged, trying to control his own anticipation. He felt like bursting. How he longed to hold his daughter again, to see her sweet face.

In the back of Alan's mind, though, he worried. Was Alana really all right? How much time would she need for healing? The concern he felt kept him praying, even as the first glimpse of the plane appeared in the sky.

"There it is!" Sharon gasped.

Alan reached down and scooped Audrey up, who was staring at the minute plane intently. "Is Allie on there?" she asked.

"She sure is," Alan answered. "She'll be here in just a few minutes."

"It's not big enough for her to be on there."

Alan laughed, the first time he had done so in weeks.

"Is Jason with her?"

Alan nodded, his admiration for the young cop growing by the second. "Yep. He's the reason Alana found her way home."

Audrey fell silent now and watched with wide eyes as the plane grew nearer and larger.

It was an eternity before the plane landed, and then as they waited for the doors to open. It seemed as if the whole town held its breath, waiting for the first glimpse of Alana. When she did step in the doorway, ready to make her flight down, the place erupted.

Alana had not expected such a reaction from such a large crowd and faltered. Jason's steady arm was there, supporting and encouraging. Alana's eyes fell on her family, just a few yards away, and forgot everything else. She fairly ran down the steps, tears streaming as she did so, straight into the arms of her mother and father.

Jason stood back, watching the tearful reunion, feeling a mixture of joy and sadness. He was so relieved to have Alana back home, but he knew her life would not be as simple as it once was. On top of everything, he felt so tired.

Alana greeted her loved ones, taking and giving embraces at every turn. She cried until she was dry, and then cried some more. The reporters respectfully stayed out of the way while she reunited with those that she had missed, and when everyone was ready, Wade Harmon had a police escort ready to see that the Crewes made it safely back home. Alana sat in the back seat between her parents. Her siblings were following in another police car.

Neither Sharon nor Alan asked questions. She felt safe and sheltered with her father's arm around her shoulders, and her mother's hand clasped tightly with her own. Alana rested her head against Alan, suddenly so weary. Her heart was full, in danger of bursting. What she had prayed for had finally come true. She was home.

In the midst of the excitement, Jason had been rather forgotten, but he understood and didn't mind. He slipped away as soon as he could, after he knew that Alana was well on her way home. He avoided the journalists and cameras. All he wanted to do was go home and fall into bed, to sleep for a week.

When he got there, though, Wade was there, sitting on the step outside his door.

"Welcome home, Banks," he greeted.

"Thanks," Jason answered tiredly.

"I won't stay long," Wade said. "I just wanted to congratulate you on your success. I don't think there are very many who could have done what you did. You found Alana and revealed Marlon Romano's whereabouts to boot."

Jason rubbed his face. "I didn't do it on my own."

Wade could see his fatigue. "I better go. You get some rest and come back to work on Monday."

"Thanks, Captain," Jason said as the older man took his leave. He stepped into his house, drawing in the familiar scent. He wasted no time getting dressed but went straight to his bed and collapsed, knowing nothing more until the next morning.

If asked to, Alana would have had difficulty describing the next few days. Memories assailed her, dreams haunted her at night, reporters hounded her for her story. At times, she wondered how she was ever going to get over it, but with God's help, and the support of her family, she knew that she was healing, be it ever so slowly.

She had two days of uninterrupted time with her family before her friends began to call. Appreciating their courtesy, Alana suddenly wanted to see them. Thus it was that on Friday evening, Curtis, Dinah, Belinda, and Tommy were at the house, all sitting in the living room.

"How are you feeling, Alana?" Dinah asked, her lovely eyes clouded over.

Alana smiled. "Still tired and very drained, but *so* glad to be home."

Dinah shook her head. "I couldn't stand it, not knowing what was happening to you."

"Dinah," Curtis spoke. "She may not want to go there."

Surprising, Alana found that she was willing to talk. She needed to share and these dear people seemed the likely sources. "No, it's okay." She licked her lips. "I never knew anyone could live through so much."

"And come out so strong," Curtis pointed out.

"I don't feel so strong."

"Because you're still getting over it," Belinda spoke up. "Give yourself some time. You'll realize it."

Alana took a deep breath. "I'm still having trouble sleeping. I keep seeing Marlon…"

"That's understandable," Curtis assured. "Look, I can't even begin to imagine what happened to you while you were gone. But I know this. Anytime someone goes through a traumatic experience like you've gone through, it takes time, sometimes a long time, to get through it. Just remember this. No matter how bad you feel, you've got friends right here that will help you out any time you ask."

Alana was touched. "You guys don't realize how much I've missed you."

Dinah reached over and gave her a squeeze. "Not any more than we missed you. I can guarantee that."

The Mexican and American authorities were in close contact over the case of Marlon Romano. Marlon was transferred back to the states to be tried for his past accusations, as well as the abduction and captivity of Alana Crewe. If for any reason he was to be acquitted or released, the Mexican law enforcement would promptly charge him for the crimes he committed while on their soil—abduction, assault, attempted murder, and a host of other charges.

It would be at least several months before the trials would end. This meant many interviews and interrogations for both Alana and Jason. It would be quite a while before either could put this whole ordeal behind them.

Jason especially worried about Alana. What would she have to go through on the stand, telling all that had happened to her while in Marlon's custody? How would that affect her? He knew for a fact that it would be extremely painful for her to describe some of the things that she had experienced.

But, it was a necessary part to see that Marlon was put away for his crimes. Jason determined to help her all he could and offered to drive her to the station when she needed. She accepted this gratefully, as she was still unsure about driving by herself.

The time that they spent together was not strained, like they both feared it would be. They talked and discussed everything comfortably, but both noticed that something had changed between them. Their easy comradeship was missing. There was a wall now, as both tried to forget what they could not.

"Just think," Jason said, as they were driving to the courthouse, yet again. "Marlon is finally being tried because of you."

"Others were killed because of me, too," Alana replied abruptly.

Startled at her words, he contradicted her. "No, that's not true."

"But—"

He interrupted. "It's because of the lives they chose to lead that they died. It did not have anything to do with you. However, it *is* because of you that Marlon and a lot of his cronies won't be able to hurt anyone again."

He was satisfied to see her eyes clear some. Obviously this had been bothering her. "Are you worried about the trial?" he asked softly.

She shrugged slightly. "Maybe a little. Not about the outcome, but just doing it. I've never been good in front of people. I'm afraid I'll freeze up and be more of a hindrance than a help to the prosecuting side."

"You'll do fine," Jason stated. "Remember, with Christ, you can do all things. You've already proven than in the last several weeks. Look at what you've come through. This will be nothing. You know the truth. Just tell them."

Alana looked up at him, her expression unreadable. "Jason, I don't think I've ever thanked you for all you've done for me recently."

"Sure you have."

"Maybe so, but I was afraid that with everything that's happened, you wouldn't know how much I appreciate it. I couldn't have done this without you."

He was shaking his head. "Alana, you're the one that made the decision to rise to the occasion."

"But, you've been there for me, and you still are. Thank you."

Jason kept his eye on the road, knowing that if he looked at her he'd want to kiss her. "Allie, I'd do it all over again," he said softly.

The statement, as well as the feeling behind it, caught Alana. He was not looking at her, but she saw something on his face, a yearning, maybe?

Alana, stop, she scolded herself, turning her gaze out the window. *Don't start seeing things that aren't there. If you love him the way you say you do, you'd let him go. He deserves so much better.*

Fortunately for both of them, the courthouse appeared around the next corner, and they were saved from any uncomfortable silences.

Curtis could see that Jason was not himself. Ever since he came back from Mexico, there seemed to be a burden on him, when he should have been rejoicing. Yet he seemed down, troubled. He especially knew something was not right when Jason chose to sit in the back seat of the church on Sunday, instead of next to him behind the Crewes. Deciding to find out what was going on, Curtis went straight Jason's house Monday evening. Jason had just come back from work and was still dressed in his uniform.

"How was the first day back?"

Jason shook his head. "Busy. I'm buried in paperwork."

"You think you'll enjoy your job the same way you did before?"

"Why wouldn't I?"

Curtis shrugged. "I dunno. I know you were offered a different position in Kansas City. I just wondered if after all this excitement you'd decide to take it."

Sitting down across from Curtis, Jason admitted, "I can't say the thought hasn't crossed my mind."

Curtis watched him for a moment. "You want to tell me what's wrong?" He watched Jason grow still.

"Who said anything's wrong?"

"Come on, Jason," Curtis groaned. "You're not talking to just anyone here. I know you better than you know yourself. It has something to do with Alana, doesn't it?"

Jason didn't reply.

"Jason, out with it. You know from experience that holding it in doesn't do you any good."

"I know." Jason sighed deeply, running his fingers through his dark hair. "You were right, Curtis, about Alana."

Curtis raised his brows. "You love her?"

Jason nodded, his mouth grim.

"Well, why don't you do something about it instead of just sitting around here all depressed?"

"I wish it was that easy."

"Look, I know she's been through a lot, but you don't want to wait until this whole trial is over. How long could that take?"

"Curtis," Jason stopped him. "It's not that easy because she's in love with someone else."

This stunned Curtis. "What? How do you know?"

"I just know."

"Who?"

Standing and pacing agitatedly, Jason said, "One of Marlon's men."

"What?" Curtis exclaimed. "Are you nuts? That's impossible!"

"No," Jason shook his head. "Not with this guy. He was different; even I could see that. He helped her while she was down there. Risked his own life to get her out."

"And what about you?" Curtis asked. "What do you think you did going down there?"

"I got us caught," Jason muttered. "Honestly, if it hadn't been for him, we wouldn't be here today, Curtis."

Curtis stared at him. "That doesn't mean she loves him, Jase."

"She practically told me flat out that there can't be anything between us," Jason said, raising his voice.

Confused and agitated, Curtis stood to his own feet. "Did she tell you that she loves this guy?"

"No, but—"

"Then you don't know for a fact," Curtis insisted. "Jason, I've seen the way she looks at you. There's nobody else."

Sighing, Jason sat back down. "I saw them together, Curtis. Saw the way he looked at her. She was so upset at leaving him behind. No," he leaned forward, resting his elbows on his knees. "I've done what I told myself I would never do again. I let myself fall for a girl that doesn't love me. I can't do any more."

Feeling helpless, Curtis said no more. Something was not right, but he didn't know what he could do about it. He couldn't very well march up to Alana and ask her if she loved Jason. Could he?

Chapter Forty-Seven

Tuesday, May 6th

"Alana, honey, it's for you."

Alana raised herself up from the bed and took the cordless phone from her mother. "Hello?"

"Hey, Alana, it's me."

Her heart did a little flip-flop. "Hi, Jason."

"Listen, I've been making some plans, and I wanted you to know first."

Alana felt her hold on the phone tighten. "Yes?"

"I'm thinking about taking a job up in Topeka."

"Topeka?" Alana repeated, struggling to keep her voice natural. "That's a ways away."

"Yeah, I know," Jason agreed. "There's a position open, and I decided it was time for me to take it."

"A detective position?" she guessed.

"Yeah, actually it is."

Swallowing, Alana said, "Well, I'm proud of you, Jason. I'm glad you've realized what you're capable of."

"Thanks. I have you to thank for it."

"Me?"

"Yeah. Going down south to find you made me realize a lot of things about myself."

Me, too. "Well, I'm glad I could play a part in it. When do you go?"

There was a slight pause. "I'm leaving right away. I'll be back for the trial, though, so don't worry about that."

That's not what I'm worried about.

"Well, I better get back to my packing," he said then. "I just wanted you to hear it from me. I'll miss you. You're a good friend."

The words sounded forced, but Alana disregarded that. "You are, too. Take care of yourself, Jason."

Turning the phone off, Alana set it on her bed and hugged her pillow against her. "I've lost him," she murmured. Unable to stem the tears, she rolled over and cried.

Jason stared at the receiver that he had just set down, feeling his insides being wrenched. It was the hardest thing he could have done, but he knew it was for the best. Alana would get on with her life. She had a strong support team. She would be fine. It was for him that he was making this move.

Feeling like an old man, Jason went back to his room where he had clothes already packed away. He resumed his packing, praying as he did so that he was making the right decision.

"Alana, what's wrong?" Andrea asked.

Alana was sitting up in the bed, staring off into space. Her face was flushed and her eyes moist.

"Did you have another nightmare?"

"No." Alana sniffed. "Jason is moving to Topeka."

Andrea was surprised. "Why?"

Alana explained as briefly as she could.

"But, I thought the two of you were together now," Andrea said bluntly.

"No." Alana pushed the pillow away. "We're not."

"Alana Crewe, why ever not? Can't you see what a special guy he is?"

"Of course I do," Alana retorted. "I know better than anybody. But, he doesn't love me. He can't love me. Not now."

The first thing Andrea wanted to do was find Jason and pound him for hurting her sister. After that impulsive thought, she calmed down and told herself that there had to be more than what Alana was telling her.

"I'm sorry I lost your jean jacket."

Andrea stared at her. "Do you actually think I care about that? All I wanted was to have you back. I'm just sorry you had to go through so much."

Alana smiled sadly. She looked up as her brother and Audrey stepped in.

"You feeling all right?" Anthony asked.

"Better all the time."

Audrey climbed up on the bed and into her lap. The little girl seldom let Alana out of her sight now. "I'm glad you made your way back home," she said.

Alana hugged her close. "Me, too."

"Hey, listen, Alana," Anthony spoke up. "I know I haven't always been so nice to you. When you were gone I did a lot of thinking and—"

Alana raised her hand. "It's all right, Anthony. I know I'm not always the easiest person to live with, either. I never doubted that you loved me, though."

Anthony looked relieved.

A twinkle suddenly lit in Alana's eyes. "But, you still owe me twenty bucks."

They all laughed, enjoying the moment of released strain.

"Allie?" Audrey addressed when they had sobered.

"Yes, Audrey?"

"Will you read my book to me now?"

Alana took the book that was offered to her, recognizing it as the one she had promised to read to Audrey when she came home. It was on that night she had been abducted and taken away from her home.

Andrea and Anthony watched the emotions play across her face. Suddenly they cleared and she smiled at Audrey. "Yes, Audrey. I would love to read this book to you."

Curtis knocked on the Crewes' door later that day. Alana opened it rather cautiously, opening it just a crack to see who was there first.

"Come on in," she greeted with a smile.

"Where's everyone at?"

"Anthony's upstairs somewhere. Dad took the others out to lunch."

"You still nervous leaving the house?"

"Well, it's just that there are still some reporters out there that want to get a hold of me." She saw his doubtful look. "And I'm still too nervous to leave the house."

Curtis laughed.

"I'd just rather stay home until everything settles down."

"Shouldn't be too much longer," Curtis told her. "Especially after the trial." He wasted no more time. "Hey, I came over to tell you something."

"Yes?"

"Jason's leaving."

Alana motioned him into the living room. "I know."

Curtis blinked. "You do?"

"He called me this morning and told me."

"You know he's leaving and you're not doing anything about it?"

Alana was surprised. "What am I supposed to do?"

"You love him, don't you?"

"Curtis—"

"Answer me."

Alana turned from him. "What if I do? I already know nothing can come from it."

"How do you know that?"

"Because he made that clear," Alana ground out, more than a little frustrated at having to defend herself, especially to Jason's best friend. "I can't force a man to love me when he can't."

Curtis crossed his arms. "What makes you think he can't love you?"

Frowning at him, Alana wondered why she was even telling him all this. "Curtis I am not the same girl I was last month. A lot has happened to me. I don't expect any man to take me like this."

"He doesn't feel that way, Alana!" Curtis exclaimed. "He doesn't care about that at all. He thinks you're in love with someone else!"

Alana stared at him. "Who could I be in love with?"

"I don't know—some guy in Mexico that helped you out."

"Vic?" Alana covered her mouth with her hand, her face going white. "Are you serious?"

"He told me himself, Alana," Curtis confirmed. "He's crazy about you. I know it's none of my business, but I couldn't let him walk away when I know you two are supposed to be together."

Alana was barely listening to his last words. "I have to go," she murmured in a daze, looking around for her purse. "Where is he?"

"Last time I talked to him he was putting some of his stuff in storage. Hey, aren't you worried about leaving the house?" he asked, hiding a smile.

"Not anymore."

The Lawson Storage Sheds were about a mile out of Edwardsville. Alana drove straight over there, not once feeling anxiety about going so far from home. She caught sight of his truck and wanted to weep with relief. She spotted him carrying some large boxes into the shed.

He looked up at the sound of the motor. He frowned slightly and set his box down. "What's wrong?" he asked when she got out of the car.

"Nothing. At least, not with anything at home," she stammered.

Not moving, Jason watched her approach, wondering why she was here.

Alana was unsure what to do now that she was facing him. She looked up at him, feeling her heart overturn in love. What would she do without this man?

"Are you all right?" Jason asked.

"Not really," she answered. At his concerned look, she went on. "I realized that there's been a misunderstanding between us, Jason."

"There has?" Jason asked, wishing she wouldn't look at him that way. He wanted to crush her to him.

She nodded. Determined that she was not going to lose him, she set her chin and put aside her self-consciousness. In an act of boldness, she approached him and touched his face. He didn't move. "I was afraid," she whispered. "I was afraid that what Marlon's done to me had ruined my chance for love."

"Alana—"

Putting her finger on his lips, Alana stared at him, her eyes starting to fill. "I'm not in love with Vic Dane."

Instinctively, his hands came up to hold her shoulders. "What?"

She shook her head, her throat tightening. It made it difficult to speak, but she forced the words out. "I'm not. I wanted you to love me, but I couldn't ask it of you."

Jason clenched his jaw. "That was never an issue for me, Allie. To me, you're just as beautiful, just as pure, just as innocent as you ever have been." His grip tightened. "And I mean that."

"I know you do," she answered, resting her hands on his chest.

"If you ever doubt it, let me know. Don't wonder about it."

She nodded, unable to speak now.

Jason drew her in his strong embrace, kissing her soundly. Any doubts that Alana might have had fled at the fervor of his kiss. She knew now that Marlon had not taken anything away from her that God had not returned in His omnipotent grace.

Friday, May 16ᵗʰ

"Oh, you look so pretty!" Sharon exclaimed, staring at her daughter, standing in the center of the room.

Alana stared at herself in the mirror, hardly able to keep from smiling.

"Well, this is what you've been waiting for," Alan said, joining his wife at the doorway. "You ready?"

"More than you know," Alana answered.

"You better go so you won't be late," Sharon urged. "We'll meet you over there."

Alana nodded and went to her parents, giving them both a long embrace. "Thank you," she murmured.

Sharon cupped her face in her hands. "There's not a day that goes by that I don't thank God that you're back home with me."

"Me neither," Alana agreed.

She descended the steps then, holding the extra folds of her commencement gown in one hand. Her flat crowned hat was in the other. Anthony whistled at her when he saw her. "Don't you look cute!" he teased. "Jason's gonna go mad!"

"You hush up!" Alana playfully scolded.

As she drove to the college, Alana reflected on how much of a miracle it was that she was actually able to graduate at all. She could have been dead, or still in Mexico somewhere. As it was, even with her returning home when she had, there would have been no way for her to walk the aisle with the graduating class if it had not been for Dianna Akin and the College Board.

As soon as Alana's story had come to them, the board and Alana's advisor decided then and there that Alana would be allowed to graduate when she came home. There was a bit of work to do, on Alana's part, but in the end she managed to get it all done. She had appreciated the chance to put her mind to work on something besides the recent events, and she was so thankful to Dianna for her help. Now, Alana had passed her classes and was about to receive her Associate of Arts.

The auditorium was full near to bursting. The hour drew near for the graduates to enter and everyone burst into applause at the first sign of them. Alana was a third of the way back in her line, and she gave a small wave to her family. She could see that there were a lot of people from her church and job there as well.

She sat there with her heart pounding during the speeches and announcements, not really paying attention to what was being said. She silently thanked God over and over for his hand in her life.

Finally it came time for the walk down the aisle to receive her handshake and special binder that would hold her certificate. As her name was being called, she stood, hardly able to breathe. A shift in the auditorium made her look around and she paused. Everyone in the room had stood to their feet, applauding her. Even the other graduates were facing her, clapping their hands. Alana was overwhelmed and had trouble seeing where she was going due to the tears in her eyes.

The dean of the school shook her hand with both of his before giving her the binder. Dianna suddenly appeared beside him. Alana embraced the woman, thanking her for all her help.

"This is your victory, Alana," Dianna told her. "Be proud of yourself."

Alana nodded and moved on, anxious to let the ceremony continue on.

Afterwards, Alana fought to find her family in the crushing crowd. She was stopped over and over by schoolmates and acquaintances, even by strangers. Everyone had seen her face in the news and knew who she was. Everyone expressed their congratulations for her accomplishments.

It was Alan who found her first. He took her hand and pulled her from the center of the throng. "A little excited, aren't they?" he laughed, hugging her.

"Oh, Dad! I don't even know what to say!"

Everyone else gathered around them—her mother and siblings, Curtis and Dinah, Belinda and Tommy, Rachel and Tim, with their little daughter, Alana Grayce, Kenneth and Maggie Nelson, Dick Browning and Stacey Martin. All those that she cared about were there.

She jumped slightly when masculine arms suddenly encircle her from behind. "Congrats, Allie," Jason said in her ear.

Alana smiled. "Thanks."

"How do you feel?" he asked as he stepped to her side, his arm still around her.

Alana looked around her at her loved ones laughing and talking amongst themselves. "I can't even describe it," she laughed. "I want to laugh and cry at the same time."

Jason pressed a kiss to her temple. "Me, too," he whispered.

Alana slipped her arm around his waist. Alan was inviting everyone to their house for her celebration BBQ. The group moved as one towards the vehicles. As Alana walked, she realized that the horrific events in Mexico already seemed like a long time ago. She knew she still had a lot of healing to do, but she had no doubt that she would make it. God's grace had certainly been sufficient to her, even when she was miles from her own home, completely across the border to a strange country. God had indeed seen her through and was continuing to bless her. She was surrounded by family and friends and loved by a wonderful man. With that knowledge, she was ready to face life head on, even to the very ends of the earth.

Epilogue

April 13th
Two years later
San Marquez, Mexico

Alana stood on the cliff, overlooking the forest. In the background, she could see the Sierra Madre Occidental. It was strange to think that it was in these same woods and mountains that she and Jason had run from Marlon Romano. It seemed like such a long time ago, and at the same time, Alana could remember it all like it was yesterday.

It had been a long, hard ordeal. It had taken almost four months before the endless court trials were over. Marlon Romano was convicted and sent to prison for the rest of his life. Many of his henchmen were also behind bars.

Alana's story had attracted much attention. There had even been book and movie offers, which she refused. She had been unwilling to relive the abduction, nor to exploit her life. The memories had continued to haunt her until she finally sought a Christian counselor. Only then was Alana able to talk through her feelings and put the past behind her and get on with her life.

It had been her idea to visit Mexico again. She felt that it was the last step to her healing. To see this vast country from a different perspective, as a visitor, not a hostage, made her appreciate it more. There were those here that had made it possible for her to go back home.

She had met Martin Jacobs, Jason's missionary friend who had given so much help. His mission field had grown and prospered under his ministry, and with some unexpected help.

It was a tearful reunion between Alana and Felina. The Mexican girl looked like a new person, glowing, happy, and serene. Alana was pleased to find out that Felina was deeply involved with the mission now. Her quiet way of reaching out had already won many souls. Martin expressed more than once how much he appreciated Felina's help. Jason and Alana were both surprised and then overjoyed when Martin and Felina announced their engagement.

"I know there's a fifteen year age difference," Martin admitted. "But Felina's maturity surpasses many her age and she helps keep me young," he added with a wink.

Both Jason and Alana saw in the end that there was not a couple more suited to each other than Martin and Felina, and expressed their delight and best wishes.

Martin and Felina had been just as excited to hear that Jason and Alana were married now, just over a year. Martin slapped Jason on the back and declared the he had always known what Jason did not—that he was head over heels in love with Alana. Felina quietly added that she had suspected the same thing from Alana.

A noise behind her interrupted Alana's musings. She turned and faced Vic Dane, standing some yards behind her.

"Hello, Vic," she greeted gently.

He was eyeing her warily, as if expecting something else. "How are you?"

"Doing well. Everything has settled down pretty much…finally."

"That's good." Vic nodded.

"How are you doing?"

He had expected the question, but dreaded it. He knew that there was no use trying to fool Alana. She could see right through him. Always had.

"I thought for a while that I wasn't going to make it," he admitted. "But, I did."

"I knew you would," she said.

He wanted to say more, but couldn't. He had never been good with words. "I spend a lot of my time regretting the past."

"That's an easy thing to do," she said. "But don't let it ruin you. You've made restitution. Now move on. Do something with your life worthwhile. You can, you know."

There was another short nod. "I'm trying," he said with an exhale. "It's not easy."

"It never is."

There was an awkward silence. Alana looked around her at the scenery, unaware of the way Vic watched her.

She hadn't changed a bit. She was still as strong and beautiful as she had ever been, maybe even more so. It was her memory that had haunted him while in jail. Sometimes it tormented him, filling him with guilt for the part he had played in her abduction. Other times it teased him, reminding him that she was forever beyond his reach. Most of the time, however, remembering her made him want to be a better man. And that's what he was fighting to do.

"You were right about one thing," he said.

She looked at him. "About what?"

"It wasn't too late for me."

Alana's eyes widened slightly. "You did it?"

He nodded, finding amusement in her reaction. "Met a chaplain a few months back. He finally convinced me that what you said was true. God's willing to take me, mess that I am."

"I'm glad to hear that, Vic," Alana said thickly, her hands clasped in front of her. "Very glad."

"Well, I still have a long way to go, and I wouldn't have done it without you," he said, walking towards her. "Even when you should have hated me, you didn't. Thank you."

"I just saw what God saw," she said. "A hurting man who didn't believe he could be anything better, but he could. I'm glad you finally saw it, too."

Vic gave her a rare, small smile. "I better go," he said. "Thanks for seeing me." He reached out and gave her a quick hug, and then stepped back.

Jason appeared at Alana's side just then, putting his arm around her shoulders. He nodded at Vic.

Vic observed the pair with a knowing look. "Glad you finally got smart," he told Jason.

Jason chuckled. "Thanks."

"Well, I'll let you go now," Vic said abruptly. "Goodbye, Alana, Jason."

"Goodbye, Vic."

They watched him leave and Alana felt a strange mixture of joy and sadness. Vic was now a child of God, but he still seemed so lost and sad. She prayed that in time, he would learn to forgive himself and move on into the future that God had for him.

Jason drew her in front of him, letting her lean back against him. "Are you okay?" he asked, resting his chin on her head.

"I am," Alana answered after a long moment, meaning it with all her heart. "I needed to come back and make peace, mainly with myself. I don't like what happened, but it did. I think it made me stronger, though."

"Me, too," Jason added.

"God allowed something bad to turn into something good," Alana mused. "Because of what happened to me, Felina, Breanna, Stacey Martin, and Vic have all turned their lives over to God. Vic has a long way to go before he can start forgiving himself, but he's on the right track."

"Marlon Romano is behind bars," Jason continued.

"The Mexican mission is growing."

"There's a greater sense of community in the church."

"And I've learned a lot about myself."

Jason bent down and kissed her cheek. "That makes two of us."

"It was a long, hard journey though," she mused.

"Mm hmm," he agreed. "But it was a journey of beginnings, for a lot of people."

"Well," Alana smiled and took a deep breath. "I'm just glad that at the journey's end, I found you."

"No," Jason shook his head. "I found you."

Alana smiled. It was an old argument. She felt happiness well up inside her, even as she prepared to say more. "Jason?"

"Hmm?" he murmured, his face buried in her hair.

"We're going to be parents."

He froze for a long moment. Then, as if in slow motion, he turned her around to face him. "You're serious?"

Alana swallowed. "Yes. Our baby is due in November. Just in time for Thanksgiving."

Jason did not wait until then to start giving thanks. He threw his head back and laughed. "Thank you, God!" he shouted. He picked her up and swung her around several times before setting her down and kissing her soundly. Then she was back in his arms spinning in circles.

The exultation spilled over the cliff and down to the forest below. Birds paused in their singing for a moment before adding their own voices to the happy sounds. The sun seemed to be approving of their joy; white puffy clouds resembled great smiles in the sky. Past heartaches were for the moment forgotten in the light of present and future blessings and the woods that had once echoed the sounds of gunfire and anger, now rang with laughter and song.

Printed in the United States
44043LVS00003B/172-231

9 781424 115693